Praise for Linda Greenlaw and her
Jane Bunker mysteries

"Small-town life, the ___ ___ ___ ob-
sters, and the bea ___ ___ de-
lineated as Greenl ___ ___ ng
practice and lore. T ___ ___ ed
protagonist, and the ___ ___ rs are also well
developed in this sat___ying mystery."

—Booklist on *Fisherman's Bend*

"Greenlaw's experience as a Maine-based lobster-boat
captain brings verisimilitude to her descriptions of
the people, the landscape, and most of all the wild
offshore weather, all neatly rolled into a mystery with
plenty of suspects." *—Kirkus Reviews*

"This debut mystery series is to be savored on all
counts . . . Greenlaw [writes] with great joie de vivre
and incredible skill."

—Library Journal on *Slipknot*

"A sleepy Maine town, the local drunk found dead, a
detective asking too many questions . . . No, not *Murder, She Wrote*—it's [Greenlaw's] first foray into mystery, and it's riveting." *—People* on *Slipknot*

"Greenlaw proves that she's as skillful a mystery
writer as she is a fishing-boat captain—and that's
saying a lot."

—Sebastian Junger, author of *The Perfect Storm*

"Greenlaw has no trouble finding her sea legs in . . . this swiftly paced yarn."
—Entertainment Weekly on *Slipknot*

"Bestseller Greenlaw introduces an indomitable heroine, Jane Bunker, in her strong mystery debut. A cast of memorable New Englanders . . . enhances a fast-moving plot, while the nautical details will appeal to fans of Greenlaw's nonfiction books."
—Publishers Weekly on *Slipknot*

"The author's experience as a lobster-boat captain is apparent in her vivid descriptions of nor'easters and in her portrayals of the quirky residents of Maine's rural areas. An entertaining series, strong on setting."
—Booklist on *Shiver Hitch*

"One of the summer's best mystery novels . . . worth tossing in your pack!"   *—Outside* on *Shiver Hitch*

"Greenlaw's third atmospheric mystery (following *Fisherman's Bend*) combines the author's knowledge of the sea with humorous accounts of small-town life."
—Library Journal on *Shiver Hitch*

FISHERMAN'S BEND

Linda Greenlaw

St. Martin's Paperbacks

This is a work of fiction. All of the characters, organizations, and events portrayed in this novel are either products of the author's imagination or are used fictitiously.

FISHERMAN'S BEND

Copyright © 2008 by Linda Greenlaw.
Excerpt from *Shiver Hitch* copyright © 2017 by Linda Greenlaw.

For information address St. Martin's Press, 175 Fifth Avenue, New York, NY 10010.

Library of Congress Catalog Card Number: 2008019185

ISBN: 978-1-250-13578-0

Our books may be purchased in bulk for promotional, educational, or business use. Please contact your local bookseller or the Macmillan Corporate and Premium Sales Department at 1-800-221-7945, ext. 5442, or by e-mail at MacmillanSpecialMarkets@macmillan.com.

Printed in the United States of America

Hyperion hardcover edition / July 2008
St. Martin's Paperbacks edition / April 2019

St. Martin's Paperbacks are published by St. Martin's Press, 175 Fifth Avenue, New York, NY 10010.

10 9 8 7 6 5 4 3 2 1

To Bob Lynde of Gay Island Oyster

ONE

I stood at the stern facing aft and watched the walls of Cobble Harbor gently melt into the rainbow sherbet foliage of Quoddy Head. The Head, high and abrupt, proudly displayed its seasonal colors; a stand of hardwoods stretched up and around the rocky bluff like an Indian headdress. As Cal pushed the throttle up a bit, I sighed with the realization that Mother Nature's ornamentation would soon be gone—like Christmas cards plucked on January 2 from their temporary refrigerator-door home. So this was autumn in New England. I was only a child when, decades ago, my mother moved my brother and me from Acadia Island, which was just across the bay, all the way down to Florida—the most exotic place she could think of. But South Florida's orange groves didn't hold a candle to this, I thought.

The deck swayed beneath me as Cal rounded a buoy, causing me to brace my left leg. The increased speed, a cool comb that parted the hair on the back of my head, was another reminder of things to come. A weathered red navigational buoy, nun number "4," suddenly appeared at the edge of my peripheral vision, and then bobbed its matronly figure in the small swells we had caused.

We sped east across Cobscook Bay and away from Green Haven as the center of our wake seemed to zip back up what the stem had so brazenly exposed. The surface beyond the churning wake was unusually smooth and protective.

I'm Jane Bunker, a newly deputized marine insurance investigator. I moved to Green Haven, Maine, in June of this year to start a new life. The old life? Well, suffice it to say I left it in Miami. It's important to note that my change of scene was nothing like the proverbial heart left in San Francisco. If my move north were a song, it would be a slightly happier tune—no regrets. Well, almost none. Dropping my position as chief detective of Miami-Dade County in favor of that of a lowly insurance investigator was a quick, albeit calculated, descent on the career ladder. Though, since my return to Maine, I had succeeded in pulling myself up a rung, and had just picked up the title assistant deputy of Knox County. Like many of my neighbors, I now wore more than one hat. Deputy sheriff was a part-time, need-based employment. It was simple supply and demand; little criminal activity meant little need for my deputy services.

The deputy gig, still in its infancy (not unlike the marine consulting, which was also relatively new to me), was the result of a lack of interest on behalf of local law enforcement in venturing out to the remote extremities that comprised the territories I cover in my chief job of insurance gal. In this respect I was now able to kill two birds. I could survey damaged property, investigate crime scenes, and write corresponding reports. (Although math is not my strength, I do realize that according to that list, any stones I cast may take care of three birds.)

My boss at Eastern Marine Safety Consultants, Mr. Dubois, had telephoned at nine o'clock this morning with an assignment to inspect damage to some of *Quest*'s deck equipment. He said that *Quest* was a privately owned research vessel authorized by the State of Maine to survey a piece of ocean floor in Cobscook Bay. A large aquaculture outfit, North Atlantic Shell Farms, had applied to lease this particular bottom from the state with ambitions of growing oysters. Surveying the bottom was part of the application process. According to Mr. Dubois, someone had maliciously vandalized some of the deck equipment aboard the vessel. In his opinion, "some of those interbreds with too much time on their hands" had thought of this as entertainment. "Just a quick inspection, a few pictures, and a report will be fine. This is a very important customer for the insurance company. Don't get too . . . well, you know," he advised.

"Thorough?"

"Look, Jane. They don't want to press any charges. They just want to collect what's coming to them, get their equipment repaired, do their job, and get out of that chromosome deficiency zone."

"Come on. Cobble Harbor can't be that bad," I said hopefully.

"Well, it's just . . . remote."

"Worse than Green Haven?" I asked. My new hometown felt like the end of the Earth to me. After our conversation and a look at the road map, I had called Cal. To avoid accusations of double-dipping, I hired Cal to transport me to and from Cobble Harbor via his boat, *Sea Pigeon*. I offered to pay Cal the same $20 per hour that I would receive from the County Sheriff's Department for my time. Cal was happy to oblige. The pay was a bit more than he had been getting at Turners' Fish Plant before it burned to the ground, and this was an opportunity for him to get back on the water, where he had spent the majority of his working life. Sure, I could have driven my car from Green Haven to Cobble Harbor. But driving the length of the two peninsulas I would have needed to traverse would have consumed the majority of my day, not to mention a significant portion of what life remained in my 1987 Plymouth Duster. By water the distance was a very manageable seventeen miles. Economics aside, I thought a boat ride would be nice.

A chronic early bird, I had arrived at our prearranged meeting spot a full twenty minutes ahead of our scheduled rendezvous of 11:30 A.M. And I learned that Cal Dunham was even twitchier than I am when I found him already aboard *Sea Pigeon* at the public landing behind Bartlett's Store. Cal is in his early seventies, tall, but stooped from a long career as an offshore fisherman. He is a man of few words, with the wide honest face of a New Englander. After the unpleasant events following the murder of the town drunk six months ago, Cal had proven himself a steady friend. *Sea Pigeon* was tied to the dock with her engine idling smoothly. I stepped aboard, Cal untied and coiled the single dock line, and off we went toward Quoddy Head.

And I was right to think a boat ride would be nice. It *was* nice—lovely, actually. We arrived at the town dock in Cobble Harbor, as Cal said we would, at just a few minutes past noon. The *Sea Pigeon* seemed diminished in size by the looming stern of *Quest*. The larger vessel cast a square shadow into which we crept as two men appeared on the wharf to catch our dock lines. To some observers, the small mound between Cal's shoulders indicated a degree of decrepitude. But his boat-handling skills, agility, and no-nonsense demeanor revealed competence of a level that thrust helping hands back to pockets as the old man secured his boat and nodded an okay for me to step ashore. My promise to be quick was met with a smile and, "Take your time. I ain't goin' nowhere."

The long step up from *Sea Pigeon* to the dock was made easier by a large hand extended by the taller of the two men standing on the dock. The men seemed to have been waiting for me. Before the tall man released his grip, introductions were made. "You must be Jane Bunker. I'm Dane Stevens, captain of *Quest*." Black sideburns spilled from beneath a red baseball cap sporting the ship's logo, which matched the embroidered patch on the breast of his light gray sweatshirt. His dungarees appeared to have been starched with perfect creases that ended just above comfortable-looking

Sperry Top-Siders. "This is our chief archaeologist, Quentin Molnar—otherwise known as Quasar." The utterance of the nickname was delivered with a broad, white smile that confirmed that this was indeed a friendly mission. The ever important first impression was a positive one; confident and competent, Dane Stevens seemed captainly.

Quasar, on the other hand, was ill at ease. Perhaps he was one of those scientists whom you suspect is more at home in a laboratory than out in the world of human beings; Quentin Molnar squinted nervously behind thick glasses and shifted his weight from foot to foot as he spoke. "Ms. Bunker, thank you. Thanks. Ahh, thanks for coming so quickly. We appreciate your coming here. We're really very grateful. So, thank you." Quasar was absolutely disheveled. The tails of his white oxford shirt were half in and half out of severely wrinkled khakis. It was clear which side he slept on as his thick mop of reddish hair was so lopsided I fought the urge to tilt my head while he was speaking. "We were scheduled to begin work today and now vandals have really screwed us up. We've been vandalized. Vandals have screwed up our schedule." I wondered if Quasar always repeated himself, or if I was making him nervous. "I've already ordered replacement parts for what I can't fix. I can fix a lot of it. I had to order a few things, but not too much. I hope FedEx can find this place. Do you know if FedEx delivers here?"

"I don't know. I'm here to inspect the damage, send

pictures and a claim to the boat's insurance company, and file a police report. Shall we go aboard and have a look?" I asked.

"Oh, yes, of course. Yes, come. Follow me. We'll go aboard. Right this way," Quasar said as he turned and scurried toward the aluminum gangplank that connected the top of the dock to *Quest*. He shuffled across the metal pathway and hopped down onto the deck without a glance back to see if I was with him. The handsome captain motioned for me to go ahead of him with a shrug and a half smile that I took as an apology for Quasar's manners and awkwardness. Soon the three of us stood in the middle of a basketball court-sized work area surrounded by cranes, dredges, winches, a submersible, and several pieces of equipment I didn't recognize. Dane Stevens excused himself to complete some unfinished project, the details of which I don't recall. Slightly disappointed to be left alone with the nerdy archaeologist, I sighed—story of my life.

I quickly got down to the job at hand, anxious to attempt to please my boss by doing only the bare minimum, even though that was against my nature. Quasar, who became articulate on his home turf, led me around the deck in a very educational guided tour of *Quest*'s special equipment. He described in some detail the workings of the magnetoscope and the galeazzi lance, both of which appeared to have been beaten with a sledgehammer. He explained that the magnetoscope was used to detect ferrous masses on the ocean

floor and the lance was designed to remove sediment
buildup around any potential historical sites. "Historical sites? What kind of historical sites?" I asked as I
zoomed my camera in on a circuit board that was exposed and smashed. "I assumed that you'd be surveying to see if the area is suitable for aquaculture." I
turned to Quasar to see what he'd say, but I was just
being polite. Sure, I was curious to learn more. But I
needed only a few pictures and an official report, not
commentary or opinion.

"Oh, we are indeed. That's why we're here; to check
the proposed site for the oyster farmers. But in Cobscook Bay we're thinking we might find remnants of
Native American campsites. Federal and state laws
require offshore projects to hire archaeological companies to determine whether activity will harm his-
torically significant remains." Quasar pushed his
eyeglasses onto the bridge of his nose. "We're also
checking water quality, tidal flow, and other factors
and elements that make the area conducive to growing
oysters. That's all North Atlantic wants to know. They
want to be assured that the site they are applying for to
lease from the State of Maine is ripe for their purposes.
They aren't concerned about anything else."

"Indians camped offshore?" I asked, immediately
forming a negative opinion of money spent on such
foolishness.

"Sure," Quasar said, a smile on his face. "During
the last ice age the level of the ocean plummeted over
three hundred feet. But then the glaciers melted, the
sea level rose again and drowned what we hope to

find—intact underwater cultural sites. How did the first humans get to this continent? Land bridge from Siberia to Alaska following big game?" Quasar's eyes widened with impassioned energy and seemed to grow tenfold with the help of the thick lenses framed in black plastic rims. "Or was it via the coastal route from Europe? It's a debate that could be settled by finding submerged settlements with evidence of tools or food gathering." Quasar's voice had gone up a full octave. By the time Quasar had completely saturated me with his passion for archaeological expeditions, I knew that he'd only scratched the surface of his vast knowledge. Through his work he intended to support theories of whys and wheres of the earliest inhabitants of New England. Although I had all I needed to get the ball rolling toward reimbursement from *Quest*'s insurance company for all damages, I asked a few questions—more out of curiosity than anything else. I wasn't feigning interest out of politeness anymore. I was genuinely intrigued.

It was abundantly clear that Quasar's connection to aquaculture was due only to the fact that North Atlantic Shell Farms was footing the bill to allow Quasar and what I assumed would be a team of scientists the opportunity to delve below. And it was also clear that this wild-eyed archaeologist was hoping to find exactly what his employers didn't want him to discover. A historic site would definitely be a setback for a company that would prosper in establishing oyster beds on the ocean floor. As a point of interest, Quasar mentioned that the vandals had sabotaged only what was needed

for underwater exploration. None of the vessel's pro-
pulsion, electronic navigational aids, or other state-of-
the-art systems had been disturbed in any way. To his
eye, in contrast to what my boss thought about a random strike born of boredom and stupidity, this incident was a direct attack targeting the archaeological
aspect of the survey. Quasar was agitated in a way that
I found consistent with any victim of a personal attack.

Now Quasar had piqued my interest. I knew that I
wasn't supposed to bother with motive, but I couldn't
stop myself from asking, "Who would care?" And
when I saw his face fall in utter dejection, I quickly
added, "I mean, who would want to keep you from doing such important work?" Quasar attempted to drag
a freckled, bony hand through his tangled mess of red
curls, but found the spiderweb of hair too embroiled
to traverse. As he tried to pull his fingers from where
they were caught, deep in his rat's nest, he shared his
opinions and theories as though he'd been hypothesiz-
ing for some time. A lot of criminal investigating is
timing. And knowing when to ask the right question
is my forte. While Quasar was in the midst of a very
long-winded answer to my query, I decided that it was
a good thing there would be no charges pressed, as the
list of possible suspects was, in Quasar's opinion, quite
lengthy. Quasar was acutely aware of the many factions who had vested interests in Cobscook Bay and
he led me through his understanding of the situation
as we moved slowly in the direction of my ride home.

Quasar thought the damage could have been done
by any member of two large, extended families of lob-

ster fishermen who worked on Cobscook Bay, the Alleys and the Beals. It seemed that, like the legendary Hatfields and McCoys, these two families had been feuding for nearly a century. So many generations into the fight, no one remembered exactly what had caused the rift. But everyone knew that a battle was presently being waged in Cobscook Bay, and it was all in the name of lobster. According to the scientist, this was the gear war that had escalated to exceed all gear wars. This controversy had gone beyond the occasional molesting of the other side's fishing gear—lobster traps, in this case. Quasar, who had been in Cobble Harbor for only a few days, had learned of beatings, burnings, and sinkings. "A reasonable person might speculate that a threat from a third party like North Atlantic Shell Farms might cause the Alleys and Beals to join forces against their common enemy. Their sheer strength in numbers could make aquaculture impossible here if they banded together and went about defeating the project legally. But these aren't reasonable people. So it could have been either family, or both, or neither." Quasar ran a hand along the badly battered metal housing of the magnetoscope as if caressing a wound.

"And then there's the Native Americans," Quasar continued. "Both the Passamaquoddy and Maliseet tribes claim to have aboriginal rights to fish Cobscook Bay unencumbered by state or federal rules. Once the lobster traps come ashore, the Indians move into the bay to harvest sea urchins."

"Wouldn't the Native Americans encourage your

research if they felt the results would protect some . . . .
Well, if they believed there could be evidence of . . ."
I struggled with the politically correct terminology.

"Heck no!" Quasar rescued me. "Nothing is sacred
to anyone other than to the very oldest members of
either tribe. There are no jobs in this area. The Native
Americans are split on the aquaculture issue. The
enormous scope of this aquaculture might infringe on
a lot of the grounds claimed by ancestral fishing rights,
but would provide some decent jobs, too."

"Hatfields, McCoys, Passamaquoddy, Maliseet . . .
Anyone else?" I was once again grateful not to have to
get to the bottom of this one.

"I guess the major oil companies would be incon-
venienced by having to reroute ships. Many tankers
use Cobscook Bay as a shipping channel in their de-
liveries up the river." I wondered why this possibility
was secondary to feuding fishermen and disenfran-
chised Indians. "And, like anything else, there are always a number of citizens who just don't like change,"
Quasar said with a degree of resignation in his voice.
I understood his tone as a cue to wish him luck before
hopping back aboard *Sea Pigeon*.

On my way out, I poked my head through the
fo'c'sle door hoping to find the captain, but didn't.
Rather than wandering around the ship, I asked Quasar to please relay my thanks to his captain. Relieved
that my request was not met with a knowing look
from the nerdy man, I realized that he must be accustomed to his friend getting all the attention from
women. And I understood that I would not become

one of those women, as the handsome one did not appear for even a distant wave goodbye as Cal and I left the dock for the outer harbor. Oh well, I thought, I probably wouldn't return to Cobble Harbor for a long time, and the chances of running into Dane Stevens in my landlocked travels were slim.

I turned away from the *Quest* and joined Cal at the helm, where he navigated a twisted path heavily studded with the multicolored bullet floats that marked lobster traps. Buoys bowed and curtsied as they were swept aside by the water cleaved at the bow. Cal piloted and I talked. I told him about what I'd found on the *Quest* and what I'd learned from Quasar, leaving no opportunity for my hired water chauffeur to reply or comment. I talked knowing that Cal was less than a sounding board, as I'd learned that he seldom gives any indication of what he's absorbing and what he's deflecting. Cal's concentration seemed to be split between the cigarette he was enjoying and the avoidance of lobster gear while maintaining a westward course. So my talking became more like thinking aloud in the presence of someone barely paying attention.

A white speck on the horizon was the only evidence of anyone working in this hotly contested area of Cobscook Bay. This late in the afternoon, I imagined that all of the other lobster fishermen had given up work for the day. I took comfort in the solitude while rehashing facts and formulating theories. I'm often considered the queen of "mountains from molehills," I know. But I'm right at least some of the time. When I stumbled across the town drunk's body on the shore back in June, everyone else thought his death had just been an accident, but I thought there was more to it than that. After a couple instances of insurance fraud, an act of arson that took out Green Haven's primary employer, and several attempts on my life, it turned out I was right. Since then, things have been a little on the dull side.

The white speck on the horizon gradually took shape: a lone lobster boat circling around and around.

At our present speed I had assumed we would arrive back in Green Haven before dark. That meant I would have time to get home to my apartment, transcribe today's work into the computer, and send my completed report along to the insurance company. That was one nice thing about my new career, I thought. Most of the time, I could complete an assignment in one day. It was great to have such a sense of accomplishment and be able to measure success in a quantitative way each evening and wake up the following morning with a whole new perspective. Very seldom does anything linger. I was already wondering what tomorrow would bring. This work was less than exciting, but hell, hadn't I had my fill of excitement in Miami? I hoped that I would be able to hire Cal in the future. I wondered whether he'd be interested in driving me to assignments via land. Maybe I would ask him. Suddenly my thoughts were interrupted by the slowing of the *Sea Pigeon*'s engine.

I turned to face forward again and noticed that we were getting fairly close to the lobster boat I had seen on the horizon. The clean, white boat was in the perpetual, lazy, starboard circle identical to that of any boat hauling lobster traps. Cal slowed the engine down to an idle as we approached the boat, whose bow now bent away from ours. Maybe Cal knew this boat or was a friend of its captain, I thought. I wouldn't be surprised if Cal knew everyone on the bay. He'd certainly spent enough time out here in the past. Now the port side faced us as Cal threw the *Sea Pigeon*'s engine out of gear. Oh, I thought, wouldn't it be nice to surprise my landlords with lobster for dinner? I wondered how much cash I had in my pocket. Now the stern came gracefully into view—*Eva B.* Beautiful boat, I thought. And a pretty name. I wondered if the "B" stood for Beal. I felt some paper money in my pocket and figured I had enough for three lobsters as long as they weren't too big. I glanced at Cal. His face was ashen. "What?" I asked.

Cal swallowed hard and never took his eyes off the *Eva B.* I looked over the bow and directly into the cockpit of the lobster boat. A numbing of my limbs and sickness in my gut grew stronger as Cal confirmed what I saw.

"There's no one aboard her."

TWO

The absence of life aboard the *Eva B.* evoked a dark image that quickly overshadowed my other thoughts and doused my hunger for lobster. The scene was numbing in what it suggested. An abandoned boat running in a dizzying and endless loop was something I had heard about during my years working the coast of South Florida. But until now, I had never personally encountered one. Floridian stone crabbers and bandit fishermen who worked inshore would cut expenses in times of slow harvests by laying off deckhands and fishing single-handedly. Maine lobstermen often did the same. Of all their expenses—bait, fuel, gear, etc.—help was the only one a captain could leave at the dock and still be able to produce. Although fishing alone was generally considered to be unwise to the point of foolhardy, a lot of small-boat operators did it; many claimed to prefer solitude at sea. By the looks of what was unfolding in front of me, this was also the case in Cobscook Bay.

Cal pulled the throttle back to an idle as we watched the *Eva B.* complete another full circle. I prayed, as I knew Cal did, that a baseball-capped head would suddenly appear in the small rectangular doorway that led to the cutty cabin between the helm bulkhead and stem. "Maybe someone's down forward," I suggested, verbalizing our shared hope.

"It's possible," Cal said as he brushed by me and opened the half-size door that led to the small triangular storage area of our boat's cabin. Cal stepped down into the fiberglass cave, vanished into relative darkness, and then reappeared with an air horn in one hand and a rusty shotgun in the other. Cal placed the gun in the corner formed by the meeting of bulkhead and gunwale, setting its butt on the deck firmly. In answer to what I suppose was a surprised look from me, Cal stated that he never boarded another man's vessel unannounced or uninvited. "Consider this my announcement," he said as he placed the air horn on the dash, reengaged the transmission, and maneuvered to draw us nearer the *Eva B*.

"Is that thing loaded?" I asked, not yet sure whether the presence of a firearm made me feel more or less anxious.

"Should be," Cal said, grabbing the horn and giving the can of compressed air a brisk shake. "I ain't used it since the Blessing of the Fleet—Fourth of July." I understood that Cal knew full well that my question had not been in regard to the horn, so I assumed the shotgun was loaded. Of course it was, I thought. What good was an empty gun?

As we passed the *Eva B*.'s stern, Cal pressed the red plastic button, releasing a long whistle of air from the can through the six-inch, trumpet-shaped, polished aluminum horn, resulting in a very impressive ear-splitting blast. He removed his index finger from the button, cutting the blaring noise like a meat cleaver would a wet noodle. We waited and watched for several anxious seconds for a startled and embarrassed captain to scramble out and into view, perhaps waving a wrench to signal he was okay and thanking us for our concern. But no one showed. Cal gave the horn a couple of short squirts, the volume of each of which made me flinch. Sadly, my flinching was the only reaction to Cal's "announcement."

"One of us has to go aboard her," Cal said.

"I'll go," I said without hesitation, and moved behind Cal to the starboard gunwale. Of the two of us, I knew I was more able physically to perform the boat hop if calisthenics should be required. Cal nodded his consent and turned his attention to driving the *Sea Pigeon*. I briefly wondered what the temperature of the water was. I'd always heard that, all things considered, death from hypothermia wasn't a bad way to go.

As the gap narrowed between the *Sea Pigeon* and the *Eva B.*, Cal gave me last-minute instructions over his right shoulder. "Don't climb onto the rail until we're ahead of her wake. And don't jump. I'll put you right alongside her. Just knock her out of gear, and we'll raft up." The *Eva B.* had been circling long enough to have built up quite a confused chop all around her. Death as a result of being crushed between the boats would be on the more unpleasant end of the scale. And to think that just a few minutes ago this day offered

nothing more than a routine inspection of vandalized
equipment aboard a research vessel. Cal increased the
throttle and brought the *Sea Pigeon*'s starboard bow
against the *Eva B.*'s port beam just aft of her house.
Both boats were bouncing enough to make the transfer hairy. I climbed onto the rail and grabbed the edge
of the overhead for stability. The few seconds that
passed as I waited for Cal to close the V-shaped opening between the rails were filled not with fear, but with
a classic clip from an old Western racing through my
mind. Cowboy movies always had a scene like this
with our hero jumping from one horse to another, I
thought. The movie in my head was interrupted when
Cal yelled, "Now!"

At this instant, the boats were pressed together from
beam to stern. The step I made was an easy one; rail
to rail. I released my grip from the *Sea Pigeon*'s roof
and hopped down into the cockpit of the *Eva B.* Once
both of my feet were planted safely on deck, Cal peeled
away to port, signaling a reminder for me to pull the
Eva B.'s gear shift into the neutral position. I hustled
to the helm, eased the throttle control back to an idle,
and jerked the gear shift toward me so it was vertical.
With her engine disengaged, the *Eva B.* slowed from
a hearty jog to a peaceful drift as the waves created
by the two wakes moved away in circles of growing
circumference and shrinking height. Cal was now
about a hundred feet off my starboard side. He tied
fenders at *Sea Pigeon*'s stern and midship in preparation for securing to the *Eva B.,* or "rafting up" as he
had said. I kept my attention focused on the old man

and my back purposefully to the door that led to the
only compartment of the *Eva B.* that was unexposed.
I couldn't help but think that compartment was large
enough to hold a person. Yes, I was anxious.

Cal was lucky I am so comfortable on boats. Much
of my childhood leisure time was spent crawling
around the commercial docks of Miami—crawling,
like a wharf rat. I was like the proverbial bad penny in
my persistence against the advice and even scolding I
received from nearly everyone I encountered. Mer-
chant seamen, longshoremen, fishermen, sailors . . .
Men of the sea in general all advised me to stay away.
It took a while, but I was eventually able to convince
all concerned that I was safer on the waterfront than I
was on the city streets. Or at least I was *as* safe. When
ships' cooks started slipping me treats and deckhands
shared trinkets and stories in broken English of faraway ports, I knew I was in. But it wasn't until I won
over Archie that I really belonged to this salty extended
family.

Archie, a lifelong commercial fisherman whom I
now considered my best friend and mentor, gave me
my most cherished gift—an education in all things related to the sea. In return, Archie got cheap labor. Cal
reminded me of Archie, which explained my immediate fondness and trust in him. Of course, I had never
explained my boat savvy to Cal. I didn't need to. On the
water, ability is displayed in action and reaction.
Words don't cut it. So, when Cal eased the *Sea Pigeon*
alongside *Eva B.,* he didn't tell me when or how to take
a couple of wraps of a line around a cleat. I just did it.

Now that we were rafted up and drifting in the slight southwesterly breeze, I imagined we looked like an awkward catamaran. "What next?" I asked, as Cal sat on the rail of his boat, shotgun in hand, and slung a leg over the rail and into the *Eva B.*'s cockpit.

Once aboard, Cal smoothed his clothes with a sweep of an open palm and then patted a loose strand of white hair back into place. Cal was always neatly groomed. "We should check down forward before calling the Coast Guard."

"Check for what? Bodies?"

"Well, I don't know about you. But I'd be embarrassed if the Coasties came all the way from Southwest Harbor to find a tired old fisherman down there taking a nap." Cal motioned at the door in the bulkhead with the barrel of his gun, indicating to me that he expected ladies to go first. "You're the deputy." I knew as well as Cal did that if anyone *was* aboard the *Eva B.*, they were not likely to wake up from their "nap."

I approached the door with the apprehension of someone turning the crank on the side of a jack-in-the-box. The pounding in my chest was strangely comforting and exhilarating. I took one last look at Cal's decrepit weapon. I thought about how far a cry this was from the Homeland Security boardings I had been part of off the coast of Key West. Overcoming fear in the face of danger was perhaps the only aspect of my former life that I missed. I took a deep breath and willed myself to be brave the way I always had; then I threw the door open with a bang. The setting sun spilled enough light into the small cabin for me to see that all it contained were spare coils of line, buoys, buckets of oil, belts, hoses, life jackets, and cleaning supplies. "See?" I said, standing to the side of the doorway so that Cal could look, too. "Nobody home. Let's call the Coast Guard."

Cal was already straddling the crease between the boats when I turned to discuss our course of action. I followed him back over the gunwales, feeling more at ease aboard the *Sea Pigeon*. The likelihood that a man had been lost at sea from the deck of the *Eva B.* gave the boat a certain shiver factor; a creepy aura difficult to ignore. Cal hailed the Coast Guard on channel 16 of his VHF radio, switched to a working frequency at their request, and relayed our predicament. As a rule (and this episode was no exception), government agencies have strict protocols from which they will not stray—no matter how ridiculous. Like the silly frequency-switching business. I was relieved that Cal was manning the radio. While the Coast Guard dispatcher ran Cal through the usual hoops of seemingly unrelated questions, I scanned the horizon and considered different scenarios of varying plausibility.

Weather, it seemed to me, could not have been a contributing factor to the situation we had happened upon. "Are you in any immediate danger, Captain?" I detected an accent—not local—in the voice of the young Coast Guardsman I now heard over the radio. Cal gave the low-down again, quickly and with more urgency this time. Although it wasn't impossible that a freak sea or rogue wave had swept the *Eva B.*'s captain overboard, I thought it was highly unlikely. "How many persons are onboard the vessel, Captain?" Neither Cal nor I knew which vessel the dispatcher was asking about. I suspected that he didn't either. "How many persons are onboard *your* vessel, Captain?" Yes, an accent, I thought—definitely Midwestern.

Falling overboard while taking a leak was a risk, I supposed. I had heard and had stored in my memory that when lost bodies were recovered from the ocean, a high percentage of the victims' flies were open. "Are you taking on water at this time, Captain? Captain, we request that you don your personal flotation devices at this time." Cal was getting annoyed with the boy from Kansas with whom he was trying to communicate. I was amused when the veteran mariner lied by assuring the Coastie that we had indeed donned our life jackets. Cal asked again when we could expect a Coast Guard vessel to arrive on the scene and suggested that an aircraft be deployed to begin a search of the vicinity.

Cal tried valiantly to explain the situation again— that we weren't in any danger, but a man was missing at sea. I continued to ponder what might have happened. It didn't seem possible that a man of average height could accidentally fall overboard from the *Eva B.* The gunwales along the length of her work space were high enough to meet anyone at mid-thigh. No, I couldn't see an accidental falling overboard, fly down or not. The missing fisherman most probably had been dragged over the side or stern by his own lobster gear. It wasn't unusual for rescuers to recover a drowned

fisherman by hauling his gear and finding the corpse
entangled in the line. Judging from the size and number of masonry bricks built into the lobster traps
I'd seen all over Green Haven, Mark Spitz himself
wouldn't have been able to stay on the surface if he
were attached to one as it dove for the bottom. "Roger,
Captain. Please relay your present position in lat/long.
Over."

Cal looked at me and shook his head, raising his
hands in surrender before keying the radio's microphone for what I believed would be his last transmission: "Our present position is approximately ten feet
northeast of our last position given to you at precisely
sixteen hundred hours. Is there a boat under way? Has
a plane been deployed? There may be a man treading
water out here, damn it! Over."

"Roger, Captain. Stand by."

Cal left the microphone dangling from its cord from
the overhead and joined me where I sat, resting on the
starboard rail. A freshly lit cigarette soothed what the
inexperienced Coast Guardsman and red tape had
rubbed the wrong way. While Cal smoked, I pulled a
pad from my tote bag and jotted some notes, including our latitude and longitude, which were displayed
in large black digits on the face of the GPS. "Not you,
too," Cal said, lightly enough to be interpreted as a
tease.

"I just thought it would be wise to calculate our
drift," I answered without taking my eyes off the
screen. "It might help narrow the field for the search."

"Point six knots to the northeast." I should have

known Cal would be ahead of me in this game, but continued to go through the motions of calculating. I knew it might be quite some time before the Coast Guard arrived and took the *Eva B.* off our hands, so I climbed back aboard her and looked around more closely than I had initially. I started below in the cabin, where I saw nothing out of the ordinary except for an abundance of shipping supplies. It was like a little warehouse. There was a stack of cardboard boxes printed with LIVE LOBSTERS—HANDLE WITH CARE, a tape gun and a folder with preprinted shipping labels. The return address on the labels read COBSCOOK LOBSTER COMPANY, which did nothing to help ID the missing fisherman. Everything else in storage was either for maintenance and repair, or they were the usual supplies one would find aboard any lobster boat, such as lobster bands, spare banding tools, a lobster measure, a short gaff, and half a dozen blue cotton work gloves. The gloves were size large. So for all of my poking around, the size of his hands was all I learned of the missing fisherman.

Two steps up and out of the cabin I was back beside the helm. I removed the top of a small cooler, ignoring Cal's comment about the man's lunch. The cooler was filled with frozen gel packs, so it seemed obvious that the man had intended to box his catch aboard and ship the boxes as soon as he got back to port.

The color sounder mounted on the dash showed the ocean floor beneath us in a medium red horizontal line; yellow numbers illuminated the depth at twelve fathoms. In over seventy feet of water, the missing fisherman had certainly not walked home. A GPS track plotter displayed an array of colorful event marks that I assumed represented exact locations of the lobster traps. A lime green track like an endless doodle ran across the monitor in curlicues that terminated at the white blinking boat-shaped symbol; this showed our position in relation to traps and landmass. I found the button that controlled the scale of the picture on the monitor, and zoomed out until I found the far end of the corkscrewed wake. Somewhat of an electronics geek, I admired the top-of-the-line equipment aboard the *Eva B.*

"Wow," I said as I roughly estimated the time and distance the *Eva B.* had traveled since wandering off the well-beaten, lime green track. "We're more than three miles northeast of where it appears the boat strayed from the line of traps he was fishing. At point six knots, that's way too long to hope for a miracle. No one can hold their breath that long."

"Where's the goddamned plane?" Cal stood, shielded his eyes with a hand, and searched the sky. "It'll be pitch-black here in three hours. There'll be no chance to save him if he has to wait until morning."

"But a plane won't help much if he's on the bottom tangled in his own gear," I added.

"He ain't."

"Ain't what?"

"Ain't snarled in his own gear. He wasn't hauling traps. The bottom in this part of the bay is all mud.

Look at that boat," Cal said and motioned toward the *Eva B*. "She's clean as a whistle. If he had just hauled and set, there'd be a mess along the rail. And where's the bait? Everything's all tucked away nice and neat. I'd bet he went overboard cleaning her up. Most fellas put the boat in a hard circle while they tidy up after hauling, and most fellas dip a five-gallon bucket over the side for wash-down water. Maybe he lost his balance and got pulled over by the bucket. There're lobsters in the tank, so we know he *had* been hauling. But . . ." Cal stopped his rant and cocked his head to one side. Squinting toward the east he said, "Boats."

Sure enough, there were boats coming from the east. They were approaching quickly, and as they cut the distance I counted eleven. Soon the lead boat, *Ardency,* was rafting to our free side. The two men aboard *Ardency* were dressed in dark orange Grundéns, the waterproof bib overalls worn by most Green Haven fishermen. Almond-shaped black eyes peered from under visors salt-stained from adjusting with wet gloves. The captain, who appeared to be the father of the man in the stern, wasted no time with questions or small talk. He was crossing our deck before his son finished securing the stern line and then hopped from us onto the *Eva B*. Both men were slight of stature, yet had forearms beneath rolled-up flannel sleeves that looked hard enough to drive spikes. What I guessed was half of the Cobble Harbor fleet—either the Hatfields or the McCoys—soon coasted to relative stops all around us. With the circling of wagons came the odd comfort of knowing that Cal and I were not in this probable tragedy alone.

Each of the ten boats on the perimeter was manned in twos by fishermen who stood with arms crossed at chests and stared, waiting for direction. As the seconds ticked by, the younger men began to fidget a bit with what I took as anxiety and disbelief while the more weathered members of the group were stilled by a common resolve that I understood as maturity in the face of almost certainly bad news about the fate of a fellow fraternity member. I wanted to know the missing man's name and ask his age, but it seemed I would have to wait to read it in the newspaper. The man who had jumped aboard the *Eva B.* grabbed the VHF mic and began organizing what I thought would be a search party, but sounded more like a cleanup crew. No one had said a word to either Cal or me.

"All right, boys," he began in a voice deeper than what I imagined his thin frame would produce. "If we each haul between fifty and sixty traps, we can get the bulk of them to the harbor before dark. Keep the gear aboard until I find out what Lillian wants done with it. Let's all meet at the dock tomorrow after the funeral." Funeral! Tomorrow! This was too bizarre, I thought. They hadn't even *looked* for a body. How could they possibly have a service so soon? I glanced at Cal, who shot me a look that had "shut up" all over it. The muscle at the jaw on the side of the captain's face worked in and out as he gave each boat instructions over the radio while he stared at the plotter.

"Greg, southeast part of Forsaken Ground. Dan, you take the stuff on Three Fathoms. Phil, looks like there's a full load along the twenty-six line between the Tetons. . . ." And he continued until all ten boats had steamed off. Placing the microphone back into its bracket, he began shutting off all of the *Eva B.*'s electronics and then turned the key to kill the engine.

On his way back across the *Sea Pigeon,* the captain stopped, shook Cal's hand solemnly, and nodded to me. "We heard you call the Coast Guard and came out as fast as we could. Most of us were just getting in from hauling, so we were still aboard our boats. I can't thank you enough. I guess the Coast Guard expects you to stand by with his boat until they get here to tow her in. I have to hustle along now to get a load of his traps before dark. Thanks again." And with that, the man joined his son back aboard *Ardency* and began casting off the lines.

"Shouldn't some of you be searching for him?" I asked as politely as I could. "I mean, what if he's still alive and waiting for someone to pick him out of the water?"

"With all due respect, ma'am, he's not." Both men pushed against the side of *Sea Pigeon* to separate the two boats.

"How do you know?" I asked.

"He can't swim."

"Maybe he's wearing a life jacket." My voice was louder now to cover the growing distance and two diesel engines.

"He never did."

"What if he's clinging to a buoy or piece of drift-wood?" I insisted.

"He wouldn't." His hand reached for the gear shift.

"Wouldn't? Why wouldn't he?" I pleaded. "You seem to know him quite well."

"I knew him quite well. He was my brother, Parker Alley."

THREE

Although it seemed to take forever, I'm certain that the Coast Guard vessel was in sight within an hour of the *Ardency*'s casting off. *Vigilance,* a large and stately-looking ship with her telltale Coast Guard stripe—a wide red slash on either side of the bow—seemed overkill for the task at hand. As she drew near enough for Cal and me to read the name on her bow, the man on the radio finally gave up his futile attempts to hail the *Sea Pigeon.* I didn't question Cal's ignoring the many calls from the Coast Guard ship, as it was clearly getting closer with each transmission. I had learned long ago how captains feel about unsolicited input from subordinates.

Men in blue uniforms scrambled to place fat bumpers along the ship's hull and flaked lines hand over hand onto the deck, resulting in neat coils ready to heave. A man on the open flybridge called down at us through a megaphone as they drifted at a fifty-foot distance by our starboard beam. "We are preparing to come alongside, Captain."

Cal flashed a thumbs-up toward the megaphone and said softly, "I can see that, dumbass."

There was a little more scrambling before the captain finally engaged the engines and began an awkward maneuvering; first away from us, then back toward us. As it looked like *Vigilance* was coming in for a landing, the man with the megaphone ordered us to stand away from the rail they were now quickly approaching. Cal moved to the helm, where he grasped the wheel with both hands and advised me calmly, "Brace yourself." I did as I was told, joining Cal at the helm and holding on to the edge of the dash tightly. The first attempt by the Coast Guard to come alongside was a glancing blow that caused *Sea Pigeon* and *Eva B.* to career against the inflated rubber fenders between them, designed and intended for this purpose. The cooler fell from the *Eva B.*'s engine hatch with a loud crash, sending frozen gel packs skittering on the deck. No damage. As the Coast Guard ship pulled away for another try I could hear the usual noise from the bridge to the men on deck, not really blaming them for the miss, but indicating to anyone within hearing range that it was because something had not been executed properly that the captain was not able to stick the landing. His second approach was much slower. The ship eased into our starboard rail, and two young men hopped aboard and secured lines.

The next thirty minutes or so were painful. Cal relayed all of the information he had about what had transpired prior to the Coast Guard's arrival on the scene, while an electronics expert examined the *Eva*

B.'s plotter, finally coming to the conclusion that
the missing fisherman must have fallen overboard.
The men were dressed in dark blue jumpsuits and orange life vests from which dangled whistles and safety
strobe lights. Each man sported a holstered firearm.
The legs of their pants were tucked into black lace-
up combat-style boots. It appeared to me that the
Coast Guard was currently better suited to respond
to breaches of Homeland Security than search and rescue. The Coasties were young and polite and appeared
to be embarrassed by their own inexperience. I was relieved that Cal took it easy on them when they asked
their silly questions. They had protocol, checklists, and
superior officers. It was understood that the young men
were doing their jobs as they had been trained. They
showed Cal all the respect due to an ancient mariner.
Unsure of my jurisdiction as deputy sheriff, I didn't
volunteer any information, which I imagined pleased
Cal as he began to fidget with impatience. The crew
of *Vigilance* was either unwilling to make a decision
or unable to move without permission from higher-
ups, something they were finally given reluctantly over
the VHF radio after what I perceived as an ungodly
amount of time between requests.

At last, the captain of the ship was told to take the
Eva B. in tow, and he quickly ordered his men to do
so. When I asked, I was told that they would tow the
small boat to their home port and Coast Guard base in
Southwest Harbor, where they would investigate and
notify family. Neither Cal nor I mentioned that the
family needn't be notified. The captain thanked us for

being good Samaritans and gave us permission to get under way. When Cal made a move toward freeing a line, he was asked to stand back to allow the Coast Guard to do it. It wasn't a particularly pretty or smooth operation, but eventually we watched *Vigilance* turn toward the northeast with *Eva B.* tethered securely and closely behind.

I pulled the fenders aboard and stowed the small lines that had once held the *Eva B.* at our side as Cal put the engine in gear and headed toward Green Haven. Cal took one last look over his shoulder and pointed at the sky behind us with two fingers that squeezed a smoldering cigarette. "There," he said. "They've got an air search going. Nothing more we can do." The sight of the helicopter flying low over the water seemed to give Cal permission to leave the scene that trumped any from the Coast Guard. He pushed the throttle up to near full and concentrated on the landmass in the distance. Weird, I reflected, how thoughts of the missing man, Parker Alley, affected me. I was no stranger to missing, or even dead, people. But this was different. We had stumbled upon this without warning. Normally, I was the one to question witnesses. I was the one who would unravel the mystery. And leaving the scene with no answers weighed particularly heavy—like the leaded apron the dentist drapes over your torso before X-raying your teeth. Something said "foul play" to me. But I'd have to shake that thought, as there was no reason for any suspicion. A fisherman had been lost at sea. It happens. His body would wash up on the shore somewhere, and there would be closure. Perhaps the gnawing in my gut was hunger, I thought, as I pulled half a sandwich from my tote bag.

"Want half?" I asked Cal.

"Half of what? Half of half of a peanut butter sandwich I watched you eat the first half of three days ago?" Cal teased, trying to lighten my mood. "Is that all you eat? You must have been raised in an orphanage or something. You're too young to have experienced the Depression. This food rationing thing must have come from your childhood, right?"

"No," I laughed. "I just don't like waste"—I hesitated—"of any kind."

"Well, you go ahead and enjoy it. Betty will have dinner ready by the time I get home." Cal's wife, Betty, is a great home cook. Cal chuckled a bit before adding, "I'll bet you walked to school barefoot, too. Never met such a penny-pincher in my life. Must be something planted deep in your head from childhood. You were taught the value of every dime, right?" My answer was a slow and silent savoring of the stale sandwich. Peanut butter and honey—the honey was a splurge I would not confess to Cal. Amused that he thought of my predilection for cutting financial corners as some sort of effect of trauma or a psychosis, I did nothing to deny either. I was tempted to explain to Cal how the thrift all my friends chided me for was indeed a result of my raising, but not in the way he assumed. My frugality was more of a rebellion to, rather than consequence of, the way I was raised. I relaxed and nibbled the edges of crust, putting on a display for Cal, who watched in disbelief as I nursed what anyone other than a prisoner of war would consume in two bites. The truth about my childhood financial situation was actually pretty funny, I thought, as the entrance to the channel leading to Green Haven Harbor came into view. I must have been all of seven or eight when my mother first taught me the value of money.

It began when I was in the second grade. I asked my mother if "we were rich." "Rich," it seemed at that age, was perhaps the greatest adjective that one could use to describe oneself. And I was absolutely delighted when she answered in the affirmative. Yes, we were rich. We were very rich. She could have left it at that, and I would have been happy. But my mother went on to define our particular kind of wealth. She explained that we were rich in health, happiness, and family love. And, she asked rhetorically, weren't we lucky to have all that? I didn't want to burst my mother's bubble, but I wanted to see bank statements. Money, it seemed, was of no consequence. We had happiness. I think it's fair to say that my personal obsession with financial security and extreme sense of thrift were shaped largely by my mother's "warped" perception of wealth. Still, I have been guided by it, I guess—as I haven't made the most lucrative career choices. For example, Mom's primer on wealth came back to haunt her when I began working for Archie for what she considered slave wages at the age of eleven. I could, she reminded me almost daily, make more money collecting cans and bottles. But, I argued, I was *happy* working on the dock and occasionally aboard the boat. And other than those few times Archie compensated me, I remained unemployed throughout high school—living on love, sustained by happiness, bolstered by kinship.

When my mother did have money, a check from the State of Florida, which she acted surprised to find in her mail on or around the first of every month for as far back as I could remember, she spent like the legendary drunken sailor. She'd tear open the envelope and fan the long yellow check in the air, yelling, "Pay dirt!" It always bothered me that she never saved a nickel for the rest of the month. It was a ritual. "Pay dirt! Come on, Janie! Let's get your brother cleaned up and go out on the town. What do you say?" We never returned home until we had spent the entire check. The remainder of the month we ate meals bought on food stamps, except for my school lunches, which Archie subsidized so that I could avoid the "free line." Oh, and fish. We ate a lot of fish that I brought home from work. Although my mother loved fresh seafood of any kind and referred to it as "brain food," she'd sometimes joke about wishing I'd find a job on a cattle ranch.

All of this reminiscence went down with the last swallow of sandwich, which I had chewed the mandatory thirty-two times. Suddenly the VHF radio came to life with, "Motor vessel *Asprella* calling the *Eva B.* Come in, Captain." The name of Parker Alley's boat brought me quickly back to the scene at hand. I looked at Cal for his reaction, but his eyes remained on the horizon. After a pause, the ship called again. "*Eva B.*,

Eva B., the *Asprella* on channel sixteen. Channel one six, Captain. Come in, please."

Again, there was no visible sign that Cal was moved in any way by this new boat calling the *Eva B.,* but he must have sensed my anxiety as he finally said, "I thought the Coasties might respond. Guess not." Grabbing the microphone, Cal hesitated another few seconds to give the Coast Guard opportunity to answer the call. When they didn't, Cal keyed the mic and said, "*Asprella, Sea Pigeon.* Come in."

"*Asprella* back to the *Sea Pigeon.* Want to shift to channel seventy-three, Captain?"

"Roger." Cal pushed a button on the VHF, changing the channel to 73, and then hailed the *Asprella* again. When the ship's captain answered, Cal relayed that the *Eva B.* was "on the wrong end of a tow line." There was a short pause while this information was digested or discussed, and then the *Asprella's* captain explained that the *Eva B.* had been hired as their pilot boat and was to meet them to pick up the ship's pilot after they were out of the shipping zone. I was unfamiliar with Maine state law, but knew that the federal government requires all ships to take on an additional captain licensed as a pilot to guide the ship through all hazards to navigation. The pilot would be delivered to the ship offshore of any area the ship must transit and outside of any headlands of navigational hazards. The pilot would be someone with "local knowledge" of the area. In this remote area of light shipping, I assumed there were no official pilot boats, so a lobster boat was used. The *Asprella* was now out of the danger zone, so the man piloting her needed a ride ashore. The pause was now on Cal's end of the conversation. "Are you in any hurry to get home?" he asked me. When I responded that I was not, Cal keyed the mic and offered his services to the *Asprella*. "But I'm going to Green Haven. The pilot will have to make arrangements to get home from there," Cal added.

"Roger, Captain. He'll be happier in Green Haven than he would be in Nova Scotia, which is our next stop. We're coming out of Mussel Ridge Channel now and will be heading due east."

"Roger. I'll intercept your course just south of Green Haven." And with this, Cal turned the *Sea Pigeon* back offshore. Within ten minutes we could see the *Asprella* heading toward us. As the ship grew near, I could see that she was a very large and well-maintained oil tanker. Seven hundred feet of hulking steel diminished Cal's boat to suit her name. I was at sea on the back of a pigeon. The bright yellow shell painted high on the ship's superstructure was further evidence that she was indeed a member of the oil fleet. The ship's captain called Cal with some instructions, basically telling him that his intentions were to maintain course and speed at eighty-five degrees and twelve knots, allowing Cal to come along on the *Asprella*'s port side. On that side, just ahead of the bridge, there would be a rope ladder directly under which Cal was instructed to press the side of *Sea Pigeon* against some heavy chaffing gear and fenders. A deckhand would be the first to descend the ladder, lending assistance to the pilot if needed, the captain explained. Once the pilot was

safely aboard, the deck-hand would return to the
Asprella, and Cal should pull away. To these instructions Cal replied, "Roger." Knowing that we had just
been through a similar drill capturing the circling *Eva
B.,* I had great confidence in Cal's boat-handling skills
even when running up against the huge tanker. But I
was relieved to not be the one jumping ship this time.

It went just as the captain suggested it should. Cal
maneuvered alongside and against the rugged fenders
just under the rope ladder, which was more of a net of
coarse webbing, and held position there using the
throttle to keep us against the *Asprella*'s hull. A small,
sharp-faced man scrambled down and straddled the
gap between the two boats, keeping one hand and one
foot on the webbing. A canvas tote bag was lowered
on a hook to the man who took it with his free hand.
Next, the pilot appeared high above us. He was a much
bigger man and was more careful on his way down.
He looked before each step to the next rung and
seemed reluctant to force the release of each handhold.
Finally, he stepped onto the rail with a hand grasping
the deckhand's forearm, grabbed the tote bag, and
jumped into the middle of the deck with a flat-footed
thud. As soon as the deckhand saw the pilot safely on
deck, he waved and scurried back up the ladder, as ag-
ile as could be. "Adios," the pilot yelled cheerily after
the deckhand, who quickly scaled the tanker's mountainous wall. Then under his breath he muttered,
"Fuckin' monkey."

We were quiet as Cal pulled away from the expan-
sive steel tanker, I suppose because it was a bit tense.

The speed of the massive ship as it increased throttle was quite amazing, I thought. Something that big shouldn't move that fast. When we passed her stern, I noticed the *Asprella*'s hailing port was Honduras. High in the rigging I saw the Honduran flag and recalled what I had learned in grade school regarding the significance of its markings. Blue stripes represented the Pacific Ocean and Caribbean Sea and white was the land between them. I couldn't remember what the five stars depicted. I closed my eyes and saw flags from Cuba, Nicaragua, Haiti, and Honduras surrounding Old Glory on the classroom walls of Henry Flagler Elementary. Flagler, of railroad fame, was the first lesson every year—a way to create school pride and unite the factions of kids from the host of countries whose flags adorned our walls. A refugee of sorts, I fit right in with my Latino classmates, who hailed from every ethnic corner of the neighborhood. Ours was an incidental and circumstantial cultural integration—while desegregation busing was being enforced elsewhere, we were a thriving melting pot of inner-city kids unaware of *Brown v. Board of Education*. Funny, all I remembered about Henry Flagler now was that he married three times and died after falling down the stairs.

Once we were in the clear of the *Asprella*'s wake and pointed back in the direction of Green Haven, the pilot introduced himself with quite a flourish of smiles and enthusiasm, not to mention volume. "Hello, folks! The name's Kelley, Willard Kelley. I can't thank youuuuu enough. What a lovely daaaaay, isn't it?" The only urge stronger than the one to plug my ears was the one to hold my nose. Wow, I thought, Willard Kelley has been nipping something. He wasn't, as far I could tell, intoxicated. But there were signs other than his breath that indicated that he had been drinking heavily in the not too distant past. He appeared to have sobered up with a shower as his hair was slicked back and he was heavily perfumed with aftershave: Old Spice, I thought. We exchanged names and handshakes, after which Kelley referred to Cal and me using our full names, Jane Bunker and Cal Dunham, and persistently drew out a random single-syllable word to the point of irritation.

Kelley was a mammoth of a man. He towered over me and moved in close to talk. "So, my friend Parker had to be towed by the Coast Guaaaaard, did you say? My, my, that must certainly have ruined his daaaaay. Probably didn't sell his lobsters yet, either. Too bad. Bad newwwwws."

"You're a friend of Parker Alley?" I asked.

"Well, not a close friend. But he's been my pilot boat for years. Nice maaaaan. Do you know him?"

"No," I said, still wanting to know more about the missing fisherman. After a thoughtful pause to wait for Cal to launch into the story of how we happened upon the *Eva B.*, I realized that Cal was not in the mood for conversation. He had turned on the radar, as it was getting dark, and was focused on navigating us into Green Haven. I thought it might be inconsiderate to allow Kelley to believe that Parker Alley's bad luck was as simple as a broken-down boat. Thinking I could get information by giving information, I told the story, beginning with our trip and reason for going to Cobble Harbor that morning. Kelley listened with interest and interjected a few questions for more detail. He winced at appropriate places and shook his head in disbelief when I got to the part where we found the circling boat with nobody aboard. Kelley seemed genuinely saddened by the loss of a man with whom he had worked for so long.

My ploy to learn more about Parker Alley was a complete failure. The apparent loss of his business associate seemed to have shaken Kelley into a silent mode. As Cal made the boat fast to the dock in the inner harbor, where I had met him so many hours ago, Kelley crossed himself, mumbled what I interpreted as a prayer, and wiped a tear from the corner of his eye. Before heaving himself onto the rail and then onto the wharf, Kelley took a deep breath and exhaled loudly. "Thank you both for everything. I very much appreciate your caaaaaaare and time in helping meeeee and for what you did for Parker Alley." He reached into his canvas tote and pulled out a bottle of Johnnie Walker Black Label, offering it to Cal.

"No thanks. I don't drink." If only Cal knew that this was the favorite scotch of Winston Churchill, I thought, perhaps he'd accept the gift of thanks. Although I prefer the Green Label, I hoped the bottle would be offered to me. It was not. If I was going to splurge on anything, it would definitely be truly great whiskey. Johnnie disappeared into the depths of the bag, where he clinked against whatever other distilled treats were cloistered within.

"You're a better maaaaan than I, Cal Dunham. Thanks again. Now I'm off to fiiiiiind a lady friend. A gal in every port, right, ol' boy? I'm in no rush to find my way back to Cobble Harbor. All work and noooo play . . ." With this he snickered and banged Cal on the back. "Just my luck, I'm walking distance to the chicken coop. Any port in a storm. No offense, Jane Bunker."

We said our goodbyes and watched Willard Kelley disappear on foot up the dock and into the parking lot. "What a rig," Cal said with a smile as he snapped taut the hitch he'd made around a piling with the stern line. "I probably should have taken that jug and given it to you. Sorry I didn't."

"I like single malts. Don't usually drink blended whiskey," I said with an air of superiority that I am sure went unappreciated. I climbed over the rail and onto the dock.

"I wouldn't know the difference," Cal said as he joined me on the dock. We walked to Cal's truck, where he opened the door and asked, "What's next?"

Although my heart wanted to search for Parker Alley, I knew that Cal was asking about the job we'd begun in Cobble Harbor this morning. "I'll file the paperwork for the insurance claim and the police report and let you know if there will be follow-up with another trip. Other than that, I'll wait for the next assignment and call you when I need a ride. Thanks for everything, Cal. We'll settle up when I get a check from the Sheriff's Department."

"Okay. Ride home?"

Knowing that a walk up the hill would stretch my legs and clear my mind, I declined the offer of a ride and bid Cal good night. I slung the handles of my bag onto my shoulder, tucked my hands into my hip pockets, and struck out for home. Soon it would be my first winter in Maine—or at least the first one since I had been old enough to pay attention. I anticipated the cooler weather with a childish excitement. God, I thought, what if I couldn't tolerate the cold? All of those snowbirds couldn't be wrong. Snow angels and hot chocolate could be overrated. Autumn was certainly splendid, I thought, as the tempo of music through an open window quickened my pace. I hustled by the darkened doorways of the coffee shop and past the Old Maids. I imagined Marlena and Marilyn strategizing how to best hook customers into unnecessary purchases as they doted on their litter of Scottish Folds, their prized and odd cats that were fixtures as permanent as the cash register in the gals' all-purpose store.

The local businesses had shortened their hours, and would further reduce the times they were open by Thanksgiving, as the seasonal residents had left Green Haven in droves on Labor Day and were still trickling away. Many of those who would stay took great pride in their status as year-rounders, but the cachet of this had evaded me so far. I hoped it was not testimony to their toughness or need for survival skills. Full-time residents of Green Haven were quick to let you know how many generations their family had endured here. With this in mind, I realized that winter might be very difficult to bear. I'd soon know if the hardiness boasted of by the natives of this town was genetic or conditioned.

I decided not to attempt to evade the motion-sensing lights in my landlords' gift shop and sneak to my apartment unnoticed, so I walked right through the Vickersons' front door after a knock and yelled, "Hello. Anybody home?"

"Jane! Of course we're home. Where else would we be at happy hour? Come in, come in," Mrs. V called back in a tone that hinted that happy hour was well under way. I entered, closing the door behind me, and found the elderly couple whom I had come to adore— in spite of their many quirks and annoying habits— sipping highballs and splitting attention between the local nightly news and the stereo. "Where have you been, girl?" asked Alice. And before I could answer she added, "Henry, get Jane a drink."

"Great. Thanks, Mr. V. It's been a long day," I said and sank into the recliner that they always seemed to leave vacant for me.

"What'll you have?" Henry asked as he headed for the liquor cabinet.

"Whatever you're drinking will be fine, thanks."

Henry hesitated in mid-stride and reached for the volume knob on the stereo. "I love this part!" Turning the set back up, he sang along, "I picked a good one.

It looked like it could run." Although he was off-key, Henry was right on tempo with Marty Robbins's lamenting of his lost love Feleena. Henry pumped a fist in the air and announced, "That man is a musical genius!"

"Turn that down, dear," Alice whined. "Jane and I want to visit and it's almost time for the weather . . . Kevin Mannix . . . Channel six. *He's* the genius." Henry did as Alice requested and made his way to the well-stocked liquor cabinet. He returned seconds later with a healthy pour of some brown beverage over ice, handed it to me with a cocktail napkin printed with a phone number for the Betty Ford Center, and relaxed on his end of the couch. "Now, if you haven't had dinner, Jane, we have a mussel soufflé in the oven that'll be done in twenty minutes."

I considered the combination of mussels and eggs. I considered the options that might come from my fridge. "Sounds great, Mrs. V. Is this another experiment for your *All Mussel Cookbook*?" While Alice explained the recipe—ingredients and inspiration—I swirled my drink with hopes of diluting it. The *All Mussel Cookbook* had been in the works for years and the Vickersons, despite having cooked mussel dishes every night since the book's inception, seemed no closer to finishing it than when they started.

"And Henry found the most gorgeous, petite mussels right below Horseman's Point. We thought the small ones would work better in a soufflé." Alice had certainly been blessed with the gift of gab, I thought. It was incredible how she was simply never at a loss for something to say. "Of course, I couldn't go with him. Art came to visit today, and stayed." I knew that this was code for Alice having had a bad time with her arthritis, and interjected with a sympathetic groan and frown. "You'll be glad to know that I took your advice and began my medical journal yesterday," she continued as she placed her hand on a notebook on the end table beside her. "I haven't kept a diary in years, but I think you're right. It will be helpful to my doctors to see what I have been experiencing between visits." She handed the notebook to me as she continued with her schedule of upcoming appointments. The cover of the notebook showed a Raggedy Ann doll to which Alice had added a hand-drawn thermometer, Band-Aids, crutches, and facial stitches.

I half listened to Alice and thought I heard Henry snoring on the far end of the couch they shared. That was the best thing about Alice's monologues, I thought. She didn't expect any participation whatsoever. In fact, if I had something to say, which was rare, I knew to rudely interrupt. That was absolutely acceptable. I kept an eye on the television and was captivated when the ticker that ran along the bottom of the screen promised an upcoming story about a missing fisherman. At least Parker Alley is getting a bit of airtime, I thought, as Alice defined fibromyalgia. Somewhere between Alice's unexplained pain and chronic fatigue, the newscaster gained my full attention. "In a bizarre twist of cruel fate, a Cobble Harbor fisherman went missing from his boat today. Authorities have not yet found the body of thirty-nine-year-old Parker Alley. The

Coast Guard has suspended their search until morning. Alley was the father of Jason Alley, the recently deceased teen whose death is a suspected overdose and whose funeral is tomorrow. Our thoughts and prayers go out to the entire Alley family and Cobble Harbor community."

FOUR

I forced myself out of bed, teetering between feeling good about the extra hour of sleep I'd logged and a little slovenly about not having been up before the sun. Maybe it was the after-dinner drink I had accepted, as a deterrent to retiring too early, that slowed my usual morning routine. I pulled open the window shades. The grayness outside did nothing to lighten the funk in which I found myself. Precipitation so light it appeared to hover rather than spritz the ground distorted the view of the harbor in a way that seemed fitting. Yes, I thought, this is a great day for sadness and grieving and tears. A stone's throw to the east, the cozy little community of Cobble Harbor was fully exposed to all elements and emotions today. Missing persons and overdosed teens were commonplace where I come from. But even in the short while I had lived in Green Haven I had begun not only to understand, but to feel the shame and disgrace families and whole communities experience when illegal activity is close at hand. I felt bad. Well, maybe more like sad. Weird, I thought, how a mere one-hour difference in the usual start of the day could throw me out of sync. Or there was the possibility that I was changing.

My past in Miami was littered with similar incidents and statistics. The kid next door could have been killed by a rival gang, an overdose, or just a random drive-by shooting. I wouldn't learn his name. I'd know only how many others had gone the same way in whichever week he had gone down. I wouldn't even know his case number. My concentration then was at the other end of the chain—the top of the chain. I knew the life histories of all the major drug barons, all the traffickers in illegal immigrants, prostitutes, and weapons. I dealt with kingpins. I studied them. I knew what their middle initials stood for. I didn't care to know how old the deceased neighbor was, or what his hobbies were, or what he looked like stretched out in the coffin. How did the death of Jason Alley, which I learned of only last night, and the disappearance and probable death of his father pull the shades on my world into which thousands of others had never cast a shadow? Was this the compassion I had always been accused of not having? After twenty-odd years in Miami criminal justice, had my move here finally softened the stone-hearted "Let's get the bad guys at any cost" gal my colleagues loathed? Did I really lie awake last night worrying about the mother and wife of Jason and Parker? Lillian, was it? God, did I actually remember her name? I *had* changed.

Even though I had overslept, it was still too early to check in with either of my bosses. Mr. Dubois, my immediate superior at Eastern Marine Safety Consultants,

was never available to answer the phone until ten.
And the Knox County Sheriff's Department wouldn't
have anyone manning the desk for incoming calls for
another two hours. And, no, it was not okay to dial the
emergency number just because you are an impatient,
early riser. I had learned that the hard way, twice.
With a little time to kill, a mood to lighten, and a need
for caffeine, I knew the Harbor Café was the one-stop
shop to satisfy all.

Three steps out the door and into the parking lot, I
realized the weather was worse than I first gathered
from the upstairs window. It was raw; not just wet, but
cold. I pulled the front of my unbuttoned cardigan together to close the gap and hustled to my car. Sliding
behind the wheel, I rummaged through my tote bag
for the ignition key. I had not yet become accustomed
to leaving doors unlocked. I shivered and dug deeper
into the bag, frustrated by all of the accumulated clut-
ter I had picked up since the last shaking out. I had
never been one to lose things, so was quick to hit the
panic button when whatever I needed didn't surface
immediately. It was no use. I had emptied the bag onto
the seat beside me and there was no key. "Damn," I
whispered. I'd have to walk. As I pushed the door
open, I noticed the key sitting in the ignition. Wow, I
really had changed, I thought. I had better keep this
departure from the norm to myself, I thought with a
hint of glee as I turned the key and stomped on the
accelerator.

I'd had numerous conversations with fellow Green
Haveners about this practice of leaving keys in cars,

and was consistently on the losing end of what nearly always turned into a debate about safety and risk of theft. They scowled when I admonished them for their negligence. They laughed at the prospect of anyone stealing my Duster. Apparently, no one would ever be quite that desperate. They were amused with my observation that three quarters of Green Haveners drove vehicles listed in the Top Ten Most Stolen. They ignored my tips, including keeping packages out of sight, leaving windows up, putting house keys on a separate key ring, and parking in well-lit, busy areas. They barely tolerated the Post-its I stuck to their steering wheels with notes questioning their obliviousness to matters of security. Now it appeared that I had joined the ranks of the negligent. I had never been described as laid back. I was curious how far my metamorphosis from uptight cop to anarchic Mainer would go.

Absent the summer congestion, Main Street was downright roomy, I thought, as I prepared to swing wide into the parking area in front of the café. Clyde Leeman, who had grown dear to me in spite of being a major nuisance in a village idiot sort of way, stood on the sidewalk and motioned me into a spot directly opposite the coffee shop's entrance. "Cut 'er to the right. Hard right. Keep comin'," Clydie yelled so that I could hear him through the tight windows. His right hand swiveled at the wrist and rotated rapidly toward his face. "Little more. Little more. That's it. Easy." I was on the verge of laughter. There were no cars in the spots on either side of where I was parking. When he signaled me to stop by drawing an index finger across his throat, I jumped on the brake pedal so hard the Duster rocked back and forth on worn-out shocks before finally coming to rest with the front bumper against Clydie's knees. His belt buckle, a snarling bulldog bearing teeth that spelled MAC, might make a nice hood ornament, I thought.

"Hey, thanks, Clyde," I said as I shut and locked the Duster's door behind me. "Are you on your way in or out?" Clyde stood forged to open the entrance to the café.

"I'm out. She gave me the boot before I even finished my second cup." Clyde seemed to take pride in being ejected from the café by Audrey, the young woman who managed and ruled the small business with an iron fist. "I ought to complain to the owners. But I wouldn't want her to get fired. She's in one particular foul mood this morning, Miss Bunker. Be careful."

"Thanks for the warning." I nodded goodbye to Clyde as he closed the door between us a little harder than was required. The cowbells that dangled at mid-door clanged loudly, compelling the attention of the café's only two customers. The Old Maids, Marilyn and Marlena, were bellied up to their usual places at the breakfast counter.

"Who is it?" yelled Audrey angrily from the kitchen.

"It's Jane," answered the ladies in unison.

"Oh, good!" came the reaction from behind the louvered doors that hid the kitchen from view. Audrey sounded genuinely pleased that I had arrived. I like

Audrey, too. A feisty, hardworking girl of about nineteen, Audrey had formed an unlikely friendship with me. The fact that she looked like a punk rocker no longer fazed me. The fact that she didn't care what I thought about anything did. Sure, she has tattoos, pierced body parts, and spiked hair, but I still saw a bit of my youth in Audrey. She's stubborn. Just like me. She is the reason I've made the café part of my morning routine—that and the fact that I am not a cook but also understand that breakfast is the one meal not to be missed.

I joined Marilyn and Marlena at the counter and exchanged the usual pleasantries, then bemoaned the gloomy weather. Audrey came crashing through the swinging doors with a smile that stole the scene from what appeared to be her newly dyed, jet-black hair. "Hey, Jane," she said as she grabbed the glass coffeepot from its warming pad, flipped the mug right-side up on the paper placemat at my section of the counter, and filled it to the brim. "What can I get you, the special?"

Oh, I had become so predictable, I thought. Cal's comments about pinching pennies had struck a nerve. Everyone must think of me as the biggest cheapskate in town. "No, I would like eggs Benedict, please. Poached sort of medium."

"But you always have the special." Her voice went up at the end, as if she were asking a question, like Audrey was wondering if I was all right.

Delighted with her concern, I smiled and said, "I know. I just feel like eggs Benedict this morning."

"You're kidding, right? Eggs Benedict? They're eight fifty. With the tip, that'll cost you a ten spot."

Oh, I hadn't realized breakfast could cost so much. Maybe I would reconsider. No, I wouldn't let Audrey sway me. "I know it's a little splurge. I like eggs Benedict and I haven't had them in a while. Please?" Why I was defending my breakfast order, I had no idea.

Audrey placed her hands on her hips and glared at me, unwilling to give up. "You order the special every day, without even asking what it is. Now suddenly you are in the mood for the most expensive thing on the menu? What's wrong? Marlena and Marilyn both had the special for two ninety-nine apiece." Audrey turned her attention to the Old Maids with some expectation of backup.

"We did. Both of us," confirmed Marilyn.

"It was good, too," added Marlena.

"This is weird," I said and then chuckled. "Okay. You win. I've changed my mind. I'd like the special, please." I raised my coffee mug in a salute to the three women and chuckled again as Audrey disappeared into the kitchen. "What was that about?" I asked.

Marilyn leaned close and spoke softly. "The cook called in sick."

"Again," added Marlena.

"Audrey's filling in at the stove until he recovers," Marilyn confided in a whisper and jerked a thumb toward the kitchen.

"With any luck, that'll be before the lunch crowd comes in." Both women clasped their hands together and glanced at the ceiling as if God lived in the attic.

I didn't know whether their prayers went to the attention of the cook, Audrey, or the customers looking for lunch.

"Oh. Why didn't she just say so?" I asked. When I got no answer other than a stare and a shrug that I took as a reasonable explanation from adults for any actions of a nineteen-year-old girl, I asked, "So, what's the special?"

Now it was the ladies' turn to laugh. They shared a look between them before Marlena said, "Toast."

"Toast! Three-dollar toast?"

"White, whole wheat, or rye?" The question came from behind the doors.

Assuming that Audrey couldn't see me, I raised my hands in surrender. "Rye?" I asked permission.

"That figures." Disgust oozed through the slats of the door.

The next five minutes were filled with banging and slamming of untold things, resulting in a range of sounds including obscenities. The three of us anxiously awaited Audrey's return from what she must certainly have considered hell. Marlena made what amounted to a false start toward the door as Marilyn yanked the hem of her jacket, pulling her back onto the red vinyl upholstered stool between us. Majorly relieved that I would not be left without witnesses to Audrey's wrath, I stood, reached for the pot, and poured three fresh cups of coffee.

"It's probably just her age," Marilyn said as she dumped sugar into her cup and stirred. "Of course, we've been saying that since she learned to talk." Our laughter melted the frost from our side of the swinging doors and we were quickly engaged in warm, meaningless conversation.

When Audrey burst through the doors carrying a tray over one shoulder, the hush was immediate. Smiles vanished without a trace. "Okay." Audrey glanced at the contents of the tray. "Let's see . . . who ordered the toast?" She looked at me and continued, "Oh yes. You wanted the special, didn't you?" I didn't dare open my mouth. I nodded. Setting a plate with four slices of rye toast down in front of me, she said, "You do realize that you're seated in the tweed-only section." The Old Maids were, as always, wearing tweed blazers. Again, I didn't dare open my mouth.

"Was that a comment about our clothes?" Marlena sounded a bit insulted.

"No, that was a comment about Jane's. She's the one not up to code." Audrey reached back onto the tray and set down a plate of cheeses and luncheon meats, then a plate with butter and individual jellies. Next came a bowl of mixed fruit and finally a bowl of cottage cheese. And even some fried eggs.

"Wow, thanks for recommending the special. This looks great," I said before Marlena or Marilyn could react to Audrey's comment about their clothes. "All this for two ninety-nine? Nice." I meant it, too. Audrey had pulled out all the stops.

"That's a lot more special than our specials were," complained Marlena.

Audrey's hands went onto her hips again, a sure sign that she was preparing to fire another shot. I focused on buttering the rye toast and hoped that Audrey would back down. I held my breath until Audrey said nonchalantly, "So, get over it." Thankfully they did get over it. That was the end of the snapping for the time being as the ladies discussed safer things, such as the slowing of Main Street business since Labor Day. That was something the people who worked either side of Green Haven's main thoroughfare could agree upon. I couldn't help but think that Audrey wasn't herself this morning. She had always been a caustic, sharp-tongued smart-ass. And, of course, she could cook, but would have been mad about having to man the café solo. But it wasn't like her to be mean to the harmless Old Maids. I knew better than to challenge her or ask why she might be out of sorts. I blamed my own sour attitude on the weather, but doubted that the tough, resilient Audrey was sensitive to a little cold and rain. Although she was busy chopping and prepping everything that needed to be done before lunch, she still held up her end of the conversation in the way I was accustomed to and enjoyed. It wasn't until the conversation slowed to the usual drivel about our individual daily agendas that Audrey confessed the reason for her mood. "I was supposed to go to a funeral today. Now I'm stuck doing the cook's job so I can't make it."

"Who died?" Marilyn asked.

"A friend."

"Oh, I'm sorry, honey. Was it an accident?" asked Marilyn.

"Yes, I think so. I heard he overdosed on heroin."

"Jason Alley," I said without any inflection of inquiry. Audrey confirmed and wanted to know how I knew his name. "News last night," I said. "How close were you to him? I mean, how well did you know him?" I tried to sound truly concerned and I was; I didn't want Audrey to think that I was simply gathering information for an investigation. This wasn't my case; I really hoped Audrey could tell I was genuinely sympathetic.

Audrey explained that she hadn't seen Jason in over a year and that they had been members of the same youth group back when they were younger. As he lived all the way over in Cobble Harbor, they didn't ever run into each other, she said.

"Heroin in Cobble Harbor!" Marilyn exclaimed. "Unbelievable."

"You'd better believe it," Audrey remarked. "It's everywhere. It's here."

"In Green Haven? Really? Heroin?" Marilyn looked stunned.

"Heroin. Heaven dust. Aunt Hazel." Audrey recited some of the nicer common slang.

"Hell dust, poison, slime." I was able to remember more fitting terms for heroin.

Audrey countered with "Hard candy, hero, sugar."

Not to be outdone, I recalled, "Smack, shit, dirt, dope, junk."

"Sweet Jesus, Joy flakes, dyno, white china," Audrey challenged.

"Judas" was all I could come up with.

"Judas? I've never heard that one."

"Oh sure, Judas. Heroin . . . the friend that betrays you. Was Jason chasing the tiger, or was he a channel swimmer?" I asked in reference to how he took it—smoking or injecting.

"Whoa." Audrey put her hands in the air, palms facing me. "I know when I'm in over my head. I'm there. I have no idea what you're talking about. I read a lot. I don't use drugs. I didn't know Jason did. We were friends a long time ago. I'm not going to his funeral. Okay?" For a minute, I had slipped back into the hard, cold Jane mode. I took a deep breath and remembered the victim, coaxing myself back to my newly found sensitive side. The Old Maids were still stuck in the horrible thought that there were illegal drugs in their hometown. When they questioned this again, Audrey explained that not only was heroin available, but that it was very affordable. "It's as cheap as beer. Or so I've heard." This did nothing but add to the ladies' dismay.

Audrey was holding her own, but I thought I could contribute something more to the conversation from my experience in Miami. "A big part of the problem is politics and the war on drugs. Law enforcement's concentration on cocaine and marijuana has allowed heroin to slip through the cracks," I explained. "Heroin was once known as the poor black man's drug. There wasn't a lot of pressure to stop it. Let 'em die. That was the attitude. Now middle-class kids are using it in increasing numbers."

"Politics, law enforcement . . ." When her hands slid to her waist I knew Audrey was ramping up for confrontation, I could just tell. "They ought to just legalize all drugs and be done with it."

Oh, she had trod on sacred ground. "Legalize heroin? Are you out of your mind? It is so addictive! The body builds a tolerance, calling for more and more to achieve the high. That's how people die," I said.

"Physical dependence is a problem," Audrey agreed. "But the same can be said of alcohol, tobacco, sleep aids. People die using those to excess, too. Poppy seeds have been around since time began. There's never been a culture that's denied people the right to get lit up."

I couldn't believe what I was hearing. "But heroin is illegal. No one has the *right* to use it. Someone needs to go to jail," I said, sounding more like my old self.

"Of course, that's law enforcement's answer to everything. Put 'em in jail," Audrey said. "One cell costs fifty thousand dollars to build and more than twenty thousand a year to fill and maintain. Our prisons are overcrowded now with drug offenders. And my friend is still dead."

I then noticed that Audrey was crying. She wasn't mad at me. I don't think she even believed what she was saying. She's just one of those people—like me—who argue when they're sad. "Someone will go to jail. You have my word on that." Maybe I hadn't changed.

FIVE

Although I would never agree that the solution to illegal drugs was to legalize them, Audrey and I had found a small piece of common ground regarding drugs and law enforcement. Sure, the small-time dealer who would push heroin cut with flea powder to experimenting, tormented teens in order to support his own habit needed to be put out of business. But that, in my opinion, was treating the symptom, not the problem. Heroin junkies are like weeds. Once they take hold in an area, eradication is nearly impossible. Arresting his supplier would not bring justice to Jason Alley. It might delay, but would not stop, the next overdose. We needed to get his supplier's supplier.

My tendency (detractors would call it a handicap) to focus solely on the larger picture was something I had long ago convinced myself was an asset. I would not get bogged down in the small details of Cobble Harbor's drug scene. Law enforcement officers always vow to get to the bottom of the problem. My intention was always to get to the *top* of a problem. As I slid behind the wheel of the Duster, I wondered to what degree Audrey had played me. We had certainly volleyed plenty of issues over the net in the last three months; the focus from either end was always an attempt to gain information about the other's past without relinquishing much of our own. Audrey had always done homework, knowing more of my life in Miami than I did of hers in Green Haven. Of course, a nineteen-year-old doesn't have as much past as a forty-one-year-old professional who has spent more than twenty years in the public eye. But from what I had gathered, Audrey had crammed a lot of experience into her nearly two decades of life. She was remarkably mature and easy to talk to and confide in—rather rare in my limited female friendships. She knew the career I had left in Miami. She knew some of the whys. She knew how to push everyone's buttons to line them up and march to her drummer. Although I was well aware of Audrey's wily ways, I couldn't seem to resist falling prey to them this time. Sure, I could ignore the weeds in my backyard. But finding and turning off the breeze they had blown in on was my forte. I guessed Audrey knew this—and knew just how to talk me into taking action.

The first order of business, I thought, was to check in with the Sheriff's Department and see who had been assigned to investigate Jason Alley's death. With any luck, I would be asked to assist. If that ploy should prove unsuccessful, I could get to Cobble Harbor under the guise of the missing person case. Perhaps I could work with Marine Patrol in the search for Parker Alley. Surely my supervisor at the Knox County

Sheriff's Department would be inclined to assign the "new gal" this mundane chore, which would seem to consist primarily in generating a mound of paperwork. And, if all else failed, I could drive to Cobble Harbor in the role of "insurance lady." Wouldn't it be responsible and professional to follow up on the vandalism aboard *Quest?* And couldn't I then broaden the scope of my investigation as I saw fit? I entered my apartment and headed straight for the phone, excited about the prospect of getting back to what I considered the "real work" that I had sworn off in my haste to get out of Dodge. So much for leaving the past behind.

The phone's answering machine flashed a red number "2" on its display, indicating, to my surprise, that I had received two calls in the last ninety minutes. I hadn't received two calls in the past ninety *days,* I thought. Of course, the main reason for the shortage of incoming calls was the lack of outgoing calls. I was way overdue with a call to my baby brother, Wally. That call would have to wait, I thought, until I had more time. The first message was from the very impatient Mr. Dubois, who always started recordings with a big, disgusted sigh and a comment about my never being home. Tempted to skip ahead to the next message, I hesitated long enough to be ordered to Cobble Harbor on behalf of the missing Parker Alley's marine insurance company. "Recent activity in the form of policy changes in Mr. Alley's life insurance is causing some anxiety with the underwriters . . . suspicion, really. Of course, we've been hired to find some evidence that Alley killed himself as there is a suicide exclusion in term policies. Maybe he left a note or said something to someone. His kid OD'd last Wednesday. So, there's motive. When the body is recovered there may be something to rule out accidental death. Make it a priority." A click followed by the beep and a computerized voice stating the date and time gave me just seconds to appreciate the fact that I wouldn't need to make up an excuse to visit Cobble Harbor again.

The second message was from the Knox County Sheriff's Department and was another assignment requiring me to go to Cobble Harbor as soon as possible. There had been a report of a planned protest in the form of fishing boats blockading the only entrance to and exit from the harbor. The Sheriff's Department was responsible for keeping the protest peaceful, and as this was my territory I was expected to go. "A presence is all that's needed. We don't expect any problems." The tone suggested that the person leaving the message anticipated resistance on my part; like going all the way to Cobble Harbor was an enormous inconvenience. I wondered whether the fishermen were blockading in protest of new regulation or aquaculture. It didn't matter. I had just been given a second excuse to poke around and ask questions. So it was definitely no skin off my back.

I picked up the receiver to call Cal, then remembered the weather. We'd be bucking against easterly wind all the way if we took the *Sea Pigeon*. It might just be faster to drive. I hung the receiver back in its cradle. But I would need to buy gas in Ellsworth and gas is expensive. The phone was again against my ear. Of course, I would be reimbursed for travel expenses. I hesitated, the phone resting on my shoulder. A boat might come in handy to break up the blockade. But it would be an awfully damp, rough ride. Cal might appreciate another day's pay. If I went alone, I wouldn't have concerns about Cal's getting home in time for dinner. One if by land, two if by sea . . . I dialed Cal's number. No answer and no machine on the other end put my indecision into remission. I gathered a few things, including my badge, department-issued handgun (Glock model 22.40 S&W semiautomatic), and rain gear, threw them into my tote bag, and bolted back down the stairs and into the Duster.

I hadn't had much windshield time lately, I thought as I drove through town. Everything in Green Haven was so accessible on foot that I rarely used my old, faithful car. That would change with the weather. I flipped on the windshield wipers. The mooing sound from under the hood was a reminder that the wiper motor was on its last leg, and the smear directly at eye level indicated a need for new blades. This could be a long ride, I thought. Yesterday, when I had looked at a road map, I estimated the drive between Green Haven and Cobble Harbor to be two hours, while a boat ride was a mere seventeen miles. By land, the trip was the equivalent of driving the outer limits of a giant horseshoe rather than cutting across from tip to tip. When the mooing cow morphed to a rooster crowing at dawn I turned on the fan to help defog the windows and to drown out the barnyard noises made by the decrepit wiper motor; this resulted in a face full of dust and tiny particles that I imagined must have been bits of dead flying insects.

Before long I was driving the causeway leaving Green Haven proper and so entranced in fleshing out the shreds of information left on my answering machine that I was no longer annoyed by the noise or poor visibility. Pondering the notion of a boat blockade, I recalled hearing about many such protests in recent years; mainly fishing boats making last-ditch attempts to derail government regulations. It was never a victory dance, but more of a surrender ritual, and I doubted that the Cobble Harbor blockade would be an exception. It wouldn't amount to much, I was certain. This wasn't at all like Greenpeace versus France in 1985. The *Rainbow Warrior* was blown up and sunk by the French government as a permanent solution to the environmentalists' use of it to blockade shipping channels as a protest against nuclear testing. You would have thought that would have discouraged Greenpeace. But they built *Rainbow Warrior II* and she has been showing up in environmental pressure cookers ever since she first splashed water at her launching. Then I remembered a news story about surfers in Hawaii forming a human chain to stop the entrance into their harbor of a Superferry. Their gripe was that the speed of the ferry would endanger whales. So they put themselves in its path in protest. That didn't do much for the public's opinion of the surfers' sanity. Given the water temperature in Maine, I figured the

Cobble Harbor fishermen would remain aboard their boats.

Deep in thought, I glanced at the fuel gauge and then at my surroundings. I was already in the middle of Ellsworth. Ellsworth, being the only gas-selling town along the way, was quite busy this morning. I decided to wait until the return trip to fill my tank, since the rain was coming down harder now. Peaceful protest wasn't a bad thing, I supposed. And trying to stop it might be seen as censorship on the high seas. Even a motley group of fishermen has the right to protest. I recalled recently hearing Green Haven lobstermen complaining of pending gear restrictions and modifications meant to protect whales. Whales, it seemed to me, find themselves at the heart of a lot of discord—counter to their nature. To protest any regulation that even remotely helps whales is foolhardy, I thought. The only good that comes from such activity is a bit of solidarity among the sure-to-fail protestors. And it seemed to me that Cobble Harbor could use a little kumbaya in the midst of the sadness that I was sure shrouded them after the loss of a son and father so tragically and unexpectedly.

Until the body of Parker Alley was recovered and put to rest, though, there might be some degree of unrest in Cobble Harbor. In a small town, closure is needed for everyone, not just the next of kin. Following today's funeral for his son, the community of Cobble Harbor would be embroiled in the search for Parker. But I wouldn't be surprised, I thought, as the road parted acres of spruce grown so thick individual trees were indistinguishable, if Parker Alley's body had been found by the time I arrived.

I eased up on the gas pedal as the road transformed from a route with an official number to "secondary." No doubt the Coast Guard helicopters were back on the scene with their infrared ability. Infrared cameras could detect temperature differences of less than one degree. Of course, the gradient between a body and the ocean would become imperceptible once the body assumed the temperature of the water in which it was submerged. The best chance of success with that method had passed, I knew. And temperature would truly be irrelevant once the body sank. Still, after a body goes under, decomposition creates gases that will refloat the corpse, except when the water is extremely cold. In spite of all the evidence obtained through years of collecting, the activity of corpses in water is not an exact science. Although people always comb beaches looking for what the tide may have left, in this case I doubted Parker Alley's body would travel that far. Drowning victims were usually found very close to where they drowned. You don't work coastal crime scenes for as long as I had and not know these things. People disappear; corpses do not. Parker's body would show up. And the Coast Guard would probably find it.

A sign indicated twelve more miles to Cobble Harbor. I could become public enemy number one, I realized, if word got out that I was being compensated to investigate Parker Alley's death with the hope of foiling payout of his life insurance benefits to the grieving widow. Although that would never be my prime motive, convincing emotionally stressed strangers that my purposes were noble would be tricky. I would be wise to wear my deputy hat and downplay the insurance gig. If my experience in Green Haven held true up the coast, law enforcement would not be welcomed with open arms in what I assumed was another self-sufficient, self-sustaining "we take care of our own problems" kind of town. If I was there to help organize the search for Parker Alley and gained trust and access from and to certain key people, I was confident that I could avenge the death of Jason by bringing real justice. I wasn't really concerned with whether Parker had killed himself or not. My feelings after this morning's conversation with Audrey resurfaced. Cauterizing the artery that carried heroin to the extremities was not what I had in mind. Stopping the heart from pumping was.

The road wound around and up and down through cleared acres, the centers of which were marked with farmhouses—Cape Cod–architectured, clapboarded homes with brick chimneys. Nearly all of the inhabited properties were dotted with small outbuildings. Barns, outhouses, woodsheds, and lean-tos displayed an array of roofing material and pitches. Between homesteads were forests of evergreens and clusters of hardwoods whose wet leaves clung to branches that swayed in the gusty wind. The only anomaly in the picturesque vista was the yellow road sign with a black deer symbol cautioning drivers to beware. The sign was riddled with bullet holes. I hoped the shots came from a frustrated hunter and were not indicative of a violent citizenry.

Farther along was an open field strewn with boulders; erratic rocks stranded by the melting of the last glacial period. Patches of low scrubby growth I knew were blueberry bushes lay in black charcoal, freshly burned. Doused in the rain, the scorched ground wafted a stale Cuban cigar smell, which was blown into my car by the fan. A sharp bend in the road led to another farm with its own fragrance. Split-rail fences surrounded muddy-looking pastures from which black-and-white cows barely noticed me as they chewed. These were livestock farms; there was an absence of cropland. Too many rocks and ledges, I thought as I crested the long gradual hill I'd been climbing for miles.

The view from the top of the hill, even in the miserable weather, was so incredible that I stopped in the middle of the road to gaze out into Cobscook Bay. The line connecting gray sky and water was made distinguishable only by the whitecaps on the bay. From this distance, it looked like someone had shaken a paint brush out on a drop cloth. Miami's shore, all skyline and sandy beaches, could never be seen from anything natural higher than sea level. South Florida and eastern Maine elicited such different feels, different weaves of fabric altogether, that it was dumbfounding to think that they were bookends harnessing the Atlantic Seaboard. The town of Cobble Harbor must be on the eastern side of the next hill below me, I thought. Never had the differences in my old and new home states been as poignant as they were right here and now, with farms tucked into hillsides behind me and the ocean sprawling below. Sad to think that heroin was a link in common. I had my work cut out for me, I knew. Treading on brand-new turf would require new techniques and rules. Cobble Harbor would have no crack houses to storm or corner coke whores to shake for information.

On the horizon, from my vantage point, rose an island out of the ocean. All round and smooth like a polished stone, Acadia Island appeared more inviting than it did when seen from Green Haven. I'd get there before the snow flies, I vowed as I looked in my rearview mirror to ensure that I was not holding up traffic. With no one in sight in either direction, I could have stayed. But I had duties to perform.

Continuing down the road that twisted around hills like a vine on a trellis, I forced myself out of the passive meandering I had been enjoying for nearly two hours into a more alert consciousness. The road I drove dead-ended at a stop sign marking a T intersection. Although there was no sign, my sense of direction and trip to Cobble Harbor by water yesterday pointed to the left. Soon I was on what I would call Main Street. The faded yellow paint line separating two lanes of traffic disappeared as the road narrowed between large stately-looking houses on either side. Nearly all of the houses were white with black trim and shutters. Many homes were crowned with a widow's walk, the small perch on top of the roof from

which wives of sea captains could look out over the
bay when husbands were expected home from voyages.
This was the Maine you read about.

After a long row of pristine houses with picket
fences, there were a number of small businesses, indicating that I was getting close to the waterfront. Restaurants, shops, antiques, a dentist . . . all advertised
with tastefully designed and neatly painted wooden
signs. I now understood the expression "hanging out
a shingle." It dawned on me that I hadn't seen a single
human. Hell, I hadn't even seen a dog. The businesses
had lights on inside, so they were open. Perhaps everyone was at Jason Alley's funeral. It was gloomy.
The weather and the funeral would probably limit the
number of protesters, I thought. There would always
be a few diehards who lived and preached principles
while everyone else went about their business, believing but not acting. Between buildings on the right
side of the road, I could see glimpses of water. But I
couldn't find a road to get to it. Finally, just when I was
searching for a good place to turn around and try the
other direction, I saw a road marked with a sign that
read PUBLIC LANDING—FISH PIER. I couldn't imagine
anyplace else where Cobble Harbor dyed-in-the-wools
could stage a protest or launch a boat blockade. I made
the turn and hoped to find someone on the pier I could
ask. I took a deep breath and realized that I was about
to raise the curtain for Act I of a remake of an old show
starring me.

The gate that protected the pier was connected to
huge metal buildings for boat storage. As I entered the

gate and passed the buildings, I saw that the menfolk of Cobble Harbor were all present and accounted for. I had it wrong. Blue lights flashed on top of state police cars and uniformed officers with megaphones paced the aisle squished between two agitated swarms of men. The curtain was up. Did I make my entrance, or wait in the wings?

SIX

Okay, maybe that was a little dramatic. But in the spirit of "everything is relative," I must admit that I was taken aback by the scene as it was *so* different from what I had expected to find at a peaceful demonstration in Cobble Harbor, Maine, on a dismal day. Measured against other civil unrest I had witnessed, the place was not exactly crawling with cops. There were two cruisers, both with lights flashing as stated, and four officers—one of whom had a megaphone. The crowd was not an angry mob—more like an upset group. From what I could see, there were two sides engaged in what, even from my sealed car, sounded like a heated discussion. There wasn't a chance I would sit this one out. With so many people assembled in one place who might be on the verge of emotional outbursts and the disclosure of information they would otherwise have kept private, this might provide a real break. Discourse fueled by the heat of the moment might include useful information. Maybe I would gain a clue or two toward my investigations into vandalism,

Parker Alley, and (if I was really lucky) Cobble Harbor's drug connection. I found a place to park, secured my holster, donned my rain gear, pocketed my badge, and headed for the center of the fray.

I approached the group slowly, intending to blend into the outskirts and listen until I had learned enough to make my presence known. I again looked over the crowd. Strangely, a few of the men were dressed in suits and long raincoats and wore Dick Tracy hats. They didn't look like cops but they sure weren't dressed like fishermen. Perhaps there was more going on here than the small ruckus I had been promised. Before I got close enough to blend, one of the state police officers saw me coming and slipped away from his post. Positioning himself directly in my path, he planted his feet and crossed his arms at his chest. "May I help you?" he asked.

"Actually, I'm here to help *you*," I said as I took a step to the side so that I could see the other men. He shifted over in front of me, forcing my attention to his face, which clearly depicted his attitude. It wasn't at all threatening. But he was giving me the look I had come to think of as a Maine thing. Not all, but most of the Mainers I had met were so suspicious of me upon first sight that I came to feel, in their eyes, as if I were a snake-oil salesman. I could almost see new acquaintances squeezing tight their wallets in protection. Maine would not be fertile ground for scam artists, I thought.

"You brought muffins and coffee?" he asked with

a smile. His uniform pants were so wet they clung to
his shins. The circle of men behind him was loosening. The party was breaking up. I had arrived too late.

I dragged my badge from my back pocket, held it
up briefly, and shoved it back in. "No muffins. Sorry."
I stuck out my hand to offer a shake. He accepted politely and his expression bore an apology for what
could have been considered a chauvinistic remark. My
skin had grown so thick over the years that nothing
fazed me. Confidence and competence speak much
louder than screams of discrimination. "Jane Bunker.
I'm with the Knox County Sheriff's Department. I got
a call about a blockade protest and came to see that
everyone behaves. I'm really surprised to see state
police here," I said, hoping for a reply that might answer my real question: *What the hell are you doing
here?*

"Everyone is surprised. No one more than us. We
never tread on counties' territory. It takes an act of
Congress to get staties to respond to namby-pamby
stuff like this. No offense. My guess is that a senator
called the department. When deep pockets get worried, heads turn, and we get the nod. Know what I
mean?" I really didn't have any idea what the officer
was talking about, although I enjoyed the fact that
he seemed to feel the need to justify his presence to me
in what he assumed to be my turf. The guys behind
him were dispersing. I recognized one of the dark-
suit-and-trench-coat men, but couldn't quite place him.
"Looks like we'll be out of your hair soon." The officer
gave a glum nod to the man I thought I recognized as

he passed. "All these guys want is to scatter a few ashes on the water; at-sea burial, I guess you'd call it. Now that we've discouraged the blockade, I think it's safe for them to go about their memorial service for that kid." A sudden gust of wind sent a chill through me as I realized that the familiar face was that of Parker Alley's brother, whom I had met yesterday.

"Heroin in Cobble Harbor. . . . Can you believe it?" I asked.

"Don't take it personally. That shit is showing up everywhere. You've got as good a chance of stopping that as you do finding the kid's old man," he said. I would have loved to contradict him by informing him that I intended to do both, but kept my cards close and hoped for more insight. "Talk about a needle in a haystack. It's a big ocean. That's why I didn't join the Coast Guard. These guys on the *Quest*"—the officer jerked a thumb over his right shoulder toward the public dock—"they're conceited enough to *guarantee* they'll find the body if it's there. Some guarantee. *If* it's there. So, if they come up empty, they claim the body wasn't there, right? Hey, maybe they'll hire a psychic!" The officer laughed.

I joined him with a smile as an attempt to firm up my membership in the Maine law enforcement club. "I thought the research vessel was in town to do a survey for an aquaculture company. Now they're talking about towing for Parker Alley?" I asked.

"Yep, that's my understanding. The captain offered to do a search, hoping that would get him through the blockade unscathed. We were briefed, and I mean

brief. The local fishermen are split on aquaculture, the
Indians are mostly against it, reps from shipping companies that transport up the river here are fighting
it. . . . The plastic company has yet to enter the ring.
Hey, these are *your* people. You tell *me* how it unrav-
els. In the meantime, let's hope that your fishermen
stay aboard their boats. That would keep us staties
from returning to this godforsaken outpost." The tone
of this implied to me that the staties believed foul play
might be a factor in the disappearance of Parker Alley. Though maybe I was reading too much into it. Or,
more likely, he was. It would take something far more
daunting than a bunch of fishermen barricading their
home port and a possible knuckle sandwich to get state
troopers to travel this far from their usual beat. Before
I could ask, the officer's partner was beckoning him
to get into the cruiser. "Brrr." The man shivered visi-
bly as a drop of rain fell from the end of his nose.
"We're heading back to civilization now." I assumed
he meant some town north of Route 1. "I'll bet you
even have a Grange hall here. Do you?" He was in the
car before I could tell him that I didn't know.

Intrigued with who the deep pockets were and why
they had sicced the state police on Cobble Harbor, I
approached the only man remaining in the pier's parking lot. Someone had to fill in the blanks for me. Now
that what had looked like an impending debate had
been averted, and there was no need for me to think
about jumping into the middle of a confrontation, I
saw no reason to act as an authority or official of any
kind. I could just be Jane Bunker. Civilians are more

prone to chat with visitors or tourists than with the police. Yup, I would just be Jane Bunker from Green Haven. Maine locals also have great suspicion of anyone "from away," which is how they refer to those not born and bred in their state.

The man, who looked like a block of granite, must have heard me coming up behind him. He turned quickly, with his hands raised and curled in loose fists at his chin. "Whoa," I said as I fell back a step, creating a safety zone between me and this man whose nose appeared to have been broken several times. He lowered his hands slowly, closed his eyes, and exhaled a huge sigh that I took as one of relief that he hadn't flattened an innocent woman. His physique was impressive. Even in heavy, ill-fitting foul-weather gear, his body was an almost perfect rectangle. Not much of a neck, and a flattop hairdo made it impossible for me not to think of the cartoon character SpongeBob SquarePants. When he opened his eyes he hung his head in shame, shaking it slightly. Placing his right hand over his heart, he tapped his chest repeatedly and mumbled something that could have been a prayer, but could just as easily have been cursing me for startling him. This tough guy was a wreck, I thought. I had to let him off the hook. "I often get that reaction from men. But usually not this early in the relationship."

My words had the desired effect. He looked directly at me. His eyes were deep brown and liquid. He smiled, and I felt the sun. He began with an apology in a voice that contradicted my first impression of a nightclub bouncer gone to seed. Soft-spoken and articulate, his accent was a strange combination of Down East and clipped guttural. He was, he said, George Paul—one of the tribal chiefs of the Passamaquoddy Indians. If I hadn't been so immediately taken with him, I would surely have come up with a wisecrack regarding his name and half of the Beatles. But I was bowled over by him; not in a smitten sort of way, just impressed. He struck me as genuine and kind. George Paul seemed delighted to have someone listen as he talked, which he did. Unprompted, George Paul launched into an explanation of who his people were, what their situation was, and how they stood on all the issues most hotly debated in the state. He was open and honest, insisting that his people had nothing to hide, nor anything to be ashamed of. The more he talked, the more questions I had for him. He was thorough and thoughtful in answering them. Maybe a little too thorough, I thought, as he hit the fifteen-minute mark of a soliloquy in response to the question I should have asked first, namely: "What's going on here?" It had finally occurred to me that George Paul knew a lot about a lot—and the fact that he was so willing to talk was a great gift.

George Paul had begun his explanation in some year B.C. Still, he was so passionate and interesting that I barely noticed the activity aboard *Quest* behind him. He had my almost full attention as he gave the time line of the history of Native Americans in this part of the world; and when his narrative approached the present date, he did tie in the reason for his being in the parking lot. Although the information he gave didn't shed any light whatsoever on the questions I had about who was bringing heroin into the area, he did provide background I thought might ultimately be helpful to me in the performance of my day jobs. I had been sent here to keep the peace and to assist in finding a missing person and, perhaps, to determine if Parker Alley had committed suicide or, in light of what the state cop had implied, been done in. Anything I could gather from George Paul might be useful to those ends.

The first evidence of human life in this area, George Paul said, was in the Maritime Archaic period, when there were Red Paint People, so called for the large amounts of red ocher interred with their dead; tools from that era showed stains of similar red. Archaeological digs in shell heaps provided evidence that the Red Paint People hunted swordfish, which, according to a very proud George Paul, was evidence of sophisticated hunting and seafaring skills. "They were a progressive group. They went well beyond picking shellfish from the shore." Most of George Paul's ancestors were presumed wiped out in a series of tsunamis at a time when the ocean was rising and earthquakes were common. This jibed with the information that I had been told by Quasar yesterday, I realized. Just as George Paul was explaining the genealogical connection between the remaining Red Paint People and the "natives" first encountered by European explorers, I caught a glimpse of Dane Stevens, the handsome captain, as he paced the *Quest*'s work deck. I got briefly distracted as I tried to figure out how best to greet the captain so that he would want me to remain in his company after the greeting. When I turned my attention back to George Paul, he had advanced to the Abnaki and Etchemin divisions of the Algonquin nation.

What was not just fascinating but relevant to my tasks at hand was that George Paul was explaining the case for Indians having exclusive rights to a wide area of sea and seabed, including where the aquaculture farm was to go. George Paul told me that the Etchemins were seagoing peoples, and so were the Passamaquoddy, his own tribe. (George Paul was no ordinary member, he added—he was the chief.) Passamaquoddy, he explained, means "People Who Spear Pollock." The Passamaquoddy fished up and down the river, but always pitched their base camps on the east side, where, he was quick to point out, we now stood. The Etchemins inhabited the west. Prior to 1820, when Maine became a state, treaties were signed between Native Americans and the Commonwealth of Massachusetts, and included the "grant" of plots of land that would become reservations; one such plot was Pleasant Point, where George Paul had lived since he was born. George Paul had been fishing since the age of eight—sixty years. He didn't look it, so I remarked on how well preserved he was. He took the compliment in stride, never wavering from the topic. Although the Supreme Court had given Native Americans tribal sovereignty, George Paul's opinion was that it hadn't amounted to anything significant. My new friend ran down the list of rights his people were being denied; behind him, a parade of lobster boats was leaving the harbor. As uniform as a string of pearls, the boats slowly filed out through the channel—a sobering funeral procession. George Paul continued. I couldn't help but be distracted as my eyes and thoughts followed the train of mourners.

George Paul fervently believed that his tribe of Passamaquoddy should enjoy the right to harvest from the ocean as they saw fit, unencumbered by federal and state rules. I admired his conviction and courage. I found remarkable his ability to speak so passionately, and yet without anger, about all the ways his people had been wronged. This was not a rant. But I knew his cause was futile. Too much time had passed and too many foes were arrayed against him. When he pointed to a bird that soared high above and said that the osprey needed no license to feed itself, I felt the need to steer George Paul to the meat of what I wanted, and away from his haunting and romantic plea for a return to the way that things were, the way he felt they should now be.

"Did you know Parker Alley?" I asked, more or less out of the blue. I had given up trying to find a good segue.

"I knew of him, yes." Then silence. Maybe I would get somewhere, I thought. The loquacious chief was suddenly a man of few words.

"Well, what did you know of him?"

"Off the record?" he asked, making me wonder what record he thought I might be keeping.

"Of course."

"He was their ringleader. . . . The Alley family

couldn't make a move without his okay. That's the way it is around here with all of us. We look to someone to guide us, but Parker Alley was a bad man. He and his family have been brutal about keeping others out of what they consider their own private fishing grounds, which happen to be the most productive for lobster and also where North Atlantic Shell Farms are proposing to lease from the state. He was spearheading the challenge to the oyster farm proposal."

"Rallying a few dozen fishermen is not going to stop big business," I said.

"There's more behind him than fishermen. Shipping oil and cargo is big business, too. And Pine Tree Plastics will be put out of business if aquaculture gets a foothold. They've been polluting the river for decades. Toxic algae blooms caused by their discharges run right through my community. They've decimated the plant and fish life that once sustained us. It's part of aquaculture's appeal to the green world—they'll be responsible for forcing Pine Tree Plastics to adhere to regulations. 'Plastic' is a dirty word these days. Must be quite a quandary for the Greenies," he chuckled. "Aquaculture is no bargain, either." The sky grew suddenly darker and the rain was swept horizontally in the wind. I wanted to ask George Paul what he knew of Jason Alley, but suspected that, because of his age, he wouldn't offer anything useful. Thunder rumbled in the distance. It was getting difficult to hear him when the wind gusted.

Just as I was getting ready to excuse myself to head for shelter, a pickup truck pulled into the parking lot.

"There's my ride," George Paul said. "Do you need me to sign a release or something?"

"A release? For what?" I thought that I had probably misheard.

"I assumed you might need my permission to quote me in your article. You didn't even take any notes. I'm impressed!"

"I'm sorry. You obviously have me confused with someone else. I'm not a reporter," I said with a bit of embarrassment, as I wondered briefly if I had inadvertently misrepresented myself. I was fairly sure that I hadn't. "It was nice speaking with you, though."

George Paul laughed—I assumed at his own mistake. "Another dress rehearsal! Figures!" Now the driver of the truck honked the horn to hasten George Paul's goodbye. "We never get any good press. Remember the casino referendum? November fourth, 2003, is forever etched in my memory as Black Tuesday. The best economic development plan Maine has had in a century, and even Governor Baldacci renounced it. We couldn't get the papers to talk to us so we never got to make our case." Another blast from the truck's horn got his attention. He thanked me for listening and turned toward his impatient ride.

The fact that he had mistaken my identity was useful in that it resulted in his providing me essential background and a glimpse into the intricately woven fabric of the Cobble Harbor community. I wondered how long George Paul would have lingered in the inclement weather had he not been trying to get his story into print. Nice accidental ploy, I thought. Now I needed to get out of the squall that was rapidly approaching. Rain I could handle, but I always felt uneasy in an electrical storm with a hunk of metal strapped to my midsection. I didn't want to give new meaning to the phrase "packing heat."

The two figures aboard *Quest,* which I had been observing intermittently since I had first stepped out of my car, had reappeared on the back deck of the boat. They were now appropriately attired in rain suits. The bright yellow forms were hunched over and appeared to be working on some kind of a project. The forms grew and gained contour as I neared; they finally looked human as I hustled across the aluminum gangplank and landed on the deck with a hollow thud. Both men looked up from their work. Smiles from beneath hoods were welcoming. Even with the hood ties limiting the portions of face exposed, I could easily distinguish the two as Quasar the scientist and Dane Stevens the captain. As I knew they were not expecting me, and I, too, had a hood cinched tight, I felt a reintroduction was in order. "Hi! It's Jane Bunker, from yesterday. The insurance lady, remember?" Before either man could speak, a flash of lightning lit up the sky and a sharp crack of thunder loud enough to split atoms shook us all to attention. Simultaneously, the men dropped shiny chrome tools at their feet and beckoned me to follow them into the fo'c'sle.

I scurried behind them through the open door and to the ship's galley, where a teakettle spat at the cast-iron stove, forming tiny puddles that hissed and then vanished, leaving behind a fine rusty residue. The captain secured the door behind me, cutting off the sounds of the storm that was now full upon us. My fingers were so numb from the cold I could barely find the loose end of my hood string. When I did, and pulled it, a thin stream of water was squeezed from the knot and ran across the heel of my hand and up my sleeve, one of the only parts of me that had, until then, remained dry. The men removed their jackets. I followed suit, exposing a four-inch-wide dark stripe along the front of my sweater where the zipper had not even pretended to be watertight. "So much for the state-issued rain gear," I said softly.

"Cup of tea, anyone? Miss Bunker? Tea? How about a hot cup of tea?" asked Quasar in his nervous way, as he opened a cupboard and pulled out an assortment of teas from Red Rose to exotics that smelled like sweet pipe tobacco.

"Thanks. I would love one." I slid onto a bench seat across from Dane Stevens, who, with a hand gesture, invited me to sit.

"I see that you met Chief One Big Loon today," Dane said with a playful grin.

"Dane! That's so disrespectful," admonished Quasar from the counter, where he prepared three cups of tea. "He has a name. And you know it. It's George Paul. Don't be rude."

"Maybe. But he *is* crazy." Dane circled an index finger around his ear, the schoolyard symbol for "loopy" and something I hadn't seen anyone do since, oh, third grade.

"You are a bigot. You truly are a bigot."

"All I'm saying is that he's a nut."

"He's eccentric," Quasar corrected.

"Okay, you win," Dane said with a smile that showed off impeccable dental work or good genes. "But, if there was a Wal-Mart in town, they'd be missing a shopping cart." I really wanted to laugh at this, but Quasar hadn't. I certainly had not regarded George Paul as a lunatic, and had to consider the possibility that these two men were putting on an act to discredit something they assumed he said to me.

Quasar served the tea with a quart container of non-dairy creamer and a plastic bear of honey—a contrast to the fine teacups I was surprised to see aboard a boat. "I assume that FedEx found Cobble Harbor," I said as I pulled the hat off the plastic bear and squeezed a spoonful of honey from the hole in the top of his head.

"Yes, they did. They did indeed," Quasar said as he removed his steamed-up glasses and rubbed them back and forth on his shirt front; the lenses rattled as they crossed buttons. The extent of his squint indicated that he was probably legally blind without the aid of eyeglasses. He pushed the glasses back on, forcing the earpieces through the tight mass of red curls, and opened his eyes, seemingly delighted to have re-gained his sight. "Yes, FedEx delivered late yesterday afternoon. We're nearly done fixing the damaged equipment."

What followed was a long awkward silence. The three of us sat sipping tea, smiling at one another, and each of us wondered whose turn it was to say something next. I was certain that it was not mine, and I couldn't for the life of me think of anything intelligent, witty, or interesting to say. Even sarcasm had abandoned me. So we sat quietly sipping for quite a while before I thought I noticed the men sharing a strange look. As soon as they saw I had noticed, they severed eye contact and concentrated on their teacups again. The next time I caught them sending signals across the table, I gave Quasar my patented "What?" look, which no one could misinterpret. But just to make sure, I raised my hands and pulled my neck into my shoulders. "Are you going to tell her?" Quasar asked.

Dane nodded. "I talked with your boss," he said, raising his gorgeous black eyebrows and waiting for my reaction to a statement I was accustomed to hearing just prior to the filing of a formal complaint about my investigation methods.

Don't get defensive yet, I warned myself. "Which one?" I asked.

"The Knox County sheriff."

So, now the men knew I was not just the insurance gal, which was fine. "And?"

"Well, I didn't know he was your boss until I called," Dane said, sort of apologetically. "When the state police left, we got worried about what could happen if the fishermen regrouped. Quasar and I both think that the vandals were trying to keep us from doing the survey that's needed for the leasing of ocean floor from the state. That didn't stop us, so they planned the blockade. There must have been a leak or a tip-off, and now the blockade has been foiled. We're not locals. We've heard stories about how these people treat their *neighbors,* so we can only imagine how they would treat people from another part of the country." Again, there was a pause. He hadn't said anything that required me to respond, so I didn't. The captain looked at the scientist for reassurance, which came in the form of a coaxing head nod. He began anew, this time speaking faster. "The cops said we should contact the County Sheriff's Department as this kind of problem is more in line with what they—or you, I guess as it turns out—would handle." Dane stirred his tea relentlessly as Quasar nodded his head in agreement to everything he had said. "The sheriff said he had already given you a heads-up and that you should be here. And here you are."

"Here I am. Everything is copacetic. I don't plan to leave until I get to the bottom of a few things, so I'll be around." I had actually intended to return to Green Haven fairly soon after the boats involved in the memorial service had been secured back to moorings, and after I had the chance to offer condolences, and, in the process, connect with some members of the Alley family. If timing and the stars lined up just right, I figured I could then get the information from those family members that I would need to begin my investigation into the source of illegal drugs in the region. Best-case scenario was a meeting with Parker Alley's wife, I thought. Connect, go home, return . . . that was the original plan. But I could hang a bit longer if Dane Stevens and Quasar felt my presence was necessary or made them more comfortable.

"Actually, the conversation turned from our equipment to the subject of that poor missing fisherman. What your boss said was that going offshore with us to find his body was entirely within your jurisdiction and duties," Quasar blurted out. That took me by surprise, but didn't stun me. I just didn't see it coming. "North Atlantic Shell Farms is okay with us recovering the body if it's within our survey plot." I swallowed and thought for a few seconds, formulating a response that wouldn't sound negative. Quasar continued: "Your boss wants you to call him. Do you have a cell phone? Cell phones work here. They work fine. There's a tower on Swan's Island. Or you could borrow mine. It works great."

Dane Stevens dug in his pocket and fished out a crumpled scrap of paper. "Here's the eight-hundred number, in case you don't have it on you," he said, and handed me what looked like the edge of an envelope. "Here, use my phone." I would have preferred to make the call in private, but knowing what was behind the door for weather, I decided to remain right by the stove. I was prepared for the answering service to say that no one was available to take the call and advise me to leave a message or call 911 should it be an emergency, but when the beep sounded for the message, I hung up without leaving one.

"There's nobody available to take a call. When do we leave?" I asked, intentionally including myself in the trip. Now that I had a minute to digest the idea, I realized that it was a good one. Both of my bosses would be satisfied, I thought.

"As soon as this weather passes, which could be

right about now." Dane Stevens got up to look outside. "Let's cast off. Quasar, you can finish the magnetometer on the way to the site, right?"

"Yes. Yes, indeed. It won't take but a few more minutes." Quasar stood and pulled his yellow slicker back on.

"I wasn't planning to go, but that's fine," I said, resolved to do the right thing concerning both of my jobs. "When will we be back ashore?"

"As soon as we have a dead body or a completed bottom survey, whichever comes first." The captain disappeared out the door, saying he had to fire up the engines while Quasar secured the galley for departure.

"Don't worry," said Quasar. "We can't stay offshore for more than seventy-two hours. It's written in our contract. If we want to stay longer, we need to hire crew, and we can't afford employees—tight budget. In fact, if you weren't going, we would have only forty-eight hours. It's an insurance thing. I guess you understand that!"

I was being shanghaied, I thought. I was the nonpaid crew member who was buying them an extra twenty-four hours to do their job. I hoped that I was being paranoid and that Dane and Quasar really felt that I was needed in some way that related to my insurance or law enforcement jobs. But if the speed at which the ship was made ready to go was an indication, they were nervous that I would come to my senses and bail out before the lines were thrown. What the hell, I had had worse duties, I thought. Much worse. I could always make the best of any situation, I knew. I followed Quasar onto the deck, where the sun was now shining brightly. I was reminded of a saying I had recently heard: If you don't like the weather in Maine, wait a minute.

I assured Quasar that I could handle the bow and aft spring lines, and carefully walked the narrow rail around the wheelhouse to the foredeck. Out in the channel I could see the boats making their way back into port. At least the sun had come out for their homecoming. Cremation is nice and neat, and either useful or terrible if it later turns out that an autopsy is needed. Several times during my stint working homicide I had been frustrated by a cremation. By the time an autopsy was ordered, the body was already toast and the crumbs had been sprinkled in the wind. Oops.

"Let 'em go," called Dane Stevens, referring to the lines he was now ready to see cast free of the pilings. Quasar and I coiled and stowed the sections of braided nylon while the captain slowly maneuvered *Quest* away from the wharf and toward the buoys marking the north end of the narrow channel. The wind had switched to northwest with the passing of the low pressure system; steep waves, working against the incoming tide, crashed onto the man-made, rocky breakwater whose purpose was to protect the inner harbor from storm surge. Chilled from spending so much time in the rain and wind, I sat for a minute to soak up some of the sunshine and allow my rain gear to dry out in the stiff breeze. The inlet looked rough enough to send spray onto the bow, so I headed for the shelter of the bridge.

"May I borrow your phone again?" I asked the captain, who stood behind a huge spoked wheel. Impressed with the range and number of electronics and computer monitors, I thought it would be fun to learn about some of this high-tech equipment, and began looking forward to getting to work. The captain handed me the phone without a word. I could see that he was concentrating on navigating, so I stepped out the open door on the lee side of the house to make a call to my landlords, the Vickersons, to let them know I wouldn't be home tonight. In the sun and sheltered from the wind, I was happy and comfortable. I would connect with some representative of the Alley family soon enough, I thought. It might actually be better to wait. I sat on the foredeck with my back pressed against a bulkhead and dialed the phone. I was relieved to get the Vickersons' machine and thus not be stuck in conversation and interrogated about my whereabouts. I left a brief message. I closed my eyes to enjoy the warmth and thought I would remain here until we were out of the narrows and onto smooth water, and then I would join Quasar on deck.

I braced my feet and pushed my back harder against the steel bulkhead as *Quest* began rolling from side to side in increasing swells. Deep rolls turned to sudden pitching and slatting as we crawled by the breakwater that lined the west side of the channel. It would be rough for only another minute or two, I thought, as I gazed beyond the rocks spewing spray, out to where the surface glistened like polished silver.

A crash on our port side and a lurch toward the

rocks felt like quite a heavy wave had caught us broadside, but when it was followed by a loud "What the fuck?" from the wheelhouse, I jumped to my feet and scrambled inside to see what the problem was. Something was obviously terribly wrong. Dane Stevens looked more than worried as he pushed the throttles up to full ahead and turned the wheel to the left, putting the rudder hard to port. I glanced out the windows on our port side to see the top of a boat.

I hurried across the wheelhouse for a better look at what was happening. A lobster boat had its stem against our port bow and was pushing us rapidly toward the breakwater. Even though *Quest* was at full power, we were losing ground quickly. Quasar came in from the work deck and screamed, "Oh my God! What's he doing?"

"He's forcing us onto the rocks, and there's not a fuckin' thing I can do about it." Dane held the wheel hard to port, eased the throttle, and shifted into reverse in what I supposed was a desperate attempt to let the lobster boat slip by our bow. It was no use; this resulted only in increasing our speed toward the breakwater as the lobster boat persisted in propelling us closer to where the violent surf pounded. Dane put the engine back in full-speed-ahead mode, and we watched the distance to the menacing shore grow smaller still. "Quasar! Get the survival suits!" The scientist was paralyzed with fear. He didn't budge, and it didn't matter, I thought. There wasn't time to climb into the clumsy survival gear. I knew I had to do something fast, or we would be pummeled against the breakwater until the ship broke up and sank. "Quasar! Come on, snap out of it! Fifty-four-degree water!" This time the captain had shouted even louder at his friend, who still was unable to move.

That did it for me. I tore my gun from its holster and charged out onto the foredeck, where I was nearly face-to-face with a dark figure behind a windshield glaring from the sun. The other boat was truly right upon us, like some kind of demon. Aiming to the right of the figure at the helm, I squeezed off a shot that blew a hole in the Plexiglas the size of a nickel. Shifting my bead to the left, I hesitated before firing again. But the warning shot had done the trick. The lobster boat that had been driving us into the rocks suddenly drew away. And as she turned, I caught the name on her stern: *Spartacus*.

SEVEN

I watched *Spartacus* over the top of my gun and kept the sights trained on the middle of the driver's back until I was certain that he had no intention of having another go at us. He never glanced back, so I didn't get a look at his face. A police sketch rendered from my eyewitness account would bring in most of Cobble Harbor for the perp walk: adult male, average height and weight, wearing orange foul-weather gear—useless. But, I thought, as I lowered my gun and secured it back in its holster, I did have the name of the boat. One phone call would give me the name of its owner. And tracking down a person by name had always been infinitely preferable to going door-to-door with a fuzzy picture. I took a deep breath and contemplated how effortless firing the shot had been—like second nature. Slinging a gun was a knee-jerk reaction born of good training and bad experience. Chalk another one up for the latter. I gripped the handrail and peered down into the water, preparing for reentry into the wheelhouse. What would the men think of their new shipmate—a modern-day Annie Oakley with sensible shoes?

I could see the bottom down below the scarce few feet of water we were in—jagged rock and ledge that have the ability to tear open the hull of a steel boat like a can of sardines. Good thing this old tub of a vessel didn't have a deep draft, I thought. The way *Quest* rolled nonstop suggested that she had a fairly round bottom and didn't require much water to float, and the fact that we weren't sinking was a better indication yet. I watched the harbor's floor fade and disappear in the increased depth as Dane found the center of the channel again. Far behind us I could see several segments of the funeral procession landing at docks and moorings, and I wondered whether *Spartacus* had been part of the service or had just found it convenient to tag along, hoping for an opportunity to pounce. My investigation into the identity of our attacker would, of course, need to be put on hold until I was back on terra firma. And that would be sometime in the next three days. I waited outside the bridge an extra minute to allow Dane Stevens time to get squared away as I assumed this episode was far enough out of his comfort zone to warrant it. I waited another minute to fully recover from the physical aspects of my fight-or-flight reaction. I needed to transition back to my more casual and less primal self.

When I felt fully composed, I stepped into the wheelhouse and latched the door behind me. The captain was busy increasing the range of the radar, putting a waypoint in the GPS track plotter, and getting the autopilot set up. Quasar, who appeared to be in shock, stood gripping the edge of the forward console panel and staring wide-eyed at the horizon. Rather than pretend that someone hadn't just posed a serious threat to our lives, I decided to remind the two that I was, in fact, in law enforcement and was not simply to serve as their crew member. Yes, Dane Stevens was our captain. And yes, Quasar was our scientist. But I had something of value to offer, too, and had clearly already proven myself to be more than just their ticket for an extra twenty-four hours offshore or someone to put a pot of coffee on the stove. "What do you know about the *Spartacus?*" I asked, intending the question for both men. Neither answered. "Anything?" I hoped to get something of a reply, even if it was a flat "No." When Dane finally pulled his face out of the radar, he shook his head and frowned. "Have you ever seen that boat before?" I kept asking questions but wasn't getting much in return.

Again Dane shook his head. When I forced eye contact, he said, "No. I don't remember ever seeing it. But there are so many lobster boats in Cobble Harbor that it's hard to place one specific boat."

"How about you, Quasar?" I asked, trying to shake him out of his trancelike state. I placed a hand on his shoulder and asked again, "Quasar? *Spartacus?* Any recollection?"

"Yes, of course," he answered, seemingly pulling something from his memory. The captain and I waited as Quasar rubbed his chin in concentration. I was holding my breath in anticipation as Quasar slowly emerged from sub-consciousness. He tapped his right temple with an index finger, then opened his eyes wide in an *aha* expression. "The movie was released in the early sixties. It starred Kirk Douglas." Dane rolled his eyes—either in amusement or exasperation or both. I was merely disappointed. I had thought for a second Quasar was going to tell us something really useful. Quasar, unbowed, continued. "What a story. And based on fact! Spartacus was captured after deserting the Roman army and was made a slave. The biggest and strongest slaves, like Spartacus, were sent to school to become gladiators. Watching fights was the Romans' favorite form of entertainment—quite the barbaric sport. Spartacus led the slaves in a revolt against the Roman Empire in what we now know as the Servile War." I was relieved that Quasar was not showing any signs of classic shock. He was speaking coherently, albeit about something totally irrelevant. Interesting how Quasar's speech lost the nervous repetition when he was reciting fact from memory. "At the top of his game, Spartacus had one hundred and twenty thousand followers. They raised havoc for a couple of years, but were finally defeated by forces led by Crassus. It's believed that Spartacus died engaged in battle in southern Italy, but his body was never found. As an interesting aside, Pompey—"

"Quasar, shut up. That's not funny," Dane interrupted.

"It wasn't meant to be funny. I was answering Ms. Bunker's question. And if you weren't so rude, you might learn something," Quasar scolded.

"Our bodies could be smashed to bits against the breakwater right now if Jane hadn't fired her gun and convinced that guy that the next bullet was going right into his head, and you're giving a lecture on ancient Rome." Quasar hung his head slightly and pouted like a child who had been reprimanded. The captain, aware that he had hurt his friend's feelings, softened his tone as he continued. "Look Quas, if you have something pertinent to say, please do. If not, why don't you get to work on the gear? We'll be on-site in thirty minutes. We haven't given up on that bonus yet, have we?"

"Right. I'm going. I'm going," Quasar replied. "We have a bonus to collect. A bonus. Let's just pretend that didn't happen back there." Quasar moved toward the door slowly, talking as he went, supposedly to himself, yet just loud enough for Dane and me to hear every word. "Pertinent, what could be *more* pertinent? What I was *trying* to get to before I was so rudely interrupted was what Spartacus represents. It's the classic struggle: good versus evil, oppressed versus oppressors, peasants versus aristocracy. The good people of Cobble Harbor think we're the bad guys. No wonder we're under attack. . . ." And his voice trailed away and faded into silence as he disappeared around the corner. I was relieved to hear the mention of a bonus, which I assumed was some financial reward for meeting a schedule. The quicker, the better, I thought.

Alone for the first time with the attractive captain, I hoped I would not revert to the idiocy I had come to expect from myself whenever I found myself in the company of a potential suitor. Suitor? I hated myself for the thought! And I also hated myself for using, even in my head, such a weird old-fashioned word. Why do

I become like some Jane Austen character the minute I start to fancy someone? The absence of a ring on his finger and the fact that he had just referred to me by my first name had led me to premature, immature castles-in-the-sky musing about whether he found me at all enchanting. That I had never been described in that way before did nothing to keep me from hoping that he was, right now, in *his* head, applying that very word to me. It was just a few short months ago, I reminded myself, that I had had a near miss in a love connection with Green Haven's most eligible bachelor. My role in sending his brother to prison hadn't done much to get our relationship out of the blocks, I knew. My brand of "justice above all" had fouled every good relationship I had ever almost had, but my dismal record never stopped me from trying to start new ones.

"Good ol' Quas. He's a very sympathetic guy," explained Dane, as if he felt the need to apologize for his friend. "Sometimes his feelings make it hard for him to make wise business decisions. He can be very irritating. I'm sorry. He makes me insane most of the time."

"Why do you continue to work with him?" I asked, glad to be drawn out of my fantasies. (Though I couldn't help smiling when it occurred to me how cute it would be to be part of a couple called Dane and Jane.)

Without any hesitation, Dane looked me square in the eye and said, "Because he's the best there is. I guaranteed the Alley family we'd come back with a body. And we will. We will because Quasar never misses. He's a genius. The only problem is that the genius has a conscience and acute sense of social justice. He's ready to back out of this project. I can tell. The only reason he's aboard now is to find closure for the grieving family." Then, as an afterthought, he added, "Well, that, and the fact that he wouldn't leave me holding the bag. We were college roommates, so we've been butting heads for a long time. We'll survive Cobble Harbor and be off to our next contract. I guess you could say he's my best friend, even if he drives me crazy."

Well, maybe I was a better match for a guy like Quasar, I thought. Smart, good at what he does, a real sense of what's right, and he follows his convictions . . . Too bad he's so funny-looking, I thought. No, too bad I'm so shallow. Dane continued. "He's brilliant, really. I've yet to stump him on any topic. Even Spartacus . . ." Oh no, my worst nightmare was coming to life. The object of my budding romantic interest was interested in me only as a possible mate for his nerdy best pal. I had to stop him before he got to the part about what a wonderful father Quasar would make.

The thought of giving birth to little Quasars did not appeal to me. What if they were girls? Little Quasar girls. "So, we don't yet know who tried to run us ashore," I said, scrambling for the safety of a comfortable topic. "But we do have plenty of people with motive."

"Yeah. It's becoming clear that there is a lot of opposition to this aquaculture project. People can get

pretty emotional when they come up against new en-
terprises. Progress is the enemy, you know? They see
change as dumping on their heritage, and in a place
like Cobble Harbor heritage is worshipped like a god."
I knew this was true. I had experienced the identical
situation in Green Haven with a proposed wind farm.
But, I thought, it wasn't quite as simple as Dane suggested. There were folks like George Paul, whom I had
just met, who would embrace some change, like a casino. There are always two sides, and sometimes three.

Quest was sliding along easily in the calm water;
the gently rolling waves provided a slight, shallow dip
from port to starboard and back, just like a hand on a
cradle. The sloshing sound of her blunt bow, plowing
rather than cutting a path, was a peaceful accompani-
ment to the tranquillity all around. The captain covered his mouth with a hand to conceal a huge, silent
yawn that I hoped was due to the temporary lull and
not indicative of the quality of my company. "Oh, excuse me," he said. "I'll go put on a pot of coffee if
you're okay keeping a lookout for a few minutes." Impressed that he had not suggested that I make the coffee, I happily volunteered to do so, saying that I needed
to learn my way around the boat. I asked to borrow
his phone again, as mine was in my car, and he gladly
lent it.

As I stepped out, I admired the way the sun had
transformed the day so completely. Harbor seals
stared, their heads like pears sculpted in black marble, and then quickly dropped beneath the surface as
if through a trapdoor, leaving behind concentric rings

of ripples. A night or two at sea in these conditions would be delightful, I thought. It had been years since I had had the pleasure of darkness offshore. Well, I had spent some time hiding in a bilge this past June, I reminded myself. But this would be different. This would be like old times fishing with Archie in the Gulf Stream, when we would go offshore far enough to escape any trace of the bright city. Arch would douse the deck lights, and we'd sit on the fish hold hatch, dangling our legs and marveling at the greatest show on Earth. He'd be up for parole in another year. He'd been framed. Though I couldn't prove it.

The clanging of steel on steel from a wrench dropped on deck shook me from my thoughts and brought me back to the mission at hand. I made a quick call to the Sheriff's Department to request they run a check on *Spartacus* and learned that the folks of Cobble Harbor are a bit more sophisticated in their criminal activity than I had imagined. The boat had been reported stolen just a few short hours ago by its owner, Willard Kelley, the tipsy pilot Cal and I had taken ashore from the *Asprella*. Buyer's remorse; I wish I hadn't bought into this trip now that there was a concrete lead and a place to begin my investigation ashore. Too late, I thought. I would just have to make the best of it. On the other hand, I realized if I hadn't made the trip then I wouldn't have been aboard to witness the ramming and get the lead. So it was all evening out.

An open can of Maxwell House was in the cupboard directly above the automatic drip machine. Secured to the bulkhead with a bungee cord, Mr. Coffee appeared to be safe in any sea conditions. I knew from my various fishing experiences that caffeine is one of the two most important ingredients for maintaining crew morale—the other being nicotine. Of course, bountiful catches and great weather help, too, but since these aren't sold at any chandlery, smart cooks stock up on java and butts. I dumped coffee into a paper filter and filled the pot with water from the tap at the galley sink, both in amounts to make a full, strong pot.

After pushing the button to start the brewing, I walked the length of the gangway toward the bow, opening doors as I went. Three double staterooms and a large bathroom with head and shower completed the tour. The stateroom closest to the bow appeared to be unoccupied, so I assumed that was where I'd lay my head when the time came. I hadn't had any warning, so of course I had no pillow or sleeping bag. Hell, I had no clothes—not even a toothbrush. I had been in worse places with less, I thought, as I closed the door and went back to the galley to check on the coffee. The machine was working, but ever so slowly. Rather than stand and watch, I joined Quasar on the work deck. "How's it coming?" I asked as I approached.

"All done! Just finished! A lot of the damage was superficial. We're in business now. We're good to go. I'm just waiting for the captain to give me the word that we're on-site and I'm ready to get this show on the road."

"Dane is very confident that you'll find the body of Parker Alley. Do you search for bodies often?" I asked. Why did I phrase it that way? I worried that my question sounded like a cheesy pickup line. I turned away from Quasar and inspected a hydraulic winch that appeared to be used to launch the ROV (remotely operated vehicle).

"Most of our work is in surveying bottom and doing water-quality tests. We measure and chart tide, current, and salinity, and note sea life—stuff like that. We get a lot of jobs through the Army Corps of Engineers. When someone applies for a permit to build a dock or dredge a channel, we put in a bid for the survey."

"But you have done searches for missing people, haven't you?"

"Oh yes. We have been hired to find drowning victims, and we've been quite successful. Very successful, in fact. Eight for eight. Perfect score."

I relaxed with this information. "Wow, Dane said you were good. One hundred percent success rate on eight assignments? Here's hoping for number nine." I crossed my fingers.

"Of course, two of the victims were trapped in a plane that went down off Cape Hatteras. That was an easy one. But still, we've had seven successful missions of this type. I shouldn't take much of the credit. It's the captain's expertise in narrowing the field of search. I'm just the technician. Dane is the man. He's very well respected in the world of oceanography, marine biology, and marine salvage. He may come off as a bit gruff, but his bark is worse than his bite. He's a great guy, really. I've known him for a long time. He's a wonderful friend, and . . ." Oh no, I thought. This can't be happening. The nerd isn't the slightest bit interested in me. He's talking up his friend. If it wasn't so depressing, I'd have to laugh. At least I wouldn't have to worry about locking my stateroom door tonight.

"Coffee?" I asked. Quasar wasn't ready for caffeine just yet, he said, but he was certain that Dane would love a cup, black. So I left him on deck surrounded by his machinery to bring coffee to the bridge. After delivering to the captain and returning his cell phone, I was sent by strong suggestion back down to the deck, where I might be useful to Quasar when it came time to launch the ROV. I wasn't there five minutes when Quasar thought of a reason to send me topside again. Before I could hop to it, I felt the boat slow to an idle. Dane joined us on deck and saved me the humiliation of watching him conjure up another task requiring me to be with his friend.

"We're close to the first track line. I'll give you a hand with the side scanner first," Dane said as he twisted the valve on the hydraulic motor that controlled a large winch wrapped full of half-inch-diameter cable. The motor turned slowly, backing wire off the spool until there was a loop of slack on the deck. Dane turned the motor off and joined Quasar in the stern, where he was untying something that looked like a miniature submarine that was attached to the end of the cable. Both men eased the towfish, or "fish" as they called it, out of its bracket and rested it on the rail. "Jane, could you operate the winch?" Without answering, I grasped the brass handle that I had just observed Dane using. "Inboard is up. Please take up the slack until the fish is hanging from that bollard," Dane said as he motioned to a large block over his right shoulder. I did as he requested, twisting the valve open until the winch moved, slowly wrapping the slack wire back onto the spool until the wire was tight enough to pull the fish off the rail and hold it under the block. "Perfect. I'll give you the word to lower the fish into the water. We want to tow at twenty fathoms, Quas."

Dane quickly vanished back into the wheelhouse, leaving Quasar and me at the winch to wait for his command. "What does the towfish do?" I asked. Quasar, as I had already learned, enjoyed explaining things about the equipment and engaging in any kind of chat that bore no resemblance to normal conversation. He quickly gave a description that I knew represented his best attempt at using layman's terms, but he still seemed to be struggling with dumbing it down sufficiently for me to understand. I learned that the fish was the housing unit for a side-scan sonar, one of three machines in *Quest*'s acoustic imaging system. The fish was designed to "swim" as it was towed at different depths through the water behind the vessel. Similar to the depth sounder, which shoots an acoustic pulse straight down from a transducer on the ship's hull, a side scanner sends pulses across the seabed, covering a wider swath in each pass or along each track line. Pulses strike the seabed and are reflected back to the vessel, where they are received by the transducer and converted to an electrical signal, which is traced on a paper chart recorder and analyzed by the technician. The depth sounder is used to determine the depth of water under the boat so that the operator knows when to lower or raise the tow-fish.

Track lines, Quasar explained, were adjacent and parallel imaginary lines that covered the search area. Dane had already determined the area and the distance between the lines to be tracked, so we were about to engage in a systematic search. He'd figured out with the Coast Guard about search parameters for Parker Alley using information from the electronics aboard *Eva B*. Flawless navigation made possible by GPS meant that *Quest* would not stray from the lines or leave gaps in the area to be searched. Fortunately, the area where it was believed they would be most likely to find Parker Alley's body overlapped the area they had been hired to survey for North Atlantic Shell Farms; two birds, one stone—or, rather, one towfish.

"When do we get to use this other stuff?" I asked enthusiastically.

"It will take almost twenty-four hours to cover the area with the acoustic gear. Then we should go over it with the proton precession magnetometer. And, ideally, I would like to try a few passes with the sub-bottom profiler over any lines where there's an indication of ferrous materials."

"Oh" was all I could muster with the realization that I really was in this thing for three days. Dane called out for us to lower the fish, and Quasar explained that the wire was marked with spray paint at five-fathom intervals. So I would need to stop the winch when the fourth mark was at the block. He pointed out the brake and asked that I tighten it once the wire was towing the fish at the proper depth. I agreed that I could handle this job, and he ran to the bridge to watch the chart recorder for "anomalies."

Manning the winch, as it turned out, was fairly inactive duty. But it took me several hours to figure out that I did not need to stand with my hand on the brake, ready to release it to change the depth of the towfish at a moment's notice. It was dark by the time I relaxed enough to sit on a basket full of line up by the boat's exhaust stack, which radiated enough heat to keep me warm well after the sun went west. Every thirty minutes or so, the boat would change direction, making sharp 180-degree U-turns that batted the waxing gibbous moon back and forth over the gallows frame that towered above the stern deck. Boredom with what I was doing and curiosity about what the men were doing finally got the best of me. Under the guise of thoughtfulness, I barged into the wheelhouse with a cup of coffee in each hand and a bag of cookies under one arm.

The wheelhouse was dimly lit by electronics. Quasar sat with his face pressed nearly against a machine that was drawing a graph that resembled the feed out of a heart monitor. "Hope I'm not interrupting anything," I said as I looked for a spot to put down the coffees. I headed for the light over the chart table, and Dane sprang to his feet. He beat me to the table, closing an open book and turning it over so that I could see only the back cover. "Your brand of pornography?"

I teased as I looked at the picture of a sinking four-masted schooner that he appeared to have been embarrassed about me seeing.

"Yes, sort of," he laughed. "It's *Unfinished Voyages* by John Perry Fish. It's a history of shipwrecks in the Northeast. I didn't know whether you were superstitious or not and might regard it as a bad omen or evil talisman." Then he laughed loudly and added, "After our encounter with *Spartacus,* I guess I should have known that a book wouldn't spook you." He removed the book from the table, motioned for me to set the cups down, and slid the volume into a magazine pocket on the side of his chair. "Oh, thanks. It's going to be a long night. Why don't you go lie down and get some sleep? We'll wake you if we need your help."

I know when I'm not wanted, and I realized pretty quickly that they really didn't want me staying up with or dating them. I said that I wasn't really tired but would try to get a nap. Quasar thanked me for the coffee without taking his eyes off the graph or his thumb off the remote sending unit button, which was harnessed to the plotter by a thin cord. These men were serious professionals doing their jobs, and I should leave them alone, I thought. But I wanted to contribute what I could. I doubted that I would fall asleep while others were working; it just isn't my style. But sensing their strong desire to see me retire for the evening, I vowed to try to stay out of their hair until daylight, when I would poke around the galley for something breakfast-like for the three of us.

Once settled in my stateroom, I rolled my rain pants up to serve as a pillow and covered my torso with my jacket. But I was nowhere near dozing. Upset that I was at sea, wasting time when I could be gathering information on the heroin trafficking, I tossed from side to side, fighting alertness while I assumed the men above waged war with drowsiness. Maybe I could do a shift for one of them. How much coffee could they consume before it no longer did the trick? I could certainly run a boat well enough to follow a line on a plotter. And I'm a quick study. I could learn what to look for on the various monitors, and wake the men when I found something. They could both sleep while I conducted the search. If I didn't fall asleep soon, I would suggest that.

I must have fallen asleep at some point, since Quasar woke me with a knock on my stateroom door. "Miss Bunker, are you awake?" The door opened a crack and Quasar spoke through the opening without looking in. "Miss Bunker, are you awake?"

I hopped out of the bunk and opened the door the rest of the way. "Yes, I'm awake. I couldn't sleep," I lied. "What is it?"

"We've located something that could be your man. I mean it might be. We're not sure, but it could be. I hate to say probably, but more than likely. I'd be surprised if it's not him. It's within a hundred feet of the exact center of the area Dane scoped out for the search. Too much of a coincidence to be a false alarm. . . . I hope it's him. Very likely could be. We're preparing to tow a net over the spot to see if we can scoop it up and thought you would want to be on deck."

"I'm right behind you," I said as I followed Quasar out onto the deck, where the sun was just rising. So I had slept for a fair while, I realized.

The captain quickly explained what I needed to do to help. First, we needed to retrieve the towfish and secure it in its bracket, which we did. Next we would have to make some adjustments to the net the men usually used for "sea sampling"—that is, for seeing what kinds of fish were swimming in a particular area, a survey requirement of the Department of Marine Resources. "We'll take up a couple of links on each end of the chain," Dane explained. "That will keep the net's lower jaw, if you will, from digging into the mud and rocks. If that's a body down there, we don't want to drag it along the bottom and then up to the surface with a bunch of rocks. It wouldn't be pretty." I didn't bother telling the men that I actually had vast experience with net adjustment after years aboard commercial fishing boats. I simply listened and did as I was told, and soon we were setting the net out over the stern. The net's configuration was one I had never seen before, towed from one wire instead of the usual two. I learned that it was a Skipper Drew design called an OLAK, which they said stood for "One Legged Ass Kicker." As I backed off the winch, lowering the net into the water, I hoped it would live up to its name this morning.

The captain returned to the nerve center of the operation, where I knew he would be concentrating on towing the net over the spot where he believed the body of Parker Alley lay. Quasar and I hung out on deck while the boat moved steadily toward the sun, which was now fully above the horizon. Soon the boat spun around and towed back in the opposite direction. "He always makes two passes, just to be sure," Quasar confided. "I suspect he had it on the first run, but there's no way of knowing. Some boats have cameras they can launch with the net and see everything that goes in, but we don't. That's why he makes the second pass. Just in case. The net cameras are expensive. It's a lot cheaper to make a second pass. Parker Alley is probably already in the net, but without the camera, there's no way to know for sure." Quasar was fidgeting nervously.

"I thought most drowning victims were recovered by divers."

"We really aren't interested in making our livings pulling dead bodies out of the ocean. This is not what we like to do. Dead bodies are not our thing. North Atlantic Shell Farms thought this would help with public relations. And divers are expensive. We can't afford divers. We're a low-budget operation. We may need to hire some divers later depending on what the data of the survey shows. We have equipment. Do you dive? We have our own compressor to fill tanks. Are you certified?" I shook my head and stared over the stern at our wake. I prayed that Quasar was right about already having the body in the net. There were so many questions that I couldn't get answered until my feet hit shore, and I knew my impatience with this trip would grow exponentially. And Quasar's repetitions were starting to annoy me.

Quest's engine slowed to an idle, while my pulse sped up in anticipation. Dane arrived on deck and ordered me to release the winch's brake and begin to bring the net up. As I did so, the men stood on either side of the stern and looked aft. "Keep a slow, steady strain on the wire. That's a good speed," the captain said, then quickly watched the water behind the boat again. When the last mark approached the winch, I slowed the winch slightly, as I knew the net must be close to the stern now. I watched Dane as he pointed an index finger at the sky and drew a circle around and around, the signal I recognized as an order to keep the net coming up. When the finger dropped into the hand, making it a tight fist, I shut the valve off, stopping the winch from turning. "Now back off the boom winch. The valve is on the bulkhead behind you." I found the valve and followed his commands, going back and forth between the two valves, until the net had been disconnected from the tow wire and the mouth had been secured, by a hook, to the winch on the boom high above the stern deck.

"Okay, Jane, take it up slow." As the mouth of the net was pulled up, the webbing behind it followed up over the stern, until the very end of the funnel slid onto the deck and hung, swinging slightly, just a few feet in the air. "Bingo. Got him," Dane said, sounding quite relieved in spite of all of his confidence. I joined the men as Quasar gave the purse line, which cinched the end of the net, a quick jerk, popping open a clip that allowed Parker Alley to fall onto the deck like a dead fish. Although a dead man was precisely what we were expecting, we were all taken aback by the large steel rod that pierced his chest and what appeared to be blood or red paint on the side of his face and clothes.

EIGHT

My shipmates were intent on covering up the corpse as quickly as possible and so, in the absence of a proper body bag, produced a down-filled sleeping bag from within the fo'c'sle. This kind of sleep was probably not what L.L.Bean had intended for the users of their product, but Dane and Quasar had no qualms. I suspected that their haste to conceal Parker Alley was twofold. First of all, until you've seen a large number of dead strangers, the presence of a corpse is creepy and, as with the accident scene syndrome, compelling in a way that makes it difficult to remove your eyes. Unless you are conducting an investigation or an autopsy, there is some guilt involved in checking out a dead body. Out of sight, out of mind, I thought as the men gently lifted the body onto the open bag, placing it on its side so as not to disturb the steel, wooden-handled rod that ran completely through his upper abdomen, bayonet style. Second reason? Covering a dead body just seems the right thing to do and shows proper respect for the dead.

Quasar folded the navy blue, down-filled nylon

over Parker Alley, and Dane operated the zipper that ran the length of the bag, miraculously, without a catch. I was still somewhat amazed that they had found Parker, and so very quickly. Either these guys are very good, or extremely lucky, I thought. I have always been somewhat relieved when things go according to plan, especially at sea. When Dane had casually mentioned the subject of superstition, I felt a bit of a pang of guilt; everyone knows that women are considered to be bad luck aboard a boat. Kindly, no one said anything. The thinking, or lack thereof, goes like this: When Lady Luck sets sail, she morphs into Jonah, and is held responsible for every bad thing that happens from foul weather to poor fishing to downright disaster. I've always been welcomed aboard boats, as I have learned that men like to have an excuse handy for when things go awry. Don't get me wrong: I have never been blamed for someone else's mistake, nor would I stand for that. Like Mother Nature, I have been held unjustly responsible only for the big stuff.

Accidental death was now a tough sell, I thought as I followed the men up to the bridge. Murder? There was no evidence of that. Parker Alley had been alone. And with so many boats working within radio or even visual contact, foul play was unlikely, I thought. Homicide would have to be ruled out. Suicide? Tough to fall chest-first onto a spike like that and then keel over into the water. But not impossible. If Parker Alley had indeed committed suicide in a grief-stricken or depressed state following the death of his young son, he certainly didn't take any chances on the success of his first swimming lesson. While hari-kari may have been considered an honorable death in some Eastern cultures, suicide in any form is shameful in ours. The only explanation I could imagine for Parker Alley's thoroughness in his self-destruction was, perhaps, his maritime heritage. Would it be considered an embarrassment for a fisherman to die with everyone thinking that he had accidentally fallen overboard? The amount of pride people take in their saltiness and seafaring abilities, nurtured over generations, could conceivably seduce someone on the brink to wish to leave no chance that people would think his death was caused by a misstep or incompetence. Better to show the world that this was quite intentional and remove all doubt of ineptitude. And yet how could he have been sure his body would be found? Maybe he just assumed as much.

The remains of what appeared to have been red paint, definitely not blood, formed a long smudge that ran the length of the corpse's left side and gave the indication that Parker Alley was right-handed. Otherwise he couldn't have painted the stripe on himself. Of course, I made the obvious connection to George Paul's history lesson, recalling the early Native American Red Paint People. But I couldn't figure out what kind of a statement Parker Alley was trying to make with the paint and it baffled me. Trying fully to understand the thoughts and intentions that would precipitate this kind of ultimate, violent self-destruction is often foolhardy, I know. But it's what I do.

People who haven't spent too much time around dead bodies are often reluctant to speak within their earshot, as if they could hear, and this was certainly the case aboard *Quest*. Nothing was said until we were all in the wheelhouse and the door had been secured. There was no real discussion, only a statement issued by the captain detailing our new course of action. He had decided that it would be best to steam to Southwest Harbor, where the nearest Coast Guard station was, and basically get rid of Parker Alley and me. He was almost that blunt. Keeping in mind our send-off from Cobble Harbor less than twenty-four hours ago, it seemed like a wise point of disembarkation for me, whether I was with or without a body. I was anxious to get ashore for many reasons and assumed that I could hire or hitch a ride to collect my car. So the captain got no argument from me.

I agreed to call the sheriff to report the recovery of the body and to have him inform the next of kin. My call was accepted, and I learned that the county coroner would also be notified, as protocol necessitated the corpse be officially pronounced dead prior to anyone removing it from the vessel. We were just two hours out of Southwest Harbor, so this seemed like a good plan.

I borrowed a sheet of paper and a pen from Quasar, as I had left mine in the Duster back in Cobble Harbor. The first thing I wrote down was "Bait Iron." Quasar, who was reading over my shoulder, questioned my notation. I informed him that this was the common term for the wooden-handled instrument with which the corpse was skewered. I recognized the rod as a bait iron, the kind used aboard many lobster boats to spear whole baitfish onto a line so that they could be held fast in the proper spot in a trap, and theorized that this one had been the personal property of Parker Alley. Next, I asked Dane for the precise latitude and longitude where he had "caught" the body, for accurate paperwork and to check against the location where Cal and I had happened upon the abandoned boat two days ago. Other than noting date and time and the other facts, there wasn't a whole lot I could do in the line of duty until my feet hit the ground in Southwest Harbor. There was no urgent reason to call Mr. Dubois regarding what should be said to the underwriters of Parker Alley's life-insurance policy, and it shouldn't be done anyway until I had filed a proper police report. When you wear two hats, you have to make sure to remember which goes on first. The insurance folks would be the only people pleased to learn that accidental drowning had been ruled out. Parker Alley's last thoughts had certainly not included his widow's financial security. A simple jump into the water would have left open the possibility that his death would be ruled accidental and would have made it possible for her to collect.

The wheelhouse was uncomfortably quiet as the green puddle of landmass over the bow rose from the bay and took shape as if melting in reverse. "Is this detour going to screw up your bonus?" I asked, intentionally breaking the silence. Quasar seemed both surprised and ill at ease with my question about his compensation; I assumed that he'd forgotten that Dane had mentioned the bonus in front of me the day before, when he was trying to shake the scientist into action during the breakwater scare.

"I hope not," replied the captain. Then the men looked at each other with what I felt was a bit of distrust, as if they both suspected the other of having foolishly shared a confidence. With a slight shrug that could have been forgiveness or apathy, Dane continued with an explanation. "Aquaculture is a hot topic these days and there's a window of opportunity for public input. If North Atlantic Shell Farms can get their ducks in a row faster than the opposition can organize a fight, their chances of pushing the proposal through is good. Our data is a required part of the application for leasing the bottom from the State of Maine. Like most of our contracted work, there's a small bonus in completing the job by a certain date. We still have two days and the weather report is good. So, as long as we don't dally in Southwest Harbor, we could make it."

"Any bonus for desired results?" I asked.

"No," Dane replied in a tone that indicated that he had been asked the question before, perhaps posing it himself. "No money for shading data. North Atlantic has done their homework. They know that this area of Cobscook Bay has ideal growing conditions for oysters and that all variables that Quasar and I will measure and record will pass muster. Our work is a formality. The only obstacle to the proposal is the public's opinion of it."

"Well, so far it appears that at least some of the public is not on board to the project," I said with a chuckle.

"And fortunately, our paychecks do not hinge on the success of the proposal. It doesn't matter to us whether they grow oysters or not. That would only lead to suspicions that we fudge data. We're not about that." I believed him. Dane pushed a button on the autopilot, shutting it off, and began steering the boat by hand as we neared the first set of channel markers. Here were two nice-enough fellows trying to make an honest living, and struggling at that, finding themselves on the bottom floor of a contentious project, which made them into targets. Quasar had summarized the situation best in his Spartacus analogy. The residents of Cobble Harbor who opposed big business, or change, or aquaculture specifically, would naturally see Quasar and Dane as foot soldiers of "the bad guys," and Quasar was certainly justified in his feelings of being "under attack." All the more reason to be landing in neighboring Southwest Harbor. I wasn't finding any comfort in my vague recollection of ancient history. As I recalled, yes, Spartacus and his band of rebel slaves had indeed defeated many Roman soldiers against outstanding odds, but in the end he failed in his attempt to flee Italy and that failure had cost him his life. Of course, Quasar had that history down cold.

I was so wrapped up in thoughts of Spartacus and also figuring out how best to organize my time once we hit shore that I scarcely noticed the beauty of the day and the surroundings as Dane Stevens navigated a wide channel that led to a junction of intersecting waterways. Quasar had binoculars pressed against his eyeglasses. He scanned the shoreline back and forth with a slow, sweeping 180-degree arc. The captain spotted the Coast Guard station and had chosen the channel that would take us there long before Quasar pointed it out. Floating docks were connected to high piers that lined the shore all along the face of the brick buildings that housed the Coast Guard base. Two of the larger government vessels were tied to the pier, while a number of small boats hung on floats. The *Eva B.* was tethered alone to the farthest float in the compound, as if she'd been quarantined. Moorings were held by skiffs and dinghies, all of which appeared to have been left by the fishing fleet, as they lacked the Coast Guard color scheme that signified and glorified every other floating object in the area. A flagpole towering above all displayed the appropriate symbols of our location: U.S. Coast Guard Group, Southwest Harbor, Maine.

Young men and women dressed in dark blue uniforms were busy with scrapers, paintbrushes, and garden tools as they manicured buildings, boats, and grounds; they were carbon copies of one another from their necks down to, and including, pant legs that bloused above boot tops into which they were neatly tucked. Two men stopped what they were doing on an adjacent float and hustled to the pier where we were coming in so that they could help catch lines. They

wore dark blue ball caps embroidered across the front
with yellow block letters: U.S. COAST GUARD, each hat
read, and included the official insignia. The men
greeted us with serious nods. High tide and a perfect
docking by our captain made line tossing easy for
Quasar and me. The young men placed eye splices
down over pilings, and Quasar and I took tight wraps
with bitter ends of four lines around prospective
cleats. Then all bustle stopped momentarily, a clear
indication that word of *Quest*'s cargo had preceded
our arrival.

"Thank you, gentlemen," Dane Stevens said as he
emerged through the starboard wheelhouse door and
down three steps onto the work deck. His thank-you
was a dismissal, and the young Coast Guardsmen took
it as such. They asked if there was anything they could
do to assist and seemed relieved to hear that we were
all set and just waiting for the coroner to show up.
They tore their eyes from the sleeping bag and walked
back up the pier and into a central grassy area. Once
there, they were quickly joined by half a dozen others
who were, no doubt, full of questions and wanted the
advance team to confirm or deny the rumors they had
all heard about a dead body. I found it strangely re-
freshing that a corpse in their general vicinity had the
effect that it did. The young men and women were distracted from work and their constant watch on the
station's entrance gate suggested that they were disturbed by the scene. How different, I thought, from
Miami, where I had on occasion seen pedestrians step

over a body lacking posture on a curb and never break stride or miss a sip of their Starbucks. "It might be a while before the coroner shows up," Dane said. "Do you see any reason for us to hang around? I mean, if you need us, we're happy to stay. But otherwise, time is really growing short. You'll be okay, right?"

"Well." I tried not to sound disappointed. "Well, the only problem is that we aren't supposed to move the body from the boat until there's an official death pronouncement." The three of us stood and stared at one another with expressions that spoke with some volume about how ridiculous that was. "Let's pretend I didn't say that. This has already been a huge inconvenience to you and, yes, I'll be fine waiting here. The tide is going to start ebbing soon. Help me with the body and I'll throw your lines." It felt better being in favor of what was inevitable. Plus, being a proactive, take-charge girl who was willing to bend the rules was more becoming than being a whining stickler, I thought as I lifted what I knew was the foot end of the corpse. The three of us set the bagged body onto the pier with ease. We all shook hands, bid thanks, and said farewells. Dane Stevens and I exchanged phone numbers at his request, something that I naturally read more into than the stated, obvious reason: I would almost certainly need to follow up with him on official matters relating to the corpse and investigation, and to complete paperwork, and his employer might need to reach me. As Quasar slackened lines, I lifted the looped ends from the pilings, freeing *Quest* to venture back offshore. "I'll return your sleeping bag to you," I called through the open door as the boat pulled away. I watched until I saw nothing but stern; I was like the girl left behind at the railroad station. Out like a lamb, I thought. My wistful hopes of romance dissipated, like a green, twinkling, outgoing tide over sandy shallows. "Bye," I mumbled. I looked down, and the sparkle-filled backdrop was gone. The lump in the blue bag brought reality screaming back into focus with some velocity.

My stomach growled. Other than a couple of Little Debbie snack cakes I had helped myself to from a box I found on the galley table, I hadn't eaten today. I couldn't in good conscience leave Parker Alley here while I looked for food. There must be a mess hall or commissary on the premises. I looked around at the buildings. Maybe some of the onlookers would find the courage to come close enough to say hello and ask if they could do anything for me. Maybe not, I thought, as the closest group of three turned away when I looked in their direction. I would just have to wait. I began walking up and down the pier, never more than fifty feet in either direction from Parker Alley. It wasn't a nervous back-and-forth pacing as much as it was a time-passing activity. I find that thoughts come easier to me while I'm doing something mindless, like walking or driving. And I had a lot of thinking to do.

I soon grew tired of pacing and thinking. I had basically run through every possible scenario that might explain what had transpired over the past two days, rehashed all forty-one years of my life, and come up with an entire self-improvement strategy by the time I decided to sit and rest on a short piling beside the corpse. My knee-high rubber boots were sock eaters, having chewed the white cotton that had hugged my calves and spit it out into the toes, where it cramped all five digits of each foot. Kicking off the boots, I retrieved and replaced my socks, then pulled the boots back on and began humming an Otis Redding tune. I was glad I didn't own a wristwatch. Even the Coast Guard had grown bored with the not-unfolding scene and everyone had resumed their various maintenance activities. By the time I had chirped through the whistling part of the song for about the fifteenth round, a black hearselike vehicle pulled slowly through the gate, followed by a large silver pickup truck. They had a leg up on Green Haven, I thought. At least they had a hearse instead of a converted bakery truck.

I stood and waited by the body while the hearse backed toward the end of the pier. When it was as close as it could get to where I stood, two men emerged, one from each side of the front seat. They nodded in my direction, and then waited for someone to climb out of the truck that had parked just ahead of them. The truck was a crew cab. The inside of the large cab appeared to be full of people whom I assumed were Alleys, since I recognized the man who was now shaking hands with the coroner as the brother of the deceased, the fellow I had originally met offshore with Cal, and the same person I had seen yesterday in Cobble Harbor dressed for the funeral. One of the men opened the back of the hearse and pulled a backboard type of stretcher from inside and carried it down the pier toward me. The other two men followed close behind.

Quick introductions confirmed the driver of the hearse was indeed the county coroner, whose job was to pronounce Parker Alley dead. The man with him was the Alleys' family doctor, who had agreed to issue a medical certificate of death by drowning to eliminate the postmortem examination and allow the family to get on with the closing of this horrid chapter. Obviously, they knew nothing of the spike. Maybe, though, they could still get away with saying death by drowning and not by suicide. Who knew what you could do in these small towns?

I learned that Parker's brother was named Evan Alley, as all three men introduced themselves to Knox County Deputy Sheriff Jane Bunker—that is, me. I warned Evan to prepare himself before the bag was opened. He said that he appreciated my concern, but he didn't believe anything could faze him at this point. He said that he was just a walking zombie and wanted to put this in the past for his entire family.

"Let's get to it," said the coroner as he knelt down beside the sleeping bag and began to work the zipper. He unzipped nearly the full length of the bag before finally unveiling the corpse with a quick peel of the sides of the bag.

Evan Alley's reaction was as I expected it might be, in spite of his initial calm and assurance that he was ready for anything. He gasped and the color drained from his face. He grabbed the front of his own shirt and beat it in and out as if trying to get air. He turned and began walking toward the truck. It must have been awful for him to see his brother's body, especially with a bait iron through it. But I was the one who was surprised when I heard what he was wailing. "It ain't him," he cried. "That body ain't him."

NINE

I don't stun easily, but I felt as though someone had pulled a chair out from under me. If this was not Parker Alley, who was it? And where was Parker Alley? The coroner, doctor, and I stood speechlessly and watched the scene unfolding by the side of the pickup truck, from which the family had emerged. There were tears of what I imagined were extreme frustration and disbelief, and hugs of support. I wanted to introduce myself to the Alleys and set up a time to talk with Lillian, whom I assumed was the woman in the center of the group, the one who was now dabbing the corners of her eyes with a handkerchief. But I knew I should wait for at least a few minutes to allow them a bit of privacy as they absorbed this mixed news. How would it feel, I wondered, for a wife to be on the receiving end of a negative ID? Would there now exist a glimmer of hope that your husband was still alive? Or are your hopes of closure dashed in bitter disappointment?

I shifted my focus to the corpse. Funny, I hadn't thought to look at the man's face until now. In the brief time on the *Quest*'s deck before he was covered, I had concentrated on the means of death rather than the dead. Jet-black hair, a small mustache, and a slight slant in the shape of his eyes; he certainly didn't look like someone central casting would have sent over to play the part of a member of the Alley clan and resident of Cobble Harbor, Maine. I pried an eye open. It was as black as I had ever seen in someone living or dead. I checked the pockets of his jeans and denim shirt, hoping for some clue to his identity, but came up empty. Unzipping the foot end of the sleeping bag, I exposed black socks and black Nike sneakers. I patted down the corpse's legs—nothing. In my experience, anytime an adult male is found with absolutely nothing in his possession—no wallet, no cigarettes, and no loose change—it is because someone has handled the corpse before the cops. "Do you know who this is?" I asked the men.

Neither man had any idea of the identity of the corpse. "So much for the quick ID, death certificate, and ride to the funeral parlor," said the coroner. "Give me a hand loading him up, would you please? I'll drop the doc back at his office and head to the morgue in Augusta."

"Will there be an autopsy report available for me to see?" I asked.

"There will certainly be an inquest. We'll need statements from you and the captain of the vessel that recovered the body. Our budget doesn't allow for many full autopsies, but we'll do a clinical inspection with toxicology." He pulled his wallet from his back pocket and handed me a business card. "You can call my office in forty-eight hours to have a copy faxed to the Sheriff's Department. In the meantime, it looks as though you'll be busy finding a missing person and a murderer."

Murder, although it was quite obvious, was something that until now I had been hoping could be explained away. Now that the coroner had said the word, there was no denying that this probably could not have been a suicide. A murder investigation would certainly distract me from my goal of damming the flow of illegal drugs into my territory. Of course, this apparent murder could be related to drugs, I realized. But right now, until I had some very basic facts, I knew I shouldn't even be trying to make a connection. I had to think for a second about why I was so much more interested in solving the drug case than in finding a murderer. It wasn't that I couldn't get excited about helping to convict a killer—of course I could. But that would simply mean getting justice for someone who was, well, let's face it, already dead. If I was able to stop the heroin from coming in, I would be helping prevent future deaths.

"Before we zip him back up, I'd like to see if anyone can ID him," I said as I took a step toward the truck. When I got no objection, I turned away from the coroner to see the Alley family coming down the pier single file, with Evan in the lead. The coroner, doctor, and I fell into place quite naturally to shield the fully exposed corpse from view.

"Miss Bunker, this is some of the rest of my family. I thought you'd need to talk with them, and they all want to have a look at the body," Evan said, and then introduced the three other people to the coroner and me. They already seemed familiar with the doctor. The young man was Evan's son, as I had assumed upon seeing them together aboard *Ardency* at the scene of the circling boat two days before. The middle-aged man was another brother, Jack, the youngest of three Alley boys. Lillian was a striking woman with classic facial features—high cheekbones and skin that appeared to dislike the sun. Her green eyes were rimmed red; she looked like she had been crying straight through from when her son had died until now, and she held herself in a way that suggested she wasn't sure if her crying would ever end. When I extended my right hand to her for a shake, she grasped the outside of it with her left and gave it a tight squeeze, as her right hand was now holding her nephew's arm for support. "I warned her about the body," Evan said of Lillian. "But she wants to help if she can."

"I'm a big girl," Lillian said. "What can be worse than seeing your son in a casket? Besides, Parker and I have been married since we were kids. I know better than anyone who his friends and enemies are. If it's someone who knew Parker, I'll know who it is." The coroner and I separated, leaving a wide gap between us through which Lillian passed with her nephew. She released her grip on the young man's arm when they were next to the body and then she circled slowly, looking at him from every angle. After a few minutes, she carefully pulled the sleeping bag back over the top of the body. "I've never seen him, but that could be my husband's bait iron in his chest."

"Lillian, you don't *know* that," Evan said, sounding as if he were pleading with her not to say anything more. "That's ridiculous. Every lobster boat on the coast of Maine has a tool just like that aboard. It could be mine."

"Look, Evan: Parker is missing; they searched for him and found this guy instead. This isn't New York Harbor, and these people aren't stupid." I refrained from thanking her for the compliment. "Parker is not a violent man, but he would defend himself." She was now addressing me specifically. "If he killed this guy, it was self-defense and he is still alive, right?" My opinion was that Lillian was grasping at any hope, but she could be delusional and actually believe that her husband would be home for dinner tonight. I knew from past experience that people clinging to hope, even to the remotest possibility, are always far more likely to talk than people who have come to terms with a loss. I needed to have some time with her before the last glimmer of optimism faded away. "Do you plan to continue looking for my husband, Ms. Bunker?"

"Indeed I do," I answered. "If your husband is alive, we need to move quickly. Missing persons who aren't located within the first seventy-two hours of their disappearance have a tendency to remain missing. I could get search warrants for your house and the boat, and can requisition your records, but that would waste precious time."

"How can we help?" Lillian was now enlisting her family members, who did not resist.

"I'll need access to everything—phone records, bank statements, financial portfolios, tax returns, receipts, personal computer, personal correspondence in any form—everything. I'll need a list and contact information of friends and enemies." So far all of this was met with eye contact and a nod to each item I mentioned. "I'll need to talk with anyone who may have seen Parker the day he disappeared." Lillian seemed genuinely interested in not only cooperating but participating in the investigation, as she pointed at Evan and let him know, in a loud whisper, that she expected him to be able to supply those names. Now, I thought, was the proper time to push my luck with Lillian. "And as painful as it might be for you, I will have to ask questions about your son." I genuinely felt bad about asking and opening up such a fresh wound, but my investigation into the drug problem also needed to move swiftly or any leads would probably evaporate.

Lillian grew about two inches in height due to the sudden tensing of every muscle in her body. I knew I had pushed too hard too soon. Sadness in her green eyes was replaced with anger as she said, "You'll leave Jason out of this, or you'll get no help from me." Like any mother, Lillian was naturally willing to throw anyone or anything under the bus to protect the memory of her child. I apologized and agreed to concentrate only on finding Parker—for now.

The men seemed uncomfortable, having just been faced with a situation that could have escalated to something very ugly, very quickly; they got busy putting the corpse into a real body bag and then placing the whole kit and kaboodle onto a litter and into the back of the hearse. While they did, I tried to distract Lillian and get her to forget her near rage with lists of things for her to do and information to gather. As long as we stayed on the subject of how to expedite my investigation into the whereabouts of Parker Alley, well, then we were fine. With what I knew so far—the circling boat, the absence of its captain, and the corpse with a bait iron through its chest, found just where a body would be if it fell off Parker's vessel—I had a hard time pretending that I might be looking for a missing person and not a murderer and/or another corpse. I recalled the message left by Mr. Dubois about changes to Parker Alley's life insurance policy and understood that such adjustments could indicate many things. But my search for the alive-and-well Parker Alley would give me cover as I charged into the innards of Cobble Harbor; I hoped the show would be worth the price of admission. And, although searching for missing persons is really more about paperwork than real investigating (now, busting drug rings—that's genuine detective work!), Parker Alley was my responsibility, alive or dead. I was, after all, deputy sheriff and insurance consultant.

By the time the door of the hearse was slammed shut, Lillian and I were speaking civilly and had agreed that she would get to work on her end as soon as she got home that afternoon. I was to meet her the following day at ten A.M., at her house, to which she gave me simple directions from the town dock. She climbed into the front passenger side of the truck as Jack took the driver's side and the nephew hopped into the backseat. My silent wondering as to where Evan would sit was answered after the truck left him behind in the parking area. "The Coast Guard has released Parker's boat, so I'll steam her home to Cobble Harbor," he explained.

"Can I catch a ride with you?" I asked, remembering that I needed to get to Cobble Harbor to pick up my car.

"My wife would not appreciate that. Sorry." He looked genuinely embarrassed to deny me the lift.

"Oh," was about all I could say to that. "Well, I will need to get aboard the *Eva B.* to take a look around for the insurance company," I added truthfully.

"Maybe you should catch a ride with the coroner. He has to go right by your car to take the doc back to work," Evan suggested. "I'll have the boat back home before you get there and will leave her tied at the town dock. You can go aboard and do whatever you need to do."

I had a suspicion that Evan didn't want me aboard his brother's boat for some reason other than a jealous wife, but the coroner and doctor were getting into the hearse, and I really needed a ride. I didn't imagine Southwest Harbor had taxi service. I had already been aboard the *Eva B.*, and she'd been at the Coast Guard station for nearly two days. So what would the harm be in waiting a couple more hours to do a thorough inspection? I chased the hearse as it slowly pulled away, catching it before the gate, and giving the Coast Guardsmen another scene to ponder.

The coroner and doctor talked freely in my presence, or I should say they talked across me as I sat between them on the bench-style front seat of the hearse. Although I had been willing to ride in back with the corpse, I was pleased when the doctor opened his door and offered me a place up front with the living. The coroner had begun the inquest and I was glad to hear what the Alleys' family doctor had to say about the clan; most of the Alleys were his patients. They were good people, in his opinion. Everyone was shocked by the death of Jason. In fact, his had been the first and only overdose from heroin or any other illegal substance in the area that the doctor knew of. Drugs had always been a factor in Bangor, which was far more metropolitan than the remote towns situated on the ends of these long, twisting peninsulas like the one we were now traveling, the doctor said. He knew of a few methadone clinics in Maine—in Bangor, South Portland, Waterville, and Westbrook—but everyone always said that no such clinic was needed in this vicinity. And until just recently, the doctor had believed that to be so: "The traditional belief was always that the drugs just never made it down here from Bangor. But with the traffic this area sees in the summer from every major city in the country, I guess it was only a matter of time." Interesting, I thought, that the summer community bore responsibility for the local drug trade in the doctor's eyes. "And now we've got a murderer on the loose. What next?"

The coroner asked more questions about the Alley family, but the doctor didn't seem to have much more to add. All he could say was that they seemed to be quite a healthy group, as they appeared only for scheduled yearly physicals. They didn't even smoke or drink, the doctor confided, and this was most unusual among the year-rounders who relied solely on lobster fishing for their livelihood. "Slow fishing drives most of them to drink, which they can't afford for all of the reasons we're aware of. The Alleys are good fishermen, and Parker is known all over town as top dog. I wouldn't say he's well liked, but that's common. You know, a jealousy thing." A little soft prodding by the coroner on the subject of enemies had the doctor admitting that, while he wasn't in the know enough to provide names other than "Beals," which echoed Quasar's opinion of a long-running family feud, he did understand that lobster fishing was a cutthroat business in which only those willing to cut throats survived. What he didn't say, but he clearly implied, was that Parker must have been plenty willing to cut throats to be known as the best.

The car grew quiet, leaving us with our individual thoughts. Mine focused mainly on the view of the town of Southwest Harbor through the car windows. Southwest is unlike Green Haven or Cobble Harbor in that it's a well-known tourist destination, as is Bar Harbor, which is on the same island as Southwest. And just about everyone on planet Earth who has heard of the State of Maine associates it with Bar Harbor, pronounced without the "r"s. Funny, I had never imagined a hearse traveling at greater than a turtle's pace. Through the years, I had been stuck directly behind the hearse in many a motorcade for a fallen comrade and shudder to think that I actually complained about the lack of speed and looked at my wristwatch constantly. One of the vows I took when I left Miami was to deep-six the watch, which I had done with the idealistic notion that a timepiece would have no value if I had no schedule to keep. Little did I know that I would indeed have a schedule. But I would have had no trouble keeping it this afternoon. Someone was in a hurry. The doctor or the coroner—or maybe both.

From the inside of the hearse looking out, the surroundings seemed to be flashing by at great velocity. I noticed a number of inns and B and Bs, now restored to funky, retro antiquity, one of the signs of a flourishing gay community. I remembered when the same transformation took hold in South Beach. Defunct businesses and dilapidated buildings suddenly came to life with a definite flair and tastefulness that was not exclusive to the gay community, but certainly was a hallmark of it. Everything was beautiful until the place started attracting more and more of the fast-lane crowd. Yes, I thought, this was the way South Miami looked twenty years ago. I hoped that Southwest Harbor could stop the wheels of change right here, before the straight fashionistas moved in.

Happily, there wasn't any evidence of fashionistas yet. Plaid flannel billowed around bodies that had not been near a gym; bodies that paused in the doorways and parking lots of the small restaurants and gift shops that lined the road on the way out of town. The storefront windows of a boutique we passed did not display clinging synthetics designed to accentuate runway-ready figures. Nope: Denim, cotton, and wool were the fabrics on hand—practical, functional, comfortable—and "high-end, modest conservative" was yet again the look in vogue this season, and all of the store's mannequins were dressed accordingly. The people I saw were draped in and covered by, rather than poured into and scantily clad by, their clothes. The wardrobe boss in Southwest Harbor liked colors other than black.

At the heart of the town, the quintessential New England church stood with perfect posture, stark in its whiteness and with a pencil-sharp steeple that cast a long shadow; the tip of the shadow pointed directly to the small cemetery next door. My mother would have regarded that as a sign from God. Yes, I thought, we're all heading there whether we enter through the front doors or not. But some of us have work to do first. For a period in my life, my mother was a member of what I fondly referred to as "the religion of the month club." She'd dress my brother and me up in our best clothes and drag us to whatever institution promised that it would save us all. The first sermon in our new religion was always like spring for my mother: an awakening of possibilities. The next service was summer, in that we were all made aware of the hard work we had to do to save our souls, a kind of religious "make hay while the sun shines." Fall, also known as visit number three, found my mother disillusioned, and winter, visit four, brought total discontentment. Four visits each church—that was the routine. I knew it well. Fortunately my mother didn't believe in giving money to the church, because we never had any to spare—not even for Jesus. It was a shame my mother was never able to find what she was looking for. I watched the cemetery disappear down the right side of the hearse.

The coroner had turned on the car's radio, and we listened to the usual gung ho, over-the-top enthusiasm of a local announcer between sets of oldies. When we made a hard left turn off Route 1, I began to recognize the road. It was the one that led to Cobble Harbor; we were close to my disembarkation point. I was aware that the coroner was not from Cobble Harbor, and so assumed correctly that he wasn't familiar with local politics. So it was understandable that the coroner never asked the doctor his opinion of the aquaculture project's possible role in the disappearance of Parker and the murder of the unidentified man riding with us. Not wanting to step on the coroner's toes but eager to hear what the doctor thought, I interrupted America's "A Horse with No Name." (And how dare they put a song from the seventies on an oldies channel, anyway?) "What's your take on the oyster farm, Doc?"

"That's a real can of worms," he said. "My personal opinion is that it would be good to have some industry in town other than lobster, and most of us are opposed to going after more tourist traffic. But the fishing families, Anglo and Indian alike, are dead set against losing the area proposed. It's the only thing the Anglos and Indians agree on. They both see aquaculture as a step toward losing their heritage—part of which is the fight between them for fishing rights."

"Do you think either side is capable of murder?" I asked. There was that red paint on the corpse. And I again recalled George Paul's phrase "the Red Paint People."

"No. Gear wars have escalated in the past to the point of sabotage and threats, but no one has ever gotten physical beyond a punch in the nose. The proposed area for the oyster farm has been closed to fishing since the last battle over rights, because the state saw the potential for things to get out of hand. It was like two kids fighting over a toy—if you can't share, we'll take it away. Amazingly enough, both sides preferred that to dividing it equally."

"But what about the degree of anger over this particular project? I mean, sure, the fishermen will get only so violent when fighting with one another over who gets exclusive fishing rights, but don't people get way more riled in opposition to a force from the outside?"

"If you are asking whether I think the man behind us was killed in the battle over aquaculture, I have no idea. I can only tell you that he isn't a local. I'm the only doctor in town. If that man had lived in Cobble Harbor, I'd know him." The hearse pulled into the parking lot, where there were many cars and

trucks, the Duster among them. The doctor held the
door while I slid out, creepy sleeping bag in hand, and
bid both men thanks and goodbye. They urged me to
be in touch should I need any information I thought
they could provide and drove off. My first move was
to the Duster; I wanted to stow the sleeping bag and
retrieve my cell phone and notebook. Once I had these
things, I headed toward the dock, where I could see
the *Eva B.* She was there just as Evan Alley had promised she'd be. As I walked, I stared at the cell phone's
display screen, hoping for enough of a signal to call
Dane Stevens and inform him that we were still missing Parker Alley's body. The appearance of three
bars had me digging in my pocket for his number.
The battery life indicator showed a deathbed's gasp
worth of juice remaining. I dialed and hoped. When I
got no answer, I left a message with the surprising
news and asked for a callback. At least they would
learn they needed to keep looking the minute Dane
picked up his messages.

My first mission aboard the *Eva B.* was to find the
bait iron. I searched the entire work space, but found
nothing resembling a tool with which a man could
spear a fish and thread it onto the bait line in a lobster
trap. There was a chance it could be stowed below. I
opened the door exposing the forward compartment.
Empty, completely empty—not only was there no bait
iron, there was also no sign of the abundant shipping
supplies I had seen two days ago. Boxes, insulation,
tape, labels—not there; even the cooler that held the
gel packs was gone.

TEN

Either Parker alley was a neat freak, or some folks had gone out of their way to scrub every inch of his boat. Under the wash rails, where you can usually find some remnants of bait, blood, mud, or one of the many grassy seaweeds that come up from the bottom on lobster traps, the fiberglass looked fresh out of the mold. One of the first lessons I had learned in criminal investigation was not to let a big reverse faze me. Of course, I needed to remind myself of this throughout my career and now. The fact that the *Eva B.* had been either burglarized or cleaned up could be a clue itself that could help me solve the Parker Alley mystery—maybe even a more significant clue than any I might have found if nothing had been taken or scrubbed away. Suddenly, I had the chilling feeling that someone was watching me. Possibly paranoia, I thought as I went about my business. Another lesson I had learned long ago was never to let on that you are aware of being watched. I put the eerie sensation of being seen through binoculars out of my head, and hoped that whatever surveillance device was trained on me—if

any—was not the crosshaired sighting mechanism
of a gun.

It was hard to believe that someone could have
come aboard right under the Coast Guard's nose without being noticed and steal stacks of white, insulated
FedEx boxes and all of the accompanying supplies.
Although there was the possibility that brother Evan
had taken the missing supplies for his personal use, or
had the thought to begin emptying the boat knowing
that Lillian would be putting it on the market, it just
didn't seem likely; I guessed, rather, that they had been
jettisoned for some reason en route from Southwest to
Cobble Harbor. It's a strange and unexplainable personal quirk, but when I think I am being watched, I
guard my thoughts closely as if the surveillance could
penetrate my skull and read my mind. Again, reminding myself of how foolish this was, I continued in both
thought and action. It wasn't like I had uncovered
anything yet that should make me nervous. But the
sensation of being watched from afar was enough to
make me keep studying the boat. Why would someone be watching if nothing on the craft was suspect?

It's traditionally the stern man's job to clean up the
boat, I thought, as I lifted hatches and inspected com-
partments. And the stern man is quite often the son or
daughter of the captain. I wondered whether Jason had
been fishing with his father right before he overdosed.
And I wondered if anyone was with Parker the day he
disappeared. Everyone, including Cal and me, had assumed that Parker had been alone aboard his boat.
But I'm not sure why we all assumed that. Certainly

if anyone else had been aboard, they would have been reported missing, too. The doctor was of the opinion that Parker was the high-liner in the area, but that would be impossible unless he frequently had help. I knew from my varied experience aboard commercial boats that top producers have topnotch help, and no one lobstering alone, no matter how good, can keep pace with a good two-man team. Keeping this in mind, I assumed that Parker Alley would usually have at least one stern man, and may have even employed two to keep up a rapid pace with the traps coming aboard and the lobsters to be measured and banded. Although I hadn't done a thorough inspection of the *Eva B.* when Cal put me aboard the other day, Cal had pointed out that she was too clean to have been hauling traps when the fisherman went missing. I had been so emotionally invested in the possibility that a man might be struggling for his life, and so flabbergasted that no one appeared to be concerned, that I scarcely took note of the condition of the boat.

The parts of the *Eva B.* that showed signs of fishing activity—the plates of the hydraulic hauler that pinch the line between them as it turns, the block through which the line travels from the water to the hauler, and the hauling patch, which is a thick piece of fiberglass on the hull where the traps sometimes bump when they are hauled from the surface—all appeared to have some wear. But, I thought, not enough to suggest that Parker Alley was a hard-charger and top producer. Productivity is always a function of a combination of factors, the most important of which

is effort. The more traps a man hauls, the more lobsters he will catch. There are the old-school guys who
will claim to fish smarter, and catch more pounds per
trap, than the men who just bull through the gear—
hauling and dumping, as they say. But at the end of
the season, it's always the guys who handle the greatest number of traps who come out on top financially,
in spite of bigger overhead. I knew that the majority
of the inshore fleet worked a season that ran from
May through December, so if that schedule held in
Cobble Harbor, it stood to reason that Parker Alley
was not fresh out of the boatyard but well into the
season. I couldn't say exactly what was amiss, but felt
that things didn't add up. The major thing bothering
me was the too-clean boat.

By the time I had surveyed the engine compartment, steering gear, rudder post, through-hull fittings, bilges, battery connections, stuffing box, bilge
pump, alarms, twelve-volt electrical system, fuel man-
ifold, and engine exhaust, my suspicion that someone
had done a destroy-the-evidence bleaching had dwin-
dled. It was clear that Parker maintained his boat to
the nth degree. Grease fittings were wiped clean, the
bilge sparkled, and the battery terminals were im-
maculate. The tools were well organized and wrenches
gleamed; even the grease gun, which in every boat I've
ever been on causes you to shudder before you grab
it, was spotless. Anyone who kept a clean grease gun
would certainly not allow blood or bait to remain in
any corner or crevice. If someone had come aboard
to steal things for resale, they would certainly have

taken tools and left shipping supplies behind, I thought. A little disappointed not to find a smoking gun, I had to admit that I normally tended to read too much into everything. Perhaps I was even imagining being watched. If I was here doing a straight survey for insurance, and not looking for clues, I might not feel as though someone were spying on me.

The *Eva B.*'s safety equipment was more than adequate and beyond the legal minimum standards. Two portable chemical fire extinguishers were in good serviceable condition and inspection tags were up to date. Four life jackets and two survival/immersion suits were USCG approved and in excellent condition. The Coast Guard–required ring buoy, properly marked with the vessel's name and strips of reflective tape, was hung with a neatly coiled piece of braided line that was secured with a fisherman's bend to the orange life ring, ready to heave to a man overboard. Visual distress signals (flares and orange smoke) were stowed in a watertight box, and the first-aid kit was first rate. Check, check, check, I thought as I went through the surveyor's list. Parker Alley was, indeed, a neat freak. By the looks of all the safety gear and first-aid items, he had in mind to stay alive in the face of any problems that might come his way while offshore. As I walked to my car, I couldn't help thinking about Jason Alley and wondering about Parker's state of mind following his son's death. I also couldn't help thinking that the sensation of being the subject of surveillance was stronger now, as if I were closer to the source.

Thoughts of father and son occupied me all the
way to Ellsworth, where I drove the Duster for gas.
Sure, I thought, as I pumped fuel worth its weight in
gold into the dusty tank, the loss of a child has to be
horrifically tough—it's ruined many a person and
destroys most marriages faced with it. But I had never
seen it result in suicide, if that's what this was. I have
handled more cases involving the death of a child than
I can count, and the parents were always wrecked.
You'd expect nothing less. But I always had a sense
that they would find some way to go on with some
semblance of their lives. And I think that most of them
did. I'm sure that there were suicides later; but I never
saw one within the first week. Were family ties that
much stronger here? Was premature death that much
more unusual here than in Miami? But why would that
matter? When it's your son or your daughter, what
do statistics mean to you?

I went back and forth and back and forth in my
mind from what I knew, but just didn't see Parker Alley taking his own life from grief. I wanted very badly
to connect death of son and subsequent disappearance
of father, but couldn't build a theory on so few facts
and such scarce evidence. The only concrete things I
had were an OD'd kid, an unidentified corpse, and a
missing fisherman. Still, a son and father perishing in
such a short time frame: There had to be some connection. I've never bought stock in coincidence, and I
couldn't buy it now.

As I turned south and headed down the homestretch

for Green Haven, I made a mental list of what I needed
to do the next day. I did have a few things to follow up
on that could lead somewhere. Perhaps the medical examiner's office would have an ID sooner than the
coroner anticipated. That would be my first call, I
thought. I had an appointment with Lillian Alley that
I was most looking forward to. Mother of dead son and
wife of missing man—Lillian was my most important
contact. I needed to call or track down Willard Kelley
to ask about the report of his stolen boat, *Spartacus*. I
hoped that I would hear from Dane Stevens regarding
the message I left on his phone, but if I didn't, I would
have to get in touch with him even if it meant using
the Coast Guard to radio him. I would need to call Cal
tonight when I got home to see if he would be available to taxi me aboard *Sea Pigeon* back to Cobble
Harbor. This last thought came when I glanced at the
fuel gauge and wished I had sprung for another gallon
or two.

Dusk bloomed slow and high in the sky, and fell
like a dark curtain onto a horizon that finally lost its
red glow of footlights as the curtain met the stage. I
have always loved this time of day. Not quite dark
enough for headlights; everything was soft, but would
soon stiffen into a sludge that could not be penetrated
without them. My favorite hour is celebrated each
and every day in Key West, I recalled. Mallory Square
saluted every sunset in grand style—tourists would
come from far and near to watch the sun go down, the
same sun that they could observe from their homes for

free. Key West had cornered the market on sunset and it was a thriving business. True Mainers don't celebrate the end of daylight. They're more inclined to appreciate sun-*rise*. Switching on the lights, I realized that the days were indeed getting shorter and knew that the decreased daylight cut into the lobstermen's profits—as it's illegal to haul traps after dark. Yes, fishermen must curse this time of day.

I could see headlights at a distance behind me in the rearview mirror. They seemed to be gaining on me at a rapid clip. I drove slowly, since the road was so winding and still relatively unfamiliar to me. I had heard the locals complaining of "summer drivers" who held them up by observing the speed limit, and sped up a bit as it was clear that the driver of the truck now on my bumper was impatient. I vowed to register the Duster and get Maine plates before venturing out of town again. The driver followed ridiculously close; I imagined that he was irritated and cursing the out-of-stater in front of him. I increased my speed to fifty-five—ten miles an hour over the posted limit. Still the lights were too close to my bumper for my comfort. At sixty-five miles per hour, I was getting nervous. Probably a couple of teenagers feeling their oats, I thought. I had heard the screeching of tires night after night on the hill outside my apartment and had seen the swirling black rubber street art. I pressed the accelerator to the floor when I was on a straightaway. The lights in my mirror went to high, nearly blinding me. I was unable to increase the space between the two bumpers as I approached a sharp turn that I had to slow down for. The trailing vehicle gently nudged the back of the Duster, backed off a few feet, then rammed against my bumper again. Not cool.

If this was what the local kids did for excitement, I wanted no more of it. I wasn't terrified; I had been menaced by cars before. But I knew I was in particular danger due to my unfamiliarity with the road. And in the past when I had been in the process of being run off the road, I was in a high-performance vehicle that could shake anything, not a dilapidated old dog like the Duster. It did appear now that the pickup truck meant business. A couple of nudges on the next two corners were hairy—keeping the Duster on the road in the tight turns was becoming a struggle. The second hit sounded as if it took out a taillight. I decided to slow down well below the speed limit and hope the driver would tire of this game and go find someone else to play with. I slowed to twenty-five miles per hour, assuming the truck would shoot past me at the next opportunity, and the occupants would flip me the bird and disappear into the night. Instead, the truck peeled off to the right, down what looked like a private dirt road. I could see dust fly in the lights before they vanished behind a thickly wooded lot.

Loosening my grip on the wheel, I took a deep breath and felt my heart rate ease back to normal. So I almost certainly had been watched while I was aboard the *Eva B*. As for what had just happened—it felt more like a warning than a full-fledged attack. Maybe I was close to uncovering something after all. Maybe when the *Spartacus* had attacked the boat I was on with Dane and Quasar, the assault had been intended for me and had nothing to do with aquaculture. And if so, the occupants of the truck were aware that I was armed and willing to do more than just bear that constitutional right.

Reminding myself that the dirt road the truck had taken could loop back onto the road on which I drove, I couldn't let my guard down yet. For the next few miles, I drove slowly, taking time to peer down all roads to my right, looking for headlights. I realized that the driver of the truck had been smart enough not to allow me to see a license plate. I wasn't completely comfortable until I reached the causeway that led directly into Green Haven. The man-made causeway was a series of S curves lined on either side by granite blocks I supposed were meant to keep cars on the road and out of the water that lapped the edges at high tide. I relaxed when I hit the south end of the causeway, knowing that I had only three miles to go before I'd be pulling into the lot outside my apartment. I imagined the Vickersons were enjoying their first cocktails by now and would invite me to join them. I wondered what mussel dish they had concocted for tonight's dinner and knew that whatever it was, I would eat it. My stomach growled.

A large shadow appeared in the fringe of my headlights' beam. The shadow moved into the middle of the road and became something quite substantial. I slammed on the brakes and jerked the steering wheel to the right, managing to avoid contact with the deer that jumped in a single, effortless bound back into the woods. The Duster came to a full stop perpendicular to the road and straddled both lanes. The headlights lit up the stand of straggly spruce trees into which I had seen the white underside of the doe's tail vanish. The clump of trees was surrounded by what looked like thoroughly cleared land. I waited and watched for the deer to spring out into the opening on either side of the trees. When nothing moved, I thought of the "deer in the headlights" phenomenon. It was a rather tiny patch of woods. Why couldn't I see the deer's eyes shining brightly in the Duster's lights? I pulled off the road and onto a narrow gravel shoulder, keeping my attention on the trees for motion. How could an animal of that size vanish with one leap? The doe had certainly not vanished. The deer must be close, but I just couldn't see her. As nervous as I was about being pursued, and now riled up by the near miss with a deer, I decided to take a few seconds to get my wits about me before getting back on the road.

The doe's heart must be pounding as hard as mine. After all, she was the one who could have been killed. This brought to mind Parker Alley. Fear is the best motivation for successful and creative disappearing acts, I thought—fear and greed. The same goes for murder—fear and greed are in the top three motives. Was Parker Alley dead, or had he simply disappeared? Had I been as close to him as I now was to the deer and simply not seen him? Until he surfaced, dead or alive, there would be much speculation and intrigue

in Cobble Harbor. His disappearance would never get
the attention that came when Amelia Earhart or Jimmy
Hoffa went missing, of course. Parker Alley was just
a fisherman. He would never have a cultlike following
like D. B. Cooper, who disappeared in 1971 after hi-
jacking an airplane, collecting $200,000 ransom, and
parachuting into the Washington State wilderness,
never to be seen again. And yet, if folks here started
to think of him as more missing than dead, it would
certainly be the cause of a lot of chatter.

The short minute to stop and think had done the
trick. My nerve endings had stopped jingling and I was
breathing normally. Realizing that I was probably putting myself in danger by spending time parked at the
side of the road looking for that one lucky deer, I decided to hightail it back to town.

I soon found myself within Green Haven proper,
where the occasional streetlamp illuminated dimly
and fleetingly the interior of my car. Back in my own
neighborhood, I allowed my mind to wander a bit as I
drove up the hill toward home. A string of unsolved
missing-persons cases that I had worked on in Florida
had similarities to my new case. All of the people in
question had been alone at sea—four cases in a row
of people gone missing while sailing single-handedly.
Their boats had all been found abandoned. The first
was deemed an accidental falling overboard, the second was considered suicide, the third a copycat, and
the fourth . . . well by the time the fourth boat was
found unmanned, the investigation of the first had
turned up some dirt on the missing sailor. Digging

deeper, my investigative team learned that all four had reasons to disappear. Bank accounts, investments, properties—everything had been liquidated shortly after the people went missing and before anyone got suspicious. We believed that all of them had staged their own deaths until body number two was found and it was clear that the man had been tortured. When a second body floated in in the same condition, we knew we had a serial situation to deal with. Televised news of the second corpse and a leaky police department put an end to the killings at sea for a while. Months later, three boats were found in four days off North Carolina. The next, three months after that, were off Delaware, bringing the count to ten. No more bodies were found, but assets disappeared quicker than officials could secure them. The absence of corpses in the more recent cases was an indication, to those involved in seeking justice, that the perpetrators had perfected the art of body disposal. Maybe the murderous party had moved up the coast to fresh ground, I thought as I climbed the stairs to my apartment. It had been three months since the last strike.

I flipped on all the lights. Just then, it dawned on me that I was stretching too far. I must certainly be overtired, and lack of nutrition had probably resulted in blood sugar low enough to cause my mind to run ridiculously amok. There was no reason for me to believe that there was any connection between the disappearance of Parker Alley and the other ten cases that were never solved. That's the cop in me, I thought, always trying to close a case—even at the expense of

the facts. There was no chance of pounding this square
peg into that round hole, even with a bigger hammer.
Parker Alley was not in the same financial strata as the
others who had gone missing off boats. All ten of them
had been independently wealthy and sailing expensive
vessels, not lobster boats or anything like them. Born
into wealth, none of the ten had ever worked a single
day. None of them had ever gotten married or had children. That may have influenced the amount of energy
we put into our investigations, something I'm loath to
admit. When there's no pressure from a family, it's
easier to drop the ball. Someone had done their homework on the victims, that's for sure.

It was then that I noticed a note had been left on
my sofa.

Dear Jane,
      I have taken the Mrs. on an epicurean expedi-
   tion to Nova Scotia. We hear the mussels are
   fabulous there—and much less expensive than
   the local. We expect to be back by Friday with
   samples unless we get waylaid. So until then, I
   guess you're on your own kiddo!
      Mr. V

My first thought was, Hooray! My second thought
was, Who will feed me? And my final thought was,
When have the Vickersons ever paid for mussels? Rav-
enous to the point of nausea, I had to eat right away. I
practically ran down the stairs, through the gift shop,
and out to the parking area. With the luck I'd had in

the Duster so far today—between the game of chicken and the near collision with a full-grown Bambi—I thought it would be wise to walk to the café and see what Audrey had on special. I hustled right along, my pace quickened by hunger and anticipation of being entertained by Audrey's antics. Five minutes later I was bursting through the door of the fully lit and totally empty restaurant. The clang of the cowbells swinging on the door brought Audrey from the kitchen to greet me, her only customer. She hadn't spiked her hair up today, and aside from the glitter on her cheeks and her gigantic yin and yang earrings, she looked sort of normal.

"Hi, Jane! Come in and have a seat. Where've you been? We missed you this morning. The Old Maids and I debated the cultural importance of rap music." Audrey rolled her eyes and smiled as she pointed to a seat at the counter, where I assumed she wanted me to sit. Before I could answer her question as to my recent whereabouts, she put her hands on her hips and gave me a serious once-over. Shaking her head, she said, "If you ever want your status to change, you really need to be more careful about how you come out in public."

"Status?" I asked. I looked down at the clothes I had worn for the last two days. They had been soaked wet and then slept in and looked it. I wondered how bad my hair was.

"Yup, status. You know, single and available, bordering on desperate."

"I'm too hungry to refute the desperate part," I said

with a grin and then quickly pulled my lips down over my teeth before Audrey commented on my oral hygiene. "What's the special?"

"Well, if you came in here more often at night instead of mooching off your landlords, you'd know that Wednesday is Chinese night. That's why we have no customers—it's awful."

"Well, that explains the earrings. I thought Wednesday was Prince Spaghetti day."

"Italian night is Friday, not Wednesday. Don't ask. This is the chef's way of going out on a culinary limb, being bold enough to serve fried rice on the traditional pasta day." Audrey slapped a sheet of paper on the counter in front of me; it was the menu. "You like my earrings? Taijitu—commoners say yin and yang. These symbolize the foundation of the entire universe. Harmony in nature, balance in life; it's all about the unity of opposites. Would you like to borrow them? Anytime but Wednesday."

"If you think they'd help improve my status," I said as I read the menu. "I'm starving. I'll start with an appetizer. What would you recommend—the egg roll or the soup?"

"That's asking me to choose the lesser of two evils. They're equally bad."

"I'll take one of each."

"Perfect." Audrey whisked the menu from my hand and disappeared through the swinging doors to the kitchen.

"I'll take an order of fried rice, too," I yelled after

her. Her response was muffled, but the tone was somewhere in between a condolence and a "You'll be sorry." It was indeed unusual to be the only patron. I was glad to learn that Audrey was her usual wise-cracking self—even when she had an audience of just one. Usually, she had the Old Maids and Clyde Leeman as her targets, and a large and appreciative crowd. I was happy to have my own turn to be the butt of her jokes and teasing. Though only nineteen, Audrey is precociously self-assured and comfortable in her own tattooed and pierced skin. Most people her age who go to such lengths to alter themselves physically are either hiding something or simply trying to fit in with their peers. But our Audrey was the real deal—fully authentic. From the moment I met her, I felt that Audrey was destined for greatness. I, like everyone else in town, wanted her to like me, and was glad that she did.

With appetizers in hand, and representation of the entire universe dangling from her earlobes, Audrey pushed back through the saloon-style doors. "So, Marilyn comes in this morning with an iPod dangling from her hairy ears. I almost threw up. Seeing someone that old listening to music with anything more modern than a box with a hand crank is disgusting. It's like realizing that your parents had sex," she said as she set the food at my place setting.

That must have been what led to the rap discussion. I stirred the cup of soup with my teaspoon. The liquid was gray, and there were no chunks of anything in it.

I slurped a spoonful. "This tastes like dishwater," I said, pushing the cup away and pulling the egg roll closer.

"Great! Is it hot enough?"

"Just right."

"That's what we like to hear. Your fried rice is up. Can I get you some mustard for the egg roll?"

Assuming her next question would be whether I preferred French's or Grey Poupon, I shook my head and nibbled the edge of the egg roll, testing before inhaling. The egg roll wasn't half bad. I ate it in three bites and looked forward to the rice. When the plate of what was advertised as fried rice was set in front of me, I couldn't help looking at Audrey with a questioning raised eyebrow. She cocked her head to one side and forced the cheesiest grin I had ever seen. "Bon appétit," she whispered and continued to stare as I picked up my fork and gingerly sampled the dish.

"Are you sure you didn't mix my order up with someone else's? This isn't fried rice."

"Right. It's leftover white rice from last night's chicken special with some soy sauce on it. Waste not, want not," she quoted. "Or in this case, perhaps just the latter." Although she didn't let on, I could tell that Audrey was amazed that I was able to eat the rice. It really didn't have any taste at all, but it satisfied my hunger and I was fairly confident that it was the safest main course on the menu that night. "Listen, I can hear Marlena calling their cats," Audrey said, cupping an ear with her hand. "They get a little nervous on Wednesdays, living so close to the Chinese kitchen."

Now I laughed. The rice had kept my hunger at bay, and I was ready for pie and coffee. Audrey promptly cleaned and reset my place and served what looked like half an apple pie to me. It was delicious. The only things I could always count on at the café were coffee and pie. As bad as the meal was, it was nice to eat something other than mussels for dinner. Audrey left me to enjoy dessert while she breezed around the room, setting up tables for the breakfast crowd. When she returned, she poured me another cup of coffee and said, "So where have you been? When you left here yesterday, you were headed to Cobble Harbor to make a drug bust. How'd that go?"

So much had transpired in the last thirty-six hours. This was an opportunity to hash all of it over with a good listener and possibly catch something I had missed. I told Audrey everything, leaving out no detail. I described the scene in the parking lot where I met George Paul and told her about *Quest, Spartacus,* and the dead body. She listened politely as I went through my experience in Southwest Harbor and the surprise I had when I learned that the corpse was not Parker Alley. I told her about the truck that rammed me, then disappeared. I even told her about the deer. I went through my mental list of follow-up tasks for the next day, realizing for the first time how ambitious the list was. "Wow," was Audrey's response when I finally looked for one. I admitted that I was pretty anxious about talking to Lillian.

Recalling that Audrey had said that Jason was a friend of hers, I saw an opportunity to ask a few

questions that I couldn't put to Lillian, who had made
it crystal clear that the topic of her son was strictly
off-limits. "Did Jason work for his father in the stern
of his boat?"

"Are you kidding? Jason absolutely despised his
father. Absolutely despised him."

ELEVEN

The cowbells jangled against the door as two young couples entered the café, stealing my chance to ask Audrey if she knew why Jason hated his father so much. My romantic ideal of the Maine father and son being an inseparable team was shattered like the Duster's taillight. Disenchanted and full of apple pie, I stared absently at the paper placemat while Audrey directed the foursome to a nice table by the window, where she suggested they "keep an eye out for a cat if you have a hankering for anything other than the tofu or the vegetable lo mein." The group laughed. They apparently hadn't eaten here before.

Every business in Green Haven advertised on the toffee-colored placemats here at the café. Even the Old Maids, whose shop across the street had a gas pump outside and carried everything from hardware to panty hose—a true Maine variety store—made sure their store was featured on the mat in the same brown, boxy typography that everyone used, but with a small picture of one of the ladies' prized Scottish Fold cats. The cats had nothing to do with their business, as they certainly didn't breed them or sell them; but you could always count on seeing one or two curled up at the cash register or wandering the aisles. And a cat certainly made for a prettier ad than a picture of a gas pump would have, and might attract some strangers looking for pet supplies, which, mysteriously, the Old Maids didn't stock. Once a customer was in the store, Marilyn and Marlena could sell that person a myriad of useless un-pet-related goods, and shame them into tossing pocket change into a jar to raise funds for some unfortunate local or to support Green Haven's Little Leaguers. A coffee stain circled the space marked YOUR AD HERE, leading me to believe there was room for another business in town. Maybe I should start my own private-investigating service. I had always wanted to be self-employed, but could never quite reconcile myself to giving up a sure thing, like a paycheck twice a month. Besides, I didn't imagine there was much need for a private eye in a place where people sweep things under rugs and forget about them. I had read every ad twice by the time Audrey had served Cokes to the two couples and taken their food orders. Finally, she returned to refill my mug with a little more coffee.

I placed my hand over the cup and thanked her before she poured. I explained that I was sure the next couple of days would be hectic, and I needed to go home and get a good night's sleep, something that would be impossible if I caffeinated myself any more. She cheerfully whipped my check from the pocket in her apron and slapped it on the counter with a flourish that, as always, exemplified her abundance of energy and highlighted my lack of it. She disappeared into the kitchen, saying that she hoped to see me back for coffee in the morning before I could question the high price of the soup that I couldn't drink and whether I should actually have to pay for it at all. Oh well, she had been generous with the pie. I plunked a salt shaker on my last ten-dollar bill, exited the café, and headed home.

Exhaustion caught up with me before I crested the first hill, but I forced myself to pick up the pace and made it home in short order. Dragging myself up the stairs, I knew I had only one thing to do before hopping into bed. I needed to call Cal and line up a boat ride to Cobble Harbor for tomorrow morning. After scolding me for calling so late—eight o'clock—his wife, Betty, put Cal on the phone. A short chat included Cal's teasing me about my gourmet dinner and assuring me that Chinese night at the café was indeed a prime example of getting what you pay for. Cal then accepted my offer of work tomorrow, as I knew he would, and agreed to meet at seven thirty for a quick coffee before boarding the *Sea Pigeon*. I hung up the house phone and glanced at my cell. I was surprised to see that someone had left a message, and then delighted to hear Dane Stevens's voice on my voice mail reporting that he had gotten my message and that he and Quasar would certainly pay close attention, and notify me first if they noticed anything out of the ordinary. He thanked me for rescuing his sleeping bag from the corpse, and said that he was sure we'd see each other soon. That was hopeful, I thought.

Sleep came easily. I woke as the first light climbed in orange streaks over the hills on the eastern horizon and settled, filling in the valleys like a syrupy juice before thinning and allowing blue sky to appear. I was refreshed and excited about the day ahead. And what a beauty it was! My mood indicated that my batteries had been properly charged. The benefits of a good night's sleep are relatively unsung in today's world of spas, energy drinks, and herbal supplements. And the best thing about sleep: It's free.

I wasn't surprised to find Cal already seated and sipping a cup of tea when I arrived at the café fifteen minutes before our scheduled meeting time. I took the stool beside him that he had clearly saved for me; every other seat was occupied and a few people hung inside the door waiting. A cup of coffee appeared from nowhere accompanied by a ghostly voice that made some smart crack about status and desperation. "Want to split a bagel?" I asked Cal. "I can expense it."

"Let's go Dutch treat," Cal offered, as a plate piled high with eggs, sausage, fried potatoes, and toast was set in front of him. "You'll probably want the second half of that bread doughnut for your lunch."

"Is that the special?" I asked Audrey as I pointed to Cal's feast. I was happy to see that she had retired yin and yang and had replaced them with multiple studs.

"That's the six ninety-nine."

"Whoa! That's too high for me. What's the special

this morning?" I asked, feeling like I wanted to splurge, but knowing I'd be riddled with guilt.

"The special is *two* ninety-nine. Want it?" she asked as she dashed by in the opposite direction.

"But what *is* the special? Eggs? Pancakes?"

A loud voice called from the kitchen that an order was up, hastening Audrey's pace in that direction. She opened her eyes wide in question and hesitated just long enough for me to say, "Yes, please."

"One special" was all I heard from the kitchen as the doors swung closed behind Audrey. It sure smelled good in here this morning. I wasn't a picky eater, and I knew that breakfast was always good at the café. So it was fine that I had no idea what I had ordered. When Audrey reappeared with a bagel and cream cheese, I was pleased, but thought it was a bit expensive. "What kind of juice would you like?" she asked.

"No thanks, Aud. I don't care for any."

"It's included with the special."

"Can I have—"

"No substituting."

"Do you have V8?" I asked.

"Tomato."

"Grapefruit?"

"We're out. Orange?"

"No thanks. I don't feel like orange," I said and tried to decide whether I would like tomato after all.

"What *do* you feel like?" Audrey looked a little irritated now as she really needed to hustle to tend to all of her customers.

"Scrambled eggs," I answered honestly. Audrey

seemed fed up with my lack of cooperation. She curled
her top lip and scurried away to clear a table that had
just been vacated. "What's eating her?" I asked Cal,
who only shrugged in reply. I spread the cream cheese
on my bagel and munched away, trying to get Audrey's
attention each time she passed to ask for the tomato
juice I had coming. I'd be damned if I would pay three
bucks for just a bagel. I would drink the juice even if
I didn't enjoy it. I had just finished the last bite of the
first half of the bagel when Audrey presented a tall
juice glass filled to the brim with steaming, fluffy,
scrambled eggs. "Thanks," I said with a smile that
went unnoticed as Audrey turned toward the kitchen
with an armload of dirty dishes.

Cal was finishing his second cup of tea and looking at his watch when I heard a familiar voice I couldn't
quite place. Wrapping my leftover bagel half in a napkin and sticking it in my bag, I looked around to see
from whom the distinct voice had come. "Sounds like
the pilot, Willard Kelley," Cal said just as I spotted
the hulking figure taking up one side of a booth designed for four diners. Cal was right on. Kelley was
louder than he needed to be, as men often are who
have spent too much time around diesel engines. I told
Cal that I would meet him at the dock in a few minutes as I had a bit of business to attend to with the
pilot. Cal left what I thought was a ridiculously large
tip, making me feel better about shorting Audrey a
few cents to avoid having to ask her to make change
for a larger bill. She'd appreciate that, I was sure.

Kelley recognized me as I approached and smiled

a friendly hello. He appeared to be fresh out of the shower. His graying hair was parted too close to his ear, requiring some kind of goop to defy the natural tendency of gravity. We made a bit of small talk, through which I learned that Willard Kelley was here meeting with his new pilot boat captain and with the man's stern help. He introduced the men. Kelley had a cruise ship coming in to Bar Harbor and needed a ride out. Just like at our first meeting, I couldn't determine whether Kelley was half drunk or fully hungover. They had to leave soon, he explained. I told him that I was assigned to file a police report for his stolen boat, to which he replied, "No need, dear. I won't beeeeee pressing any charges. The boat's back on her mooring, safe as caaaan be." I went on to explain that *Spartacus* had been involved in a little criminal mischief while reported stolen and asked if he had any ideas about who had borrowed her, to which he replied, "I can guarantee you it was the Indian chief."

"George Paul?" I asked.

"That would beeee the one. That guy has quite an enormous sense of entitlement! He helps himself toooooo anything and everything. It has something to doooo with their ideas of ownership. The lazy bastards don't haaaaave anything because they don't work. And they resent anyone who does."

I thanked Kelley for his time and asked how I might get in touch to follow up. He explained that since his new captain lived in Green Haven, he'd be in town quite often on his way to or from a ship. He liked the café and figured this would become his new haunt. I thought this was unlikely. As soon as Audrey became irritated with his volume and weird way of speaking, not to mention his enlightened opinions, she would run him out. I had now decided that Willard Kelley didn't just make a bad first impression; the more you got to know him, the tougher he was to like. So I would not give him any friendly advice regarding how to handle—or, rather, stay out of the way of—Audrey. Secretly hoping that she would find some reason to lash into him this very morning, I hurried out and down to the dock where Cal had the *Sea Pigeon* warming up. He had already let the bow and spring lines go. The pretty little boat leaned lightly against her stern line, like a dog into a collar when bored with heeling.

I pointed at the stern line. Cal nodded, indicating that, yes, he was ready for me to cast us adrift. I stepped aboard, holding the line that I had removed from a cleat on the dock, and we were off. Just about every mooring in the commercial harbor was held by a skiff or rowboat, which meant that the fishermen of Green Haven were out in force today, anxious to benefit from prices that were finally rising after the high-season glut. The mood of the entire town fluctuated along with the market price and supply of lobster. Virtually every person in Green Haven—even people far removed from fishing—was in tune with the industry. Amazing, the degree to which the ugly little crustaceans referred to by the locals as "bugs" rule Down East Maine. The Old Maids could quote market price on any given day and recite statistics of flux and stasis in landings going back a decade.

As we exited the channel and entered the bay, Cal pushed up the throttle to a comfortable steam. The *Sea Pigeon* seemed to lift the hem of her skirt out of the spray created by the increased speed. She skipped lightly between blue puddles that reflected every ray of sun. "This is a great boat, Cal," I said in admiration for the *Sea Pigeon*'s grace. Cal smiled in thanks; I had given him one of the greatest compliments you can give to someone who has dedicated himself to the sea. I had never spoken to Cal about his life. But I knew that he had won the respect of everyone in town for his accomplishments offshore. Cal was, I thought, the epitome of the able-bodied seaman, even now in his seventies. And he handled the *Sea Pigeon* with a touch as light as that of a man on his wife's back while leading her through a waltz to their song. He reminded me of my poor pal Archie, stuck in that damn Florida prison. Cal lit a cigarette, and I wished he didn't smoke.

We were soon slowing to an idle and rounding the first channel marker leading to Cobble Harbor. The *Sea Pigeon* settled deeply, pulling the surface up like a blanket. Swinging around and through alternating red nuns and green cans, we left the thoroughfare and headed for the town dock. Like Green Haven's, Cobble Harbor's commercial fleet was enjoying this calm day offshore. As late fall approached, it would bring great wind, and fair days like this would become scarce. Cal weaved a crooked path to the dock through

a mooring field littered with rowboats. A gentle landing allowed me to reach a piling with the stern line,
and I quickly looped it with a clove hitch. Cal wrapped
a midship line around a piling and then back to the
cleat from whence it came. He then made it fast with
a jerk and called it good. He killed the engine and
looked quite deliberately at his wristwatch.

"I have no idea how long I'll be, Cal. But I assume
it'll be afternoon before you see me back here." I
climbed from the boat to the dock.

"Take your time. I ain't going nowhere," he said in
his usual pleasant way. "Except maybe to poke around
town a bit for lunch. I won't worry about you, but when
should I start worrying? Where will you be?"

I thought it was sweet that Cal would be concerned
and decided that I would meet him back here at three
o'clock to touch base. I explained that I should be ready
to head home by then, but if I hadn't quite finished
with Lillian, I would at least let him know at that point
how much longer I'd be. He agreed with the plan and
asked for Lillian's address just in case. I didn't have
an address, but gave Cal the same directions to find
her house that she had given me. Cal was the perfect
partner, I thought, as I approached the parking area between the docks and Main Street. Unlike some of the
partners I had been assigned through the years who
were anxious to stab me in my back as opposed to covering it, Cal had no desire whatsoever to take over my
job. But then again, who would want my current job?
Deputy sheriff was not exactly a coveted position, and
the insurance gig had gone unfilled and unapplied for

until I decided to see if they wanted me to try it. Neither position had prestige or power. There wasn't even much pay.

The parking lot was full to capacity—mostly pickup trucks with bumper stickers promoting local seafood or ridiculing tourism or the federal government. As I turned onto Main Street, I heard an engine start behind me. I made my way to the sidewalk just as the truck turned onto the street headed in the opposite direction, nearly on my heels. The proximity of the vehicle made me turn around to look. I wasn't sure, but it certainly could have been the same truck that George Paul had jumped into the other day. But it could just as easily not have been the same truck. So what was the point of noticing the truck? I wondered. I guess it had struck me as strange that a truck would suddenly leave a full parking lot when I hadn't seen anyone around or any movement since we came into the dock. It occurred to me that I was slipping into my usual habit of overthinking things. What if Willard Kelley had been correct about George Paul stealing his boat? And maybe I had been the target, rather than aquaculture, after all. But what on earth would George Paul have against me? Ridiculous, I realized. It just *seemed* like someone had been hanging out in the parking lot until we had arrived. Real spies were far more discreet. Even local Maine ones.

I turned left onto Quarry Road and walked the half mile Lillian had guessed was the approximate distance to Cobble Harbor's public square. Park benches made with slabs of speckled granite looked as though they

had sunk into plush, green moss. A right turn when I
was across from the fishermen's monument and a left
up a long hill brought me to the end of a narrow road.
The gate, although clearly marked PRIVATE, was wide
open. I entered as Lillian had said I should, and walked
around a sharp bend in the road that opened up to a
stately home in a clearing. Funny, I would have assumed this was a summer house belonging to a wealthy
Bostonian or New Yorker, not the home of the missing
fisherman.

Lillian stood waiting behind a screen door in the
center of a room with many large windows. The screen
occluded, but couldn't conceal, the sadness in her face.
She opened and held the door for me as I entered.
Antiques and art melded and gave the house a refined
feel. Elegant, yet homey—a combination not usually
pulled off so tastefully. My eye was caught by wondrous sea creatures, sculpted from stone. I would have
to ask her who had created them. Lillian ran a hand
the length of a marble seal that almost seemed to preen
with the attention. I complimented the piece. "Edgar
Holmes—all of them. This was our first purchase, and
we made it before he was discovered. The beauty is
simple and innocent. I think that's why I can't walk
by without touching this one," she said. "I named him
Oscar," she added as she held the seal's chin in her
palm. It did seem like she had to make a real effort to
pull her hand away, and I guessed that was due largely
to what the rest of the day promised. She can't have
been looking forward to our conversation.

I followed Lillian through a long hallway dotted

with seascapes in oil. "I think I have everything you asked to see," she said as we entered the kitchen. "And I've requested updated statements from banks, credit cards, and the phone company, which they have all promised to e-mail today." Stacks of file folders covered most of the square kitchen table, and a laptop computer sat on a linen placemat at a seat I assumed was hers. A cordless phone lay on an open notebook next to a ceramic shell that held pens and pencils. "Shall I put on a pot of coffee?" she asked.

"Thanks, that would be nice." I pulled one of the eight Windsor chairs from the table and took a seat by a window that overlooked Cobscook Bay. "Your place is lovely. I hope you don't mind my saying that it's so much more than I expected. I guess I have a mental image—stereotype—of a fisherman's house. And it's just not like this at all."

"Modest was not what Parker wanted. He's an extremely hard worker and a very shrewd businessman. You'll see when you get into that stack that he made some good investments and has more than lobster traps providing for us." She opened a door exposing a large, full pantry. "That's not to take away from his ability to catch fish. He's good at what he does and always went the extra mile to make the most of it. He even ships his catch himself to avoid the middleman." I was aware that Lillian was waffling between present and past tense when talking about her husband. She found an electric coffee grinder and a glass French press and placed them on the counter between us. Real coffee, I thought excitedly. I hadn't had a decent cup since I left Miami, a city where connoisseurs raved about their favorite blends and where I fell in love with plain old delicious Dunkin' Donuts java. I hadn't found gourmet coffee in Green Haven, and wouldn't pay for it if I did, and the nearest Dunkin' Donuts is miles away.

Lillian swung open the freezer side of the most spacious side-by-side unit I could imagine. The freezer was jam-packed from top to bottom with zippered one-gallon plastic bags, each one appearing to be crammed full of coffee beans. She grabbed a bag, almost causing a landslide, and then closed the door. "Wow," I said. "Do you have trouble sleeping? I don't think I have ever seen that much coffee."

Her green eyes hinted at a sparkle. "Isn't it ridiculous?" she asked. She opened the door of the freezer again, looked in at all the bags, and then shook her head with a laugh. "There's no room for anything else! Parker is always being given bags of coffee beans as gifts from the ships he delivers the pilot to. When he first started hiring himself out as the person who would deliver the pilot to the ships to guide them into the harbor and then pick the pilot up once they were safely at sea again, the ships were always giving him bottles of liquor in appreciation for his service. He said it was one of the perks. Only thing was, we don't drink. He finally told them that we couldn't give away any more booze, so they began with the coffee beans. We have beans from all over South and Central America. We've given tons away as gifts, and still have more than we'll ever use." Her explanation made me recall the scotch whiskey Willard Kelley had in his bag when Cal and I picked him up from the *Asprella*. "These are my favorite beans; they're from Guatemala." Lillian held up what must have been five pounds of very black, oily-looking beans. "Would you like to take some home when you go?"

"I would love to. Thanks," I said. This was a treat that I could share with my landlords when they got home from their mussel-scouting trip. I quickly got down to the business of tackling the file folders to get a sense of Parker Alley on paper. I really wanted to question Lillian, but didn't think I should start in quite yet. Everything was fairly well organized. Statements were in chronological order with the most recent on top. Lillian kept me company as I read. We both sipped coffee until the pot was empty. I couldn't find anything unusual—except for the large amount of money they had. The fishermen I had known who owned and operated their own small boats barely survived. Parker Alley was indeed a smart investor. Archie had always told me that a hardworking fisherman who didn't blow his money on the usual bad habits and addictions could do very well. But until now, I had never really seen an example of that. I found where Parker's life insurance policy had been upped from $100,000 to $200,000—certainly the timing could be seen as a red flag, I thought. But the amount did nothing to arouse suspicion in light of the value of the entire portfolio. I continued to pore through the pages well past the time that my stomach suggested lunch. "Have you had a chance to put together a list of your husband's

enemies, or been able to figure out if anyone might
have wanted to do him harm?" I asked when I couldn't
stand waiting any longer.

Lillian tucked a loose tendril of auburn hair back
into the knot on the back of her head from which it
had escaped. She concentrated on swishing around in
the bottom of her START YOUR DAY WITH THE LORD
mug what would be a last sip of coffee. Although she
appeared to be thinking, I suspected she was avoiding thought. She began to weep. I waited patiently for
a response. Her hands began to shake and she sobbed.
She had seemed so strong yesterday. Maybe it was just
too soon. Eventually, she wiped the tears from her
cheeks and eyes, swallowed, and took a deep breath.
Good, I thought, she was pulling herself together. "I
want to find your husband. I just need something, anything. A list of his enemies would be very helpful."

"Evan is putting that together for you. But the list
will be incomplete," she stated as a matter of fact.

"Really? How so?" I asked.

"Evan won't have included my name—and it belongs right at the top."

TWELVE

Although I was certain that I'd heard Lillian correctly when she said that her own name should be at the top of the list of her husband's enemies, I asked her if she could repeat what she'd just said, hoping that she would do so and tell me more. She did and did. Like most confessions, hers was tearful. Unlike most, this was one I had not anticipated. It seemed that Lillian Alley was convinced that she had driven her husband to take his own life. "We had a terrible fight," she began. "The night before Parker went missing, I called him a coward and said that if he were any kind of man at all, he would kill himself and be done with his miserable life."

"Did you fight often?" I asked. Lillian said that she and Parker never fought. In fact, they never even argued. She was distraught about the death of their son, she let her emotions get wildly out of hand, and she lost control of her senses. A discussion about nothing turned into a bitter argument that ended with her suggestion that Parker remove himself from this world. He had stayed up all night, she said. And she had lain awake, too, into the wee hours. She finally fell asleep at daybreak and didn't awaken until mid-morning. When she got up, Parker was gone; she presumed he was making a pilot run or hauling lobster traps. She never imagined he would actually harm himself.

Lillian was miserable waiting for her husband's daily radio call. It never came. "I figured he was still upset and didn't want to talk to me. I would never have thought that my hateful words would get to him like that. Then I found the note." Lillian stood and reached into her hip pocket, retrieving a slip of paper. She handed it to me to read.

"You know that in addition to being deputy sheriff, I work as a consultant for insurance companies. Let's just say that once I read this note, I would be required to file a report about its existence. And if your insurance company has proof that Parker's death was a suicide, then they don't have to pay one cent of the policy benefits you would be owed if they came to the conclusion that his death was an accident." I held the note in an open palm for her to take back and destroy if she so chose. I'm all for doing my job, but wanted to make sure I wasn't taking advantage of a widow's grief.

"That money means nothing. I want the truth to come out. I want you to find Parker's body. He was a great man and deserves a proper burial. You've seen the accounts—Parker left me very secure financially. I don't need the pittance the insurance company would love to save. My husband was a good man. And he was a great fisherman. He never would have died in an accident and never would have fallen overboard. He killed himself grieving for our son. I'm afraid I pushed him. But what could be more honorable than a man who can't live without his son?"

I unfolded the shipping receipt and read the scrawled note:

Dear Lillian,

You are right. I am a coward. I hope you'll someday be able to forgive me. Your life will be better without me. I have always loved you and always will.

Parker

I refolded the note and stuck it in my bag. "Where did you find it?" I asked.

"In his lunch pail. I was feeling so bad about the fight and everything I had said that I got out of bed and wrote him a note apologizing." Lillian's emotions had stabilized. She was calm and clearly wanted to tell her story. She was convinced that she was responsible for her husband's death. That wasn't something she could share with their family. I was clearly the first person with whom she'd been able to share her terrible secret. "I always pack Parker's lunch the night before and put it in the refrigerator out in his workshop. He leaves before daylight. So I put my note in with his lunch knowing that he would get it at ten when he breaks for a sandwich. He didn't take his lunch pail, but he took my note and left his for me."

"May I see the workshop?" I asked. Of course Lillian was very cooperative, as she now was feeling like a heavy weight had been lifted from her shoulders. I explained to her that, legally, she was not guilty of anything, and reminded her that people fight and say things they don't mean. I certainly wasn't trying to clear her conscience, but until I was able to uncover the truth, I needed Lillian to be frank with me about everything. And becoming her friend would facilitate that end more than acting like a hard-nosed cop would. If she trusted me, maybe I could get her to open up about her son.

"But I told Parker that I *hated* him. That had to kill him. It would me." I followed Lillian through a back door of the kitchen into a large shop. "Parker spent most of his time at home out here." She flipped on some fluorescent lights. "He was a workaholic. He loved his work more than life itself."

I wandered the floor of the shop and was impressed with the array of tools and the workstations he had organized. At the far end of the room was an air compressor and some type of mechanical contraption that I didn't recognize. Everything surrounding this station was covered with a thick layer of dust. "It doesn't look as though he had used this equipment lately," I said, mostly to myself and not expecting an answer.

"No, you're right. This is where Parker built his lobster traps. Like most young fishing families, we started out with nothing but an old wooden boat and a few rickety traps. Parker had to build his own gear to save money. He took great pride in doing everything possible to cut out the middleman and maximize our income. Look"—Lillian pointed to a workbench to my left—"he even made his own freezer packs for shipping his lobsters and scallops. At first, doing everything himself was a necessity. We were really just scraping by."

"What else, other than fishing, was Parker involved in?" I was still finding it hard to believe that hauling lobster traps—even if you've cut out the middleman—could provide for a family in this style.

"Just work. That's it. No hobbies or anything, if that's what you mean. He fished and saved money, bought a better boat and then a better boat, the same as everyone else around here. A few years ago, Parker had the opportunity to work as the pilot boat, which really helped us out financially. He was the only boat servicing Cobs Bay Pilots, so he had a couple runs a week. Every time a tanker needed to go up the river to the refinery or a cruise ship had a scheduled stop in Bar Harbor, Parker was moonlighting. We were doing fine without the pilot work, but that extra money was all invested and has done well." She stopped long enough to think for a few seconds then added, "The only other thing Parker had going on was that he participated as a volunteer in the U.S. Coast Guard Auxiliary."

"What did that consist of?"

"First of all, Parker never volunteered for anything. He was too busy making money. Some government program provides fuel money for people with boats who agree to patrol and report anything suspicious. No one spends more time on the water than Parker did, so it seemed like a good fit for him to be keeping an eye out, and he was reimbursed for the fuel he would be burning fishing or piloting anyway."

"Did he ever report or mention any suspicious activity to you?"

"No, in fact everyone involved knows it's sort of a way of getting money for nothing from the government. Apparently any seacoast town where there is no military base has been determined by the experts to be at greater risk for terrorist activity. Cobble Harbor? Terrorist attack? It's laughable." Lillian leaned over a chest freezer and opened it, exposing more coffee beans and a small basket filled with freezer packs for shipping. "Having said that, I have to admit that my first thought when I saw the dead man yesterday was that he must be a terrorist and that Parker had killed him. For a brief moment, I thought my husband would be revered as a hero." Lillian hesitated and looked as though her next breath caught in her chest. Her eyes welled up again, but she fought the tears and held them back. "Then I came to my senses and realized that I was still unable to face the fact that Parker had killed himself and that I may have had a lot to do with it. What would terrorists target in Cobble Harbor—the sardine cannery? And with all of the fishermen on the water, someone would have seen a boat that didn't belong."

I was aware of the different incentives offered in the name of Homeland Security, and agreed that Cobble Harbor was the least likely target for terrorism that I could imagine. I walked the perimeter of the shop once more. Parker Alley's shop was in the same condition that his boat had been—superorganized, every tool in a special place, even a custom-built rack to hold delicate scales for weighing. If everything Lillian had said was truthful and accurate, it was quite probable that Parker had committed suicide. And I did have the note he'd written. That didn't explain the corpse, though, with the bait iron in its chest. Maybe there was no connection. It would certainly be helpful to hear from Dane and Quasar that they were headed into Southwest with another body for the family to ID, I thought. Now who was grasping at straws?

After I checked out Parker's inventory of shipping supplies, which were exactly the same kind of supplies I had seen aboard the *Eva B.,* Lillian and I left the shop, returning to her kitchen table without a word. There wasn't much more I could do here without a list of enemies to question and without the promised e-mails from the banks and credit card companies, which I thought I should peruse to see if there was any deviation from the norm. I wanted to begin learning about her son, Jason, and the circumstances surrounding his overdose, but even though Lillian had calmed considerably, I couldn't take her there yet. She had said the account information had been promised by the end of the business day, which probably meant five P.M. on the dot. But I needed to head back to the *Sea Pigeon* soon; if I didn't, I ran the risk of worrying Cal needlessly. "From what you've told me, I don't think your husband would consider you enemy number one," I said. "In fact, I would guess the opposite to be true."

"I think when you mentioned the list, it was an opening for me to blurt all that out before I lost my nerve," Lillian said. That was exactly how I read it. "Evan is putting a list together and will drop it off on his way home from fishing this evening. I can't imagine anything will come of it. I guess Parker had some enemies, mostly people who are jealous of the fruits of his labor. He was certainly center stage in the opposition to the oyster farm, and he had an ongoing feud with the Passamaquoddy Indians over fishing grounds and rights, but those things have never escalated beyond slashed tires or spray paint."

The clock on her microwave oven indicated that it was now 2:40, so I explained that I would be leaving as I needed to catch a ride from the dock at three. I printed my phone numbers—home and cell—on the back of an envelope and asked that she please call me when the information came in and to then also read me the list of names her brother-in-law came up with. She agreed to do so and thanked me for spending so much time with her. "I hope you'll find Parker soon. I need to get on with my life somehow. Right now, I don't know where to begin. For the past seventeen years I've been Parker's wife and Jason's mother. Now I am neither." Although she had mentioned her son's name, I would wait for our next meeting to bring him up myself.

Lillian walked me through the house and held the screen door open for me. Armed with coffee beans and a suicide note, I walked with a brisk pace, hoping to arrive at the *Sea Pigeon* before Cal had even a second of concern. I dug into the bottom of my tote bag and found my cell phone. I turned it on and stared at the signal strength bars as I walked. Three bars, but no messages—par for the course, I thought. I dialed my home number and entered the two-digit code to play messages that might have been left on my machine in the apartment. "You have one new message," the machine squawked. I waited for the message to play and crossed my fingers in prayer to hear Dane Stevens.

"Hello, Deputy Bunker. This is Sheila from the Knox County Sheriff's Department. The Office of the Chief Medical Examiner called and asked us to notify you that fingerprints have confirmed a positive ID on case number two-two-seven-four-fiver. We have a name and passport number. Please call at your earliest convenience. Thank you." Sheila left a number, which I scratched onto the sidewalk with a piece of gravel. This was so exciting, I thought. Finally a breakthrough; I wasn't expecting any word on John Doe this soon. What were the chances of having fingerprints on file? As I dialed the number for the sheriff's office, a truck pulled up beside me and came to a stop. I pushed the red button on my phone, severing the connection but storing the number for when I had privacy.

George Paul leaned across the front seat and rolled down the passenger-side window. "Can I give you a lift?" I had a feeling that this was the truck I had seen leaving the parking lot earlier. Physically, George Paul appeared to have the ability to crush cars with his bare hands, but he carried himself with a rare kind of

gentleness. I wanted to ask him where he went after
our discussion at the pier the day *Spartacus* attempted
to drive *Quest* onto the rocks of the breakwater, but
was more anxious to make the phone call to learn the
ID of the corpse.

"No thank you. I'm only going to the town dock."

"I'm heading right there. Come on, get in." He
opened the door and waited. I hesitated. "Your friend
is expecting you back aboard by three, and it's"—he
checked his wristwatch—"five minutes to." Although
my suspicion of George Paul was growing, the fact
that he had spoken with Cal made me feel a bit easier about climbing into the truck with him. Dane Stevens thought he was a nutcase, and Willard Kelley
claimed that he was a thief. Two reasons not to accept
the ride, I thought as I pulled myself up and in and
slammed the door. I left the window open and rested
an elbow in the door frame. George Paul drove slowly,
his hands dwarfing the steering wheel.

"Nice truck," I said.

"Thanks. It's not mine. I'm borrowing it." I wondered if I was riding in a stolen vehicle. Since I wasn't
in town to investigate that, I really didn't care. "How
was your boat ride the other day?" he asked. That
could have been interpreted as a signal for me to get
the hell out of the truck. If he knew that we were
menaced on the water, then it was a question with a
sinister edge. If he didn't know, then it was just a question. I decided it was the latter and that George Paul
was fishing.

"Fine. How was yours?"

"Fine, thanks. Did you and your friends find what you were hoping to?" he asked.

"Oh, we found something all right. But not exactly what we had hoped for. They're still very confident that the survey will be successful." My mind's eye flashed on an image of the corpse with the faded streak of that red substance, which ran nearly the length of the body. I tensed while again making a connection with George Paul's explanation of the Red Paint People's burial ritual. George Paul held a key to some part of this mystery, I was certain. We arrived in the parking lot, and George pulled into the only empty spot and shut the engine off.

"So the boys must still be looking to make their bonus, right?" he asked as we both opened our doors. I noted that he left the keys dangling in the truck's ignition—just as the drivers had done in nearly every other vehicle in the lot, I assumed, if the folks of Cobble Hill behaved the way people did back in Green Haven.

"There's still time, yes." There was something coy in his manner, and I couldn't figure out what, if anything, he was hiding. When we first met, George Paul had mistaken me for a newspaper journalist and was incredibly talkative. I wondered if he now knew that I was an officer of the law. I certainly wasn't going to volunteer that fact.

I thanked him for the ride and we parted company, taking off by foot in opposite directions. As I walked by the front of the truck, I noticed a smashed headlight and dented grill. This was probably the truck that had harassed me and broken the Duster's taillight. I wondered who George Paul had borrowed it from and who had been behind the wheel of the truck and trying to run me off the road or scare me away from whatever I had gotten too close to. I stopped to enter the license plate number into my cell phone to run later. "It belongs to Parker Alley," George Paul volunteered. I hadn't noticed that he'd stopped and turned back to face me. "I didn't think he'd miss it."

THIRTEEN

No matter what anyone told me about George Paul, I couldn't help but like him. He looked like a guy who had spent years sparring with Foreman and Ali; he and I didn't seem to share a lot in common, and I couldn't exactly call him a friend as he was still most accurately described as some guy I'd met in a parking lot. But I just liked him in the same sort of way that I like John Daly—the bad boy of the PGA. I've always been that way—I like who I like. This personality trait first surfaced in middle school when I found myself going steady with Stanley Rodriguez, a kid who basically laid permanent claim to the class dunce cap and who was widely believed to have "cooties." I didn't care. Again, I like who I like.

Happily, the flip side is not part of my makeup. I almost never *dis*like people for no reason at all. When I dislike someone, I have a darn good reason. So did it bother me that I had just sent a small wave of thanks to a man who had yelled across a parking lot for all to hear that he had given me a ride in a truck stolen from a man who was likely on the bottom of the ocean? Not really. George Paul would remain in my mind a good guy until he proved himself otherwise. I was expecting a comment from Cal as I approached the stern of the *Sea Pigeon* and wasn't disappointed. "Didn't your mother warn you about taking rides with strangers?" he asked.

"George Paul isn't a stranger. I met him the other day. Besides, I didn't want to keep you waiting or worry you."

"He's a creep." Another party weighs in, I thought. When I didn't respond, Cal continued. "He was sure concerned about what you were doing at Lillian Alley's house. Of course, I didn't tell him, because I don't know anything. Didn't stop him from asking questions though. Creepy."

So, I thought, George Paul must have followed me to Lillian's. Unwilling to debate "creepy" with Cal, I decided to change the subject. "Let's get out of here. I'm starving. Let the lines go?"

"Sure," Cal said as he loosened a line from the cleat closest to him. I slackened the stern line from a cleat and pulled the bitter end around a piling and back aboard where I coiled and stowed it on a hook under the rail. Cal knocked the boat in gear with the helm hard to starboard, kicking the stern to port and away from the dock. He reversed the engine enough to back the *Sea Pigeon* a distance from the pilings to a low him to pull out while turning to port and to avoid contact with anything solid. Once we were clear of the dock, I grabbed my cell phone from my bag and prayed. Damn! No service. I would have to wait until we made

the corner around the steep headland and had a shot
at the cell tower on Swan's Island. I tucked the phone
back into my bag to avoid staring at it like a teenager
waiting for a text message.

Cal tugged a cigarette from a fresh pack in his
breast pocket and tucked it into the corner of his lips.
He raised an index finger in the air, suggesting I
wait for something that had just dawned on him. He
grabbed a brown paper bag from the console against
the windshield and handed it to me. "There's a nice
sandwich shop about a block from the dock," he said.
"I figured that doughnut would be wearing thin on you
by now. So I got you something. You ain't one of them
vegetarians, are you?"

"No. I'm a carnivore." I wasn't surprised that Cal
had asked. About all he'd ever seen me eat was peanut butter and bread. Opening the cellophane wrap,
I allowed the halves of the sandwich to separate, exposing an inch of pink roast beef. "Wow. Thanks
Cal. Want half?" He shook his head and lit his cigarette. He enjoyed his smoke while I indulged in beef.
How long had it been, I wondered, since I had eaten
roast beef? This must have cost a fortune. I would
add a small bonus to Cal's check this week, I thought.
Well, that was if it didn't cost too much to repair the
Duster's taillight. I could order the lens and bulb from
the Old Maids and repair it myself. That would save the
labor of a mechanic. The thought of finances tempted
me to wrap the second half of the sandwich and save
it for dinner. But that might be rude. So I happily ate
the whole thing.

Feeling stronger with a belly full of sandwich, I concentrated on organizing my thoughts. I felt that I had collected fragments of the whole picture but was unable to put anything together. If I could just start the puzzle in one corner, I could build from there. It was seldom that I had this much information and still could not formulate a viable theory to tie everything together. Right now I would be satisfied with a solid hunch, even one that might need to be discarded after I had the next clue. But I didn't even have that. I closed my eyes and saw the pieces: Parker Alley, John Doe, George Paul, North Atlantic Shell Farms, Lillian, fishing rights, heroin, and Jason. I shuffled, rearranged, stacked, and played sleight-of-hand games with the pieces. But nothing clicked. Suddenly the *Sea Pigeon* lurched hard to starboard. I grabbed the edge of the console and hung on as we rolled to port and back to starboard in the wake of a passing boat.

When the *Sea Pigeon* settled down, I turned to see the boat behind us. The *Ardency,* Evan Alley's boat, steamed away, throwing a mountainous wake. The captain and stern man never glanced back. "Looks like someone's in a hurry to get to the barn," Cal laughed, happy that I had been jarred from my trance. That made two of us. I added Evan to my puzzle pieces. I remembered how he had been so cool the day his brother's boat was found circling. He had absolutely zero interest in searching for his brother and displayed no hope of finding Parker alive. Yes, Evan deserved some close attention.

I pulled the phone from my tote and held it to the

sky in an offering to the god of cellular service. Three signal-strength bars rose from the depths. I hit the button recalling the number for the Sheriff's Department, pushed the green SEND, and walked to the stern, where the engine noise was less bothersome. After two rings, a female voice identified herself as Sheila and asked how she might direct my call.

"Hi, Sheila. This is Deputy Bunker returning your call. I understand you have some information for me regarding a John Doe." I was nervous with anticipation.

"Ah, yes. Let's see. Bunker . . . Oh, here it is. Augusta faxed this and asked me to forward it to you. The man's name is Jorge Aguilar. He was born in November 1970 in Champerico, Guatemala. He was employed by Central American Oil, aboard a tanker that is in and out of U.S. waters. So his fingerprints were on file with Homeland Security."

"Does the report name the tanker?" I asked.

"Well, let's see. I have a passport number. . . . No. Here's a customs form. It's six months old, but at that time he was aboard the *Asprella*. Is that helpful?"

"Yes. Thanks, Sheila. Please let the sheriff know that I'm on this case and will report back with any developments." I thanked Sheila again before we hung up and she seemed genuinely pleased to be of some assistance. I didn't imagine much of her work included dead people from Guatemala.

I joined Cal back at the helm as he eased the throttle to enter the channel that would lead us to the dock in Green Haven. "Cal," I said. "Where was the *Asprella* heading after we picked up Willard Kelley the other day?"

"Halifax, Nova Scotia."

"Is that far from here?" I asked.

"It would be aboard this rig. But I suppose it's like next door for a tanker. They steam at twenty-five knots. Why?"

Why? That was a good question. I answered it in a rather long-winded fashion. I worked backward from the information provided by Sheila. I suppose this was a way for me to think out loud and fill Cal in on everything that I had kept from him until now. I tried to sort things out as I told Cal the details of what I had learned over the last three days, hoping that when I finished, the solution to the puzzle would suddenly be clear. When I got to the part about George Paul's explanation of the Red Paint ritual and the connection I had made to the corpse, Cal laughed. I couldn't imagine what he found funny. "What? It could have been someone framing the Passamaquoddy, right?" I urged Cal to tell me what he thought.

"The red stuff on the dead guy must have been copper paint. You know, that red antifouling paint everyone uses on the bottom of their boats? Originally, you were looking for someone you believed had fallen overboard, right?" This was embarrassing, I thought. Of course—it was just paint from the bottom of a boat. Cal continued. "Copper paint—of course, they don't put real copper in it anymore, they just call it that. Still, it makes a wicked red mess on anything that comes into contact with it. I've ruined more clothes coppering the bottom of this boat." The conversation was interrupted; we had just arrived at the dock and needed to concentrate on securing *Sea Pigeon*.

As we walked toward Cal's truck, I mentioned that I had to get in touch with Willard Kelley to learn when the *Asprella* would be in the area again. "Good luck." Cal seemed to be tired and had lost interest in the case. He was happy being the chauffeur. I told Cal that I would let him know in the morning what our next assignment would be. I suspected we would need to return to Cobble Harbor to check on some of the names Evan Alley might come up with, especially those of his brother's enemies. I reminded myself of Cal's age and understood that he was anxious to get home to dinner and an early bedtime. I bid Cal good night, thanking him again for the sandwich. "Kelley's a creep, too" were his parting words. Cal, like most people of his age, gets a little cranky when he's tired, I thought.

We sure had lost a lot of daylight since I had first arrived in Green Haven, I thought, as Cal's brake lights flashed at the stop sign at the junction of the parking lot and Main Street. Anxious to get home to try to locate Willard Kelley and to touch base on the phone with Lillian, I hurried along. By the time I reached the top of the hill, I was gasping for air, and I was totally out of breath when I reached the stairs to my apartment. I had learned the hard way not to call anyone after five P.M. Mainers are strict about dinnertime, and they like to eat early. Most of the people I knew sat down for dinner promptly at five, and anyone foolish enough to interrupt the meal got an earful. I understood

that fishermen rise at three A.M. and, in order to get
their full eight hours, need to turn in by seven. Even
the folks who don't fish keep the same schedule. Except for my landlords. Henry and Alice prided themselves on their late dinnertime and fancied themselves
European. I knew that this was because they liked a
two-hour cocktail hour, a double they called it, and
didn't feel they could start drinking until five, which
pushed supper to the ungodly hour of seven, something basically unheard of in this town.

But the Vickersons were still away, so I was on my
own. I pushed open the door, flipped on some lights,
and then dropped my bag in a chair and checked the
answering machine. No messages. I loosened the
buckle on my gun holster, removed it, and hung it on
the wooden peg that Mr. V had mounted on the wall
among three others for coats. I would secure the gun
in its locked case later. Was it just four months ago that
I had vowed never to carry a gun again? Well, I had
lied. My vows were meaningless. I hadn't made a New
Year's resolution in ages, because they inevitably
brought on deep depression when I breached my contract with myself. I never kept any vow I made unless
it was to someone other than me. That was different.
And yet I had given Audrey my word the other day that
I would put someone in jail. And right now, I seemed
to be getting further from that promise. Audrey would
never mention it, nor would she rub my nose in the
fact that I hadn't been able to deliver. But I'd bet she
hadn't forgotten what I had pledged. I certainly wouldn't
forget.

I sat at the table with a paper and pen and leafed through the relatively few pages of the local phone book looking for Willard Kelley or Cobscook Bay Pilots. There were a few Kelleys in the "Greater Bar Harbor Region," but no Willard. I struck gold in the Yellow Pages. There was indeed a listing for Cobscook Bay Pilots, Inc., that included two numbers—one for the usual business hours and another for nights and weekends. I quickly dialed the second number, assuming it would forward to Willard Kelley's home phone. A woman, I assumed Willard Kelley's wife, answered.

"Hello, Mrs. Kelley?"

"Yes."

"Hi, Mrs. Kelley. This is Deputy Bunker from the Knox County Sheriff's Department. I'm looking for a Willard Kelley. Is this the correct number?" I asked as politely as I could.

"What will you try next? Give me a break. If you want to whore around with my husband, that's your problem. He's probably dead drunk by now. Stop calling me! Get it?" *Crash!* The phone was slammed down. I removed the receiver from my ear and stared at it in disbelief. Did that really just happen? I had to try again. I dialed the same number and got the same "Hello."

"Hi, Mrs. Kelley. Please don't hang up. This is Jane Bunker. I am a deputy sheriff here in Green Haven and am involved in an investigation, and I urgently need to get the schedule for a tanker your husband pilots."

"Really?"

"Yes, Mrs. Kelley. I'm not looking for your husband.

But I do need that schedule. I can come to your home with a warrant if you would prefer."

"No, that's not necessary. Which ship are you looking for?" she asked.

"The *Asprella*."

"I'm the secretary here, among other things. I should be able to help you out. What did you say your name was?"

"Jane Bunker. Deputy Sheriff Jane Bunker. I work for the Knox County Sheriff's Department."

"Bunker, okay. Willard had a double today. He took one of the Carnival cruise ships into Bar Harbor this morning and is scheduled to meet the *Asprella* right about now to take her up the river to Bucksport. He'll stay aboard while they pump, then take her back offshore later tonight. She won't be back again until next month. Sorry about hanging up on you."

"That's quite all right. Thanks for your cooperation, Mrs. Kelley." We hung up in a civilized manner this time. Either right now or not until next month! I'd better get a move on. I wondered where I would find the ship once I got to Bucksport, but couldn't take the time to figure that out right now. I had to get going. I strapped my gun back around my midsection, threw on a jacket, grabbed my tote bag, and ran out the door.

I nearly choked when I calculated how much gas I would burn in the four-hour round-trip to Bucksport. If I weren't in such a hurry I could at least ease up on the accelerator. But I needed to get there quickly. The sooner I was aboard the ship and asking questions about Jorge Aguilar, the better. Time is not a friend of a murder investigator. Guilty parties can create very elaborate and convincing alibis given enough time. They can buy witnesses, too. I stepped on the gas pedal even harder. I knew I would be reimbursed for my expenses. This was exciting. I tried to contain my nerves as I drove. I pushed the Duster like I was being chased by something out of a nightmare. This was exhilarating. Maybe this was a feeling that I'd been missing and hadn't realized it. Pure adrenaline. Two hours, two hours to Bucksport. I prayed the *Asprella* would still be in port. Two hours faded to one hour. I skidded around corners, flew off bumps, and squealed tires on straightaways. The old Duster was in top form. How many middle-aged women got to do this? I was crazed and I loved it.

The light distinguishing Bucksport from the surrounding blackness was a dull haze. Rising from individual bright spots and joining hands, the town's lights dimmed as they spread upward, forming a cloudy veil that appeared to protect everything under it. As I entered the town and got under the umbrella, the haze cleared. From the middle of a bridge I could see a large terminal on the west side of the Penobscot River surrounded by tremendous tanks that looked like overgrown silos. Tugboats were bridling up to the only ship at the terminal. The bright yellow shell on the ship's stack left no doubt. It was the *Asprella*. All I had to do was figure out how to get there, I thought.

I knew I had to turn right. I drove slowly off the bridge and continued on the main drag until I found a significant right turn—one that looked like it could support some tractor-trailer traffic. I had guessed correctly. A chain-link fence hemmed in the tank farm and wharf. A guard shack was manned by an elderly gentleman who tried to tell me I was in the wrong place until I showed him my badge. He waved me through and directed me to park in a spot marked VIS-ITOR. I ran from the parking area to the wharf and sprinted to the section alongside the *Asprella*. A small hydraulic boom was winching up the aluminum gang-plank that connected the ship to the top of the dock. I waved to the man running the winch, asking him to stop. "I need to board the ship!" I yelled. He stopped and waited for me to come close enough to talk. "I need to board that ship, right away."

"Do you have an ID, or a visitor's pass?" I whipped out my badge and introduced myself as the Knox County Sheriff, leaving out the deputy part in the interest of brevity. He lowered the gangplank, allowed me to board, and cranked it back up and away.

The deck of the *Asprella* was the size of a football field. Large pipes ran in mazelike confusion to pump boxes and valves that I stepped over as I worked my way toward a set of stairs that went up to the bridge. I needed to find the captain. The ship was made fast to the wharf by steel cables that were now being slacked off of drums to release the ship for departure. The tug-boats strained against steel bridles, waiting to take control of the tanker and escort her down the river to the ocean. I banged a couple of hardy knocks on the steel door at the top of the stairs and let myself in. The bridge was massive, and although the overhead lamps

had been doused, the electronics—all in duplicate—
emitted enough light for me to comfortably see three
men. I introduced myself, showing the badge, and
asked to see the captain.

A uniformed gentleman shook my hand and asked
what I was doing aboard his ship. I explained as briefly
as I could that I was investigating the death of Jorge
Aguilar and that U.S. Customs records showed that he
was employed aboard the *Asprella*. The captain looked
pained with the news of the death and quietly introduced the other men as his first and second mates.
"Jorge was one of our crew. This is most upsetting. We
will, of course, cooperate with your investigation, but
right now we're casting off."

"That's okay," I said, relieved that I had indeed
found someone who might provide at least one more
piece of the puzzle. "I'll hop off at your next stop. I
just need a little time to ask some questions of you and
Jorge's shipmates."

A voice from the remote radio on the captain's belt
said that all lines were clear. The captain took the radio from his hip and handed it to the first mate, who
keyed the microphone and said, "Roger." The ship
started to move sideways away from the wharf, pulled
by the powerful tugs. The captain asked his men to
man the helm and radio while the tugs navigated the
Asprella to the mouth of the river; once there, the ship
would be under her own power.

"I have about thirty minutes before I have to pay attention. You, on the other hand, have plenty of time.
Our next port is in Central America. Unless you want

to jump off with the pilot once we're out of Maine state waters, you can make yourself comfortable in my quarters. I'll move in with the chief engineer."

Central America? I hadn't given this plan much thought, I now realized. "I'll jump with the pilot. It's Willard Kelley, right? Where is he?" The captain explained that "Willy" had had a long day and was freshening up, which I understood to be sobering up. I figured if Willard could get from the ship to the lobster boat in his condition, then I would certainly have no trouble doing the same. "Isn't he supposed to be piloting the ship right now?" I asked. The captain explained that, yes, that was the law. But it seemed that the piloting gig was a formality that cost shipping companies tens of thousands of dollars a year, and totally unnecessary after a captain has been in and out of any given port once. "How long before I bail out?" I asked. The captain explained that I would have ninety minutes before the pilot boat was alongside, and led me to the officers' dining room, where we sat at a small table and were served coffee and pastries by a man who looked a lot like Jorge Aguilar.

Before I revealed the little I knew about the circumstances surrounding Jorge's death, I asked the captain to tell me if and when he had first noticed or been notified that one of his crew members was not around. By the time the captain finished speaking, I had come to regard him as a decent and honest man, which was my first impression anyway. I was pretty certain that he hadn't taken part in, nor had he any knowledge of, wrongdoing aboard his ship. It seemed that the captain had received a call from the home office in Venezuela that Jorge Aguilar's wife was very ill and it was necessary, if Jorge was to see his wife alive, for him to go home to Guatemala right away. The captain excused Jorge from his contract and made arrangements for his travel. The captain bought Jorge a bus ticket from Bangor, Maine, to Boston and plane fare to Guatemala with his own personal credit card; Jorge was to pay him back when he could.

The travel arrangements for Jorge included a ride on the pilot boat. That was the fastest way to get Jorge ashore, since the pilot was on his way to meet the ship to bring her into Machiasport when they got the news about Jorge's wife. The plan had been for the pilot to board the ship, and for Jorge to leave the ship and board the lobster boat to go ashore, where the boat's captain would drive him to the bus station in Bangor. The captain knew that the pilot boat Willard Kelley had been using was the *Eva B.*, and that was the boat that delivered Kelley on that trip. "Did you see Jorge get aboard the *Eva B.*?" I asked.

"Unfortunately not. The shape of the *Asprella*'s hull hides the pilot boat once it gets within striking distance. My job is to maintain course and speed while the lobster boat does the maneuvering alongside and away after transfer. I can't see a thing from the bridge and rely on radio transmissions from the deck. The first I see of Willard is when he climbs over the rail onto the deck and the last I see of him is in the opposite direction."

"That sounds a little hairy."

"It can be, in bad weather. We've never had a mis-hap, but the minute or so when the pilot is going up or down the ladder out of my sight and the radio is quiet can be fairly long and agonizing."

"Who *can* see the pilot boat and full transfer?" I asked, wondering who to question next. This, I learned, varied from transfer to transfer. The captain said that a couple of crew members always stood at the rail of the ship to assist if needed. In fact, sometimes a man would travel down the ladder to help with the pilot's bag so that the pilot could use both hands while climb-ing on and off the ladder. One of the crew members was responsible for radio transmissions to the bridge—sort of remote eyes for the captain, he said. So it was immediately clear that I needed to speak with the crew members responsible for the pilot and Jorge's transfer on that leg of their trip three days ago. And I didn't have much time to get what I needed from them. The captain had to resume his responsibilities on the bridge now, so I followed him back up to find Willard Kelley slumped on a bench seat in a corner.

The light that came in through the wheelhouse door from the gangway snapped Willard Kelley to a more attentive posture. He struggled to his feet and greeted me in an overly friendly way. He embraced me with a bear hug that could have crushed my ribs had I not been of hardy stock. He smelled of aftershave and mouthwash, and his hair had been glued into place against a wet-looking forehead. "Jane! How nice to seeeeee you. The mates told me that you were here and why. Such sad neeeeews about Jorge. He was a good man."

I pressed my palms against his chest, forcing him to release his grip on my shoulders. He teetered, but quickly found his sea legs and balanced, holding the edge of a radar screen. "Hello, Mr. Kelley." I tried for a professional tone somewhere between friendly and brusque. "The captain has explained the arrangements he made for Jorge's travel, and what I need from you is a statement as to when you last saw him. My understanding, if I have it right, is that you were boarding the *Asprella* and Jorge Aguilar was disembarking this ship and boarding the *Eva B.* to be taken ashore."

"Yes, yes, that's all correct. Jorge and I were like two ships passing in the night—and it waaaaas at night as I recall. I can check for an exaaaact time in my log. Jorge scrambled down the side of the ship, I handed him my baaaag, which he placed on the hook to be hauled aboard by his cohorts up on deck. I ascended the ladder, climbed over the rail, and never looked baaaack."

"So you can't say for certain whether Jorge Aguilar made it aboard the *Eva B.* or not, right? He could have slipped and fallen between the ladder and the ship, correct?"

"That's right."

"Was your pilot boat captain Parker Alley on that trip?" I asked, knowing that it had to have been.

"Yes indeed, it waaaaaaas. Good old Parker. Any luck recovering his body?"

"Not yet. Do you recall who the other crew members were on the deck of the ship when Jorge left? I need to speak with someone who could say he saw him actually get aboard the *Eva B*."

"These guys aaaall look alike to me. I can't tell one from another."

"Okay. May I have some time with your crew, Captain?" I asked.

I explained to the captain what I needed and he asked his second mate to assemble the eight members of the ship's crew, including the cook, in their mess area. I waited on the bridge for the mate to return and show me the way. The radio was noisy with tugboat traffic, mostly from the two hooked up to the *Asprella*—one towing from the bow and the other secured to her hip—which were making preparations to let the ship go. The captain warned me that the pilot boat would be alongside in about twenty minutes. I was thinking that twenty minutes would probably be long enough for me to ask a few questions. "Only one problem," interjected Willard Kelley. "They don't speak English." I assured Willard that I was comfortable with Spanish, which seemed to annoy him slightly.

Eight men sat at a long galley table and rubbed their eyes in sleepiness. My request had clearly required waking most of them. *"Discúlpenme por interrumpir su descanso. Necesito su ayuda. Tengo que hacerles unas preguntas muy importantes."* I apologized for interrupting their sleep, emphasizing the importance of my visit and my need for their help. I didn't feel as though I had anyone's attention. They looked bored and suspicious; I realized they probably thought I was from immigration and was there to cause trouble, but they had probably been questioned by immigration many times in the past and had all their papers in good order. *"Encontraron muerto a su compañero Jorge Aguilar."* I dropped the bomb regarding their shipmate.

A group gasp and looks of shock assured me that they indeed comprehended what I had said and were now interested in helping. I knew full well that he was probably one of their good friends and I hated giving them the news so abruptly. But time was short. *"¿Cómo? ¡No puede ser!,"* cried a young man in disbelief. There were a few tears and many of the men crossed themselves and mumbled prayers. I told the men that I was aware of the fact that Jorge Aguilar had intended to go home to see his sick wife, and asked who was on deck duty the night he was to start his trip home aboard the *Eva B*.

Two hands shot up instantly. *"Yo era el que estaba de guardia."* One of the hand-raisers said he was one of two crew members on watch that night. The other said he was the second man on watch.

"¿Alguno de ustedes vio cuando abordó el Eva B.*?"* I asked if either man had actually seen Jorge get aboard the small boat. Both men confirmed that they had indeed seen Jorge safely aboard the *Eva B*.

"¿Saben si Jorge andaba metido en líos? ¿O si estaba amenazado?" I asked if the men were aware of any trouble that Jorge might have been in and if they knew of anyone who would want to kill him. Eight

heads shook emphatic negatives and the men all frowned in greater shock when they understood that Jorge's death might not have been an accident. I followed up with questions about Jorge's mental state and asked if he might have been suicidal. *"¿No estaría deprimido? ¿No se habrá suicidado?"* More head shaking and sour looks were accompanied by one voice that stated the opinion that no, Jorge was not sad. He was going home to see his children, who made him very happy.

"Pero que Jorge supiera que su esposa estaba grave podía tenerlo deprimido, ¿no?" I reminded the group that Jorge's wife was very sick, and insisted that this would naturally be a cause of great sadness.

"El suicidio es un pecado mortal." The retort from one of the men that suicide was a mortal sin was irrefutable. Just then the second mate returned and announced that the pilot boat was approaching. This was my exit cue unless I wanted to visit Central America, which I did not. I thanked the group, wished them safe passage, and followed the mate out onto the deck. Two of the crew members came along; it was their turn to oversee the transfer. The mate said goodbye and disappeared up to the bridge, where I assumed he had more important duties to perform.

Willard Kelley leaned against the rail unsteadily. He looked as though his hard night was catching up with him. I was sure he was bound for a terrific hangover once he came out of his drunken stupor. The wind had picked up to a brisk twenty knots or so. The ship was not bothered in the least by the chop, but the running lights of the pilot boat bobbed up and down spasmodically. I was nervous about Kelley making it down the side of the ship and onto the deck of the lobster boat in his present state. The ladder was made of rope and was swinging fore and aft. I assumed that the fisherman captaining the small boat was relatively new to this task, and hoped he had superb boat-handling skills. The ship held course and sped directly into the wind while the lobster boat closed the gap between the two vessels. When the small boat was almost against the *Asprella*'s hull, Willard said, "Wait until I am on the bottom rung before you come dooooown and don't dally."

One of the crew members took Willard's bag and asked for mine, which I gladly handed over. He placed both bags on a hook tied to a coil of rope and lowered it over the side and into the waiting arms of the lobster boat's stern man as Kelley hoisted himself over the rail and onto the ladder. I watched as Kelley made his way down. He hesitated. The ladder was swinging rather violently, with his weight enhancing the pendulum effect. The crew members motioned for me to get moving. I slipped a leg over the rail and placed a foot on the first rung of the ladder. Once I had turned around facing the ship and had both hands solidly around rope, I was quite comfortable even with the swinging motion. I started down the ladder, and waited a few rungs above Kelley for him to make the leap aboard the boat. He seemed to take forever. He was waiting for the perfect opportunity, which might not come, I thought. Finally, he released his grip and fell into the boat, knocking the captain away from the wheel.

I watched anxiously as the two men untangled themselves. With nobody at the wheel, the lobster boat had now peeled away from the *Asprella*'s hull, leaving me dangling over the open ocean. The boat drove away, and then started to circle back to make a fresh landing. The waves had increased, making maneuvers more difficult. I wondered whether I should remain here or go back aboard the ship and wait for the lobster boat to come back alongside. There was some shouting between the lobster boat's captain, the stern man, and Kelley. They seemed a bit frantic, which did nothing for my confidence. They didn't seem to be making much headway. I looked up to the top of the ladder for some advice from the crew. The deck lights were very bright, nearly blinding me. To my horror, I could see the blade of a knife sawing one side of the ladder. *Pop*—it parted. I was now hanging by a virtual thread on a ladder that was heaving back and forth with some velocity. I clung to the ladder for my life. Climbing back aboard was no longer an option. Going overboard in the dark from a steaming ship was certain death. The small boat was coming closer ever so slowly. The knife was working feverishly against the last strand of the rope that held the ladder to the ship. I was all about gut reactions now. I pulled my gun from its holster and took aim just above the knife, where I assumed a head must be hidden by the glaring lights.

FOURTEEN

B ut then another instinct took over and I paused before firing what could easily be a lethal shot. The ship was changing course, raising the bar for the new pilot boat captain to make and maintain contact with the *Asprella*. But still I didn't fire. I kept my gun and attention fixed on the top of the ladder and prayed that the few strands of hemp remaining would hold. The ship continued to turn. The crew must have radioed the bridge that we were clear. The wind was now blowing directly on my back, pressing me against the hull so that I could no longer see anything above but a black steel wall. And then I realized that I was now dangling right over the lobster boat. I quickly holstered my gun and was snatched like a rag doll from the ladder by the back of my jacket.

I came down hard on my right side directly on and perpendicular to the rail of the lobster boat, which had been at the top of a surge when Willard Kelley grabbed and pulled me to safety. A wave of icy water walloped me full in the face. Kelley and the young stern man helped me off the rail and onto my feet while the captain steered away from the ship. I leaned against the bulkhead, holding my ribs, which I was sure were broken, and watched the *Asprella* slip into darkness while cool saltwater dripped down the back of my neck. "Well, that was what we would call a cluster fuck," said Willard, as he relaxed and exhaled a huge, fully intoxicated breath. "Good job everyone, good jooooob," he continued. I guessed from his reaction that he hadn't seen my gun or the knife while looking up into the bright deck lights. "Nobody's hurt. That's the important thing." I begged to differ, but kept my mouth shut while Willard entertained us with a number of stories of harrowing transfers that made this one seem like child's play.

As Willard regaled the captain and his stern man with tales of blizzards and hurricanes, I suppressed the pain in my rib cage by concentrating on how I would conduct the next leg of this investigation. It wouldn't be possible to interrogate further the crew of the *Asprella,* since they would soon be long gone, and I was certain that the ship would have a crew change before returning to this region a month from now. I couldn't pick the man with the knife out of a lineup of the eight I had seen at the galley table; the lights in my eyes were too bright. He could have been one of the two who were supervising the transfer but he also could have been one of the remaining six. And I had believed the men who claimed to have seen Jorge Aguilar safely aboard the *Eva B.* were being truthful, but now I couldn't be sure.

Every wave that hit the side of the boat jarred my

side, sending pain so severe it buckled my knees.
When the stern man got busy preparing to grab a
mooring in Green Haven Harbor, Willard sidled over
to me, placed a heavy arm across my shoulders, and
quietly asked if I was okay. I assured him that I would
be fine, explaining that I had reinjured some ribs that
I had broken months ago. "Did you learn anything
useful from the monkeys about their fellow country-
man?" he asked. I shook my head in reply and decided
not to take the bait on the "monkey" comment. "Well,
I'm not surprised thaaaaaat they were uncooperative.
You know, if Aguilar had been found dead in his own
country, there would be noooo investigation. Human
life isn't held at a premium where they come from."

So Willard was basically telling me that I was wasting my time putting any effort into an attempt to find
out what had happened to Jorge. Nice. The stern man
was on the bow with a long gaff. I watched him hook
the mooring and place the loop over the bit on the bow.
He walked back to the cockpit, towing the skiff along
like a stubborn leashed dog. The captain shut the boat
down for the night. He appeared to be quite frazzled,
and I imagined he was questioning his aptitude and
stomach for this new job. We all climbed into the skiff;
the stern man then started the outboard motor with one
easy pull and ferried us ashore to a small dock at the
west end of town and far side of the working harbor.
Willard offered me a hand out of the skiff, which I accepted. He pulled me onto the dock like I weighed
nothing, aggravating the pain in my ribs that had, until then, subsided to a dull ache.

I gladly accepted a ride from Willard, knowing that Cal would disapprove of my traveling with another "creep." But I was a long way from the apartment and beginning to feel the hour that it must be. I directed Willard along Main Street, up the hill, and into the Vickersons' small parking lot, which was conspicuously empty in the absence of the Vickersons' Caddy and my Duster. I would need to get a ride tomorrow from Cal so I could go retrieve my trusty vehicle from the dock at Bucksport. "Where's your partner tonight?" Willard asked before I had a chance to thank him and escape.

"Cal's in bed, I hope."

"Keeping the bed warm for you, is he?"

Jesus, I thought, this guy is repulsive. I would have allowed him to think that Cal and I shared a bed if Cal had not been happily married, but I knew how rumors flew in a small town. "No. He's at his house with his wife. Thanks for the ride. See you around." I opened the door and winced in pain.

"Gawd. You really are hurting aren't you? Heeeere, take this." Willard pulled a bottle of Johnnie Walker from his bag. "It's great pain medicine." I took the bottle to avoid any further discussion and thanked him again. Just before I could slam the door closed, he asked, "Would you like a little company?"

"No thank you," I said firmly, as I walked away from the car and into the gift shop, feeling better after I was inside and out of Willard's sight. His headlights remained shining on the building until I was safely in my apartment with the door locked behind me. I pulled down the shades and received a quick honk from the horn as Willard left the parking lot. I suspected he would find some company with the woman his wife had mistaken me for. For a second, the hungry feeling in my stomach masked the hurt that plagued my torso. Although I would not divulge to Audrey the fact that I had been propositioned tonight, I felt as though I had just proved that I wasn't nearly as desperate as she made me out to be. In fact, I was not desperate at all. I just happened to be alone. It's not a bad thing. I liked being alone. If I repeated that over and over, it might come true, I thought.

If I ever felt I needed booze to ease pain, physical or other kinds, I would quit drinking forever, I vowed, as I put the scotch in a cupboard to enjoy another time. And that was a vow I would keep. Sometime when I had someone to share it with, I'd have a real treat. Maybe I could share it with Henry and Alice when they returned on Friday. The thought was quite depressing. I like being alone, I repeated. I was surprised to find a bag of coffee beans in my tote. I stowed them in the cupboard, along with the bag Lillian had given me. Strange that the crew would have wanted me to have a gift and then try to kill me. Obviously, not every member of the crew was involved, I reasoned. Might just be a couple of bad apples. Or perhaps Willard Kelley had been the target. The answering machine said that I had two messages—two more reasons to believe that I was not really alone; two people had been thinking of me. The first was from Lillian Alley. She sounded upset and said she hoped I could be at her place at ten in the morning. Unless I called and made other arrangements, she would assume I was coming. The clock on the microwave oven showed that it was now one A.M. and certainly too late to call Lillian. The other message was from Cal. He said that he would be at the café for coffee at seven A.M. If I needed him to work tomorrow I could find him there. As easy as that, my day was planned. I emptied my pockets in preparation for getting undressed, cleaned up, and into bed. To add to my mood was Parker Alley's suicide note. The guy really was a workaholic, I thought. Who else would scribble their final words on the back of a FedEx shipping receipt? Carl Bagley of Lynn, Massachusetts, had quite a feast coming to him—ten pounds of lobster. I couldn't afford the local lobsters. You had to be a pretty big sport to pay to have ten pounds of them FedExed right to you. I threw my dirty clothes in a heap on the floor.

I nearly scalded myself in the shower, and it felt good. Tension rose from my muscles with the steam and frustration spilled down the drain at my feet. I forced all thoughts, formulas, theories, speculations, and fears from my head as I tucked myself into bed. I had only five hours before I would have to be up, and five hours of sound sleep would refresh me enough to have a clear mind with which to begin again. The Guatemalan crew tried to sneak into my consciousness just before I drifted off, but I locked them out to be dealt with tomorrow. Lillian must have been upset by something Evan came up with, I thought. Maybe

Parker had a secret mistress. That was my last thought before the alarm sounded.

I reached to silence the ringer and was reminded of my ribs. Ouch! Jesus, I thought, I must have really done a number on myself. My standard ten minutes from bed to door was increased to fifteen this morning as I found dressing and brushing my teeth left-handed a bit awkward. Nonetheless, I was in the café before Cal had finished his first cup of tea. "Good morning, everyone," I said to Cal, Marilyn, Marlena, and Audrey. They all smiled friendly greetings as I took the stool between Cal and Marlena.

"What did *you* do last night?" Audrey asked with a playful grin. "You look awful!"

"Thanks," I said, delighted to hear my first voice of the morning, even if it was just Audrey reminding me that I looked like hell. I guess I was pretty lonely. "Coffee, please."

"Ha! It's gonna take more than coffee this morning! Do you even *own* a mirror?" The Old Maids seemed to be enjoying this, as I figured my appearance had taken the heat off them. Cal looked a little embarrassed and squeezed his tea bag relentlessly. "Seriously, just between the"—Audrey looked to my right and then to my left—"five of us. You need a little"—she puckered her lips and I dreaded hearing her opinion of my needs—"TLC."

"Audrey," I said with a smile, "I need caffeine. Please?"

Audrey flipped a mug into the air, caught it by its

handle, and poured it full. She then placed it in front of me with gusto as she looked me square in the eye and said, "No. You need more than caffeine. You need the service that only Juan Valdez himself can supply." I started to laugh and immediately grabbed my ribs in pain.

"Are you all right?" Cal asked.

"Yes, I'm fine. I'll be fine. I just slept wrong."

"Slept *wrong?* You mean like a stiff neck?" Audrey blurted out. "You look like you—" The door of the café opened, sparing me Audrey's next shot. "Clyde Leeman! Get out!" Audrey said sternly. "I banished you for a week. Now go. Out, out, out!" I had never been so happy to see Clydie, I thought as Audrey marched from behind the counter to show Clyde the door.

"But it's been a week," Clyde protested.

"Has not."

"Has too."

"Has not." Clyde took a step closer to an empty stool, then hesitated. Audrey took a step toward Clyde and said, "Look at the calendar, Clyde." She pointed at the large month of October on the wall behind the counter. "You see the big 'C L' in the middle of the red circle with the slash through it on last Tuesday?"

"Yes."

"The 'C L' stands for Clyde Leeman. That's you. You're banished until Tuesday according to my records," Audrey stated with some authority.

"Can I get a coffee to go?"

"Sure. Pull around to our drive-thru window."

"Okay, thanks." And Clyde left, looking somewhat triumphant. We all sat and stared at one another.

When we heard the door of his truck open and close, and the engine start, Audrey looked scared. She ran for the door. "Oh my God. Someone has to stop him! There's no telling where he'll end up! Wait, Clyde! There's no drive-thru!" When Audrey didn't come back right away I pictured her chasing Clyde's truck down Main Street.

After a few healthy slugs of coffee, I told Cal I thought we should get going. We left a couple of bucks on the counter, wished the ladies a nice day, and left. Audrey stood on the sidewalk chatting up a very nice-looking young man. She pretended not to know us, turning her back slightly. Here was the perfect opportunity to embarrass Audrey! What could I say . . . I made a move in her general direction and Cal caught my arm. "You'll be sorry," he whispered. He was right. I changed course and headed for the dock with Cal.

It was another beautiful day. We would be in Cobble Harbor by nine thirty, allowing me a full thirty minutes to walk to Lillian's house, and I knew that I would need them, as I wasn't moving as quickly as usual. Once we were under way, Cal lit a cigarette. I wanted to tell him where I had been last night and what had happened, but really felt that he would prefer to be left in the dark. "So, what happened to your ribs?" he asked. I wondered if he was curious, or was just being thoughtful.

"Do you really want to know?"

"I wouldn't have asked if I didn't." So I told Cal the

whole story—all but the knife part. And I left out the
scene where Willard was hitting on me and asking
whether Cal and I were an item. I didn't mention the
fact that I had accepted a bottle of scotch either. Come
to think of it, I wasn't all that forthcoming. However,
I did answer his question honestly by explaining exactly how I had smashed my ribs, and I did mention
that I needed Cal's help in rescuing my car from the
lot in Bucksport. Cal finished his cigarette. I finished
my story. And we were at the dock in Cobble Harbor.

"Same time, same station?" I asked Cal, suggesting
we again meet back at the *Sea Pigeon* at three.

"Good" was all he said as he watched me walk
away toward the rows of parked pickups. I couldn't resist searching the lot for Parker Alley's truck, the one
that George Paul had borrowed some time after it had
been orphaned. When I found the truck, I also found
the Passamaquoddy's tribal chief sitting proudly behind
the wheel. I smiled and nodded. George Paul waved.
What the hell, I might as well go right up to the truck
and say hello. There was no sense having him waste
fuel following me when I could just tell him where I
was going. Maybe he would finally tell me why he was
so interested in my investigation.

I approached his open window and said, "Hi." He
put the book he was reading on the dashboard and
complimented the weather. I couldn't help but notice
the cover of the book. It was *Unfinished Voyages,* the
same book that Dane Stevens had been reading aboard
Quest. It was clearly a popular volume. I vowed to

check it out of the library in Green Haven, if it was still on the shelves and not already circulating.

"Are you heading to Lillian's again today?" he asked.

"Yes. Are you going to follow me again today?"

"No. I can't. I'm waiting for my ship to come in," George Paul said quite seriously, and stared out at the horizon.

"Okay. Well, I guess I'll see you later." I backed away from the window and headed toward the road. Maybe everyone was right about this guy. Maybe he was a nut and kind of creepy. I expected to see George Paul's name on the enemy list that I hoped Evan had delivered to Lillian. I wondered if George Paul had made the top ten. It was likely, I thought, that the list would be quite lengthy. When there are no immediate suspects or archenemies, this kind of list usually becomes so voluminous that anyone who ever looked at the victim sideways finds him- or herself on it. Enemy lists rarely produce successful results, but often lead to clues that do. I hoped this would be the case today. Otherwise, I would have to throw in the towel on the murder and the disappearance until more evidence surfaced—which could be never. In the past, I had a track record to brag about. Cases I was assigned didn't hang around long enough to get cold. This thought bolstered my flagging confidence.

Lillian stood behind the screen door. But something was different today. She flung open the screen and jerked her head toward the interior, commanding me

to follow her without speaking. She walked with a
heavy step and had lost that ethereal grace that had so
impressed me before. Rather than caressing Oscar, the
marble seal, she smacked him solidly on the back and
kept right on walking. I entered the kitchen behind her
and saw that the counters and table were buried in paper. There were folders, notebooks, reports, and hun-
dreds of loose pages. Lillian placed her hands on her
hips and said, "It's gone. All of our money is gone.
Whoever killed my husband has robbed us blind."

It was quite a stunning reversal. And I've almost
never seen a human being so changed in a day. She
looked older, sadder, and defeated. "Okay," I said, hoping that my calm manner would in some way reassure
her. "Let's go over everything. This is going to take a
while. Maybe you should put on a pot of coffee." I
rolled up my sleeves and got started on the piles of
paper in front of me, checking all the recent activity
against previous statements. First I organized everything into categories. Then I began going through the
stacks with a calculator. Numbers are not my thing, so
I had to do a lot of rechecking and recalculating. It
seemed that I had been there forever and had barely
peeled the first layer. I suggested that Lillian call her
accountant or financial adviser to help, and she said
she had done that. But she begged me to see if there
was anything I could learn about the crime. And I
knew that I might get some clues or helpful information from the statements and that she would be more
likely to be forthcoming if I had her alone. "So, did
Evan ever come up with that list?"

"Oh yes. It's useless. It's right here somewhere. I'll find it for you. He didn't leave anybody out." I told her that I figured that might happen and that I would still like to see the list. She searched a little longer and finally found it. There must have been fifty names on it. The next phase could take months, I thought. Lillian began crying. Not a soft, ladylike weeping as she had done yesterday, but a real heart-wrenching bawl. "Now I have no family and no money. How could someone do such a thing? I'll have to sell this house. You'll find the murderer, won't you?"

"Lillian, have you forgotten about the suicide note?" I tried to be as gentle as possible in reminding Lillian of this.

"They could have forced him to write it. They might have threatened to kill *me*. Parker would lay down his life for me." This sentiment brought on a fresh batch of tears. And then there was a knock on the door, followed by a man's voice calling Lillian. She wiped the tears away and yelled to the man to come in. "That's Evan. I asked him to come over. God, I need him to sell the *Eva B.* quickly." Evan entered, shook my hand, and thanked me for helping Lillian. He said that he was willing to assist in any way that he could. I thought he would need to start by coming clean about the events surrounding his brother's disappearance. I had a hunch, and pieces were falling into place. While Lillian informed her brother-in-law of the shocking news that all of Parker's money had been stolen, and discussed what should be sold and when, I excused

myself to make a phone call. I had a little research
project for Sheila at the Sheriff's Department.

Sheila promised to call back in ten minutes with information. I returned to the kitchen, where Evan
seemed to be processing all the recent developments.
He tried to offer Lillian hope that the money could be
recovered; he was sure that the banks and institutions
must be partly to blame. "And what about Parker's life
insurance?" Evan asked. "When can Lillian collect
that?"

"With a suicide note and no body, it's tough. Your
brother had just doubled the payout of the policy. I
wouldn't count on anything from the insurance company," I said.

"We'll have to sell everything," Lillian cried.
"Parker worked so hard to provide for us. This is so
unfair. All of his time and effort, his entire life, for
nothing."

My phone rang, interrupting Lillian. Sheila confirmed what I had suspected. I thanked her, and she
again expressed her pleasure in helping and told me
she was eager to assist in the future. Now, how best to
relay what I had to tell Lillian? I decided that being
fairly blunt probably was the best course. "Lillian, I
know that you are very upset, which I fully understand, and that all you see in all of this paper are the
zeros at the bottom of the columns. But if you look at
the dates of the final transactions, everything was
liquidated prior to Parker's disappearance." This
news was met with blank stares from both Lillian and
Evan. "And that call was from the Sheriff's Depart-

ment. Someone traveled by bus and airplane using tickets purchased for Jorge Aguilar—that's the name of the body you were asked to ID." Evan sat down, held his head in his hands, and closed his eyes. "I believe that your husband drained your accounts, staged his own death, and disappeared using the tickets and identity of Jorge Aguilar."

Lillian appeared to be stunned. I couldn't tell whether she understood what I had said. Evan opened his eyes, took a deep breath, and said, "I'm so sorry. I guess it's time for the truth. I have been struggling with this for days. I haven't slept a wink, and neither has my son." Finally, I thought, Evan is going to fill in some of the blanks. And he did. He confessed that his brother had come alongside, boat to boat, the morning of the disappearance. Parker had pleaded with Evan to take him ashore to an abandoned dock where no one would see them. Parker had said that he was in trouble and that he was afraid for his life, but didn't say why. He said that he needed to go away while things cooled down, and planned eventually to call Lillian so she wouldn't be distraught over his fake suicide. Evan claimed not to know anything more, and I believed him. "Lillian, I am sorry. I have to go find Little Ev and let him know that I've come forward with the truth. The lie has been killing him." And then for me, he added, "He's very fond of his aunt Lillian. Oh, and that's why I was so adamant that no one look for him, why I said that I was sure he was dead when we met at sea that first day. I feel terrible for all the trouble I've caused." With this, Evan left.

The slamming of the screen door behind Evan was like the snapping of a hypnotist's fingers, waking Lillian from a deep trance. "But why?" She believed that I knew; in fact, I didn't. But I had a theory.

"I don't know, Lillian. Sadly, people do things like this for many reasons. We may never learn why your husband skipped out. Some sort of trouble he couldn't get out of without making it appear as though he had died? The death of your son could have sent him over the edge."

All of the emotions that Lillian had conveyed up until then—grief, sorrow, remorse, confusion—suddenly morphed into blind rage. She stood and pushed the stacks of paper from the counters and table onto the floor where she stomped on them. "He hated Jason! That bastard! He humiliated and ridiculed his own flesh and blood! And he beat him. He thought Jason was weak and not enough of a man, not good enough in sports, not strong enough. No wonder my sweet baby used drugs. He needed to escape the abuse of his father. You have to track him down. I'll kill him!" I had neither the nerve nor the heart to explain to Lillian that this case was now beyond my jurisdiction. If Parker had flown to Guatemala, the feds would have to pick up his scent. I had reached the end of the road in my search for the missing fisherman.

But now I knew why Jason hated his father; it was, sadly, because his father hated him.

FIFTEEN

The thing I most appreciated about Cal was his willingness and ability to listen. He seldom interrupted me and never broke my train of thought. He just listened. He didn't make facial expressions to influence the next word to come from my mouth, nor did he ever appear uninterested or bored. He just plain listened. Cal kept his opinions to himself, except when I asked or was way off base—like I had been with the red paint. By the time we arrived back in Green Haven from Cobble Harbor, I had said all that I could, and Cal had probably heard more than enough. It had been a long week, and I was pretty well exhausted.

So the Parker Alley case had reached a conclusion. Any resident of Cobble Harbor still waiting for a body to wash ashore could relax. Lillian was broke, but she had some closure. I would hand everything to the state police; I assumed they would in turn bring in the feds to locate and extradite Parker Alley on charges including murder one. The only thing that remained a mystery was the why, and I now had more than a hunch on which to follow up. Not today though. It was five in the afternoon, and I was tapped out. Cal and I parted company in our usual manner, he in his truck and me on foot. Cal agreed to call me after he had a chance to speak with his wife about tomorrow's schedule, and hoped to get me to Bucksport for the Duster. I assured him that I was in no particular rush to rescue my car, and might need a day or two to catch up on the insurance work I had neglected, not to mention needing time to sleep and rest my ribs.

I might be mistaken for a regular Mainer tonight, I thought as I crawled up the hill to my place. An early dinner and bed before the street lamps came on sounded extremely appealing. I knew from past experience that my ribs would bother me for some time to come. But there was no reason to see a doctor. I could tolerate the pain. I had before. However, I did almost give myself a reason to seek medical help when I tripped on the bottom step of the stairs to my apartment. I'm sort of clumsy when I'm tired. I caught my balance, though, so didn't do any damage to my already-injured frame.

A big red "2" was flashing on my answering machine again. I figured I was due to hear from Mr. Dubois about the boat surveys I hadn't done. Preferring to hear his reprimand now and not spoil a fresh day tomorrow, I pushed PLAY. "Hi, Janie, dear. It's Mrs. V calling. We're having the most wonderful time. And the mussels we've had! Henry isn't much good after dark . . . driving that is. So we are staying in Ellsworth tonight and will see you in the morning. Bye, dear."

That was thoughtful. Gee, it must be Friday already, I realized.

The second message was from none other than the handsome captain, Dane Stevens. I was delighted to hear his voice. He said that Quasar and he had completed their work and were not feeling particularly welcome in Cobble Harbor, so they were making landfall in Green Haven instead. They hoped that I could join them for dinner and return the sleeping bag. They knew of only one place to eat—the café—and would be there around six, and were looking forward to seeing me. Wow. Dinner out, even at the café, would be nice. And a chance to see Dane Stevens, and even Quasar, was nice, too. Friday night is all-you-can-eat fish night. Great! Oh my God! I didn't have much time to get myself presentable. After Audrey's comments this morning, I realized that fifteen minutes hadn't quite done the trick.

I hopped in and out of the shower and began the Holy Grail-like search for something decent to wear. By the time I figured out that I wasn't happy with anything I owned, I had emptied the contents of my bureau drawers and my closet onto the bed. Digging through the sad pile, I found the lesser of all evils in a newish pair of jeans and a light blue blouse that had somehow lived its life without obtaining a coffee stain. I tied a black sweater around my shoulders the way I had seen sailboaters do. Slipping into a pair of black flats, I checked myself in the mirror, knowing that I had to go with whatever the end result was, as I

had no time to change. Not bad. I pulled the down-
filled sleeping bag from under my bed, rolled it into a
ball, and headed out. This was not an official date, I
reminded myself, more of a meeting to return a sleeping bag.

When I entered the café, my first thought was to
give thanks to Cal for not allowing me to humiliate
Audrey this morning while she was with the young
suitor. I was well aware of her propensity for payback.
As expected, Audrey, who works every shift of every
day, was front and center as I closed the door behind
me. She gave me a puzzled look and said, "Hey, I know
the service is slow. But come on! A sleeping bag?"

"Hi, Aud." I chose the more familiar nickname,
hoping to stay in her good graces tonight. I held the
bag out. "I'm returning it to a friend."

"You have a friend?" She sounded rather skeptical.
I saw the men seated behind her at a table for four, and
waved a hello.

"Yes, there he is." I nodded toward the table.

"The one with the glasses, right?"

"No. The other one." I didn't consider this a lie, as
Dane Stevens was my friend, sort of. And this *was* his
sleeping bag.

I was sure Audrey was going to ask if I was kidding, but she surprised me with, "You vixen!"

"Look, Aud, I would really appreciate it if you—"

"Don't worry." She cut me off before I begged her
not to embarrass me. "I won't say a thing. Who do I
look like, the Grinch? I wouldn't do *anything* to jeopardize this annual event for you." Fortunately an order

was up in the kitchen. Audrey sauntered off, allowing me to join Dane and Quasar at their table.

They both got to their feet to greet me with light, one-armed hugs. We sat and were immediately engaged in conversation; three people off duty and off the record. I gave the men a brief summary of what had happened since they had left me with the corpse in Southwest Harbor. "We couldn't believe it when you left the message saying that it wasn't the right guy," said Quasar. "Unbelievable. Who would have believed it was not the right guy? After that, we were a little trigger-happy. I'll bet we launched the net a dozen times thinking we had another body. We were sure anxious after that news. I still can't believe it was the wrong guy. Weren't we trigger-happy, Dane?"

"And every time we hauled the net back aboard, we were relieved that we didn't have another body," Dane Stevens chimed in. Audrey appeared with a pitcher of water, filled our glasses, and asked if we were ready to order. We all decided on the fish and chips. When she moved to the next table, I breathed again, and Dane continued. "So who was the dead guy?"

I ran around that loop of the story in record time, answering the question, but not in much detail, since I didn't think the part about being aboard the *Asprella* put me in the best light. Waving a gun and breaking ribs are not the most flattering images to share with someone you hope is finding you attractive. "On to nicer topics! Your job for the oyster farm is complete. Congratulations! Will you be getting the bonus?" I asked.

The men shared an awkward moment, making and breaking eye contact. They seemed to be deciding how to answer and who would do the talking. I was ready to change the subject when Audrey saved us all with our meals. She left again quickly. We all got very busy passing tartar sauce, ketchup, and salt. I was not amused with Audrey's artwork. My fish had been cut and arranged to form a perfect heart in the center of my plate, and a few fries had been placed to make an arrow that pierced the heart, Cupid style. My eyes darted to Quasar's and Dane's dinners. I was glad to see that the fish on their plates hadn't been arranged in any special way. I ate mine quickly, partly because I was famished and partly to destroy the creation of my immature friend. My question about the men's work had absolutely deflated the buoyant atmosphere we had enjoyed before I asked it. Now we were quiet, and I couldn't think of anything to say.

Quasar cracked first. "Let's just tell her, Dane. It's not a secret anymore." My first thought was that they were getting ready to come out of the closet. "It will be in the paper tomorrow. We have good news," Quasar said to me. By the time Dane smiled and agreed that there was no reason for secrets anymore, I was totally intrigued. They started with an apology for not telling me sooner, but added that they just couldn't. Now the men were excited and telling all, interrupting each other to avoid missing any details. It seemed that the "bonus" the men had been pushing for was sunken treasure. As bizarre as that sounded, by the time they had finished, it made perfect sense to me.

In the late 1700s, the ships that comprised the Northeast fleet were busy exporting rum and fish to Africa and bringing home gold and ivory. Although importing slaves had been banned in 1788, some ships still engaged in that awful trade. The Embargo Act of 1807 closed all shipping from the Northeast; the result was a huge increase in smuggling and piracy. Sometime before the War of 1812—the dates were sketchy—a fully loaded schooner, the *Abigail,* went down in Cobscook Bay. Because trading had been made illegal, there was no paperwork, only rumors of what had gone down with the ship. Dane and Quasar had researched and found a journal kept by a member of the *Abigail*'s crew that verified a cache of gold and gave a detailed description of the land he had swum to nearby. When *Quest* was hired to do a survey for the oyster farm, Dane and Quasar had the perfect opportunity to chase a dream.

The men confided that George Paul shared the same knowledge; his information was passed down from early generations of native Maine Indians who had hosted the shipwrecked crew until they were rescued by another schooner. George Paul had no resources to attempt to recover the gold. So he had been working to get legislation passed to declare the offshore site the property of his people, which would have barred aquaculture and everything else, and would have given him time to raise money for a search for the treasure. Dane and Quasar knew that George Paul had sabotaged their deck equipment and that he had tried to run *Quest* onto the rocks to delay their find and

subsequent claim to salvage rights. That explained a
lot, I thought, including the book on shipwrecks I had
seen both Dane and George Paul reading. It also explained why George Paul had been following me and
had tried to scare me a bit when he used the truck to
try to push me off the road; he had seen me spending
time with Dane and Quasar and knew that my job as
deputy gave them a certain amount of protection.

But I was pleased to hear that Dane and Quasar had
no hard feelings toward George Paul and that, in fact,
they were going to give the lion's share of the haul to
establish a local Native American cultural center and
also a fund for sustainable economic development.
Their interest was far more in history than in getting
rich. And I was also pleased to discover that I had no
hard feelings toward George Paul either. I don't think
he had it in him to hurt me or them.

We'd finished dessert and coffee, and I was tired.
Dane and Quasar would be working out of Green Haven for the next month or so, which I was very pleased
to learn. There would be ample opportunity to get to
know Dane Stevens better. We planned to meet for
coffee in the morning, and I excused myself after being forbidden to contribute to the dinner bill. The men
stayed behind for another cup of coffee when I turned
down their offer to walk me home, and I escaped unscathed while Audrey was in the kitchen, though I
assumed I would be in for a fair bit of teasing over
breakfast.

I admonished myself as soon as I realized that I had
left my apartment unlocked. Was I that tired, or had I

been foolishly fuzzy-headed with the prospect of dinner with Dane Stevens? Either way, it wouldn't happen again, I vowed, as I closed the door behind me and reached for the lights. A hand covered my mouth and jerked me close to a warm body. The pain in my side crippled me, and I felt faint. I was never totally out, but I was woozy enough from the shock of the pain that I was unable to put up a fight. Before I knew it, I was strong-armed into a chair and duct taped so that I couldn't move. As I gathered my wits, I knew I needed to remain calm. The shadow of a large figure moved slowly around the kitchen. Screaming would be of no use. The Vickersons were in Ellsworth and no one else lived within earshot.

The small table lamp was switched on, illuminating the face of the man who stood over it. Willard Kelley glared at me. I saw my gun under the lamp beside the phone. I hadn't locked it up, something I never forget to do. I was mad at myself for that. Willard paced back and forth on the linoleum a few times, never taking his eyes from mine. He checked cupboards until he found the unopened bottle of Johnnie Walker, pulled the other chair over, and sat facing me. He was jittery, but I'm guessing he thought the whiskey would smooth the shaking in his hands. He drank directly from the bottle, and the alcohol loosened his tongue. "Deputy Bunker has beeeeen very busy."

"What do you want?" I asked.

"Information."

"There are easier and more lawful ways to get information," I suggested. "Could you loosen the tape on my wrists? My ribs are killing me." I tried to establish a bit of rapport with my captor and wanted to see if I could get him to empathize a bit with me.

"When I'm done with you, you won't beeeeee feeling a thing." Now Willard teetered in the chair a bit and slurred his speech. The booze had already had an effect. He must have been pretty drunk already. This was not good. Drunk people act crazy. The telephone rang. "Who might thaaaat be?" He reached across to the end table and started hitting buttons on the answering machine to silence the ringing, but had no luck. The ringing persisted.

"If I don't answer, someone might get worried and come to check on me." Willard grabbed the phone, held the receiver to my ear, and aimed my gun at the other side of my head as a reminder.

"Hello," I said as normally as I could, knowing that a drunk had a loaded gun pressed to my temple. It was Cal. He was calling to tell me that Betty wanted to do some shopping tomorrow and that they would be happy to take me to Bucksport to pick up the Duster since they had some errands to run in that area. "Great, Cal. I'll treat you both to a really expensive lunch."

"Betty isn't crazy about fast food," Cal teased.

"I'm not talking McDonald's. I'm talking lobster. A great bottle of wine. My treat. Sky's the limit, pal. Good night." As I hoped, Kelley put the gun down when he placed the phone back on the table.

"I want to know what you know, and whoooo else knows it," Willard said.

"Well, I have everything figured out—including

your involvement. And I've already told the whole thing to the sheriff." I figured my best chance of escape lay in convincing him that his cover was already blown and he would be caught no matter what, but be in much worse shape if he harmed me before he was caught. I hoped he would buy it. So I continued, "Obviously, part or all of the *Asprella*'s crew were bringing Parker Alley heroin packed in bags of coffee beans, and he was distributing it around the region stashed inside the freezer packs he FedExed with his lobster. No dog can sniff heroin when it's masked by two heavy scents like coffee and lobster. When Alley's kid died from an overdose, he got jumpy and started preparing his exit strategy. He was worried local law enforcement might start snooping around his home. Someone—I assume the kingpin of the heroin gang—also got nervous. Maybe the gang leader figured that Parker was skimming heroin from the shipments and selling it locally. So the gang leader sent Jorge Aguilar to kill him. The sick wife was a sham to set Jorge aboard the *Eva B*. Parker was tipped off, though—I assume by you—and he killed Aguilar the second he got off the big ship and onto the lobster boat. Parker'd already cashed out all of his savings and was prepared to stage his own death, steal Aguilar's ID, and skip the country using tickets intended for Aguilar.

"How am I doing?" I asked.

"You nailed it," he said. "If he hadn't gotten greedy! Parker double-crossed the connection. Heeee was skimming a little off the top and handing it tooo a

local guy. That was the heroin that his poor stupid kid
OD'd on. God, heeeee hated that kid. You got to love
that the kid got his revenge in death—if the kid hadn't
OD'd, then the gang never would have figured out that
Parker was selling loooocally. Parker and I agreed he
would kill Aguilar, but he wasn't supposed to disappear with all the money. Of course, I was supposed to
get a cut of the local sale and Parker was saaaaving
my cut for me. Now he's double-crossed meeee. He's
left meeee holding the bag."

"If the Guatemalans don't find him, the FBI will.
Either way, it's bad news for Parker Alley. If you cooperate as a witness, you could get off fairly light and
have protection." I thought I was making sense to him
as he got up and paced again. Now he was intoxicated
to the point of being unsteady. If I could just get my
hands free, I was sure that I could get my gun before
he did. But my mind didn't stay on that—it drifted to
the incident on the boat when I'd cracked my ribs. Who
knew how many of the ship's crew were in on the drug
dealing? Maybe all of them. And why had Willard
saved me from falling into the water? Probably because the new pilot and stern man weren't in on any
of this and he had to be seen making an effort to
help me. That must have been the argument they had
about whether to come back around for me; Willard
was probably stalling to give the crew more time to
cut the ropes.

My thoughts were interrupted by Willard as he
picked up his bag and sat back down. "I don't believe

you told anyone. I think you're lying. I think you're theeeee only one who knows."

"Why would I keep something like this to myself? Of course I told my boss."

"I don't thinnnnnk you did. If you had, the whole town would already beeee swarming with cops and feds." He pulled a syringe from his bag. "I think that when the lady chief detective from Miami dies in her apartment from annnnn overdose of heroin, her secret will die with her. Your corpse will be so full of holes, you'll look like a pin cushion. And there's enough dope in that bag of coffee I gaaaave you last night to make you look like the reeeeal dealer around here." He stooped and unplugged the phone line from the jack in the wall.

There was no doubt in my mind now that he would inject me with the heroin. This was not the way I wanted to go. A bead of sweat rolled down the side of my face, tickling my cheek.

Willard placed the phone line around my upper arm and twisted it tight. "My wife will testify that youuuuu called, asking for the ship's schedule. Witnesses can place you at the wharf in Bucksport aaaand aboard the *Asprella*. Don't you think your stories of happening upon the abandoned *Eva B.* and being aboard *Quest* when Jorge was found are a bit tooooo coincidental for anyone to believe?"

Jesus, I thought, I didn't want to die this way. Only Archie would know beyond any doubt that I had been framed. And who would listen to him, his cell mate?

No one else knew me well enough to question the scene. Sure, my new acquaintances would be surprised that I used heroin and would tell everyone, "She seemed like such a nice woman." And how would this be explained to my brother, Wally? Just as I felt the needle pierce the skin on my forearm, the door to my apartment burst open, startling Kelley and causing him to stumble backward. I kicked the small table, sending my gun to the floor and out of his reach. I turned to see Cal grab the gun and hold it on Kelley while Dane Stevens and Quasar wrestled the big man to the floor. The syringe had fallen from my arm before Kelley depressed the plunger. The answering machine beeped a warning that time was running out. Kelley had apparently accidentally hit the RECORD button when he was fumbling to shut off the ringer. So he had inadvertently taped his entire confession.

Quasar peeled the duct tape from my wrists and midsection, releasing me from the chair. Thank God for Cal, I thought, who not only got my signal, but stopped by the café for reinforcements. I gave Cal my biggest smile, in spite of the pain in my ribs, to assure him that I was fine. Cal replied, "You owe me and Betty lunch. Lobster. Wine. Sky's the limit, right?"

Author's Note

The fisherman's bend is another name for the knot known as the anchor bend. Its most common use is in securing one end of a length of line to the ring at the end of an anchor's shank. It is also handy when making fast a fender to a pipe-style railing. Although most knot-tying sources say "rope," unless you're a cowboy, the correct nautical terminology is "line" or "warp." The fisherman's bend is a tough one to explain in writing, but I'll give it a shot. To tie the knot, pass the bitter end of the line around a post, or through a ring, twice—keeping slack in the second turn. Then pass the bitter end around the standing part of the line and through the slack round turn. Continue around the standing part and tuck the bitter end under itself. If you are dying to tie this knot, I would suggest Googling "Fisherman's Bend," and watching one of the many animations offered. I own a copy of *The Ashley Book of Knots,* and recommend it to knot enthusiasts.

This book was fun to write in that it gave me the opportunity to research some things that have always been of interest to me. There is so much information available on the Internet! The sites that I found useful in learning about Native Americans in Maine were

www.nativelanguages.org/maine.htm and
www.nativeamericans.com/penobscot.htm

The best information on oyster aquaculture was at
www.maineaquaculture.org/home

The sites dedicated to illegal drug use were staggering in number and content. I checked out several of them and found all of them to be eye-opening.

Acknowledgments

Thanks to all who stepped up with clutch performances in the final leg of this voyage; first and foremost, my editor and friend Will Schwalbe. Huge thanks to the dynamic team at the Stuart Krichevsky Literary Agency—Stuart Krichevsky, Shana Cohen, and Kathryne Wick—who were seemingly undaunted by my many requests for help and need of encouragement.

Special thanks to Murray Gray for his answers to my questions about his career and experiences as a ship's pilot in Penobscot Bay. Many thanks to my friend and neighbor Anna Jacobs, for her English to Spanish translations.

Thanks to all of the folks at Hyperion, especially Will Balliett, Brendan Duffy, Jane Comins, Phil Rose, and my very good friend and publicist, Christine Ragasa.

Thanks to my parents, Martha and James Greenlaw, for proofreading and cheering me on.

Thank you, Simon, for your patience.

Read on for an excerpt from

SHIVER HITCH
by Linda Greenlaw

ONE

Except for the time I was digging my own grave at gunpoint on the edge of Biscayne National Park, I hadn't much experience with a shovel. Now, my first winter in Maine was providing a cram course in the form of snow. Back in Miami, a sore back was the least of my concerns. And when I was able to crack the gun-toting drug lord's head with the back of the shovel and run for the mangroves, the real terror began. That night spent hiding, half submerged, I was unable to decide which was worse: leeches or mosquitoes. Neither of those was a threat here in deep, dark February in sleepy, frozen Green Haven, Maine.

I had been warned, and was fully expecting and prepared for a "wicked" winter, or so I thought. The locals whose holy books are *The Farmers' Almanac* and *Uncle Henry's,* who had advised me that there would be a record amount of snowfall—as forecast in "FA"—and that I could get whatever I needed to cope with it in "UH," must now be enjoying the fact that I had been skeptical. Of course it didn't help that my parking space seemed to be at the vortex of a snow funnel. Every time the wind blew out of the northeast, which accompanied most large storms, my 1987 Plymouth Duster had been buried. To be honest, my car is actually a Plymouth Tourismo. Plymouth did not make a Duster in 1987. I just think a Duster is more my style—less extravagant, more practical. Today, just the tip of the antenna marked the car entombed in flakes so big I could almost see their individual differences. I laughed to myself. My present situation was a far cry from chief detective of Miami-Dade County. If anyone from my past could see me now—Jane Bunker, bundled up like a goddamned Eskimo—living in an apartment over a trinket-selling tourist trap in this remote outpost—making ends meet financially (just barely) with a combination of insurance consulting/ investigation and a job as the assistant deputy sheriff of Knox County—shoveling snow!

My landlords, Alice and Henry Vickerson—Mr. and Mrs. V to me—had been gracious in offering me the use of their snow blower. But that offer had come with the stipulation that it not be fired up until eight A.M., the time at which "anyone with an ounce of civility" should wake. I suspected the ounce of civility was in direct correlation to the ounces of Scotch whiskey consumed the night before, but might also have been age related. The eight A.M. mandate, in conjunction with the price of gasoline to power the blower, had me, at six sharp, digging a path with a red plastic shovel from the door of The Lobster Trappe (the V's gift shop over which I reside) to the antenna under which lived my wheels. Not that I am opposed to

Scotch. I have been known to imbibe. But I am frugal; some would say "cheap."

When a crease of golden light warmed the eastern horizon, I figured I had been shoveling for nearly an hour. Not that I was counting, but I was aware that we were gaining over a full minute of daylight every twenty-four hours. I yearned for the four A.M. sunrise that would come again with the spring solstice. I thrive in daylight. And, I've come to find out, I am not crazy about the cold. Mr. V had secured a big, red, lobster thermometer ("Lobster Thermadore," as advertised in the shop) on the largest spruce tree on the lot. The black line whose height signified the temperature barely showed on the tail, displaying a frigid eight degrees this morning. Exercise within multiple layers of clothing resulted in full warmth by the time I had exposed the hood of the Duster, allowing me distractive thoughts while I found the car's doors.

Maine had become home, again, sort of. Although I still struggled when asked about my past, I had at least confided in the Vickersons and my new friends enough to stop their incessant questions that were born out of curiosity and rumor. People make more of what is unsaid than what is said. Not one to wear my heart on my sleeve, I am weirded out by strangers who bear their souls over a cup of coffee in public, or share intimate and minute details of their daily existence over social media. The surge in popularity of reality TV has everyone thinking their lives are ready for prime time. Just eight months ago, I was the new kid in town. What preceded my arrival was the knowledge that I had

been born on Acadia Island, was basically kidnapped
by my own mother (along with my baby brother, Wally),
and was transplanted to Miami, where I grew up in a
predominantly Latino section of the city and worked
as a police detective until this past June. Rumors of a
highly decorated career in drug enforcement cut short
by some undefined, yet insurmountable scandal may
have been exaggerated. But I have never been one to
kiss and tell.

Although I hadn't yet visited Acadia Island since
my move back to Maine, I could see it, as I stood to
rest my back in the distance across the bay, looming
mysteriously over smaller islands and ledges that dotted the way between it and Green Haven. Someday, I
thought, I would initiate a family reunion. Someday,
when I could stomach the possibility of having a door
slammed in my face. Or worse yet, learning that the
Bunkers were not the catalyst that sent my mother
sneaking off in the middle of the night, settling at the
farthest reach of the Eastern Seaboard, into the loo-
ney bin, and finally to suicide. The way my mother told
it qualified her for sainthood. To my five-year-old
mind, she had been heroic. At forty-three, I wasn't as
convinced. What I "knew" was this: My mother had
disappointed my father's family when she gave birth
to a girl, as boys were needed to perpetuate both the
Bunker name and the heritage of lobster fishing. The
Bunkers had fought long and hard to acquire and protect their private sliver of the ocean floor that provided
their livelihood and identity, and needed to seed the
future with young Bunker men willing and able to

carry on the territorial war. I always wondered how my life would have been different if the Bunkers had considered women capable of fishing and fighting. No matter, because when dear Wally was born and it was clear that he was a Down syndrome baby, that was the final blow to our "family." My mother, according to her, was treated like a pariah until she found the courage to escape. Nearly forty years later, here I was, a short boat ride to the truth, but unable to climb aboard; my fear of disillusionment crippling. Or perhaps it was confirmation I feared.

My move to Maine from Florida was indeed a knee-jerk reaction, and one that brought with it an inherent dichotomy that I straddled awkwardly. What remained constant in my life was my affinity for the law. This passion for fighting crime and solving cases ranging from petty theft to first-degree murder was what bolstered me through all lows. In the short time I had been in Maine, I had seen the crime rate change dramatically. Although the downeast coastal villages were quaint, sleepy havens where tourists enjoyed tranquillity and lobster rolls, there had been an explosion of drug use and overdoses among the young population of year-round residents. Meth labs were being discovered weekly, and synthetic opioids had become the new heroin. I had cut my law enforcement teeth in the era of the War on Drugs in Miami, the highest drug trafficking area in the Continental US. The older folks who live here are shocked by the seemingly rabid increase in drug-related topics in their local newscasts and print. But when you see young people harvesting a very abundant and lucrative resource like the Maine lobster, it was just a matter of time before the drug lords would tap into that cache. Timing may indeed be everything. Or is it location, location, location? Time and place. I was in the right place at the right time to make a difference, I thought.

When I was able to pry the driver's side door of the Duster open wide enough to squeeze in, I did. Three pumps on the gas pedal with a foot clad in the requisite, insulated L.L.Bean boot, a twist of the key in the ignition, and "Vroom," off she went—purring contentedly. I hated wasting gas, but thought it might be okay to let the engine idle while I dug out the back tires and dished out a couple of wheel wells behind them and out to the main road. The price of gasoline in Down East Maine was all the motivation I needed to throw snow with a real hustle. Just as I was finishing the job, the phone inside the house rang, piercing the stillness of the icy air. I leaned the shovel against the rear bumper and started toward the house. One ring later, the phone stopped. Two rings and a hang up was the code I had worked out with my boss at Marine Safety Consultants, Mr. Dubois, and was my signal to call him back pronto.

Cell phones are all but useless in this particular nook of coast, so my personal calls all come through a "party line" that I share with the Vickersons. The code was worked out in an attempt to gain a bit of privacy. At first, Mr. and Mrs. V had been discreet about listening in on my calls. But once the cat was out of the bag, rather than stop doing it, they became more blatantly nosy—even jumping into conversations to offer opinions. Most of my first-time callers end up saying "Who the hell is that?" before the end of the conversation. I then have to be polite and introduce whichever one of my octogenarian landlords happened to be near the phone when it rang. At the start it was disconcerting, then it really began to piss me off. Now, I laugh. And of course outsmart them.

Torn between allowing the Duster to remain running and thus climbing into a toasty warm car and shutting it off to feed my frugality, I opted for frugality. Besides saving gas, I needed to toughen up, I thought as I made my way back to the house. Carefully closing the door behind me so as not to wake my landlords, I brushed snow from the bottom of my pant legs that were frozen stiff, and pulled my feet from my insulated "Beanies" with the lobster claw boot jack. Yup, The Lobster Trappe sold anything and everything lobster related. There were lobster trap birdhouses, lobster beanbags, lobster coloring books, lobster cork screws . . . Well, you get the picture. The shop was now in its off-season, so the Vickersons were busy researching new items to add to their inventory, which led to many interesting conversations at their dinner table, where I had an open invitation to be any night at 7:30—five o'clock if I wanted cocktails. I tiptoed my wool socks across the shop and started up the stairs to my apartment. Halfway up, the door below that connected to the main house opened and I heard a very cheery, "Good morning, Janey!"

"Hi Mrs. V. I hope I didn't wake you."

"No dear, the phone did. Two rings and a hang up. Must be your boss. Better call him back right away." Oh no, I thought, they were on to me. I wondered how many conversations they had tapped into since I had schemed the code. The Vickersons were so good to me in every way that I had never been able to bring myself to scold them for eavesdropping. What the heck, I thought, at eighty-two and eighty-six, if they find pleasure injecting themselves into my fairly unexciting life, so be it. It's not as if the happenings in Down East Maine and outer islands (my territory in both my insurance and deputy gigs) required security clearance. The last two assignments I had been given by Mr. Dubois were surveying minor damage to lobster boats in a late January blizzard. One boat's mooring parted and it was blown into another boat before landing luckily on the only patch of sand beach in the county. And the only task I had been assigned as deputy sheriff since September was following up on leads that often led to busting meth labs, arresting addicts and hopefully beginning to snuff out what had reached epidemic proportions. Often, the entire community knows about a case or incident before I do, I realized. The Vickersons just like to be in the loop. I assured Alice that I had come in to call my boss, and hoped I could discreetly give Mr. Dubois a head's up that they were listening before they jumped in.

"Hello?"

"Hi, Mr. Dubois. Jane Bunker here, *we* are returning your call."

"Alice?" Mr. Dubois asked.

"Present," Mrs. V said promptly.

"Henry?"

"Standing by," answered Mr. V dutifully. Oh God, I thought, now there wasn't even any pretending. The only thing keeping me from being terminated from either of my jobs was the total lack of anyone else to do them. That, and the fact that I *am* good at what I do.

"Okay team, here's the deal," the boss started. "Jane, I need you to go out to Acadia Island to survey damage suffered in a house fire. It's a summer home owned by a good customer for whom we insure several properties, three vehicles, a boat, and a business. The fire was just last night, and I want to move quickly to accommodate these people."

"Since when do we survey house fires? I thought you handled only marine-related insurance?" I asked to stall, and hoped to conceal an oncoming loss of composure about a trip to Acadia.

"It's called bundling, dear," interjected Mr. V. "Everyone is having to gain bandwidth in *any* business to stay afloat. Insurance is very competitive. Alice and I have all of our insurances under one roof as well—it's the only way we can afford it all."

"Besides," Mrs. V weighed in, "you really should go to Acadia and get that demon off your back."

"I think you mean monkey, dear," Mr. V corrected. "And maybe Jane needs to let sleeping dogs lie."

"Either way," Mr. Dubois interrupted what I had come to know as ping-pong proverbs before Alice could send one back over the net, "I assume the place is a total loss. Not much in the way of firefighting on

these islands—all volunteer, and no real training or
equipment. All I need from you is to go out and take
lots of pictures to document what I already know," said
Mr. Dubois.

"Yes sir, I'll get out there ASAP." Yet again, I am
reduced to a photographer, I thought.

"Great. When you get off at the dock, take a right
on the main road, in about half a mile you'll see a
yellow Cape on the right. The Proctors are expecting
someone from the Agency. They are caretakers for the
Kohls, whose house you'll be surveying. They will get
you where you need to be and back to the dock," the
boss instructed. I breathed an audible sigh of relief
when I registered "Proctor"—not any of the family
names associated with my kin.

We all said our goodbyes and hung up, leaving me
to contemplate the trip "home." Within seconds the
phone rang again. I grabbed it and was not at all
surprised to be speaking with the Vickersons. They
advised me of the ferry schedule to and from Acadia,
adding that I had already missed the first boat out to
the island. The winter ferry schedule to Acadia did
not give a passenger many options—the "early boat"
departed from South Haven (a ten-minute ride from
home) at seven A.M., and the "late boat" was a three
P.M. departure from South Haven. Following the forty-
minute cruise out, the Vickersons informed me, the
boat would remain at the dock on Acadia just long
enough to unload people and freight, before returning
to the mainland. I thanked my landlords for the info,
and told them I would find an alternate ride out, snap

a load of pictures, and return on the last and only remaining ferry this evening. "Better get a wiggle on," advised Mrs. V. "Time is of the essence."

"What's the rush? Remember, haste makes waste," instructed Mr. V.

"He who hesitates is lost," admonished Mrs. V.

"Fools rush in where angels fear to tread!"

"The early bird gets the worm!"

"Good things come to those who wait."

"Tide and time wait for no man. And damn few women! There, top that, Henry," Alice challenged.

"I need to deice the Duster. I'll let you know my plans, thanks!" I wasn't quite sure what I was thanking them for, but slammed the phone down, bolted down the stairs, yanked on my boots, and hustled to my chilly and waiting Duster. For all I knew, the old folks were still volleying proverbs. Their game used to irritate me. Now I enjoyed it, I thought as I quietly quipped, "A stitch in time, saves nine."

My warm gloves melted the thin layer of frost on the car's steering wheel, leaving distinct handprints at ten and two. Nothing upsets me more than waste, I reminded myself as I waited for the Duster's defroster to clear a porthole in the windshield. I don't mean global, all-encompassing misuse and extravagance. That does not concern me. I only pay heed to the wastefulness of which I am responsible—me, myself, and I. Perhaps a gut reaction to my very unusual childhood; my personal frugality is just that—personal. I don't preach. I don't boast. I don't admire extreme economy in others. I find nothing more annoying than conversation regarding the "great deal" someone got on something following a compliment on that something, or the fuel economy of any particular hybrid automobile. Nor do I care about membership on the Fortune 500 list, or who the top-paid athlete is at any given time. My mother's routine of frittering away the monthly welfare check from the State of Florida in a single day, leaving us to "get creative" for the remaining thirty days to the next installment left its mark. Not that I didn't enjoy and look forward to the first of every month and whatever my mother had planned for us, but I knew at a very early age that my mother suffered with chronic immaturity with money. We ate and enjoyed government cheese, and the neighborhood ladies were forever dropping leftovers off for us, which sustained our family of three until I was old enough to work. I heard but didn't agree with the same ladies' whispered, negative opinions of how Wally and I were being raised. The ladies whose husbands worked long, hard hours, barely making ends meet, knew the value of a dollar. And I remember the look of envy in their children's eyes each and every month when we arrived home by taxi—not the bus, a taxi—armed with gifts, souvenirs, and stories of adventure. They said we couldn't afford such extravagance as a day at the circus. My mother said we couldn't afford not to. I'll never know which is true. But this morning, had I left the car running for fifteen minutes while I was on the phone, I would have been sick to my stomach.

Publicly, I am not big on sentimental journeys. My wanderlust is limited to the future. Privately, I spend a lot of time wondering about my roots, especially since moving to Green Haven. The only family I have left is Wally, I thought. Five years my junior, and an adult with Down syndrome, living in an assisted, yet independent situation, my baby brother has always been more well balanced and adjusted than I have been. He makes friends easier than I do. All of the reasons that I had for *not* uprooting him to come along to Maine when I bailed, were the exact same reasons why I should have done so. He's happy there, I justified as I backed out of the driveway. But Wally is always happy. The last shrink I saw before the big move north told me that I was overprotective of my brother. Maybe so. I just couldn't risk dragging him off into the unknown where, if my mother had been truthful, he would be mistreated by mean people blinded by ignorance—and those were blood relatives! Now I faced the probability of actually meeting what remains of the Bunkers, and hoped some of the hatefulness my mother spoke of had withered in the past thirty-eight years. I reminded myself that this trip to Acadia was not a quest for the truth or an opportunity for a family reunion. It was work, period.

Normally I would walk the mile to the Harbor Café, but there had been so much snow lately, it was banked high on either side of the street, leaving a gap so narrow that an oncoming vehicle presented a challenge. No sidewalks and not much time to find my buddy Cal were reasons enough to forgo the exercise today. As I nosed the Duster into a too-small parking space, I hoped this latest snow had not disrupted Cal's morning ritual of coffee and a newspaper at the café. Cal had quickly become my go-to guy for just about everything, including a boat ride, which was foremost on my request list this morning. Cowbells swinging on the inside of the café's door announced my entrance along with a good gust of cold, fresh air that formed a wispy vapor where it mixed with air permeated with donut grease. The place was crowded, and I stood in the doorway looking for Cal while I wiped snow from my boots onto a not-so-welcoming doormat that read "Many Have Eaten Here. Few Have Died."

"Close the door!" Yelled a chorus of apparently chilly breakfast guests. Pushing the door closed behind me, I spied at the counter the back of Cal's head with its thinning white hair. Luckily, the only empty seat was next to him. Unluckily, the seat was unoccupied because of the presence of Clyde Leeman, the unofficial town crier, on the other side of it. I tried to be discreet about putting my back to Clydie when I took the stool between him and Cal, like the people on the airplane who stick their face in a book to avoid having to speak to their seat mate. I liked Clydie well enough, just wasn't up to his nonstop complaining and nonsensical jabbering. It was clear to me how and why Clydie had developed a very thick skin. It was virtually impossible to insult the man. And believe me, everyone tried.

"Hi, Cal," I said pleasantly, as he lowered the newspaper onto the counter, exposing his quick smile, and removed his glasses to reveal twinkling, blue eyes that defied his age. Cal had a natural ability to make everyone feel as though he was genuinely happy to see them, even when he wasn't. Before Cal could speak, Clydie broke in with his usual, too loud voice.

"Well, hellooooo, Ms. Bunker! You must be freezing. You ain't in Kansas anymore, are ya? Hey, I hope you don't have to pee. The pipes are froze in the bathroom." With that, the couple seated on the other side of him got up to leave.

"Clyde Leeman!" shouted Audrey, my favorite (and only) waitress in the café. "Will you stop with the announcements? Every time you open your pie hole, a customer leaves." The sassy, heavily tattooed and pierced Audrey was headed my way with a cup of coffee. Clearing a used paper place mat printed with local advertisements with her right hand, she plunked the full cup onto a clean one with her left, and slid it in front of me.

"Well, I just think it's good to let people know that your toilets are not working. What if someone has an emergency? This coffee is like mud! If anyone makes the mistake of a second cup, you're gonna have an awful mess," Clyde yelled.

"I thought the out-of-order sign on the door was sufficient," Audrey said. "But I guess that would require the ability to read." Audrey rolled her eyes, and sighed in exasperation. "Want the usual, Janey?" She asked, seemingly hopeful to exclude Clyde from anymore conversation. I hesitated, not knowing what my usual was. I didn't recall being that predictable.

"I can read!" Clydie defended himself. "And you'd

better avoid the prunes this morning, if you know what I mean, Ms. Bunker. Those pipes is froze solid. They won't get a flush down until April at this rate."

"Why don't you take some of that hot air into the bathroom and thaw the pipes?" Audrey asked sarcastically.

All the talk revolving around the status of the toilet was making me nauseous. I quickly agreed that I wanted my usual, whatever that was.

"English or day old?" Asked Audrey. When I met this with a puzzled look, she elaborated. "Your usual is the least expensive item on the menu. Today that's a tie between a toasted English muffin and yesterday's special muffin."

"What was yesterday's special muffin?"

"Raspberry, a buck fifty."

"What's today's special muffin?"

"Apricot bran, two bucks."

"I'll have the toasted English, please," I said.

"Ha!" Clyde chimed in. "Good idea to avoid bran with the nonfunctioning facilities." Just as I thought Audrey would pour coffee into Clyde's lap, the cowbells announced another customer, causing Clyde's head to swivel toward the door. The incoming customer looked around in vain for a place to sit other than next to Clyde, and shrugging hopelessly, shuffled over and took the least coveted seat in the café. As Clyde began chewing an ear off the guy, I turned my attention to Cal.

"Cal, I need a favor," I said.

"You name it. I'm your guy," Cal replied immediately, never breaking eye contact. To my mind, only the best of friends will agree to a favor before knowing what it is. This was testament to the mutual trust we shared; trust that had been won quickly and tested frequently. Not that I had been involved with many investigations since my arrival in Green Haven, but when I had, Cal had been at my service in any way needed.

"It's an easy one today. I need a ride to Acadia Island this morning. Seems that I missed the boat, so to speak." I went on to explain my mission to document damage caused by a house fire, and my plan to grab the late ferry back ashore later. Cal confirmed that I was in luck. He was happy to accommodate my request, especially at the expense of the insurance company who would reimburse all expenditures. I had learned that Cal was delighted to collect money from an insurance company with whom the vast majority of cash flow had always gone in the opposite direction. And since his retirement from a number of careers including commercial fishing, Cal had the time and appreciated a little extra money.

"Besides," Cal added, "the *Sea Pigeon* needs to stretch her legs a bit. And it's a great day for a boat ride. I haven't been to Acadia in years. No reason to go."

Me either, I thought to myself as Audrey delivered a toasted English muffin.

"Not my business, but . . ." Audrey started and hesitated long enough to give me an opportunity to cut her off, which I did not. I really liked Audrey. She is young and quirky, but has great insight—well beyond her nearly two decades of life. And I had confided in her to a small extent about my connection to Acadia, so figured that I had made it her business by doing so. "Are you hoping to catch a glimpse of the mysterious Bunker clan?"

"No," I chuckled. "I wouldn't know a Bunker if I was sitting next to one." I extended my arms to both sides, indicating that Cal and Clydie were more family to me than anyone on Acadia.

A long pause accompanied by Audrey shaking her head was finally filled with, "OMG. The only thing keeping me from genealogy research is the slight possibility that I could be related to Clydie." Cal's shoulders bounced up and down with a silent laugh. "Well, I want a full report tomorrow, girlfriend," Audrey said as she smacked the counter with my tab. Cal ordered a couple of muffins to take to his wife before Audrey was out of hearing range, and we laid out a plan.

I was to go home and ask the Vickersons to deliver the Duster to South Haven so that I would have it upon my return to the mainland this evening. Cal would pick me up at the Lobster Trappe and we would ride together to the dock where his boat was secured. He would get me to the island by ten, giving me plenty of time to take pictures and catch the last boat off. I liked simplicity. And I liked the fact that I would be home in time to join Mr. and Mrs. V for drinks and dinner.

Cal and I paid our respective tabs and stood to leave just as the cowbells rang out. Marilyn and Marlena, or "the old maids" as they were affectionately referred to, stepped in single file; Marlena cradling one of the couple's numerous blue-ribbon Scottish Fold cats. A chorus of "close the door" was met with quick action, and the ladies, whom everyone assumed were gay, came over to take the stools Cal and I had vacated. The sixty-ish gals were regulars at the café, allowing them lenience with pets. Any resident of Green Haven who had engaged in conversation with either of the women knew a lot about Scottish Folds. Even I, in my brief time here, had learned that these cats cried with a silent meow and stood on their hind feet like otters.

Marlena and Marilyn owned Green Haven's only hardware store and gas pump, and were legendary for gouging the locals who had no other shopping options. (My introduction to them several months ago had left me with a comparison to the Baldwin Sisters from *The Waltons,* which I had never been able to shake.) Marilyn had a distinct look: gray hair pulled into a neat braid; Marlena looked like a man. Both of the women had a penchant for tweed. And both pulled off an arrogance that privileged education and upbringing afford by being quite philanthropic.

Before we could exchange pleasantries, Clydie took the floor at full volume. "Hey Aud," he yelled across the counter to a clearly disgusted Audrey. "That's it! The solution to the problem is kitty litter. If it's good enough for the highfalutin Sir Walter Bunny of Wheat Island, it's plenty good enough for the clientele here."

I choked back a giggle with the reminder of the name of this particular cat. I thought I recalled being

told that the ladies' numerous Scottish Folds had
been trained to use the toilet, too, but may have imagined that part. Audrey looked stunned, and claimed
that it was shock at the inclusion of "clientele" in the
dimwit's vocabulary. This was not enough to throw
Clyde off his game, though. He added, "Put a litter
box back there, and I'll bring in my clam rake for
you to use as a pooper scooper." Audrey scowled and
snapped a pointed index finger at the door while Marlena and Marilyn looked on in confusion. Clydie, who
was banished from the café nearly weekly, donned his
coat and hat, and wished everyone a nice day. Clydie's
exit scene was complete when he drew Audrey's attention to two customers who were sitting crossed-
legged suggesting that they might need the restroom.

The door closing behind us clipped fragmented
conversations of the village idiot and other daily customers, small talk that I had become accustomed to
since my arrival in Green Haven and my frequenting
the only breakfast joint in town. Cal was right behind
me in his pickup truck as I weaved the way back to
my place through high banks of snow made fresh
white with this morning's windfall. Although it had
been a full nine months since my move here from Miami, I still marveled at the differences. It wasn't the
obvious, opposite ends of the spectrum differences of
the physical surroundings that I found astonishing. It
wasn't subzero temperatures, record inches of snow, or
the remoteness of this ultra-rural location that drew the
biggest dissimilarities to the life I had left behind in
South Florida; it was the subtleties. It was the fact that

I had a sense of community here. I had a circle of people with whom I lived that I actually cared about. And they cared about me. In Miami, when a coworker asked how I was doing, they expected nothing more than a cursory "Fine, thanks," and would be put off by anything more. The best and worst times of my life had been defined publically as "Fine, thanks."

Here in Green Haven, when acquaintances asked why I had never married, it was not the accusatory tone that I had become weary of in Miami. It was asked out of real caring and wanting to know my story. As quirky as it was, Green Haven was starting to feel more like home to me than anything I had ever known. Maybe it's just a good place for misfits, I thought as I pulled myself out of the Duster and signaled to Cal that I would be a minute as I walked toward the Lobster Trappe. The Vickersons' Cadillac sports a bumper sticker that reads "Some of us are here because we're not all there," which sums it up completely. Certainly the regulars at the café were quite a collection of oddballs. And I couldn't help but wonder if mavericks gravitated here, or if the place had made them that way. Classic chicken or egg, I thought. And something that didn't need resolving. Either way, I knew that Green Haven was a place that embraced, more than tolerated people like me who are less mainstream—whatever the hell that means, I thought as I knocked and let myself into the Vickersons. It had taken me over forty years, but I was learning that home is a feeling, not a place. And I had actually succeeded in starting life over in spite of the naysayers of my past who warned that I could not do so simply by saying "Goodbye and good riddance."

Knocking twice on the door with the back of my left hand, I twisted the knob and flung it open with my right, and barged into the landlord's knickknack-filled home. The place was a virtual menagerie of nautical novelties, souvenirs, and small collections displayed in what Mrs. V liked to call "Salty Chic." It was immediately clear that I had caught the Vickersons in mid celebration of something. Mr. V did a fairly dramatic fist pump while his wife danced around gleefully. Their mood was so joyful, that I couldn't help but laugh. "Oh Janey! You just missed the best phone call of our lives!" shouted Mrs. V.

"Publishers' Clearing House?" I asked playfully.

"No," Mrs. V said, nearly out of breath. She clasped her hands together and placed them tightly under her chin. "Wally's coming to live with us!"

"*My brother?*"

"If you get on...
I can keep you...

Petrified, she conn...
eyes. Gorgeous. A... ...she
wanted to be with a... ...other time.

The stranger held out his hand. "We really need to go now, sweetheart. You coming?"

She straddled the back of the motorcycle. The bike sprang to life and her arms shot around him. There wasn't any give to his body when her fingers locked together across his hard abs. She closed her eyes and buried her face against his black jacket. She wanted to see nothing, especially the gruesome picture the shooting had left in her mind.

"Hold on tight."

Had she left the safety of the house for a dangerous daredevil?

DATE DUE

BULLETPROOF BADGE

ANGI MORGAN

204037

Tim, thanks for doing the dishes.
A special thanks to Cindi D & Tamami for bouncing ideas around.
Another to Janie for all the late nights. Always to my pal Jan
(you know why). And a special shout-out to Brenda R
for the constant reader support over the last five years!

ISBN-13: 978-0-373-69886-8

Bulletproof Badge

Copyright © 2016 by Angela Platt

Recycling programs
for this product may
not exist in your area.

HARLEQUIN®

™ www.Harlequin.com

Printed in U.S.A.

Angi Morgan writes Harlequin Intrigue novels "where honor and danger collide with love." She combines actual Texas settings with characters who are in realistic and dangerous situations. Angi and her husband live in north Texas, with only the four-legged "kids" left in the house to interrupt her writing. They recently began volunteering for a local Labrador retriever foster program. Visit her website, angimorgan.com, or hang out with her on Facebook.

Books by Angi Morgan

Texas Rangers: Elite Troop

Bulletproof Badge

West Texas Watchmen

The Sheriff
The Cattleman
The Ranger

Texas Family Reckoning

Navy SEAL Surrender
The Renegade Rancher

Harlequin Intrigue

Hill Country Holdup
.38 Caliber Cover-Up
Dangerous Memories
Protecting Their Child
The Marine's Last Defense

Visit the Author Profile page at Harlequin.com for more titles.

CAST OF CHARACTERS

Garrison Travis—A rookie Texas Ranger who has focused his entire life on achieving one goal after his father's life was cut short in the line of duty. His charming attitude normally melts women's hearts until he meets the one woman who sees right through him.

Kenderly Tyler—The definition of *wrong place, wrong time*. A cosmetologist who has just landed on her feet with her business. Raised by a foster mother, she's now alone in the world making friends and establishing her life. She can't afford to be a state's witness. She'll lose everything.

Jesse Ryder—Lieutenant in the Texas Rangers, Company F. Garrison's best friend from childhood.

Aiden Oaks—Captain in the Texas Rangers, headquartered in Austin.

Josh Parker—Major in the Texas Rangers. In charge of Company F, based in Waco.

Bryce Johnson—Lieutenant in the Texas Rangers. Company F's authority on Texas organized crime.

Tenoreno Family—Texas organized crime family. Isabella Tenoreno, wife to Paul, has been murdered.

Rosco Family—Texas organized crime family. Trinity Rosco, wife of Thomas, has been murdered.

Chapter One

Garrison Travis caught the kick with both his hands before it slammed into his chest. How had he given himself away? Why was this guy so dead set that neither of them get to that bedroom? He'd eventually find out during the interrogation. This moment though— He pulled the leg with him as he fell backward, rolling and placing his opponent under him.

Screams came from downstairs. Shots, upstairs and down, had started this mess. His opponent swung and missed. Garrison retaliated, sending a hard elbow to the guy's chin. It ripped the tuxedo across his shoulders. Always a good reason to rent. The company could reimburse the bridal shop. He popped to his feet. His opponent did the same.

Right cross. Uppercut. Double jabs to the ribs. He blocked them all and retreated. He was unarmed, having gone into the private event undercover as one of the waitstaff.

Where are the damn security guards or men from downstairs? Hadn't they heard the shots?

More screams. Pleading through the closed door off of the upstairs landing. He rolled across the plush carpet struggling to get free. He'd been heading to that bedroom with a tray of sangria when he'd heard the shots from the back of the house. He'd sent the text message to his captain from the staircase that shots had been fired. He didn't have backup, but where were Tenoreno's men?

The three glasses were crushed across the white carpet, leaving dark red stains. If he could get to the door...

"Come on, man. Somebody's in trouble." Why was this guard trying to prevent him from getting to those women?

Right jab. Right jab. His opponent's face flew back along with his feet. A give-it-all-he-had left to the belly doubled the guy in half. Muffled cries and threats from inside the room. He had to end this and get inside. He raised his knee into the guy's chin. Eyes rolling back in his head, his opponent sank to floor. One more kick to his jaw guaranteed he was out cold.

Two succinct pops behind the solid oak door. A blood-curdling scream. He checked the downed guard for a weapon. Nothing. Last pocket had the key to the door. He got it in the lock, turned and burst inside.

Two women lay dead. Executed.

The intruder had a fistful of hair in one hand and a gun pointed at a third woman's head. He sported the same rent-a-monkey tux, but had added a face hood to conceal himself.

Slamming the door into the wall was enough to divert the direction of the barrel and make the bastard let the blond hair go. Garrison dropped and rolled, the monkey suit fired, missed. The woman picked up a metal case, swung, connected. The pistol flew under the bed. The case burst open spraying makeup supplies in every direction.

The monkey suit focused his attention on Garrison. Outweighed by forty pounds, Garrison locked his fists and swung them like a bat against a jaw as solid as rock. The bigger man barely staggered back a step.

But he did stagger, giving Garrison enough time to pounce. A double punch connected with ribs. His knee jabbed the man's thigh. Once. Then twice. And then the gunman threw a punch that hit Garrison square in the chest like a battering ram, slamming his head into the solid door.

The hooded monkey suit left through the balcony doors while Garrison was momentarily stunned. Tingling on his cheeks. A faraway plea for him to wake up. Both brought him fully to his senses.

"Get up. We've got to go," the woman whispered. Her makeup had smeared from the tears running down her face. "Come on."

Garrison took in the room. The lady of the house and her guest were lying holding hands on the floor. Both shot execution style in the back of the head. The other shots from downstairs must have been this guy's cue to take care of the extended family.

Top Texas organized crime boss wives. Dead instead of extracted. The captain was going to have his head on one of these silver platters.

"What are you waiting for? They're coming up the stairs, and I don't know what to do."

He got to his feet. "Close and lock the door."

There was nothing he could do for either woman. While the one left alive did as she was told, he reached under the bed with the hankie from his tux pocket and retrieved monkey suit's gun. The man had been in gloves, but maybe they'd get lucky.

Then again, they had a witness. He swiped the business card from the dresser. Kenderly Tyler, hair and makeup. Long multicolored golden or ash-blond hair past her shoulders, oval face and dark chocolate eyes. She was a little taller than his shoulder. He memorized the way she looked, every shapely curve covered in shiny sequins.

The doorknob shook. Shoulders slammed against the wood. His eyes fell to the gun in his hand. The Tenoreno men wouldn't ask questions. They'd shoot first.

"Kenderly?" He'd ask her why she'd waited for him once they were safe. Teary eyes questioned what he wanted. He jerked his head toward the balcony.

Following the gunman's path, they ducked into the cooling Texas sun. He kept her back against the brick, blocked her from anyone's view on the ground with his body. He could see down the open roads that his backup was nowhere in sight. The gunman was next to the pool house. Unless he wanted both crime families coming after him forever, he'd eventually need something to prove there was another person in the house. He dug into his front pocket, swiped the phone and took a series of pictures.

Heading the opposite direction next to the garage would take them to his bike. And right next to an older Volkswagen Beetle where two armed guards stood. They weren't waiting for them. At least not yet.

Which way? Follow the killer or protect his witness? Not a real question.

If the family got hold of her, he'd never find her again. They may even think she'd pulled the trigger or that he had. That settled which direction they'd run. He swung his legs over the side, dangling like a baited worm on a hook before he dropped and sprang up from the grass.

He looked up at the blonde who tossed him a small jeweled box, then a purse. She shook her hair away from her face as soon as she hiked a leg over the banister. He pointed to her shoes, which she flicked off, hitting the ground next to him. He scooped them up and shoved them in his pockets along with the box.

"Grab the bottom with your hands. Then lower, and I'll catch you." He tried to shout in a whisper. He kept looking over his shoulder expecting a gun in his kidney at any second.

Kenderly Tyler wasn't exactly ladylike coming down. At least she stifled her short scream the two feet she fell into his arms. There wasn't any type of special moment or slow-motion feel as she slid through his grasp to the grass. She pushed back, picked up her purse and ran.

The men breached the room right behind her escape. Moans, cries, questions shouted to God... Garrison caught up with her before she darted across the drive-way. He tucked her behind him, gave her a shush signal and evaluated their position.

They hugged the house, avoiding the guards. All point-ing their guns around corners and opening car doors. Tak-ing their time. Didn't they want to find the gunmen? It was one thing to sign up to fight in Tenoreno's army. It was much different when that army went to war. Shoot. His job would be easier if he could just shout at them to search for the killer by the pool.

The guards were armed to the teeth and outfitted bet-ter than the Secret Service. How the hell had they allowed the gunmen on to the property in the first place? Why had the gunman executed the women? Had the shots fired downstairs taken out the rival organized crime bosses, too?

Just as he thought they'd be in the clear, his witness darted around him and headed straight to the Volkswa-gen. Too many questions had distracted him. He needed to secure Kenderly Tyler and hightail it back to Com-pany F.

ONE STEP AT a time and she'd make it. Kenderly's hands shook, rattling the keys as she tried to push one into the car door. She just needed inside. She saw the man who had let her in the gate earlier. He held up his hand for her to stop.

No way. She couldn't stay with all the guns and… death. She ignored him and sat behind the wheel. He put his finger in his ear, then looked at her again and began running. His rifle bounced across his chest until he held it against his ribs.

The keys rattled. Her body was shaking now. Isabella and Trinity were dead. She would have been next. They were going to kill her. If she hadn't been cleaning up in the bathroom, she would already be faceless and…and…

The man with a rifle yanked the door open and grabbed a fistful of her hair, tugging. She'd forgotten to lock the door, but somehow she'd already put on her seat belt so she was stuck. He reached across and popped the lock, then yanked again. All she could do was grab his wrist to keep her hair attached to her head.

The image of the dead women fixed on the back of her eyelids. Every time she blinked she saw the blood and gore. He pulled her hair to get her to move, but she was about to be terribly sick.

With blurred vision, she leaned forward and lost what little was in her stomach. The man hopped out of her way. Hearing more fighting above her head, she continued to retch. Someone pulled back her hair, put an arm around her waist and helped her stand. He led her off the white gravel drive. Past the man who had yanked her hair, now unconscious on the green grass. Its cool shaded lushness registered under her bare feet.

"Water?" she squeaked out.

"Can't help you with that," a deep Texas twang answered. "But if you get on the back of my bike, I can keep you alive."

As weary as she was, that popped her head up. Petrified, she connected with a pair of jade-green eyes, sandy short brown hair and a casual self-confident smile that didn't belong in her surreal afternoon.

Gorgeous. Absolutely the type of man she wanted to be with any other time. He dangled her shoes in front of her, and she slipped them on.

The stranger held out his hand. "We really need to go now, sweetheart. You coming?"

Yes. But she didn't think she said it out loud. She straddled the back of the motorcycle in her short skirt and heels. Two large, strong hands grabbed her thighs, pulled her closer and placed her feet on two metal rods. Her sequined skirt was up as high as it could be without revealing anything, but now wasn't the time to care.

The motorcycle sprang to life, and her arms shot around him. There wasn't any give to his body when her fingers locked together across his hard abs. She closed her eyes and buried her face against his black jacket. She wanted to see nothing, especially the gruesome picture the shooting had left in her mind.

The motorcycle screeched to a halt, sliding sideways in the gravel. Her rescuer slowly took off across the field, avoiding the closed front gate.

"Hold on tight."

She didn't think she could hold tighter until her bottom was airborne over the first incline. Had she left the safety of the house for a dangerous daredevil? Had it been safe at the house? Absolutely not. And how did she know for certain this man wasn't a part of the...the...

Go ahead and say it. Murders! The man dressed in black had murdered two people right in front of her, then stared openmouthed as she'd screamed. This wasn't the killer. His dark green eyes proved that. The man she'd fought with was just as tall, but his eyes were black with hatred.

She'd never forget those eyes.

They flew over the next small hill, landing hard on both tires.

"Slow down before your kill us!" she shouted in his ear.

"Can't. They're following. May start shooting."

She turned behind them, her hair whipped across her face. Sure enough, a black SUV bounced over the rolling hills of the Texas lake country. The motorcycle skidded, and she held tighter. If the men shot at them, she'd be dead. Period.

Her rescuer turned sharply, heading toward a tree line. "Where are you going?"

"Where they can't."

The trees were so thick she didn't think they could get through, either. He slowed a little, but zigzagged, tilting them from side to side, making her want to put her feet out to drag along the ground. She kept them secured and kept her body smooshed against the stranger's back, moving like a second layer with him.

Bushes whacked at her legs as they zoomed past. The branches stung but suddenly stopped. The first thing she saw was the perfectly smooth carpet of green. She looked behind them, and no one followed. The SUV turned and followed on the other side of the trees for a few seconds before turning away.

"Hey!"

Someone shouted, making her look forward. They were on a golf course, bouncing yet again over the greenway to a cart path. Once there, the ride was smoother, but her hero didn't slow. If anything, he went even faster. It was a Friday night at dusk, and the golfers were finishing their rounds. So they were few and far between on the earlier holes they'd zipped past.

Kenderly only relaxed a little. This time when her eyes closed, they were burning with tears for Isabella. No one deserved to die that way.

He was right. Her hero. They couldn't stop. Her unnamed rescuer popped over curbs, into a parking lot and on to the street. He ran stop signs, passed other cars as if they were standing still and just kept going.

Once on Highway 71 leading back to Austin, he wrapped his long fingers around her thigh and gently tugged her close again. His subtle message was that their wild ride wasn't over. She moved, resting her head once more on his back. They rocketed through the wind, which didn't allow for talking.

She couldn't have answered any of his questions or any of the thousands running through her mind. Isabella had given her a small jewelry case and told her not to open it for three days.

Oh no! The case! She'd dropped it somewhere. She'd been so out of it by losing her cookies all over the guard's feet that she'd forgotten. What had Isabella not wanted anyone to know? Why was she supposed to wait three days? Kenderly wasn't sure she'd ever know now.

Her hero stroked her frozen forearm, slowly warming it back to life against his chest. When she cried harder, he held on to her hands tighter.

It didn't matter who he was. He'd probably saved her life. Okay, he'd definitely saved her life. But that was only one reason she was thankful. The stranger's actions in the past few minutes were more intimacy and kindness than she'd felt in years.

Chapter Two

The arm under Garrison's hand was no longer frozen. Early spring in Texas was fine with lots of sunshine on you, but once it got dark—and speeding in excess of seventy miles per hour—you could get chilled to the bone.

"You can let me off anywhere," she said as he slowly merged with city traffic near the university hangouts.

"I don't think so, sweetie. No discussion necessary." He sped up again to limit the conversation.

"But I need to go back. I have to."

Darting between stopped cars, the horns blared as he pushed safely through red lights. He had to keep moving, so she couldn't jump off. Go back? She was the ranger's big break, and he couldn't let her disappear.

"Let me go at the next corner, or I'll start screaming my head off," she shouted, piercing his ear.

"We have a head start, but we're still being followed." It was logical to think so. There was only one road back to Austin from the crime scene. It didn't make sense that Tenoreno's men would give up because of a row of trees. He slowed the bike to a more normal speed. "After I rescued you and everything, screaming just wouldn't be cool."

"Neither is kidnapping."

"Come on, Kenderly. We both know I'm not kidnap-

ping you. I saved your a— I got you out of there safely,"
he amended. "Why the hell do you want to go back?"

"I appreciate it. I really do. But there's something I...
I just want to go home." She sat straighter, pulling away
from him.

He immediately missed her soft breasts pushed against
his back. He needed both hands to control the bike, or
he'd pull her closer again. Instead he pulled into a parking lot, darted to the side of the building and cut the engine. He twisted a bit on the seat to face her and reached
into his pocket.

"Is this what you need to go back for?" He held up the
smaller case he'd picked up from her seat. "The purse
strap got stuck on the gear shift. I couldn't get that. You
tossed this to me at the balcony."

"Oh my God, thank you so much." She reached for it,
but he kept it high above her head.

"I'm thinking I should have a look inside."

"No. You don't understand. It isn't mine."

"Then I especially need to look inside."

"Just who do you think you are? A hotshot waiter with
a fast motorcycle has no right—"

"Lieutenant Garrison Travis, Company F, Texas Rangers. Temporarily on assignment in Austin." He wanted to
pop whatever lock was on that case, but he didn't have
anything with him. "I'm sorry that you can't go home.
They'll be waiting there. They know who you are."

"But I didn't do anything." She grabbed his upper
arm. Her hand shook a bit. She was either shivering in
her short sleeves or from the shock of everything that
had happened.

"They don't know that. Plus, you saw the killer." He
shrugged out of his split jacket and flipped it around her
shoulders, holding it until she slipped her arms through

the sleeves. "You're coming home with me. It's your only option."

"Are you crazy? I don't know you. Where's your ID? Just take me to the nearest police station, and we can tell them what we saw." She swung her leg over the back of the bike and took off. "They'll protect me if I need it."

"I can help you," he called after her. "And that's smart, asking for my ID. But I don't carry it while I'm under-cover."

"You did help, and I thank you. But the police need to know what I witnessed. I'm sure I broke a law or some-thing leaving the scene of a crime." She backed up across the run-down parking lot in a short fancy skirt and his torn tux jacket. She might trip in her heels. "Why are you shaking your head at me?"

"Come on, get back on the bike." He threw one of his best smiles at her, attempting to make his witness feel more comfortable. But she wasn't reacting like the rest of the women in his life.

Maybe because she'd just seen two of her friends ex-ecuted, and someone was trying to kill her. Maybe he should change tactics.

"No."

"Well, I'll need my jacket. It's a rental." Fortunately, he'd dropped the murder weapon in the cycle's saddle-bags, so it was safe. He dug his cell from his front pants pocket. "I'm going to dial a number, and you can confirm my identity. Then I'm taking you to my place."

Garrison was afraid she'd break her neck running away from him if he got off the bike and chased her. He stayed put, got the number and pressed dial. He heard his captain answer, pressed speaker and told him, "Hang on." Then he extended the phone to his witness.

For some crazy reason, she walked back to him and took the phone. "Hello?"

"This is Captain Aiden Oaks, Texas Rangers. Who is this? Why do you have Travis's phone?"

She shrugged, searching him for answers. Garrison pointed to it and made a talk symbol with his hand.

"Someone handed it to me. Are you really a Texas Ranger? Is he?"

Garrison took the keys, opened the saddlebag, dropped the case inside and locked it. What was coming next would be pleasant for Kenderly, but not so much when Garrison confronted the captain.

"Is the smart-ass who handed you the cell riding a motorcycle, wearing a tuxedo and got a smart-alecky grin on his face?"

"I think so."

"Lieutenant Garrison Travis didn't have identification with him, miss. Did he call to assure you of something?"

She hung up and walked the phone back to him. "He says you have a smart-alecky smile. He's right."

"Ouch. I've been told this smile was reassuring. Ready to come home with me now?"

Kenderly had been through a sick ordeal and needed a lot more help than he could provide. The first step was getting her under the protection of the Rangers. And for that to happen, he had to find out exactly what she'd seen and what was in that case.

He braced the bike while she hopped on the back again. He moved his hand to bring her closer, then thought better of it, speaking over his shoulder. "You can trust me, Kenderly."

"No more running red lights."

"Not a prob."

"And you promise that I'll be safer with you than with the police?"

"You've got my word as a Texas Ranger. Nothing'll happen to you while you're with me." He started the bike and rejoined traffic before she realized he was a complete stranger and decided to yell for help. She didn't yell. She only cooperated.

Kenderly was too trusting. Or playing him.

Witness or perpetrator? He had a lightbulb moment of his own. He hadn't seen the actual shooting. He couldn't swear who pulled that trigger. The makeup artist could have unlocked the balcony doors and let the monkey-suit guy inside.

Maybe he was protecting an accomplice?

Not a chance. There was no blood spatter on her clothes. She couldn't have been near the fatal shots. He'd find out all the details when they got to his house. Just a couple of minutes and they'd be safe.

The small jewelry box would have to wait until he was at his place. He needed to ask her about everything, but was certain Captain Oaks would want to be there for the questioning.

Turning down Forty-first, he replayed the scene in his head, searching through his memory for what the murderer looked like. Approximately the same height as him, so the guy had to be six-one, maybe more. Brown eyes, huge nose that protruded under the hood. He didn't have much to go on, but the man's shoes weren't from a rental company like the tux.

Garrison had rented enough times to know how unforgiving a new pair of rental dress shoes were. Or how the older ones looked scuffed no matter how hard you shined. This guy was wearing his own.

He pulled to a stop in his driveway. Then he mentally

brought up the image of the man in black. He'd turned to him—surprised someone had entered Mrs. Tenoreno's bedroom—guilty.

Blood. Bright dark spots that couldn't be mistaken for anything else shone all over the black tux. He was confident he'd interrupted the gunman before he pulled the trigger on a third victim. Kenderly was a state's witness.

Kenderly was off the back of the bike before he'd cut the engine. He popped the kickstand, tugging her to him. He might be confident she wasn't the murderer, but he wasn't so sure she wouldn't run down the street hollering for help.

"Mind if I take the jacket back?"

Delicately, treating the ripped tux like an expensive designer jacket, she folded it in half and handed it to him. He tossed open the saddlebag and removed the gun, wrapping it protectively in the jacket's folds, then setting it on the bike seat along with the case. The evidence couldn't be out of his line of sight, and this was the best he could do. He unlocked the detached garage and lifted the heavy door, then rolled his bike inside and reversed the procedure.

"I think I have a couple of sodas inside and maybe a frozen pizza."

"I can't possibly eat." Her hand covered her lips.

"How about some soup, then? I got a cabinet of the stuff."

"Really, I'm fine." She shook her head and preceded him up the steps. "What I really need is a toothbrush."

"Got you covered. My aunt has extras from visits with her dentist. She's visiting my mom." If he could remember where she'd put them.

"Oh." She tugged at her hair, trying to smooth tangle upon wind-massacred tangle.

His Aunt Brenda's house was on the small side. What most people might call cozy. Just right for one bachelor ranger who wasn't home half the time. That is, if he really lived in Austin. He was on temporary assignment and shared a place in Waco. He opened the door and prepared for the assault.

"Hey, I forgot to ask. Do you like dogs?"

Both his monsters slid across the old linoleum, tongues out, ready to jump on their visitor, expecting a treat. Before he could yell at them to get down, Garrison set the coat-wrapped gun on the counter. He knelt at the pups' level, taking one dog under either arm.

"I adore dogs. Are they Labs? What are their names? They're so sweet." Kenderly brightened and dropped to her knees with him.

"Diabolical is more like it. Don't turn your back on them for a minute. This big black boy is Bear. The chocolate pup is his half sister, Clementine." He reached up and pulled treats from a jar, handing them to his guest. "They'll do tricks for these."

She sat at the kitchen table, patiently petting the panting Labradors. "Clementine isn't exactly what I'd call a puppy."

"Sit, Clem. Bear, you know better than that." He used hand signals to get them to sit, wanting to show them off. "She's barely a year old. Already seventy pounds of love. I didn't know how long I'd be here, and these two sort of go berserk if I don't check in every day. Excuse me while I make a phone call."

He dialed, then retrieved a new Ziploc from the cabinet while he waited for the captain to answer. "Travis? I guess the party blew to hell?"

"Yes, sir. So you've heard. The beautician, Kenderly Tyler, witnessed the whole thing. I stopped the murderer

from blowing—" He darted a look at the woman he'd rescued to see if she'd heard his slip. "I stopped him from
having a third victim. We came straight here. I didn't
think you'd want anyone to know we have her in custody."

Kenderly got the dogs another treat and repeated his
hand commands to them.

"You think she's reliable?"

"As far as I can tell. I also have the murder weapon."
He placed the gun inside the bag. "It should take you about
forty minutes to get here, sir. See you then." He dropped
his phone on the counter, and Clementine nudged the back
of his knee. "Oh no, you don't. Christy fed you an hour
ago."

"Where's the bath, and do you have a first-aid kit?"

"You okay?" During the call, she'd taken a paper towel
from the roll he left on the table and started dabbing at her
legs. "Obviously not. Those from the trees we brushed
through?"

"Yes. My legs started stinging on the golfing green."

"Let me get something."

The house really was super small. Keeping the medicine cabinet mirror open, he could still see the kitchen
table. Bear was spread-eagle on the floor waiting for
some more attention. Kenderly was staring at the gun
and not moving. He dug through the antibiotic creams,
looking for something without an expired date. No luck.

"I found some cotton, alcohol and peroxide. Best I
can do." He knelt and took a look at the long scratch at
the top of her thigh.

"It'll be fine." Kenderly's soft voice matched her
dainty frame and manner.

"Need a belt to bite down on?"

She looked a bit confused. Instead of explaining, he

poured the bottles over the scratches. Her tanned thigh used to be completely smooth, not even a freckle.

The deep scratches would cause the peroxide to sting— a lot. Garrison fanned at her leg, and she shut her eyes. He leaned in close and blew across the peroxide bubbles, hoping to ease the pain.

"How could I have gotten into this mess?" She fanned her cheeks in a motion his sister used years ago when trying not to cry. "When I woke up this morning, I never imagined I'd have two dogs at my feet, be sitting in a funny little kitchen with peroxide dripping down my thigh and have a complete stranger blowing up my skirt."

"I don't really know what to say after that." He choked to keep from busting out laughing. Two Band-Aids across the deepest scratch and they were done.

She covered her face, looking embarrassed. "I didn't mean to complain about a scratch when Isabella… She's… Oh, gosh, I can't stay here."

Garrison lifted her to her feet, against his chest and into his arms. "Go ahead and cry. I won't stop you. You're safe here." He couldn't just tell her she would be okay. He had to make her feel as though she was safe, and he didn't know another way.

She shoved at his shoulders, and he let her go. "What am I doing here? If they're following us, how can we possibly be safe?"

"You witnessed a murder, and we need to get your statement. The captain will be here soon, and we'll have some decisions. Until then, let's wait in the other room."

He led the way to the living area, just big enough for a small couch, arm chair and a television that covered most of the end wall. He loved that television and would be hauling it back to Waco after this assignment.

"Why did he shoot them?" Kenderly sat and dropped her head in her hands. "He was going to kill me, too. Wasn't he?"

"I think so."

"Why did he kill them?"

"That's what I'm hoping you can help us with, Kenderly."

"Why were you there?" She looked up quickly, accusing him of something without a word.

He flattened his lips shut and shook his head. He couldn't tell her that he was undercover tonight after an anonymous tip let them know there'd be trouble. He should have gotten the women extracted earlier instead of waiting for the cover of darkness. They'd been hoping to turn one of the families against the other. Instead, both had been hit.

"Let's start with how you knew Isabella Tenoreno."

"She came once a week into the shop where I have a chair. Wednesday she said she was having a party today and asked if I could come. I do hair and makeup for private events. This was a little different since she invited me to attend. I ended up doing her friend Trinity's hair, too."

Trinity Rosco, the wife of the rival crime family. Garrison noticed how stiff Kenderly had become. She was a terrible liar. So there was more to her story than she was letting on. "What happened after that?"

"I was gathering my things and cleaning my brushes in the bathroom. I heard something break, and Trinity screamed. At least I think it was her. The man, he already had the gun out and told them both to get to their knees."

"What language?"

"English."

"Why didn't he see you?"

"I saw the gun first thing, so I didn't open the door all the way. I should have. I should have done something. Maybe they'd still be alive." She covered her face with her hands again, crying this time.

"Don't doubt for a minute that you'd be dead now."

"I… I thought it might be a…a joke. You know? The gun didn't look real at first. But then he…he shot them. He just…shot them."

She jumped up and stood at the window. He let her. What could he say? Two women had been brutally murdered. There was nothing that would take the image away from her. He was just lucky she wasn't falling apart. She could be a hysterical mess.

"Then he found you?" he prompted.

"There were noises coming from the sitting room. I thought about calling out, but I didn't. I must have moved backward, hit something or made a noise. He found me and was pulling me over their bodies when you came into the bedroom."

"So you're a hairstylist?"

She nodded, rubbing under her eyes, smearing the mascara that had run from her tears. Personally, he didn't care for a lot of makeup on a woman, but he did appreciate her long multicolored hair and bare legs.

"I know my aunt used to talk to her hairdresser all the time," he prodded. "Did Isabella happen to mention what this special occasion was about?"

"Isabella was never at my work alone. Her bodyguard was never more than five feet away and could always hear what we were saying. This time she locked them out of the bedroom, while she changed her clothes."

"She didn't mention…anything?"

"I'm not sure I know what you're getting at. Isabella

had lots of money. Why wouldn't her husband's enemies just kidnap her?"

"That's one of the things I'm trying to find out, Kenderly."

Was there something too innocent in her wide eyes? Something she was holding back? Or was he too paranoid, after losing not one, but two women to an assassin? Naw, she was holding something back. She'd said "husband's enemies," and that meant she knew. She just didn't trust him yet.

"Is that horrible man going to try and kill me again?"

If we're lucky he'll be after us both. It was easy to think that. As a Texas Ranger he wanted the guy to find him.

It would be harder to involve an innocent woman. He'd held Kenderly's hair away from her face as she lost her cookies in the driveway. He couldn't afford to have a personal attachment.

Yeah, the sensitive guy inside him winced at the thought of using her as bait. The investigative ranger didn't have a choice. If his captain ordered it, he'd have to act.

Chapter Three

One of the most gorgeous male specimens Kenderly had ever encountered had choked while laughing at her. She wished she knew what he and his captain were talking about outside. The captain seemed to have brought news Garrison didn't really want to hear.

She'd been introduced while the murder weapon was locked away in the captain's trunk. Now she was eating toast at the kitchen window and watching the men talk.

Captain Oaks was calm, watching her from where he stood in the backyard. His hands were behind his back, as stoic and sturdy as his name. But her rescuer waved his hands, disagreeing or in disbelief. She could make out the words no and no way. Just a few minutes before he'd said "hell, no" loud enough to be heard in the next county.

Garrison adamantly refused whatever his new assignment required. The only movements that were relaxed at all were reaching down to pet Clementine or take her ball and throw it again. Such a normal action that he performed without thinking.

He hadn't broken a sweat saving her life today. Confident. Cocky. Extremely good-looking. A little arrogant. And sweet, sweet Thelma, he rode a motorcycle like it was nobody's business.

Her fingers tangled in the mess that was now her hair.

The long extensions were so matted that she couldn't unclip them from her head. The wind had done permanent damage, and it would take hours of combing to make them wearable again. She headed to the bathroom to see if she could get them loose. Bear followed and sat in the doorway, then slid to his belly.

"I suppose you're used to the door staying open," she said gently to him, stroking the old boy on the head. She looked in the mirror and almost screamed. "I look like a middle-aged drug addict."

The slate liner was smudged under her eyes and halfway down her cheeks. She had no way to repair the damage, other than removing all the makeup. She had nothing except her cell. Her makeup case, purse, keys and car had all been left at the Tenoreno estate.

How was she going to get to work? Or work without her supplies, for that matter? Everything was in that bathroom or her Beetle. Her ID, debit card, checkbook…how would she even eat until they could be replaced?

But she couldn't feel sorry for herself. Isabella and Trinity had lost much more than supplies or money.

Much more.

The men hadn't opened the jewelry case yet. It had also been locked in the captain's trunk almost immediately. Neither of them asked what was inside. They'd just assumed it was important. Probably because she'd asked to go back for it.

She took a deep breath and tried to slow her racing heart. Turning the water off, the men's voices drifted in through the slightly open window.

"You have your choice. Protect her or be the bait."

"I appreciate your confidence in me, sir. I don't think I have a choice. I don't have the skills or patience to sit and wait. And isn't it against some type of regulation or

something? Don't we need to involve a female DPS officer to be on her protection detail?" Garrison was marching back and forth across his grass.

"You're the one insisting that she needs protection
without evaluating if what she saw is admissible in court.
Or what's in that case you locked away. How dangerous
do you think the threat to her is?"

Garrison stopped pacing. His smile was gone, and he
suddenly looked grown up. The white teeth he'd flashed
all evening put her at ease, but it made him look much
younger.

"From everything you've told me about these two families, they shoot first and never bother to ask if it's the
right person. If they find her, they will kill her, sir."

"You're right, and she'll be safe. I'm giving you the
option, son. Keep your word and be a part of her detail.
Or you nail these bastards once and for all. As I said before, the Tenoreno family released a blurred picture of
you both to the media. They're going to find the fake
background information we set up for you to get the job.
It won't take them long before they track down your cover
phone. We need a decision and need a plan."

Kenderly wanted to crawl through the tiny window
and shout at both the men. They were making decisions
about her life without asking her anything. She wasn't
running off with Garrison Travis to hide. But she also
wasn't stupid enough to go home. Without money or a
place to live, the Texas Rangers were her best chance to
stay alive.

"That ID got me on the grounds. The pictures will get
me back inside. Regarding Kenderly, there isn't a choice
here," Garrison said so seriously it scared her. "Without me, you don't have a connection to the shooter. If
Kenderly comes forward, it will blow the entire opera-

tion. It's the closest we've been to bringing these crime families down in years. If they join forces, we might never get the chance again."

"As of today, the Tenorenos and Roscos were falling behind the cartels. Together…" Captain Oaks shook his head with the implication. "They'll either kill each other, taking a lot of other people along the way. Or they'll be strong enough to control seventy percent of organized crime in Texas."

"There's only one choice, then. I go back inside. Try to convince them I was just running for my life when the shots started. It would help if I had something of value to trade. I don't see anyone making an identification from the pictures. I've got my fingers crossed there's something in that jewelry box that Isabella thought was worth smuggling out with Kenderly."

She couldn't see the captain's face, but she did have a good look at Garrison's dissatisfied expression. He shoved his hand through his sandy-blond hair. He'd changed into jeans and a button-down shirt. She'd seen his badge ready to go on the kitchen table before he slid it into his back pocket.

"We'll do the initial Q and A here. We both need to hear her answers firsthand. You could come to headquarters but—"

"Got it. The fewer who know about Kenderly Tyler, the better." Garrison looked more relaxed.

Why he should be…she had no idea. He was planning on returning to the Tenoreno house surrounded by men with guns…and more guns.

"I'll make a call and get a video camera here. Then we'll get started. You okay with your cover story about why you left in such a hurry?" Captain Oaks asked.

"Easy to explain. Shots start flying, and I'm not hanging around. It might take longer to wrap my head around officials thinking I might have something to do with the murders. I'm not usually the one being hunted. I'm more the hunter type. But I can fake it."

"You're our best bet to discover the true reason for the assassinations. We can assume they don't know about the real murderer." The captain bent down to pet Clementine. "But he knows about you."

"And Kenderly. We both saw him."

"That was quick thinking to get the pictures. Maybe something will come from it. Having evidence of the murderer is your best way to get back in to see Tenoreno. He should be extremely interested in your photos."

"I don't understand why the wives were killed and not the crime bosses. It doesn't make sense. I heard shots at the back of the house, but couldn't get to both."

The captain clamped a hand on Garrison's shoulder, stopping him. The younger man didn't flinch or try to get away. It seemed friendly enough, fatherly in fact. "It's not your fault, Garrison. No one predicted they would be murdered."

"If I'd only been a couple of minutes earlier."

"According to what you told me, more lives would have been lost if you were a couple of minutes later."

"But—"

"No buts in this line of work. It was out of your control. We move on."

Kenderly liked Captain Oaks. She had no idea what some of the things they were talking about meant, but she liked him just the same. Taking his wise words to heart, she also needed to move on. There wasn't anything she could do about the past. She couldn't go back and change time or rush in and save Isabella.

All she could do was help find her friend's murderer.

"WHERE DO WE START?" Kenderly sat at the kitchen table, her hands clasped together so tightly her knuckles were turning white. "Do you need for me to write out my statement? I looked for a tablet. Oh, but I didn't go through anything. Sorry, I promise I wasn't looking through your things."

"It's okay." Garrison wanted to hug her and calm her down again. But that wasn't happening in front of his captain.

"Miss Tyler," Oaks began, "we've sent for a video camera and plan on recording your statement here. If I take you downtown, too many people will know we have you in protective custody. We'd rather continue without spreading that knowledge. That okay with you?"

Kenderly nodded and moved her hands to her lap until she swiped at a tear with the back of her knuckle. She'd washed her face. Gone was the heavy makeup he'd become used to in a very short time. Without it she looked younger.

"I have to confess… I didn't mean to eavesdrop, but the bathroom window was open. I could hear a few things."

"Like what?"

Garrison let the captain lead the discussion. He tried to keep a solemn look on his face out of respect for the two women who had died and the seriousness of the current situation. But just sitting there, Kenderly had a way of making him smile. Or the way she tugged at the stretchy skirt jerked him back to the memory of his hand on her thigh.

"I'm not sure I know what you meant by extracting. Who? Were you there to get Isabella away from that horrid man she was married to?"

She'd turned to Garrison, looking for an answer. He

popped away from leaning on the wall next to the living room. Taken totally off guard, his mind had been on the soft flesh that had been beneath his fingers. The question had him staring straight back at his commanding officer.

"Oh, my gosh, you were. Is that why you want to open her jewelry box?" She turned back to Oaks. "You see, I honestly don't know what's inside. Isabella told me to open it in three days. I thought it might be another letter to mail."

"Why do you think she said three days? And you'd mailed letters before?" Oaks brought out his pocket notepad, something he was never without.

If Garrison wanted to take notes, he'd have to get a pad from the hall closet. No way. He wasn't going to miss any part of this interview.

"I don't know why she said three days. I've been doing her hair for several years. Like I told Garrison—" Her hair flew over her shoulder when she turned toward him. "Oh wait, should I call you Lieutenant?"

"I don't mind being called Garrison." There it was again...the urge to smile.

"Like I told Garrison, it had gotten to the point that I had to ask her bodyguard to move back while I washed her hair. And they absolutely refused to let her come on her own. But I did pass notes to Trinity and mail an occasional letter."

"You passed notes for her?"

"Right. Isabella whispered to me that her husband was mad at one of her friend's husband. And he was being very strict about even allowing her to talk with her friend. So she wondered if I'd mind holding a note for her. It was very secretive. She wanted to pay me to do it, but I said no. I was getting a new customer out of the deal."

"So both Mrs. Tenoreno and Mrs. Rosco had their hair done at your shop?"

"Yes. Although, they never got to come in at the same time or the same day because of their husbands."

Garrison moved forward so Kenderly could look at him and Oaks at the same time. "Did you know what their husbands did for a living?"

She shrugged, and he realized that her hair was just above her shoulders. He could have sworn it had been longer.

"Not at the time. I looked them up online after some-body mentioned it one day." She tugged nervously at her skirt again. "I know they weren't the best of men, but that didn't have anything to do with Isabella and Trinity. After their husbands got mad at each other, they couldn't see each other."

"Did you ever read any of the notes or keep the ad-dress of something you mailed?"

"Of course I didn't read them. They were private." Kenderly looked at her lap where her hands had dropped again.

The reaction was one of embarrassment, not indig-nation.

"You didn't happen to keep copies of the addresses where Mrs. Tenoreno sent letters?"

She looked up, connecting with him on a level he didn't understand.

"Yes," she whispered. "Their husbands were—are—frightening. I sort of wanted to…well, to have some proof in case something went wrong."

"I could kiss you, Kenderly. This is sure to be a break we've been needing," Garrison said, receiving a cross look from Oaks.

"It might help us determine why they were murdered.

What are the addresses?" Oaks's pen was poised in one hand, and he pulled his cell out of his shirt pocket with the other. "We'll get units over there ASAP before Tenoreno discovers they exist. If we can get the original letters… Is that the video crew?"

Garrison saw the headlights pull into the driveway and stay lit. He went to get the kitchen door for the TDPS video crew and to signal them to kill the lights.

"No offense to the video crew, but have you ever seen any that are over six feet and two hundred and thirty pounds of muscle?" he threw over his shoulder. Every nerve he had jumped to alert.

Was it the same guy from the murder scene? He sure had the same build. He pulled his weapon and hit the switch closest to him.

Oaks immediately moved Kenderly into the bathroom, closing the door behind her. Garrison saw the machine pistol outlined from the streetlight as the guy moved closer to the shrubbery on the far side of the drive. Garrison dove, knocking Oaks to the floor. They turned the ancient wood table to its side just before his aunt's house began to be cut in half.

Chapter Four

"How many?" Oaks asked, covering his head, protecting it from the breaking glass raining on them.

"Just the one son of a bitch from Tenoreno's estate."

"How the hell did he find you here?"

Garrison didn't have an answer. Kenderly didn't have a phone on her. He had no landline, so she couldn't have called anyone. She seemed as though she wanted to cooperate, so her betraying their position didn't make sense. And he knew that Oaks didn't do it.

Or did he?

"What if they believe Isabella was communicating with authorities, sir? Is that a possibility? Is another agency involved? They could have waited for a call or followed you."

"However it happened, you've got to get her out of here. We'll wait for him to reload, then move. Toss me that dish towel," Oaks commanded. "He winged my leg, or your aunt's gravy boat cut me."

Garrison tossed the towel and admired the captain's attitude. The force of the bullets ripped through the paper-thin walls of the side of the old house. Dishes shattered inside a cabinet, and the doors burst open. Thank God for the solid table his aunt had squeezed into the tiny kitchen. Though she was clearly going to kill him when she saw what was left.

"I'll get Kenderly."

Garrison belly-crawled to the bathroom, covering his head more often than not. Just as he passed into the short hall, the gunfire stopped. He didn't wait for the captain to begin firing. He kicked open the door and pulled Kenderly from the tub.

"Out the front as soon as I give you the go-ahead."

They moved. She was silent. Oaks fired through the shattered kitchen window. The assassin ceased firing a moment longer.

"Take mine," Oaks shouted, throwing his keys to Garrison. "Phone's busted. Call it in. I'll keep him pinned down."

Garrison had a split second to follow or disobey orders. The small feminine hand latched on to his biceps reminded him they had a witness to protect. That was his first duty.

Not to mention that no one normally argued with Aiden Oaks, captain or otherwise.

Moving Kenderly's hand to his belt, he pointed at her shoes. "Take those off and run beside me. We both get on the driver's side in the street. Take these." He handed her the keys. "Unlock the door while I cover you. I'll drive. You're in the back. Unless something happens to me."

She nodded.

"Go!" Oaks shouted and fired.

Garrison jerked open the door, searching for any accomplices. No shots this direction. They were still on the side of the house. He touched Kenderly's hand, then they moved across the porch. He kept as wide a view as possible, turning, scanning. Then he saw the Tenoreno assassin to his left.

"Run. Hit the unlock button."

She did, the alarm sounded, then he heard door clicks. They got to the far side of the car before shots were fired, but it was the captain out the front door firing at their pursuer.

Both men took cover in the yard. The keys were very steadily placed in his free palm, then Kenderly got inside and lay across the floor. Oaks had their backs covered. He started the engine and got out of there as fast as he could. He tossed his phone in the back.

"Dial 911."

He turned a corner, hitting the brakes to slow the car to a below normal speed and then hearing an "ow" from Kenderly.

"What are you doing?" she asked leaning close to his shoulder. "Oh, the cops." She could see the flashing lights heading past them and skidding around the corner. "Still want me to call?"

With no more flashing lights in sight, he sped up and headed for downtown Austin. "Not if we don't have to. Oaks will be fine. No reason to give the cops my number."

"What now?"

If they were being followed, more traffic would help them get lost. He drove the car as fast as he safely could.

"That's a very good question. I can contact Oaks in a couple of hours to find out what story he spun." *And hope that he has a plan.*

"Maybe they caught Isabella's murderer." She sounded a bit frightened.

He couldn't see her face in the rearview mirror. He couldn't hold her hand, needing both of his on the wheel. She might be scared. She should be, and he had to tell her straight.

"It's more likely he's right behind us." Garrison searched all the mirrors again but couldn't see anyone following. "You should put on a seat belt."

Again with the silence, but she did as he'd suggested. Just ten minutes ago she might have been white-knuckled at his kitchen table, but she'd been talking faster than he was driving. Ready to help with a statement and volunteering new information.

Statements? Where had the video tech crew gone? They should have been there about the time the assassin showed. Another question for Oaks.

"I guess we can't call your captain to find out what happened. Didn't he say his phone was busted?"

"Yeah. They'll try to take him to the hospital. Don't know which one, though." Oaks would be okay. He was their only shot at keeping this operation alive. They just had to hang on until he could contact them.

"Are we going to just drive around until he calls us?"

He shrugged. He hadn't decided where to go. He didn't know of any rangers who were a part of this undercover operation. And then there was the leak. Somehow the assassin had found them. Garrison couldn't believe it was on his department's side of things, but he'd been taught not to rule out any possibility until he had proof.

"I don't think anyone's following, but I still have no clue how that guy found us."

He stopped at a red light and the back door opened. He was ready to yell and his hand was on the handle, but in the blink of an eye Kenderly sat next to him.

"Or how he did it so quickly? Do we still need to record my statement and open the box? Do we wait until your office can do that? Or can you use your phone?"

"We can't wait. I should get hold of a digital recorder and do this thing right. That includes a reliable witness."

"I have a friend who has several cameras. He's an amateur photographer. Don't cameras have a record button now? Will that work?"

"As long as it embeds date information, stuff like that. It's definitely better than doing nothing. He'd have to be willing to testify that we opened the case in front of him."

She waved him off like he was being silly. "No problem. He lives a boring life like me. I bet he's hanging out somewhere on Sixth Street. All we have to do is hit a couple of bars with good music, and we should find him."

"Sixth Street?" Clubbing on a Friday night on the busiest street in Austin was a fate worse than… Okay, not as bad as death. "Can't we wait for him to go home?"

"Sure. He lives across the breezeway from me," she said flippantly, knowing exactly what his reaction would be.

There was no way he was parking this car in Kenderly's lot. Between Tenoreno's men, the police and their assassin all searching for them…that wasn't going to happen. And Kenderly knew it without him saying a word.

"Looks like we're bar crawling."

"I KNOW I'M going to regret this, but I am super hungry." Kenderly hated bar food. It was greasy, normally cold and completely overpriced, but she was totally starving.

"This is the fourth place we've been inside. Do you think he went home?"

"Can I order something?" She hated to beg, but she was getting close to being that desperate.

"I'd rather find this guy and not hang around here too long."

The toast at Garrison's house had only reminded her stomach that it was empty. "Fine." She shoved her hair away from her face.

The bar was crowded and hot. A huge neon sign flashed "Keep Austin Weird" against a mirror, making her want to shade her eyes.

It was hard to breathe at armpit level. For people who were tall, they never had a problem finding each other in a crowd. For someone just over five feet two inches, it was terrible. The last thing she needed was to become light-headed, but that's exactly how she felt.

Shutting her eyes for a second brought the gory image of Isabella and Trinity. She covered her stomach with one hand and clutched her mouth with the other.

"Are you turning green or is it the lights from the dance floor?" Garrison tried to pry her hand away, and she stopped him. "Okay, that's you. Bathroom is…this direction."

Her hero excused himself with each gentle shove to part the crowd. He got her to the ladies' room in record time, cutting straight across the dance floor. And he didn't stop there. Making more excuses, he cut in front of everyone, then flashed his badge when he waltzed through the door with her.

"I've got this part on my own." She tried to push him away before the bile rose.

"Can't let you out of my sight. Sorry, miss. Give us five, will you?" Even though he sounded polite, he wasn't really asking. He guided the last person out before she could use the hand dryer.

"Seriously, Garrison, I'm okay now. Let's just leave." She tried to open the door, and he stopped it with his toe.

"You're still as white as a sheet, Kenderly. Dammit, why don't they have paper towels anymore? Can you splash your face or something?"

The image in the mirror was sort of scary-looking. No makeup, seriously pale. Cooling her skin was actually a good suggestion. "Just getting away from all the people helps tremendously."

She wet her hands and patted her cheeks, cooling her hot flesh. She took a deep breath of semiclean air. The need to throw up no longer registered, so she stood straight and faced Garrison.

"You really okay?" He placed both hands on her shoulders and searched every inch of her face. "Still think you can eat something? Will you keep it down?"

"Yeah, I'm sure. I'm sorry we haven't found my friend."

There was a knock on the door. "Management. Do we have a problem?"

Garrison flattened his lips and raised his eyebrows, sort of shrugging in the process of reaching for the door handle. He flashed his badge before they got a close look, sort of gave an explanation, and they were out on the street without the help of a bouncer after a couple of minutes.

"The cool air feels great." She twirled on the sidewalk as they headed back to their borrowed car, thankful for the crisp feeling in her lungs. "Where do we go from—"

Garrison jerked her in the opposite direction. "Stay close."

She had no idea what was happening. But after having her life threatened twice, she completely trusted the man at her side. He'd tell her when he could. They walked at a very fast pace away from the car.

"What about Isabella's jewelry case?"

"Oaks will have to take care of it. Right now the cops are too close for us to get back to his car." He cursed under his breath.

She looked up and saw the red, white and blue reflections in the windows. "Can't you explain to them who you are?"

"Not unless I want to completely blow my cover and not find the murderer." He slowed a little after they turned a corner. "Right now we're both wanted for questioning."

"So the cops don't know you're a Texas Ranger?" Kenderly looked up and saw a fast-food restaurant. "Can I borrow five dollars?"

"Right. Sure. We'll get something and sit in the back corner." Garrison ushered her through the doors and stood outside checking the street for something. He backed in the door and pulled out his wallet, handing her a twenty. "Bacon cheeseburger, ketchup, no pickles and any soda."

She placed their order and watched him at the front window looking at his phone. He was texting one minute, then talking furiously the next.

No matter what he was currently doing, Kenderly decided to follow his original instructions and sit at the back booth.

"Hey, we're closing in fifteen minutes," the teenager behind the counter called out. "You'll have to leave by then."

"No problem," Garrison let him know.

Kenderly ate her small, dry burger and fries alone. Her hero texted, made more calls and popped outside the door another time. She had no idea if he was leaving messages or holding conversations about her future. His food sat in its bag.

The drink gathered sweat and made a ring around the bottom of the medium cup. She was mesmerized with the droplets.

It kept her from wondering what might have happened if Garrison hadn't been there today. She would be dead. No question about it. She felt helpless. She dipped a fry in the ketchup, and a red drop hit the table. She froze. Even though she knew it was ketchup, she couldn't eat another bite.

The clock over the front door indicated three minutes until they closed. She should quickly use the restroom before they were kicked out. She locked the door behind her and almost immediately heard Garrison yelling on the other side.

"Kenderly, are you there?"

"Give me a second, please? I promise, I can't get away. There aren't any windows."

"We have to get out of here."

"I know, they're closing."

"Listen to me, Kenderly. Cops are gathering outside. The kid must have called us in. Our status changed from wanted for questioning to wanted for murder. It's scrolling on the television. Tenoreno has a bounty on our heads."

Chapter Five

"Do you have any idea where you're going?" Kenderly had lived in Austin most of her life, but she was getting disoriented. Garrison had turned down almost every street and doubled back and then doubled back again. She tugged him to a stop not only to get her bearings but also to catch her breath.

"I'm certain of one thing. We have to keep moving." Garrison reached for her hand, but she took a step away from him.

"I can see that you believe you're right. But I can't keep this up all night." She glanced at her watch. They'd been walking just over an hour since the burger she'd choked down. "Don't you have a plan?"

They'd blended in with college students for a while, but were alone again on the corner of Brazos and Eighth Street. It was late enough that hardly anyone was around in this area.

The thought of being scared fleeted across her mind. She certainly had good reason to feel that way, but she didn't. The Rangers had convinced her they were legit and wanted to protect her. It was hard to get used to having someone else make the decisions. Limited choices as she had, every path she'd taken was completely hers.

He flashed that perfect smile at her and tilted his head like he was actually curious about something. "Sweet-heart—"

"Stop right there. Your wicked gorgeous smile might work on the girls you're trying to pick up and sway back to your tiny little house." She caught her hand shaking as she pointed in the direction they'd come from. She quickly wove her fingers together. She might be upset, but she didn't need to show the world. Or him. "I have no choice except continue wherever you go. I know that. So you don't need to convince me of anything."

"Wicked gorgeous?" He winked.

She had to turn away from him. Appreciating his cavalier attitude was one thing, falling for the charm he oozed with every movement was quite another.

"Just give it to me straight. Bottom-line it."

"I like you, Kenderly Tyler. I really do." He sent another text and then removed the battery from his phone before sliding both back into his pocket. "Our odds aren't very good. Truth is… I didn't think we'd make it this far."

"Well, that's reassuring." If she'd had any choices she might have turned around and run from him. But there weren't any other choices.

She stood beside a set of stairs leading to a church. Sitting on the cold concrete she leaned back only to jolt forward. She'd forgotten that her heels were hooked into her skirt at the small of her back. It might have looked normal for a college student, but she felt silly.

"So, what now?"

For a split second the confident young smile disappeared, and the thoughtful Texas Ranger who had absentmindedly petted his dogs stood there. Maybe he was as lost as her?

"Oh my gosh! Clementine and Bear! Are they okay?"

"They were in the bedroom at the back of the house. I don't think the bullets penetrated that far."

"Those poor puppies. What will happen to them?"

"They have a regular dog walker. She lives across the street. But I sent a message to my buddy, Jesse, to come get them."

Disappointed that they didn't have a way to find out, she rubbed her bare feet and wasn't about to complain. Captain Oaks had been shot, and that man was trying to kill Garrison because he'd helped her.

"Can he come get us, too?" she mumbled.

But he'd heard and grinned. He casually leaned against the corner of the building. Or he tried to look casual. His body was tense. His eyes darted a different direction with each tilt of his head.

"Trouble is, no one really knew that I was at Teno-reno's place. This operation is sort of..." He shrugged.

"Off the record?"

"More like last minute and hasn't gone through all the proper channels."

Kenderly jumped up and ran across the street. "Great. This is just absolutely great. And so in character for my life."

She spun around midintersection to see her escort picking up her shoes, so she continued jogging across the road.

"Kenderly," he said sternly, running after her. "Come on. You know we have to stay together."

"So you have any idea when this is going to end?"

"Look. You're a smart gal. You know life isn't going to be the same. You might want to think about relocating."

"You aren't serious?" His lips pressed firmly into a straight line, and she knew that he was very serious. "What am I going to do?"

Placing both hands on her shoulders, one heel dangling from each, he looked at her for a good thirty seconds. If they'd been at her apartment door… If they'd been on a date or had met at the party Isabella said she could attend…

If. If. If. If things had been different, the moment might have been full of nervous anticipation instead of emotional dread.

"One step at a time, Kenderly. Just one small step. Our first is to find someplace out of the way to hang out for a while. We've got to give Oaks a chance to straighten this manhunt out."

Headlights shone on them as a car turned onto the street where they stood. Garrison ducked his head and curled her into his side. Whoever it was kept going. Loud, happy music poured from the open windows along with the laughter of the young people inside.

Why did she suddenly feel so old? She was only twenty-three, dammit.

The music faded as she watched the taillights disappear. Her fingers curled around the folds of Garrison's T-shirt. The tears came before she could completely bury her face in the soft, dark cotton.

As hard as she tried, she just couldn't stop them. Mournful tears for Isabella and Trinity. Frightened tears for herself. Angry tears that everything she'd worked for was gone.

She didn't know if he was patient about it, but her Texas Ranger wrapped his arms around her and didn't crack a joke. He didn't try to stop her. No attempts to rush things along.

His arms gave her the illusion of being secure. It was a strange feeling, with her body relaxing while her mind raced because she was so frightened.

"Sorry. I didn't mean to cry again." She tilted her head back to look up at him, expecting to see frustration or at least disappointment. There was neither.

"Ready to move out?"

She nodded. He dropped to one knee, sliding his hands down her calf and tapping on her foot.

"Oh, wow. You don't have to do that."

"Lift your foot. I'm down here all ready."

Off balance, she clung to his strong shoulder and let him slip her impractical high heels back into place.

GARRISON HAD SEEN the scrapes on Kenderly's feet. She couldn't move fast in the ridiculous heels, but she wouldn't be able to walk at all if she cut her foot. Putting them on was easier than her trying to accomplish it in the skirt he'd appreciated more on his bike.

What should he do?

"I need to check on Oaks." He stood and guided his witness up the street. He recognized where they were. The capitol wasn't too far away.

"Well, we can't walk into the hospital. Not with our faces splashed all over the TV."

"Right."

"You don't even know which one they took him to."

"Right again." He kept watch. Kept expecting the cops around every corner. They didn't have time for explanations. Should he just take Kenderly to Rangers headquarters and let them straighten the mess out? Or stick with her until the captain was giving orders again?

"And I hate to be a wimp, but I'm really tired. I don't know how much longer I can stay awake. Let alone move my legs to walk."

"Got it."

"You wouldn't happen to have an emergency credit

card, do you? I have one, but it's at my apartment. I leave it there since, of course, it's only for emergencies."

Garrison halted and checked his back pocket. He was an idiot. All this time he'd been worried about the police tracking any transactions or his phone. He didn't have to worry about that with his real name. Just his undercover identity.

"Don't worry. Your time walking the streets is over."

"If I wasn't so relieved, I'd make you correct that street-walking phrase. But I am very grateful not to walk another step. Are we grabbing a cab?"

He wouldn't mention aloud that he'd had his own wallet the entire time. He hadn't had a chance to switch them after Oaks decided to send him back to Tenoreno's.

"Are you going to call or something?" Kenderly asked, giving her skirt a habitual tug.

Her eyes looked as exhausted as she claimed. Her hair wasn't nearly as tangled as when she'd first arrived at the house. He really liked how it was so many different colors. Every place they'd been she looked like a different woman.

There were other things he liked. Of course, being responsible for her, he couldn't tell her how good she looked in sequins and silk. Or how the unrealistic heels made her legs look four inches longer.

His hands itched to touch the smooth skin of her thigh again…

"We should get a cheap motel room until I receive some orders. And maybe pick up some sweats for you."

"Sweatpants? Couldn't we just get me some jeans? But you're not talking about right now. Or are you?" She grabbed his wrist and flipped it to see his watch. "It's almost three in the morning."

"Okay. Got it." He partly listened, partly searched for

their enemy and tried to keep thinking about their options. Nothing seemed to be going their way. Not even a cab. "Where can we catch a ride?"

"Oh, good grief. We need to head back to Congress Street." She laced her fingers through his. "Just so you know. I'm not really a sweatpants type of girl."

Holding hands was standard practice. Along with dragging him across the street, heading west again. She leaned into his arm, using his body to steady the fast pace. He was proud of her for hanging in there so well. He almost opened his mouth to tell her but thought again. It somehow felt intimate to tell her.

Shoot. He needed sleep himself if he was having this type of debate in his head. More importantly, he should be making plans. Deciding where they could stay, someplace a manager wouldn't call the police.

"Would calling the police be so bad?"

"Huh? How did you know…?"

"You were mumbling. So, would it? Would calling them be so bad?"

"It would ruin our chances of catching Tenoreno."

"Well, then we're definitely not going to the police. I want that horrid man to spend the rest of his days rotting in jail. Even if he didn't pull the trigger, he was responsible."

Garrison felt Kenderly's determination through her fingers squeezing his biceps. Yep, he liked her. He felt himself smiling without anyone looking.

Nice. Wait. Not nice. She's my witness.

They spotted the cab at the same time. Their hands separated, and Kenderly's earsplitting whistle got the cabbie's attention.

"Evening."

"Hi," Kenderly responded to the driver, then looked at Garrison. "Where to?"

"I...um... I'm not sure."

The driver tapped his finger against the steering wheel, flipped the meter on, then tapped again. At least he wasn't listening to local news. Their descriptions were accurate enough, and the burger shop probably let the police know what they were wearing. At least, if Garrison was the cop assigned to their case, he would have gotten a description.

"Hey, buddy, I need to get going. So where to?"

"Take us south on I-35."

"Got a particular place in mind?" the cabbie asked.

"I can't remember the name, but I'll tell you when I see it."

"Sure," the driver said.

"You have no clue where, do you?" Kenderly whispered.

He crossed his fingers and showed them to her. She covered her mouth, but he heard the giggle.

Fifteen minutes later, there was no laughter. He checked them into a semisleazy motel. Sheets in hand, he unlocked the door facing the highway and wished he hadn't flipped on the light. It wasn't the worst place he'd stayed in, but it was far from the best.

A long sigh escaped from Kenderly next to him. "At least they didn't assume we needed it by the hour."

Chapter Six

"Coffee."

Garrison smelled his favorite morning aroma before he pulled his nose from the pillow. He raised his head, squinting as the light bounced from the metal part of a car parked in front of their room.

"Good morning." Kenderly carefully crossed her legs while sitting in the one chair in the corner of the room.

"Where'd you get a grande?" At least that's what he hoped he asked. He wasn't really sure his mouth was working at the same rate as his brain. He sprang up. "What the hell, Kenderly? You went out for coffee?"

"Well, I was desperate for food. The coffee came with."

"You're missing the point. You left this room on your own? What if you'd been seen? Our pictures are probably everywhere this morning."

Didn't say a whole lot for his skills if a hairdresser left and returned without him waking up. He might just have to leave that out of the final report.

"Well, first, I was really hungry and thought you would be, too." She pointed toward a plastic bag and a Styrofoam cup. "And second, I was very careful. I avoided cameras and wore your T-shirt."

"I can see that." She looked good in his clothes. Or partially in his clothes. She still had the dressy short skirt.

He stretched his arms above his head, tracking Kenderly's reaction. She sipped the hot drink a little too quickly, swallowing extra hard as she watched him.

"Breakfast doesn't make up for you leaving on your own."

"It was probably safer since they're looking for a man and woman traveling together. Of course, they think we're long gone from Austin and haven't connected us to the shoot-out at your house." She pushed the paper—neatly sitting under his breakfast—across the small, rickety nightstand. "At least according to the *Austonian*, which covered both stories."

"Still…"

"You were out. I really did try to wake you. I mean, just trying to get off that bed. It rocks more than my grandma's rocker."

They laughed. And she sipped again. Coffee was coffee, and he needed his morning ration. Just as he reached for the cup, his stomach growled loud enough to be heard through the thin walls.

"Goodness. I'm glad I got you the deluxe breakfast."

"I thank you for that." He pulled a biscuit off the plate and shook it at Kenderly. "But don't leave my side again until you're told. I can't protect you if you aren't there."

"Any idea how long that will be? And for the record, you could have asked politely instead of commanding."

"Do you think the person trying to kill you will ask politely?" He tried to shock some sense into her, but had a feeling that commanding Kenderly to do anything was going to be a challenge.

"You have a point."

"Of course I have a point. This isn't a game." He

scooped his cell and the battery from the top of the television—for which they'd been charged extra to have in the room. He admired Kenderly's shapely legs while waiting for it to boot up. Then he forced his eyes to scan the phone. "There's plenty of reception here, but nothing from Oaks. At least Jesse has my dogs."

"That's such a relief. I assume they're okay?"

"He didn't say otherwise." Just as a precautionary measure, he removed the battery and shoved both into his pocket. He dove into the take-out breakfast, inhaling the scrambled eggs in two bites. "I am thanking you for this because I was hungry. Just don't do it again, okay?"

"I promise. But I really did try to wake you up."

"That I'll never believe. You were up early. Did you manage to get any sleep?"

"Me? Sure. I was snug all wrapped up in the clean sheets you rented from the manager."

"Did I snore?" He shoveled in the last bite and dropped his back to the bedspread, taking a deep breath.

"Not really." She twisted her finger in the hem of his shirt. "I suppose you need this back."

"It'll probably be easier to get into a store. You know, no shirt, no service. That sort of thing." He sat and reached for his boots.

"Isn't that risky? I mean, you were worried about me getting coffee. Won't stores have security cameras? Where will we go after that?"

"We'll avoid showing our faces. But if we want to stay put somewhere, we'll need supplies. Food, clothes—"

"A toothbrush," she added.

They needed practical items to hide out. Kenderly would need things no matter who babysat her. If he was going to finish his assignment, he'd still need a way to defend himself…and a toothbrush wouldn't hurt.

"You also need out of those four-inch monsters. How were you cutting hair like that? I don't see how any woman walks around on stilts."

"Isabella hired me to *fix* their hair, not cut it. I did that Wednesday. And I told you this, she said I could come to the party afterward. But I was just going to sit by the wall and watch. Maybe have a glass of champagne, try some of the food." She shrugged her shoulders that were swallowed by his T-shirt.

He hadn't noticed how petite she was yesterday. The heels threw off her real height—like they were supposed to do. Thinking about it, she hadn't acted small. Everything about her was strong. She might have cried a couple of times, but she hadn't fallen apart.

Her words finally hit his brain. Were their sources wrong? Was it just a social gathering for the two families or had they intended to merge? "She invited you to a Tenoreno-Rosco meeting?"

"Wasn't it a party?"

"Not according to our sources. Then again, they could have been covering something up by inviting more people."

"Something like the murder of two women?"

"Yeah." He fingered the fading curtains to the side and checked the perimeter. He also noticed that Kenderly's hands tightened into fists, and there wasn't a tear in sight. "You might be right about that. Sure would be nice to know what was in that jewelry case Isabella gave you. Still no idea why she'd trust you with it?"

"I told you, she was my friend."

"And you really didn't know her husband is head of one of the biggest crime syndicate families in the South?" Garrison watched her closely.

She covered her lips with the tip of her finger and

shook her head. She was hiding something. He could feel it. Knew immediately that she was trying to lie. All the classic tells were there. She looked away, bit her lip, brought her hands closer into her body and stopped talking.

"Finished?" She began gathering the trash.

He reached across the stool-sized table and stopped her hand. "You don't have to clean up after me."

"I just need to *do* something. Anything. Did Isabella die because she gave me some letters?"

"I doubt it was that simple. It might have been what was in those letters. Or what her husband thought was in them. It could be because he was afraid of another divorce splintering the family. His son's wife left him last year. Made the news cycle for a while."

"Isabella mentioned they were petitioning the church for an annulment. Of course, even if the annulment went through, they don't know where she disappeared to."

"I believe she disappeared because she was afraid they'd take matters into their own hands."

"As in kill her so an annulment wasn't necessary?" Her entire body shook with the recognition. "Do you think Isabella was planning to leave, too? It just doesn't seem anything like her. She was more upset about the sin of divorce than her son being unhappy."

"Oh, I think he was happy. We have a file of all the women he was sleeping around with."

"So, you've been watching the Tenorenos for a while then?" Kenderly's eyebrows lifted in an arch. The sun brightened her brown eyes to the same color he liked his coffee.

"I think we'd be better off developing a definitive plan for us today. We can't stay here."

"What about Mr. Oaks? Are you worried? I know I

would be." She tapped a manicured nail at a picture of the ranch house they'd fled from. "At least he's not dead, or it would have been in the papers."

It didn't matter if he were worried about his captain or not. He had a job to do before personal feelings or distractions. Long legs or shiny pink nails or eyes the color of his coffee.

"True. First things first. We need a car."

KENDERLY CLOSED HER eyes and took another deep breath. It was necessary to keep the tears tucked away until she could hide her face in her pillow later. She'd cried after they'd gotten situated in the room. Partly feeling sorry for herself, but mainly because she couldn't get the images of Isabella and Trinity out of her mind. No movie could ever compare to the reality of their deaths.

The amount of detail she kept recalling frightened her. Seriously frightened her. The wind had caught the outside door to the rental car building, making the same sound as when the balcony doors had burst open in Isabella's room. She'd barely made it to a bench with her shaky knees.

Garrison had left the counter and helped her. He hadn't spoken, thank goodness. She wouldn't have been able to keep it together if he'd asked her anything.

He was waiting on the keys. She was waiting on her stomach to stop rolling. She jumped out of her skin when he touched her shoulder.

"Oh, God, you scared me."

"Sorry. You ready to go?"

"Sure." She accepted his outstretched hand and was surprised when he laced his long fingers through hers.

She was noticing all sorts of things about Garrison. During their conversation that morning, he'd compressed his lips when she'd mentioned Isabella's ex-daughter-in-law was missing. As if he had more information he couldn't share or knew the answer to her questions.

Noticing him was a nice distraction. It was hard to miss the way his muscles flexed with every simple movement. He had a strong, firm grip. Confident that she wouldn't shake her hand free. It made her feel safer—even if she knew it was just a pipe dream. Paul Tenoreno would never let her live. Not if he thought she had anything to do with his wife's murder.

"What if—" She grabbed Garrison's arm with her free hand, pulling them to a stop. Lowering her voice as soon as she heard it echo in the hallway, she started again. "What if they think I let that man inside the room? Is that why…" Her eyes filled, and she reached up to swipe them dry. "Dammit. It's a good thing I don't have any makeup. I doubt there's a mascara in the world that could weather this amount of tears."

"It's okay. Come on." He pointed her through the doors, urging her to walk a little faster by placing his hand in the small of her back.

"I'm right, aren't I?" She heard her nervous laughter and couldn't stop it. At least they were outside now, and it didn't bounce around the empty walls of the airport rental center.

"Hold it together until we're inside the car, will you?"

"I'm good." *Or hysterical.* "I can handle this. I've handled tough situations before. Not as tough as this, of course. But at least I thought they were tough at the time."

Garrison turned her toward him and tilted her chin up with his index finger. Their eyes met, and he held her gaze. She couldn't look away. She didn't want to.

"Don't fall apart on me now, Kenderly," he whispered.

She managed a nod. He smiled and tucked her into his side.

The car appeared, and he calmly drove them away from the airport, back toward the city. They went through another fast food drive-through. He ordered something for her and set the sack in her lap. Then a bank to make a withdrawal. And then they were on the highway.

"Do you have a plan now?" she asked, unable to keep the shakiness from her voice.

"You should eat so you'll feel better."

"I don't think a bacon cheeseburger will do much good."

"Fries might." He winked and smiled. Then he realized what he'd done and drew his brow in concentration. "Okay, look, I'll have more of a plan after I know the captain is letting someone know we're not the murderers. But I need to get you out of this county, get a throwaway phone and call Jesse. He should have an updated status. Might have a couple of suggestions where I can take you."

"What if he's not? Conscious, that is. What if Captain Oaks is out of the picture? Is there anyone else we can ask for help? Will your friend Jesse hide us?"

"One step at a time, Kenderly." He tapped the top of the food sack. "Eat."

She bit into a burger identical to the one he'd already finished. Fortunately, she could barely taste the ketchup that she hated on any sandwich. She stared out the window, watching the cars and buildings they passed. People going about their business like any other ordinary day.

There was no room to fall apart while on the run from crime bosses and assassins. How insane was it that the thought even crossed her mind? Today was supposed to be ordinary.

"I wonder if anyone at the shop canceled my appointments? Barbara Baker has a color at one and will be severely ticked off when I don't show up. And I have a new perm at four."

"That's the least of your problems," he said, both hands gripping the steering wheel tightly.

"You're right. But that was my life, my livelihood, my reputation. I've worked too hard to watch it disappear in an instant." Her head collided against the glass as he swerved to change lanes. "Hey, um…aren't you going a little fast?"

"Someone's following us."

"That's impossible. How could they find us?"

"Hold on. We're making our own exit."

She dropped the burger and held on with both hands as Garrison cut in front of two lanes of cars and slid down an embankment. Horns blared. Cars skidded. Kenderly squeezed her eyes shut as the side of the rental headed on to the access road. There were a lot of cars on the frontage road. She had no idea how Garrison turned at the last minute, missing them all.

Before she could celebrate, the car following them slid down the incline, too. Garrison had to lose him. But how? His answer was to go faster. She braced herself, but with each swerve it was harder to maintain her grip.

Each second ticked by as a series of movements. One to judge if he could dart in front of a car. One to jump ahead of another. One to apologize for putting so many lives in danger. The next one to illegally U-turn between two pickups. Another to skid through a right turn. One long moment to fishtail into a used car lot, barely missing the iron post where the gate was swung open.

All she could do was pray that the man following didn't see them turn.

When he slowed, he pulled his cell and battery out of

his pocket and held them in his palm. "Dial 911. It's the only way to get you safe. This guy's not going to stop."

"But—"

"We don't have a choice. Do it!"

She threw the sack of food into the back and reached for the phone, but it went flying.

"Grab hold!" Garrison yelled as he hit the brakes.

Kenderly had kept calm and hadn't screamed...until then.

Chapter Seven

Garrison slammed on the brakes too late to avoid the drop-off. What he thought to have been an exit ramp was just a broken piece of concrete. The wheels of the car popped over the curb and shot them into the air.

The top of a building, then a light pole, then a parking lot sloped on a hill. He watched Kenderly slam sideways. Thank God it was only about a four foot drop. The rental's undercarriage caught on the retaining wall so the air bags didn't deploy.

"Stupid. Now what?" He hit the steering wheel once, then turned to Kenderly.

She was out cold.

The person following them would have them trapped shortly. Garrison checked Kenderly's head. No blood, just a huge goose egg on her temple. He had to get them out of there.

The car was still running. He stepped on the gas, smoke billowing from the front tires. But nothing budged. Men ran across the parking lot he'd crashed through, then scrambled out of the way of a speeding car. The murdering son of a bitch from the previous day was driving the car.

Garrison jumped from the car—really jumped since it was firmly stuck. He scrambled to the passenger side.

One of the garage workers was there prying the door open. Wordlessly, he gave Garrison a leg up so he could pop the seat belt. Kenderly slumped sideways with him, and they got her free.

"Thanks for the help." Garrison caught Kenderly over his shoulder.

"She okay? The cops are on their way."

"I've got no time to explain. She's dead if we don't—"

"We got it, man." He hit his palm with the pry bar he'd used on the door. "He won't follow you this way. 'Less he's a cop."

Garrison did a questioning turn trying to decide which way to run. "Not a cop. Thanks, but I can't let you do that. He's armed—"

"The dry cleaners has a back door that's always open. The lady's safety is more important. Let us help."

It was hard to walk away, but the stranger was right. He hoped that the man following them wouldn't draw his weapon.

Down the embankment and across the lot. Every second anticipating the worst. Would he feel the impact of the bullet or hear the fatal shot first? He made it to the propped-open front door of the cleaners.

Nothing. Not even shouting. Wheels peeled out.

The murdering son of a bitch had been kept in his car by the onlookers.

"Oh, Lord. What be happenin' out there? She dead?"

The woman behind the counter might help if he asked. But they couldn't stay. "Which way?"

She jerked her thumb over her right shoulder. He ran through the maze of baskets and steam. He couldn't turn, fearing he'd whack Kenderly's head on something else. She hadn't stirred. Once he saw the open door, he ran faster.

A slight pause to verify no madman was in the alley, then up a grassy slope and across another back drive of a gas station.

What now?

The words bounced around in his brain. He'd jumped from the car, forgetting to swipe up his phone and battery. How had that bastard found them? Right that moment, it didn't matter how. It mattered that the murderer had.

He adjusted Kenderly on his shoulder, tugging at her skirt to make sure she was decent. He had no clue where to go. Dumpster? Inside? Steal a car? Make a run for it?

But he crossed all the options off as soon as he listed them. Delivery truck. He tried the door. Open. It was their only chance. He climbed into the back and maneuvered Kenderly with him as gently as possible. No way to lock the door behind him.

There was no real place to hide and no weapon unless he threw cardboard boxes. Not much of a defense for an assassin with a gun. Packages on either side of them, a special roof kept it well lit on the inside so he could see how pale Kenderly was.

"Come on, sweetheart. Wake up." Completely out and probably needed a doctor.

Tires screeched to a halt—the murderer. Metal crashed into metal—the Dumpster lid. The door raised an inch or two. Men shouted.

"You ain't stealing from my rig, you son of a bitch. Somebody call the cops."

Garrison heard a scuffle. A short one.

"That's right, run, you big lug."

Tires squealed, then the car's engine noise grew fainter.

"I'm fine, everybody. Thanks for your help. Not the

first time I dealt with some loony tunes," the owner of the truck said.

The door shut. The driver got in the front, cranked the truck and pulled out. Garrison sat out of his line of sight, pulling Kenderly into his arms. This was the only way. If the delivery guy drove straight to the police, it would be better than getting shot between the eyes.

"Kenderly," he whispered as softly as he could. He was so close that his words were cupped by the curve of her ear. "I need you to wake up now, babe."

She stirred with a short moan that the driver didn't hear over the natural noise of the truck. Garrison didn't care if he did hear. Relief saturated him as thoroughly as when he'd gotten the news he'd been accepted as a ranger.

The color was coming back to her cheeks as her eyes fluttered open. He gently covered her mouth while pressing a finger to his own. When her eyes registered, he got back close to her ear.

"Just hang tight, and we'll get out at the next stop."

Her eyes shut, and she relaxed her head against his arm. Her hand found his and latched on tightly. He should take her to the hospital. A possible concussion, maybe worse. She should be observed by doctors. His gut told him they'd be sitting ducks in a hospital.

Which wouldn't be necessary if he hadn't thought his phone was safe to use. How the hell had they been found? Who was this maniac working for?

He didn't have long to think about it since the truck pulled over and stopped. The driver consulted his clipboard, then stood facing the back where the packages were.

"What the hell are you doing in my truck? Don't tell me. The SOB back at the station was after you and you hid inside?"

"I can explain."

"I don't need no explanation. That SOB was crazy-eyed. But I can't give you a ride back to your car. It's against regs."

"Thanks for the help."

"Okay. Fine. So go already." He backed into the built-in shelves, gesturing that they should pass.

Kenderly was apparently still a little stunned. It took her a second to realize she was sitting on his lap and needed to stand first. Garrison followed, squeezing by the rather large driver.

"Excuse me," Kenderly asked. "Is that Highway 183 back there?"

"Yes, ma'am, 183 and North Lamar."

"Sweet." She took their surroundings in at a glance and walked toward the street.

"Wait a minute. Where are you going?"

"I worked nights up here for a while. A restaurant near North Capital." She faced the driver again. "A couple of miles that way, right?"

The driver had a package in his hands ready to step from the truck. He looked at Kenderly and shrugged. "I'm going that way. Stay put while I get a signature." He ran down the sidewalk into the office buildings.

"Do you think he'll get in trouble? It shouldn't take us long to walk. I think I can get us a car, and you can call your friends."

He grabbed her by the arm and spun her around harder than he'd intended. "Wait just a damn minute. They might let us use one phone while they call our location into the cops."

"I know these people. They'd never do something like that. The cops are the last people they want there."

"Money does strange things to people. Are you forgetting about the reward Tenoreno put on our heads?" She tried to shake off his grasp, but he was determined she wouldn't get free. "Give it up. You aren't going anywhere 'til I get my bearings and think this through."

"So why don't you ask to borrow the driver's phone?"

"I don't think the man likes to share. You didn't hear him get the crazy bastard chasing us to back down." The delivery man was pretty good swinging that tire iron. "You shouldn't be walking a lot. We're taking him up on the ride offer."

She rubbed her temple and winced when her fingers crossed the lump. "We're lucky to be alive. You know that, right? How did that creep find us anyway?" She took a side step to lean on the door, either trying to break free or ignoring him.

"Kenderly. Wait. I need a minute to think." He pulled her next to him, backing up to the truck, watching around them as much as he could. If they'd been followed...

"Can't we think once we're inside a building where the sun isn't blaring and making this headache worse? Besides, what's there to think about? The big bad murderer found us and tried to kill us a—"

"Now you're with me. We know he's the murderer, and he's not going to give up just because a truck driver scared him off for a few minutes."

The driver emerged from the building whistling and waved at them to get inside. He looked around all the corners as much as Garrison had. Kenderly was already inside. Garrison followed just one step ahead of the driver jumping in and throwing the truck in gear.

"They have a tracker in the truck. I can't turn off my route or I'll have some explaining to do, which I don't want to do. Get me?"

"I'm sure wherever you can drop us is fine." Kend-

erly had to raise her voice over the truck noise. She had
tried to keep standing, but ended up sitting on the floor.

His mind freed up and began working again. It finally sank in that the murderer had found them by tracking his real name, finding the rental, using it. That took
connections.

The truck stopped once more. Kenderly thanked the
driver over and over again, elbowing Garrison in the ribs
several times. He took the hint and thanked him once or
twice before holding her hand and running to the building's edge.

"I figured it out," he told her when she faced him.
"In order to find us, he has to be working for one of the
crime bosses. They're the only ones with connections
that could have sent him looking for me."

"Somehow they found out who owned your house."
Kenderly shaded her eyes. He hadn't noticed how bright
everything was reflecting off the cement lots and cars.

"Yeah. After they knew my real name, it would be a
cinch to search my credit card activity."

"Which led them to the rental car company."

"And my cell. They could have bribed or threatened
someone to locate us via the GPS in the car." He blocked
the sun from his own eyes and scanned the cars. None
of them were black. None had dark tinted windows. But
the murderer was out there.

The corner where they stood was visible from only
two directions parallel to the highway. They needed to
disappear. "Risking the restaurant is our only option. But
just so we're clear. It's a bad option."

"Believe me, Joey Crouch does not want the police
near him." She laughed and stepped away.

Garrison caught her arm. She turned to him with

brows raised, her brown eyes sparkling in spite of the headache she had. "Who is this guy to you?"

"An old friend and an old boss."

"Boyfriend? He the reason you don't work there any-more?"

"As a matter of fact, no. I finished up school and went to work full-time. I no longer needed to work nights. My life was in order, Ranger Travis. Was yours?" She walked and he let her.

Perfect timing as the delivery truck pulled by blocking anyone's view. They crossed with the light. He hurried her toward the patio of the building, scooping her over the short hedge and gently setting her on the other side.

The couple finishing their meal shot a couple of looks, but it didn't stall Kenderly. She wove her way through the tables, and he followed—one look to her and a complete spin to see if they were being followed.

"Hi, Jen. Is Joey here today?"

"Kenderly. What in the world happened to you?" The restaurant hostess with her arms full of menus laughed. "Have a rough night, hon?"

"Is he in the kitchen?"

"Where else would he be?" Jen set the stack down and took a step toward the door.

"That's okay," Kenderly said. "I know the way. I don't want to pull you away from your work."

Garrison wished he could have seen Kenderly's ex-pression, because he caught a glance of Jen's. A cross between guilt and satisfaction. Kenderly's tone sort of implicated a love triangle. One more glance at the streets. No black sedan.

Garrison had to speed walk to catch up with Kenderly before she stopped short of the kitchen. She gave an exaggerated tug on her skirt, shoved her fingers through her hair and wiped her face with both hands.

She mumbled, "I wish I had my shoes," before pushing the swinging door aside and stepping through. Garrison looked at her bare feet. He'd been so busy rescuing her, he hadn't noticed he'd left her shoes back at the car.

The staff was light at this time of day. They all greeted his witness with welcome surprise. One tall dude stood near the stove, arms crossed, black hair pushed back from his naturally tanned face. He appeared to be over thirty, but if Garrison admitted it to himself, he was good-looking enough to probably attract a young woman like Kenderly.

Not that he'd readily admit that to anyone else.

There was a hard, resentful look. As his staff—it was obvious he was in charge—looked toward him, his sternness cracked with a broad smile. Shoot. He understood how Kenderly saw through him so quickly.

Ex-boyfriend Joey had the same smile as him. Of all the stinkin' luck.

"Kenderly, darling. It's been ages and ages." If Joey's smile wasn't wide enough, he opened his arms. Why? Expecting her to run into them? "Who's this?"

"A friend. Can we talk a minute?" She avoided his arms and led the way toward a door by the dish-washing station.

Outside. Potential targets again. Kenderly might have been wishing for shoes, but he was wishing for his sidearm. He wanted to gauge this character's reaction, but he watched the perimeter and listened.

"It's been a while, Kenderly."

"Yes. We both know why, and there's no need to dredge it up."

"This my replacement?" Gone was all pretense of a happy return. There was animosity in his voice. "Or did you bring muscle to get your way?"

Maybe he hadn't cheated on her, after all.

The sounds of the highway interfered with Kenderly's mumbled words, but not with Joey's "you owe me."

"Really, baby? You going to bring that up after all this time?" Joey's voice continued getting louder with a touch of anger mixed in.

Garrison forced himself to keep his back to the conversation. He searched each passing car for the guy who'd been chasing them. The look he'd gotten had been quick and blurred, but he'd recognize him again. It wasn't enough to look for the car. He might have ditched it. So he stared, growing angrier himself at each word Joey spat.

"I owe you nothing," Kenderly answered. "In fact, I'm here to collect on that little problem you have."

"Nobody will believe you, baby. It's been two years."

"You're right. Of course, you're right. But I don't think two years is long enough to avoid prosecution for tax evasion. And don't call me baby."

There was a quick movement in Garrison's peripheral vision. He spun and caught Joey's hand on the way toward Kenderly's face. "Not a good idea, buddy."

"I wasn't going to hit her. Just try to—" He yanked his arm. "Do you mind?"

"Yeah. A lot."

Kenderly smiled, but Garrison didn't let go. "I need to borrow your car and cell. And a couple of hundred cash would be nice."

"There's no way in hell I'm doing that, b—"

Garrison dropped the man's arm but stuck a finger in his face. "Watch it."

"It's okay, honey. I've got this," she said patting his shoulder. "Joey owes me big-time. Would it help if I promised to be careful? Oh, and never mention your little off-the-books business again."

"No way, baby. I can't do that." Joey shook his head and waved them off with his hands.

"Sure you can." Garrison wouldn't strong-arm the ex-boyfriend again. Not unless he threatened Kenderly. On the other hand, there was no harm letting the man think he would. They were desperate.

Chapter Eight

Kenderly tried calmly lacing her fingers together in her lap. It didn't work. She didn't feel secure and had almost bitten through the inside of her lip. Joey's sports car didn't help. With each shift in gears, her heart revved a little higher.

The built-in safety handle would be too obvious. It would make her look scared. Dammit, she was scared. What did it hurt if Garrison knew it? She reached up, latching on with a death grip.

She was so ready for a nice slow drive in the country. Barely missing cars at every juncture was beginning to take its toll. Not to mention being shot at, running, sleeping like a mummy—when she'd slept at all. Garrison was staying with traffic, but definitely pushing the speed limit and switching lanes like a maniac. The fast corners she could manage. Just no more parking lots.

"I know it's hard, but I want to get away from that area as fast as we can."

"Do you have a destination in mind?" Kenderly used her left hand to grip the console, wedging herself in place. If she'd been more prepared the last time, she may not have hit her head. "Any place with aspirin?"

"I'm delivering you to my company in Waco. It's the

safest place for you to be. They'll take care of you, and I can come back to sort through this mess."

"That doesn't work for me." The words were out before she realized the thought was there. She didn't want him to leave her anywhere. The panic rose faster than he was driving.

"Don't be naive, Kenderly. My first duty is to get you to safety. I can't investigate the murders or find this guy who's after you as long as you're in danger."

She knew about his assignment, knew he had a duty. She felt her eyes welling with tears. Frightened of starting over again, of trying to trust yet another person who had nothing to risk but their job.

"Us. He wants to kill you, too," she reminded him, blinking the moisture away.

Garrison gave her a quick sideways look. Did he think she was crazy? Did he really think he was invisible? Of course he did. He was a Texas Ranger. Maybe he was above being scared.

"What if he finds me wherever I am? What if whoever's behind this doesn't ever stop sending killers? What if we get stopped before you get to Waco, and we're arrested on the spot? What if—"

"Whoa. That's a lot of what ifs. How about trying *what if* you trust my judgment and experience?" He let off the gas. A car actually passed him. "Taking you to Waco is a risk I'm willing to take. The men of Company F know me. Know that I'm one of them. Know that a ranger would never commit murder."

"I'd rather find out what's in the jewelry box. Don't you want to know what happened to Captain Oaks?"

"Of course I do."

"Then why don't we take a breath, slow down and maybe talk some of this through?"

"Once you're safe in Waco." He relaxed a little, draping his wrist over the top of the wheel. "Why would you want to play detective and risk that SOB finding you again?"

"Isabella was my friend."

"Who would want you to stay alive."

"But also trusted me to finish something for her. What if she gave me evidence that would convict the person who ordered her death?"

"The Rangers can take care of this…even without us."

Did she really need this man to make all the decisions regarding her life? She was out of her mind if she thought she didn't. But there was a feeling that she needed to stay in Austin. Maybe because she'd always been in charge of her own life. She couldn't dismiss Isabella's faith in her as easily as Garrison could.

"Do you trust them?" she asked. "These men you work with."

"Only with my life."

"Then how come you're wanted for murder?" Why would anyone jump to the conclusion that an undercover ranger would murder two women? Was Mr. Tenoreno truly that powerful?

"I'm certain Company F is wondering the same thing." He slowed and stopped for a red light.

"That's not really an answer. I think I'll take this." She gathered the cell with shaking fingers, not knowing completely what she would do. But she couldn't run and hide. Isabella had depended on her.

"Who are you going to—"

She got out of the car, slamming the door and cutting his words off before she could change her mind. She ran between the cars, across two lanes to the right side of the road. It would take him a few minutes to make a U-turn and come back for her.

Or at least she thought it would. She turned around to find him following. On foot. The light turned green, and cars began honking. It was a busy street, but it didn't stop him.

"Leave me alone, Garrison!" She looked around for a place to run. She had picked the only street with no store or gas station around. Just a covered bus stop.

"No way. I have a job to do."

It didn't take him long to catch her. She was barefoot and wearing a ridiculous party skirt. Horns and shouts from other drivers didn't hide their exerted breathing as they faced each other. He held on to her arms, but it didn't frighten her. His grip assured her she wasn't going anywhere without him, but the look in his eyes was admiration. Not anger.

"Come on before somebody calls the police." He cocked his head back toward Joey's car and smiled. Genuinely. Only for her. Not part of a calculated plan.

Fingers laced, he led her quickly through the cars. It didn't go unnoticed that he pressed the auto-lock as soon as he was also inside. But she wasn't going anywhere. As soon as she'd made it to the sidewalk, she knew she was in trouble. She had no idea how to go about helping Isabella on her own.

Even more than that, she had no one to turn to for help. She would just be putting her friends in danger if she went to them. She needed the Texas Rangers as much as Garrison relied on them.

A mile or so up the road, he pulled over on a residential street and twisted sideways in his seat to look at her. "I admire you, Kenderly. I really do. But you have to be reasonable about this."

"I know you're right, but running away to save myself just feels so...wrong."

He reached out and cupped both of his hands around hers resting on the console.

Hold it.

"Wait a minute." She slipped her hand from his and leaned back against the door. "I've known you a little over twenty-four hours, but this comforting thing...it's not you. What happened to the overconfident Texas Ranger on the motorcycle?"

"That's a relief. I didn't know how long I could keep that up." He winked. "I need the phone."

She handed it to him, a little confused as to what that scene was about. Garrison was a mixture of arrogance and cocky. That was definitely appealing for a while, but those men never ever turned out to be the comforting type. He wasn't a jerk. At least she didn't believe he was. But it sure would have taken a lot to prove he wasn't. That is, if they'd met under different circumstances. Was it just an act?

"I'm looking up news footage. If they're reporting on the condition of Oaks, they'll be in front of... Gotcha. Brecken Ridge Hospital. If that don't beat all. It's right back where we were last night."

"Are you calling them? They won't give you any information."

"It can't hurt to try. Somebody might slip up and let us know something."

The car automatically connected to the phone, and she heard it dialing. Garrison put a finger across his lips.

"Brecken Ridge Hospital, how may I direct your call?"

"May I have the room for Captain Aiden Oaks?"

"I'm sorry, that information is restricted. May I help with something else?"

"No, thanks."

He disconnected. He could have taken it off speaker but hadn't. He could have driven straight to Waco without any other discussion. Instead he'd parked and included her. Now what was he up to?

"He's still there, still alive. He must have been shot more seriously than he let on. I admit that I wondered if he was the primary leak that left me out to dry. Then again, Tenoreno has so many dirty cops and politicians in his pocket that I don't think Oaks would have faked an investigation."

"Somehow I don't believe you were thinking of him like that."

"I might rule Oaks out simply because he's a ranger. But I don't think we're going to get close enough for a chat to verify our roles in yesterday." He continued to scan news about the shooting from the day before. "Thing is, we're out of the loop. I don't have a way of knowing if it's better to take you to Waco. As much as I want to jump in and clear my name, my orders were to keep you safe."

He flipped the phone toward her, and she saw the headline: State Manhunt for Rogue Ranger.

"Do you really think it's a good idea to leave Austin?" She genuinely wanted to know. If this man was willing to risk his career to protect her, that meant something. She should trust him completely. Right?

It was just so hard to do. No one had really been there for her to practice that particular skill. The situation was calling for her to quickly overcome big time therapy issues…without any therapy.

"We need to talk with Jesse. We'll call, and you can pretend that you're the dog sitter. Whoever's chasing us knows all about me, so they might be monitoring his phone. We'll see if it's safe."

"How do I do that? I don't know what to ask."

He dialed. "Let him do most of the talking. If I shouldn't come home, he'll find a way to let me know."

"Jesse Ryder."

"This is…um…the dog sitter for Bear and Clementine. I just wanted to see if things were okay."

"Sure. They're happy to be here."

Kenderly shrugged her shoulders not knowing what to say. "That's…um…great. Real good."

"I appreciate you checking up on them. But, yeah, there's really no telling when they'll be able to go back to Garrison's place. Not with all this mess."

"I heard someone was shot pretty badly." Kenderly watched Garrison mouth the word package, drawing a square with his fingers.

"Captain Oaks. He's still in ICU. No one's getting in to take his statement."

"There was a…um…a package left here. Should I forward it to you?"

"Don't rush it or anything. I won't be around for the next three days. Thanks for checking on these mutts. If you want, you can check again."

"Thanks." Kenderly searched Garrison's face for confirmation of what she thought she'd heard. If she was the package, then it wasn't safe. Not for either of them. "What do we do now?"

"We find a place to stay. Ditch this car and phone before your friend calls the police."

"He won't. He's afraid of what I might say." She heard him suck in a breath. He was about to ask a serious question. "We can't get into that. Not now. I promised I wouldn't tell you about him, but I didn't promise I wouldn't drop an anonymous call to the IRS. But one problem at a time. A bed for tonight. I don't suppose you have any friends in Austin."

He shook his head. "Do you?"

"As a matter of fact. How good are you at picking locks?"

Chapter Nine

Garrison was in total awe of this woman. The news from Jesse wasn't good. The fact that they were reporting a statewide manhunt for the first Texas Ranger wanted for murder was worse. There was no way he was going down in history with *that* title.

All things considered, Kenderly was holding it together and working with him.

Without shoes.

She had made a run for it, but he didn't think that was serious. Just a moment's hesitation. She'd come back to the car quick enough and been cooperative afterward.

Not to mention calling his bluff when he'd tried to comfort her. He wasn't that guy. He'd been way too busy over the past ten years to get where he was at. Naw, comforting wasn't his style. He was more the love 'em and get too busy to call back sort of fella.

If he heard that description out loud about someone, he might call them a jerk. Okay, there was no might in that thought. He *would* call them a jerk. It didn't happen all the time, though. Yeah, he could justify it. His work since transferring to the Rangers had been secretive and intense. It hadn't left time for serious—or even nonserious—dating.

"You take a left on the next street unless you want to go to the store before we stop."

They still hadn't bought a change of clothes. Had nothing except a couple hundred bucks and the change in the console. His stomach seemed to be a bottomless pit, and Kenderly hadn't eaten since breakfast. Their outlook wasn't good at all.

"This is the apartment of a coworker who you're sure is gone for the weekend?"

"Yes. Rose took off for a family emergency Thursday. I was supposed to take her four o'clock perm. Home is in California, so she didn't know when she'd be back in town. It'll be at least a week, giving us time until we check in with your friend again. Right?"

Fifteen minutes ago he'd agreed to break into an apartment because there was no other option left for them. Jesse's message to check back later meant just that. Stay out of sight and come up for air in three days. No hotels, motels or checking out the captain's hospital room.

"There it is. The corner one."

"With the light on?"

"I'm pretty sure."

"Dammit, Kenderly. You need to be more than just pretty sure."

"I'm going to let that outburst slide because I can understand your anxiety. I've only been here once. Coworker—not best friend. I remember it was on the corner because I could see the parking lot from two windows. I also remember climbing two flights of stairs. So, yeah, I'm sure now. And for the stupid record, I leave my lights on all the time." She mumbled the last sentence.

"Sorry. I'm not good at this."

"What? Breaking and entering or communicating?"

She had his number, unlike most people. "Let's just get it over with."

Maybe they got lucky with the time of day or maybe it was because they were on the third floor. No one caught him shoving or pulling at the door. And no one barreled up the outside staircase after he'd gotten it open. The complex hadn't bothered to install secure, safe locks, and Kenderly's friend had left without latching the dead bolt.

"It's very discomforting to see how easy it was for you to get in the door," Kenderly said as she walked through.

Once inside, to turn the dead bolt he lifted the door a little, making it slip into the slot. "Your friend needs to have maintenance rehang that door."

Kenderly dropped to the couch, spreading her arms wide, sinking into the cushions. "Oh, my gosh, this feels good. How long do you think we'll be here? Do you think I could take a shower?"

Garrison shrugged, pulling the cord to close the blinds. He looked around the parking lot that had one teenager walking a dog. Other than that, it was completely quiet. Kenderly looked comfortable. Her skirt had been through the wringer, with lots of bare spots where it had lost the sequins. Her feet looked just as bad.

"Think your friend has some practical shoes you can borrow?"

"I'll check." She sat forward, then fell backward again. "Right after a nap. I'm wiped out."

He secured the second window and curtain. "Sounds like a good idea."

"Do you think they'll find us here?"

"I didn't think they'd find us before. There's no sign anyone followed. But I need to get that car away from here. I don't trust your old boyfriend."

"I don't trust him, either." She yawned. "That's why he was never a boyfriend." Her eyes were closed by the time she rested her head on the arm of the old couch.

Garrison opened the fridge and cabinets. It wasn't his normal junk food, but he could do healthy for a couple of days. They could lie low and wait for Jesse to give them the all-clear. Or the captain could straighten out his involvement. He'd leave the car and take a bus back. No one would notice him on a bus, especially since they were flashing a ten-year-old academy picture of him on the screen. The Rangers must not have released his official white Stetson picture.

"Do you think your friend has an extra key?" He waited with the freezer open for a response, then looked around the corner. "Kenderly?" He crossed to her, took a blanket from the back of the couch and covered her legs.

As brave as she'd been since they'd been thrown into each other's lives, she finally met something she couldn't handle. Exhaustion. It had taken over and claimed some sleep time. He'd wait half an hour to make sure they were really safe and leave her a note. He could take care of Joey's stuff on his own.

GARRISON KNOCKED ON the door with one knuckle. It was as quiet as he could manage with plastic grocery bags looped over his arms. If Kenderly was still asleep he'd be lurking in the dark until she could open the lock.

The flimsy door was jerked wide. He nearly fell through as Kenderly grabbed his new T-shirt sleeve and yanked him inside.

"You went shopping?"

"I left a note."

"Be back soon. You call that a note?"

"It took a while to catch a bus."

"You can't blame it on public transportation. We're really going to have to work on your communication skills, Garrison." She took a few of the bags, glanced inside and led the way to the kitchen. "I've been out of my mind flipping channels to see if there were any reports about your capture."

"I brought dinner."

"Like I could eat anything after the past three hours." Kenderly used her hands, expressing her dismay or concern or panic.

"Three hours? You must have woken up right after I left."

Blocking his entrance into the tiny kitchen, she placed her cute little fists on her sequined-covered hips and tilted her chin up to look at him. There was something in her eyes he hadn't noticed before.

Fear. During their escape, she'd been in shock. Maybe they'd been running enough that it just hadn't sunk in until now. But she looked frightened.

"I would have known how long you'd been gone if you had left the time on your note."

"Yes, ma'am." He admitted it to very few people, but he wasn't great at resolving conflicts. He took them in stride, sidestepped as often as possible, and forgot them immediately. He wanted to sidestep here, but she kept returning directly to the problem…him.

"Seriously, you tell me never to leave your side. I close my eyes for a few minutes, and you're gone. I learned one thing, though. I'm glad you came after me when I got out of the car. If I was truly on my own, I'd have no clue what to do."

She threw her arms around his waist, smashing her cheek to his chest. He didn't have to make a decision whether or not to hug her back. His hands were still full of bags.

"Promise you won't abandon me. Okay?" she asked softly.

He flinched and she let go. "I can't make that promise."

"Sorry. I didn't mean to put you on the spot." She wiped at her eyes.

He'd seen her frightened, sad, mourning, unconscious and acting like she owned the world. He hadn't seen this. She'd used the word *abandoned*. This would have been the perfect time to plug her name and date of birth into a database and see what records were spit out.

Communication.

Quickly setting the bags on the floor, he caught her shoulders before she scooted by him. The silky shirt was cool and smooth under his fingers. The roundness of her shoulders fit perfectly in the palm of his hands.

"I can't make that promise, Kenderly, because I have to do what's best for you. Keeping you safe might mean leaving you. But I won't walk away until I guarantee you're safe. You can count on me. I can promise you that."

"Thanks," she whispered. "I was just so scared. Maybe if we had some sort of plan… Some way to figure out why all of this happened, I'd feel better."

"I really did bring dinner."

"I get it. Change the subject before the strange woman can get too emotional."

"Naw. I'm just hungry. I've been smelling this chicken since I got to the store. I snuck a piece on the bus and just made my stomach growl more."

He gathered the sack handles and set them on the counter. The kitchen was a tight fit while they worked together and put away the things he'd bought. The deli fried chicken and sides were opened by Kenderly while he set one sack in the corner. They fixed their plates without Kenderly seeing the sack that held her surprise.

The TV was muted. It didn't take much to decipher what the report was stating. National headlines about two women being executed by a Texas Ranger and his stylist accomplice.

"Want me to turn it off?"

"Does your friend have cable? Is there a movie or something?" he asked to take her mind off the news.

She pointed the remote, and the screen went blank. Guess that decided what they were watching. Sure, they needed to talk. He got it. He had been hoping for a moment to not do anything. Just a few minutes to decompress.

First day with the Rangers more than one of the men had told him to enjoy the days when nothing happened. He'd been in law enforcement long enough to realize that truth on his own.

You couldn't drive forever. You had to stop to refuel. He also realized that Kenderly needed him to—dang it—communicate. At least he could eat at the same time.

"What did you do with Joey's car?"

"Left it in a parking lot, took a bus five miles away, went to the store, ate a piece of chicken on the return bus, then knocked on the door. That's it. I didn't talk with anyone or get noticed. I didn't make eye contact with the deli person. I even went through the self-checkout to avoid another person seeing my face."

She pushed her mac and cheese around her plate.

"I thought everybody liked green beans and macaroni. Eat up."

"I'm not too hungry."

He shrugged. "Eat or don't eat. It'll be there when you're ready." He was on his second piece—third if he counted the appetizer on the bus.

Kenderly dropped her fork and sank into the couch cushions, pulling the blanket up to her chin. It was clear that she was attempting to be patient. If it had been him, he'd be pacing the floor demanding answers. He knew what she wanted to ask but didn't know to ask.

"There were a lot of patrol cops and Texas Highway Patrol." He swallowed his last bite and wiped his hands. "Joey might not have reported the car stolen, but I still don't trust him."

"Agreed and I understand why you didn't wait for me to wake up. But you reminded me this morning not to leave your side. So it seemed strange to me. I panicked and had no clue what to do if something did happen to you."

"Sorry 'bout that. If we're separated, you call Jesse. You can trust him. After these accusations, he knows not to turn you over to the police." He needed to make certain nothing happened. They needed a plan, and he needed time to think of one. "It was better to leave you here. They're looking for a couple and ignored a guy without a car buying groceries."

"Well, no one's busting down the door, so I guess you're right."

He laughed. He couldn't help it since she was so matter-of-fact about it. He'd taken great pains to guarantee no one followed and busted down the door.

"I don't see what's so funny about me being frightened to death. Or that someone's trying to kill me. Or that we're both wanted for murder. There's just not anything funny about it at all, in my opinion."

"I didn't mean—let's forget it and chill. How about that movie?"

Kenderly popped up from the old couch quicker than toast from a toaster. She shoved her fingers into her hair, sort of with a low, irksome long "ugh," followed by a short "ow." Her arm was bent at an awkward angle.

"Dang it, my ring's stuck." She yanked a couple of more times. It was stuck and getting worse.

"Come back over here and I can help."

"No." She tugged some more.

"Don't be a spoilsport." When she didn't budge, he stood and crossed the room with a couple of steps. "Hold on or you'll tear it out by the roots." He gently worked the tangled strands free. "I could have sworn that your hair was longer yesterday."

"Hair extensions."

He smoothed the multicolored blond strands. "It made you look different."

She covered her face. "I feel weird without my regular makeup on."

"I think you look better. Not that you didn't before. I mean… Hell, I think you're just as pretty without it."

"Thanks. I think." She rolled her eyes.

Not good, man. He opened his mouth to try to take his foot out, but she stopped him.

"I'll accept it as a compliment." She disappeared around the corner and came back with a yeast roll. "I know I look different. That's why I do it."

"I'll never get why a woman wants to look that different. Now, someone on the run using a disguise makes perfect—"

She whipped around, her mouth dropping open to match his.

"Do you think?"

"Could you?"

They spoke together.

"I'm sure Rose has everything I need here." Kenderly took lids off of boxes of supplies stacked against the kitchen wall. "What are you thinking? Would it be too obvious if we dyed our hair dark? Would they be looking for us like that? Do they teach you to expect changed appearances in Ranger school?"

Garrison let her chatter away with ideas and questions. She assumed they'd be running. It was a natural progression. But for him, it was natural to investigate. With a couple of calls he could find out where the captain's car had ended up. Or if it might still be on the street.

If it had been towed, it wouldn't surprise anybody if *Mrs. Oaks* showed up to drive it home. Looking at how excited Kenderly was, he knew she could pull this off. Easy. They could retrieve the jewelry box and maybe a major clue to help solve the murders.

And if she gets caught? Is that a risk worth taking?

Chapter Ten

"You're nuts. Completely and totally nuts. There's no way I'm going to walk into a police station that might be full of men who report to Paul Tenoreno. No way. No. You don't trust them. Why should I?"

"You won't go into the station. If the cops have the car, there's no way they'd let us inside the vehicle. It'll be evidence. No, odds are the car was towed and is at an impound lot. We'd need cash to pay the fee."

Kenderly had tried reasoning with Garrison. She'd presented what she thought was a solid debate about how she wasn't trained for undercover work or even pretending to be married for half an hour. He—in all his arrogant, self-confident glory—had said she could do it. Just like that, he'd turned her simple makeover into a secret agent plastic mask that would hide them from the world.

"I can't do the level of work you're expecting. They'll see right through it. If we get caught, it'll be all my fault."

Garrison sat backward in the little chair from the dinette. This time the smile on his face was at her—what he'd called an overreaction. Not once but at least twice.

Infuriating was putting it mildly. And now he was just smiling. Not saying a word and just smiling.

"How can I argue with you if you won't say anything?"

She put it out there, but she didn't really hope for an argument. She prayed he'd change his plans.

"I think you were doing okay there by yourself. Don't mind me at all."

Kenderly walked around the table, nervous as the caged white tiger she'd seen at the zoo when she was a kid. "Why don't I put makeup on you and *you* be Captain Oaks's wife? You're the one with all the experience."

He burst out laughing. "Not in heels," he managed to get out between heehaws. "I've never been undercover in heels."

"Oh good grief. You truly are serious about me doing this."

He stood and followed her to the couch. They were in close quarters, so she sat immediately, sinking on to the broken-down cushions. At least she was farther from him than if she'd remained standing. She was either going to grab his face between her hands and shake some sense into him or shower his face with kisses, thanking him for saving her life multiple times.

And how would she manage that? She slipped her fingers over her lips at the thought. No! She would not kiss him out of the blue like her body wanted to.

Not in a million years. Not innocently or passionately. He'd interpret the gesture as an invitation. It was the genuine laughter. He'd looked so real and relaxed and sexy. "No, no and no again."

"Hey, take it easy. I understand you're scared. There's no real reason to even think about it. The towing company for that part of Austin is closed, and I can't verify where the car is until the morning. So just relax." He dropped to the couch, remote in hand, finally flipping channels searching for that movie he wanted to watch.

Kenderly remained quiet, but not for the reasons he'd suggested. She needed some deep breaths and a few moments to catch her runaway thoughts. Why did she want to kiss him a half hour after believing he'd abandoned her? It didn't make sense. But of course, none of the past two days made much sense to her.

Garrison Travis was totally all wrong for her. They knew nothing about each other and probably would never have even met if he hadn't saved her life. She was grateful he had. And tremendously grateful that he hadn't just dropped her off to be dealt with by the police until he knew the entire story.

Danger. Vulnerability. Trying to solve the mystery. And if she allowed herself to think that way, excitement had brought them together. A relationship couldn't be built on adrenaline.

So, no. Kissing him wasn't an option or something she actually desired. Not really. She was exhausted. Her mind was just going down a familiar path while in the company of a handsome man. Even if she hadn't been in a man's company for a very long time. It didn't make a difference.

Then why were her insides doing a little dance? Okay, a very big dance. She drew in another deep breath, holding a throw pillow against her chest. Desire took over. The need to scoot across the cushions and have strong arms engulf her in their protection was tremendous. She curled her feet in the space between them and used the pillow for her head.

"You don't have to watch this. You could get a shower if you want. I'll take the couch tonight. You can take your friend's bed."

It would get her out of the room. Away from temptation.

Without a word, she hurried from his close proximity and locked herself in the bathroom.

Sweet, sweet Thelma...she was in big time trouble.

As soon as Kenderly left the room, Garrison remembered the surprises he'd brought from the store for her. Too late. He heard the shower and wasn't about to interrupt. He gathered the sack he'd dropped out of her sight and decided to put her things on the bed.

Pink, pink and twenty more shades of pink. The bedroom was covered in it and trimmed in more of it. Right down to a pink scarf with roses and beads covering the lamp shade. He clicked the switch, turning the bedside lamp on and then another to shut off the bright light from overhead.

Then he put the clothes he'd bought on the silky spread. Kenderly was correct that her friend had everything handy to change their appearances. There were a couple of wigs on the dresser, other hairpieces—they looked like long braids—pinned to a bulletin board, and some sort of makeup sat on every available inch of a mirrored table.

His plan would work if Kenderly let him coach her through a couple of techniques. If the car had been impounded, though, that was a different animal altogether. It wouldn't do any good to get inside the car. Everything would have already been taken and logged as evidence. If the car had just been towed, there'd be nothing to it. Just sweet-talk the attendant to get her purse out. No prob.

Maybe he could change her mind over an omelet. He fingered the short curly black wig on the Styrofoam head. The hair felt real to his untrained touch. It would look real to anyone watching. No one would suspect that she was Kenderly Tyler.

The shower cut off. Time for him to retreat to the couch before his witness went all weird on him again.

KENDERLY WASN'T ABOUT to show her face in the living room. Her adrenaline-filled veins wanted release like nothing she'd experienced before. The more she tried to downplay her desire for Garrison, the worse it became.

Cold showers might work for men, but all it had done for her aching body was give it the idea to warm up next to the man in the next room. She couldn't put her ratty clothes back on. What used to be her favorite satin shirt and skirt was trash can filler. She hoped Rose wouldn't mind her borrowing some things. Starting with pajamas.

With her head wrapped in a towel and another large comfy one around her body, she opened the hall door and barreled right into Garrison.

"Sorry." His hands caught her as she sort of bounced off his chest and tripped backward over her own feet. "Hey, you okay?"

The towel around her hair fell to the floor, and the one around her middle was barely secured by a pinch of her fingers. "I'm fine. What are you doing? Checking the windows?"

"No. I did that before I left you here alone."

"Okay. I should… If you'd excuse me." They did a little dance moving the same direction to let each other pass.

"Hold it." Garrison grabbed her shoulders, turning her sideways. He mirrored her. "There."

The palms of his hands burned her icy skin. A quick look up told her Garrison felt the fire as much as she did. For once there was no smile on his face. He smoldered as his hands tightened, moving her slightly against the hall wall.

"This is going to break at least fifty regulations."

She knew what *this* meant, and she didn't care about regulations. She'd been dying to get her lips next to his since waking up that morning. How many thoughts of consequences could she have in the amount of time it took him to crash into her mouth?

Garrison trapped her with a hand pressed against the wall to either side. He didn't need to worry about her going anywhere. She couldn't. Curiosity or hunger... neither would let her move a step away.

Then he was there. His lips covered hers. She tilted her head back, giving him full access to her mouth. He took it. Devoured it. Moist, hot heat saturated her...everything as his lips took control.

Thoughts were over. Pure unadulterated feeling took the lead.

Sounds from the back of her throat bubbled up, awakening something that had been dormant long before her past couple of boyfriends. Was it the feeling of finally being alive after coming so close to losing her life?

She had no idea and didn't want to think too hard about it. The sensation was more than a little wonderful.

Garrison lifted his head, gently sucking her bottom lip through his teeth and sending cold chills down her spine.

His hand had moved to pinch the towel just under her arm where she apparently had forgotten about it. He guided her fingers back to the spot and let go, taking a step toward the living room as he did.

"'Night, 'night, sweet Kenderly," he whispered like the breeze.

"Good night," slipped from her breathy voice before she could fully open her eyes again. She dashed into the bedroom, shutting the door and leaning her back against it as if Garrison was hot on her trail.

If he had been, she would have let him in. It was the simple truth. But he didn't follow. She was disappointed and didn't want to think about it. Of course that's all she could think about as she took a sheet from the top closet shelf, intending to wrap herself on top of the covers.

She turned to the bed and saw the clothes and a cute pair of white sneakers. She flipped them over, and they were only a half size too big. The underwear was remarkably accurate, as were the jeans.

Somewhere between opening the bikini panties and the simple beige sweater, she began crying. She skipped the PJs and cried into her friend's pillow.

Fitful sleep finally came as she twisted, turned and then twisted again.

THERE WAS NO way he was sleeping after that total surrender in the hallway. Garrison fought with himself to stay put on the couch.

"Stupid. Impulsive. Idiot. You're an idiot, Garrison Travis." He might have whispered the words into the dark, but he heard his best friend's voice screaming them at him.

They'd worked so hard to become rangers. Jesse, Avery and he had gone to college and the academy together. They'd all been accepted as TX DPS officers. All climbed the ranks, tested, learned more in every class they could manage on their schedule.

When his sister didn't make the final roster, things changed. They hadn't really been the same since. The last thing she'd said to him before trading her DPS badge for one as a small-town deputy was not to screw up.

Kissing a witness was a royal screwup.

None of his fellow rangers in Company F would look on it as anything else.

Captain Oaks would let him have it. One look from his captain and Garrison would be falling all over himself apologizing. He couldn't let it happen again. He glanced at the clock. It had only been twenty minutes, but he might as well get a shower. No way was he going to sleep for a while.

The frightening part of kissing Kenderly wasn't a reprimand. It wasn't breaking the rules. It was falling for her. He was on the edge, and it was a long way down.

When he tasted her kiss again, he'd be at her mercy. That was a place he couldn't afford to be. He needed to be at the top of his game.

He lifted the shade at the windows. It was late on a Saturday night, and nothing was moving. A door opened across the complex, and the same dog walker was slowing his dog, trying to keep the massive mutt from pulling him down the stairs.

A quiet neighborhood. He dropped his head against the wall thinking about what his family must be going through. Not to mention his aunt's house that might need to be demolished. Jesse would assure everyone that Garrison wasn't guilty. Would that be enough? They'd all thought he pushed things too hard and fast to meet his goals. Would they still have faith in him?

Shower. Then sleep. No thinking about Kenderly. A plan in the morning. And finding another place for them to stay or disappear for another couple of days. He turned the water as hot as he could stand.

Cold showers to relax were a myth in his mind, since they made his body tense. A hot hard spray normally had the desired effect of easing his tense muscles and nerves. Almost. He almost had a peaceful minute when he closed his eyes. But Kenderly's face was plastered on the back of his eyelids.

Once there, the tiny upturn to her nose, the perfect shape of her cheekbones and the cute arch of her eyebrows refused to leave. He relived every soft curve of her mouth. Each imperfection of her lips that he'd pulled under his own had him clamoring for more. Ultimate softness and a response that had him shaking to the tips of his Western boots, or bare feet at the moment.

Why couldn't it have been a kiss that he didn't want a second or third or fourth. He toweled dry and wrapped it around his hips. His new clothes were on the table. Stepping into the hall, he heard a whimper... Kenderly's. Mumbling. No one could have gotten into the apartment, but he had to be certain. He turned the bedroom doorknob slowly and pushed it open.

Kenderly was tangled in a sheet, lying on top of the bed. Dressed only in her undergarments, her smooth flesh called to him. He resisted. When he did touch her, it wouldn't be while she was sleeping. She'd be awake for every soft caress, every firm deliberate stroke.

He tugged the sheet free and covered her legs, adding the comforter to prevent a chill. With a finger, he hooked her long hair behind her ear and got a smile for a reward.

Yep. The next time their bodies were together...she'd definitely know and remember.

Chapter Eleven

Waco, Texas

Jesse Ryder tried to act as if he was comfortable instead of hanging off a cliff by his fingernails while he stood at the back of the room. No one asked if he'd had contact with his best friend. The major had given him a couple of looks, so it was just a matter of time before it happened. But Jesse keeping his mouth shut wasn't unusual. Garrison usually had enough words for the both of them.

The first question on everybody's mind was why Garrison was in Austin. The second was how the hell whatever operation he was involved with had gone so belly-up. The third was why he was running. No one had accused Garrison Travis of crossing the line. They wouldn't. He was one of them. A Texas Ranger.

Texas Rangers didn't cross that line.

Yet he'd run and taken a witness or accomplice or perpetrator. No one knew for certain. No matter how much they believed in him, they were in the dark.

As the rest of the company left their commanding officer's office with late night assignments, Josh Parker nodded in Jesse's direction. *Here it comes.* His loyalty would be questioned along with the rest of his life's direction.

He and Garrison were closer than a lot of brothers. How could he keep the man's secrets and not break his oath?

"You know the powers-that-be argued against allowing you and Travis to stay in the same company. They didn't think it was a wise decision. I wanted you both." Parker took his seat behind his desk. "I thought you were a good team. So, what's going on?"

A familiar sight was to see the major tip his chair back, prop his worn boots on the solid oak desk corner—heels off the edge so as not to scuff the wood—and doze. Thing was, no one cared. He was an outstanding ranger, wise beyond his years, and those cat naps normally resulted in an inspiring realization about cases.

There hadn't been any napping this afternoon, but that same look of awareness was apparent in his eyes.

"We appreciated it, sir, but I don't know what's going on."

"It says in both your files that you've been friends since grade school. Is that going to be a problem?"

"No, sir."

"So your loyalty to your best friend isn't going to put him in more danger or trouble?"

"I swore an oath to uphold the—"

"I know what the oath is, Ryder." The major gestured for him to take a chair. Then pointed to the frame hanging above the door. "I look at it every day."

Jesse sat. Attempting to appear as comfortable as possible, still feeling like each of his fingers was popping off that cliff's edge into an abyss. He didn't need to look behind him to know the major's deceased wife had embroidered the motto. "Of course you do, sir."

"I also know that you've had contact with Travis."

"No, sir, I have not. A woman called around two this

afternoon, claiming they were his dog sitter. I wasn't certain the caller was credible."

"You don't think it was the dog sitter. You didn't think that was necessary information to pass along to us?"

"I knew it would be relevant at some point, sir. Before Austin headquarters brought us in on the investigation, I didn't know if it was important or not."

"Skip it. What did she say? You think it was the hairdresser, Kenderly Tyler?" Parker took a plain yellow pencil and threaded it through his fingers.

"I can't be certain, sir. She didn't identify herself. She asked about the dogs. I said they were okay and we hung up. I drove to Austin and brought them back last night. They're with Travis's mom and aunt. Waco PD is watching the house for now."

"He cares about his dogs enough to risk burning a phone, and that's all that was said?" Parker sat forward, leaning on the formidable ancient desk. "This is where you make it or break it, Ryder. You know what I'm implying?"

Jesse knew exactly what his commanding officer asked. Where would his ultimate loyalty lie? If roles were reversed, he knew exactly what his best friend's decision would be.

"I indicated to the woman that it might be better to check on the dogs in three days."

"And that satisfied her? She didn't say anything else?"

"That was it, sir. I figured we'd have a direction by that time." He'd also hoped that Garrison could stay alive and avoid apprehension for that many days.

Parker slapped the desk's surface and grinned ear to ear. "They don't know squat in Austin. Oaks is still unconscious and might need a second surgery. So they're keeping him that way. Whatever the captain had going on wasn't being shared with headquarters. It happens sometimes when we're forced to move fast."

"What do you want me to do, sir?"

"You're to follow my exact orders. Got that? Travis is a smart man. It's clear to me that he wanted to know if it was safe to bring his witness here. Oaks must have a reason not to trust the men he's working with in Austin."

"I came to that same conclusion."

Jesse caught glimpses of men watching the office. The blinds weren't drawn, and anyone could see a calm conversation happening. They'd all be as curious as hell why, and none of them would hear a word. They may be watching through glass, but their major spoke in a low voice that just didn't travel well.

"Then make it safe. The Tenoreno family is a dangerous one. You heard me say the police believe they located Travis using his rental car, which he abandoned near I-35." He scratched his chin, rocking back in the desk chair. "When did they call?"

"My call was after that time frame. She didn't seem panicked. She was hesitating enough that someone may have been feeding her what to say."

"Good to know. If Tenoreno has Travis's name and information, they may go after his family for leverage. Might not care that he's a ranger." Parker stood.

Jesse stood half a second later, uncertain if he were a part of that family threat or if he were to handle it. He chose the latter. "I can arrange a protective detail. He… um…has a sister in the Panhandle. She's a deputy and won't want to be pulled from duty."

"Get it done. We can't give either crime family a way to threaten him further. You drove to Austin and back. You were up all night. I'd send you home for sleep, but

need you close. You stay put. Understood? In the building until I say otherwise."

"Yes, sir." Relief went through him that he wasn't suspended. Grounded maybe, but not suspended.

Back at his desk, it took longer than he wanted, but
Jesse made arrangements for the Travis family to be
moved from Waco and protected. Avery wasn't as easy. He
was waiting for verification her fellow officers had located
her. It would be harder for the sheriff Avery worked for
to keep her under wraps. Jesse suggested that she might
be thrown in the Dalhart lockup for her own safety. Boy,
he'd love a picture if it happened.

The files were thick on the Tenoreno and Rosco families and piled on the desk opposite his own. Bryce Johnson was the resident expert. Crimes over the past decade
could be linked to them, but nothing ever stuck.

The family's representative had told police that Kenderly Tyler was there as Mrs. Tenoreno's hairdresser. In the
photos of her escaping on the motorcycle with Garrison,
she was wearing silk and sequins. A hairdresser wouldn't
have been going to the dinner. He studied the crime scene
photos of the two murdered women he'd left visible on
his computer screen.

Their deaths were statements. Assassinations. The
shooter had made them get to their knees, taken his time
to pull the trigger. Maybe told them why. The hairdresser
might have heard.

"But who ordered it?" he mumbled out loud.

"That's the million dollar question. Or billions. The
families are worth billions." Johnson was neck deep in
files. "A legitimate theory is that a new player wants them
to take each other out by ordering their wives' deaths.
They haven't yet, but a declaration of war might not be
far off."

"But why was Garrison there?"

"The Austin PD is just as confused about Travis and Oaks's involvement. We're assuming they were working together. The police are assuming Travis went rogue. They are stretching that whopper as far as they can. I'm wondering if someone needs to drive down there and remind them we're on the same side."

"The media has it that Travis ambushed Oaks. After the first reporter posed it as a hypothetical, the rest began replaying it as an exaggerated fact." Jesse had explained to Garrison's mom and aunt that they couldn't believe anything about the case on television.

"I guess we're holding the information that Travis had a fake ID. Oaks put it in the system himself. That's why it didn't hold up long under scrutiny when Tenoreno's people looked into him." Bryce continued to type on his computer. "Do you think it's suspicious that Travis took a witness back to where he was staying?

"It was his aunt's house. Tells me that Oaks didn't trust someone along the way. Why he bypassed standard operating procedures... He must have needed a new face neither crime family would recognize as the law."

"Logical. It would be easier if we knew if Travis was at the meeting to eavesdrop or to extract." Johnson tapped away on his keyboard. "Things have been rocky with the Tenorenos since their daughter-in-law disappeared. Can't help but wonder if she's in hiding or buried in the desert across the border."

Jesse rolled his pen across his knuckles, imitating the major. He scrolled through the available photos again. The rental car threw him. It was perched across a cement retaining wall separating two parking lots that were different levels.

What the hell chased Garrison over the edge, and

where did he go from there? The image of Garrison joining a body in the desert kicked in Jesse's chest, making
it hard to breathe or sit. He scrambled from behind his
desk like a rat had scurried under it.

"Man, I need to do something instead of just sitting
here staring at pictures. My best friend is out there with
a price on his head."

"Working the evidence is doing something, Ryder.
We figure this out, we'll nail them." He shut the file and
handed it to Jesse. "For good."

"Yeah, but will we be burying the man I consider my
brother along with it?"

"You've done what you can to protect them. Now
we move forward, find the killer and clear Travis of the
bogus charges."

Jesse wasn't one hundred percent certain he could accomplish that as an armchair investigator, but it was better than being suspended. He hoped Garrison wouldn't
wait three days to call in. Now that the company was
aware of the situation, they'd be there to protect him until
his name was cleared.

They just needed to know where he was first.

Chapter Twelve

Kenderly adjusted the curly wig one last time on Garrison's head. He suggested the wig changed him more radically than dyeing his hair, and he was right. She had a scarf covering her hair and huge sunglasses to add to her costume when they went outside.

Both their styles might be a little retro '70s but were absolutely accepted in Austin. The wig changed Garrison's overall appearance. He'd been tall compared to her while she was barefoot, now he was ridiculously lofty.

Their complexions were more like beach lovers, four or five shades darker than they should be if properly applying makeup. It looked so fake to her. She was completely filled with doubts about being able to pull this off. She was bound to totally muck up retrieving the jewelry box.

"Do you really think this is going to work?"

He pointed to the mirror. "No one's going to recognize us. No way. I could pass my twin sister on the street, and she wouldn't know me."

"You have a twin? Seriously? That's so cool."

"Yeah, most people think so. Just imagine not ever celebrating your birthday alone with your friends. Believe me, it's demoralizing when you're an eight-year-old boy and forced to ask girls to your party."

"I bet that's not the case now."

They got to the front door where he kept his hand on the knob, delaying their departure. "I'll admit that Avery is sort of cool. You'll like her. She's nothing like me."

"I'm sure I will." A layer of the unknown disappeared between them. He'd made fun of himself but also shared. Progress, but they were still strangers. "You're sure the key you found in Rose's desk works on the door?"

Kenderly didn't have his confidence that everything would work out perfectly. She shouldn't have allowed him to talk her into trying to find the captain's car. If he touched her again he might just discover she was shaking down to the tennis shoes he'd bought her.

"Yes. I've checked it twice. Remember who to call if something goes wrong or we get separated?"

"Your friend Jesse at Company F in Waco. I'm to tell him I'm Christy, the dog sitter."

"Right. But nothing's going wrong since no one is going to recognize us looking like this."

And the police wouldn't expect two fugitives to return downtown. Or at least she hoped they wouldn't.

Maybe she was more willing to help than she believed. If it was possible to find the jewelry box and discover what Isabella wanted her to have, then she was definitely willing to try.

"You ready?" he asked.

The sincerity of his expression and deep concern in his eyes made her melt. She didn't totally understand the need he had to risk his life to keep a total stranger safe or recover the jewelry box that may or may not have evidence inside. But in that moment she understood the attraction of every fairy tale where a handsome prince rescued the maiden in distress.

"Wait." She latched her free hand on to his arm. "Garrison, I know why I'm taking this risk. But why should you? If you just stay out of sight for a few days, your ranger friends will clear your name. Now, don't laugh. You've told me they will, and I have to believe they will. So it's just a matter of time. Tell me. Explain why we shouldn't stay here and watch television until Rose gets back."

He leaned against the door instead of opening it. "When the murderer showed up at my aunt's house instead of the real videographer, the captain and I had doubts about who we could trust. The Rangers. Sure. It goes without saying that we'd never doubt them. But the others." He shrugged.

"One day you're going to have to explain that loyalty sentiment. I've never experienced it. Who else would have known?"

"Other agencies are involved trying to gather evidence against these two crime families. Local PD to the FBI. It's never been a secret. And somewhere along the line, the Tenoreno organization found a person who could be cracked…or bought. There goes our security. Why am I willing to go after your jewelry box? We don't know who this mole is. What if they breach the team that invento- ries the car? We can't take a chance that the box might disappear. We'd never know if it's important or not."

"You want to get to it before the people who betrayed you. All right, then. Thanks for explaining this time." She tried to open the door.

Garrison covered her hand with his, but he remained leaning against the thin door. "You don't have to do this if you're too scared."

"It's not that I'm scared as much as…" She lowered her voice to a whisper, almost afraid to admit the truth. "I don't want to mess up. I don't want us to get caught."

He shook his head, dismissing her fear as he pushed a

lock of her hair under the scarf, leaning forward slightly. "You have the most expressive eyes."

Was he about to kiss her? She loved the flutter of anticipation in her tummy and her racing pulse. Would it feel as good as last night? He leaned closer with a mischievous but genuine grin. He used his thumb to smooth her cheek.

"There was a weird spot of makeup," he whispered and continued his descent to drop his lips closer to her ear. "If I kiss you right now, you know we're not going anywhere. So I'm not going to kiss you. Not until I know we have time to finish."

The man was too sexy for words. And too darn practical. He also needed to be taught a very important lesson. He wasn't completely in charge…at least not about when they should kiss.

Kenderly slipped her hand from his, and before he could straighten to his full height, she stroked the back of his neck. His eyes brightened with surprise, and before he could finish arching an eyebrow, she pressed her lips to his.

He might be able to wait, but why should she? The sexual tension would distract her and make concentrating on his instructions impossible.

So she kissed him. His arms wrapped around her waist. His strength brought her chest into his body, her feet lifted from the carpet. Their mouths slashed against each other. Open. Closed. Noses softly bumping as they turned their heads, not caring about anything else.

The flutter in her belly spread across her shoulders and breasts. She paused half a second to look into the blazing fires that were now his eyes. His skin temperature grew. She could feel the heat, or maybe it was her own.

Her feet, snug in the new tennis shoes, floated to the

ground. Her hands drifted down his arms, stopping at the muscles under her fingertips. He was breathing hard and inching away, ready to stop.

So she kissed him again. And he kissed her back. Madly. Hungrily.

She might have touched him first with her lips, but he had total control. His nails gently grazed her scalp as he shoved the scarf from her head. His palms cupped her cheeks as he caressed her lips with one sensuous kiss after another. She untucked his shirt, needing more of his burning flesh under her hands.

"Dammit, you taste good," he said between their lips, continuing their exploration.

"You bought minty toothpaste," she answered between each new sensation.

"Yeah." Then he shook his head as his tongue tasted her again. "No. This is all you." Another taste. "Yep, all you."

No one had ever kissed her like this. Not. Ever.

Garrison kept her next to him, his lips firmly against hers as his knuckle grazed her breastbone. Even through her shirt she felt her skin sizzle with anticipation. The tension she'd felt since last night… Well, there wasn't a measurement she could put to it that would be accurate.

It was so intense, so fast, so…much.

His kisses moved close to her ear and then down the back of her neck where there wasn't any makeup.

"Wait," she panted. "The makeup. You were…you were right."

"About?" He nipped her at the curve where her shoulder met her throat.

"We need to take care of…you know that thing." She hoped he knew because she certainly didn't anymore. He sucked a little on her sensitive skin, and her knees went weak. His arm around her waist secured her next to him.

Take care of what?

He swung his mouth to hers again. She couldn't think…just feel. As quick as the last kiss began, it ended.

GARRISON STAGGERED BACK, catching himself with the door.

He could think enough to reach out and keep Kenderly from crashing in the opposite direction but not much past that. He stiffened his elbow at the last second to keep from bringing her supple body against him. Tempting him again.

Damn, he wanted her. He hurt, he craved her so badly.

At arm's length he was still tempted.

He didn't think she wanted to stop any more than he did. She'd continued to kiss him while she said wait. His lips had taken a different path. Given her a chance. She could have asked him to stop at any point. It would have been easier than forcing his body to back away on its own. He'd warned her that this would happen.

The pull between them was stronger than anything he'd experienced.

But somewhere in the backs of both their minds, they knew they had to put this on hold. The contents of the jewelry box were important. They needed to get to the car before anyone else realized it was there.

Kenderly's breasts rose and fell with her rapid breathing. He could feel her hand shaking in his. Or maybe his was shaking in hers. Didn't matter. He had a job to do, and she had to stick with him. She'd pass out or hyperventilate if she didn't slow her breathing down.

"How's my makeup?" He grinned at her, expecting the same reaction as always. A laugh and a scolding remark.

She took a deep, long breath, throwing her head back a little. Stretching her neck in a way that made him want to forget about retrieving the evidence and dive back into their kiss.

"Sweet, sweet Thelma. Is being flippant your reaction to every situation? Do you feel anything other than your smile splitting your face in half?"

"What about you? Can't you just enjoy the moment? I thought we had a pretty good one, so I smiled. What the hell's wrong with that?" He was lost.

Having avoided women who could potentially make him turn down this road, he'd never traveled to a place where it mattered what someone thought. Laughter and a smile had always worked before. Every situation.

"Nothing. It doesn't matter. Let's just go and get this over with." She covered her face with her hands, then dropped them before spoiling her makeup. "I'm messed up. It's not like we actually care about each other anyway."

Whatever it was, it probably mattered a hell of a lot more than he could figure out. The two of them had crossed so many lines in two days that his sense of direction was fouled up. Lost was a good word for what he was experiencing. Or maybe it was just plain inadequacy.

She pulled her scarf back into place, adjusting it and dabbing the dark black outline of her eyes. He twisted the dead bolt and opened the door a crack, then slammed it shut.

"Hold on a minute."

"What now?" Kenderly tilted her head back to look at him.

Bonehead of a move as it might have been, he stopped himself from bending toward her for another kiss. He stopped the action, but not the desire.

"I, um… I've never been around a woman like you. That's hard to admit. But I picked up on it real fast. So you might give me a break for the learning curve." God, he sounded like a wimp. "I've lost track of what we're really talking about."

She laughed, then reached up and straightened the wig sitting on his head. A curly black mess he'd forgotten all about.

"Then maybe we need to get back on track and take care of business." She placed her hands on her hips, acting proud of her work transforming his looks.

Ridiculous and lost. "Will I be a jerk if we leave now?"

"Not at all," she whispered.

That elusive remark was put on a hook in his mind. He had every intention of finding out what the hell they'd been talking about. Just not at this moment.

Right now, he had to put their lives in danger to see if he could eventually keep her safe.

Chapter Thirteen

The light blue sedan was still on the street where Garrison had parked it late Friday night. The key was in his pocket, and he'd seen Oaks punch in the code to the lockbox where he'd placed the jewelry box. So getting the jewelry box wouldn't be that difficult.

Unless the cops or anyone else following them was waiting for them to come back to it. The police might not know the significance of the car, but the SOB who had shot at them knew they'd left his aunt's house in it.

"Are we supposed to act like we don't know each other?" she asked behind her grande café au lait skinny extra foam.

The name of her coffee made him want to laugh, but he held back, draping his arm around her shoulders instead. "Sure we do. If anyone's watching, they saw us get coffee together and sit together. Yeah, we can talk."

"So the reason we're just not getting into the car and driving away—because that would be much more convenient than riding public transportation—is that someone might be watching the car."

"Right."

"And if they're not, why don't we take it?"

He and Kenderly had grabbed coffee and were sitting on a bench near the parked car. "One or both groups might have attached a tracker. We can't risk it."

"Aw, yes." She sipped. "The old tracking device ploy."

The bench they'd chosen didn't have a cover. His face itched from the sun shining in his eyes.

"We've been here half an hour, and I've barely seen anyone around at all. I feel exposed like this. Can't we just get this done and leave?"

"We agreed—"

"No. You dictated. I'm sitting next to you as a result. This is your decision."

"Whoa there. We're in this together. If you want to leave, then we will. There are better things at the apartment I'd like to…explore." Yeah, he looked her body over. Deliberately. Slowly. He was attempting to take her mind off their situation. He might have, but he also got a look that needed no interpretation.

"Please, take me seriously."

A couple of minutes later, a guy who looked like a regular Joe passed with his hands in his pockets. A couple left the bar across the street. The bar didn't seem open, so they might have worked there.

Little things caught his attention. Like Kenderly's shoes already had scuff marks on them. He'd noted that the jeans he'd purchased fit her, which meant the underwear worked, too. For some reason he'd never had a problem guessing a woman's size.

"I am so glad it's not hot out here. I feel like my face would melt off." She fanned her cheeks like a beauty queen.

"I feel the same way. So I can joke now?"

"I don't think you could stop if someone were sticking bamboo shoots under your nails."

"I think that's where I'd draw the line." Garrison's fingers curled into fists as he thought about what it might feel like. "I bet it's hard to laugh when you're screaming. Although, it might give the interrogators a shock if I did."

"I bet…" The words rolled around while she turned to him with a grin. "I bet you could pull that off. Laughing is the first place you go. Is there anything you don't laugh at?"

"There would have to be incentive to stop."

"I bet you couldn't do it."

"Do what exactly?" Although he turned his face slightly to her, movement in the bar window caught most of his attention. A guy wearing a ball cap low over his eyes kept darting close to the glass.

"I bet you can't go two hours without attempting to charm someone."

Easy as pie. There was no one around to charm. Except Kenderly. "What do I get when I win?"

"You mean when I win. Anything you want, no questions asked."

"I can think of quite a few things. Foot massage. Back massage. Foot massage again."

"Whatever you want for the rest of the day."

"It's a bet."

Their plan was to sit for an hour and observe the car. Sip coffee and take a look to see if anyone was watching the sedan. He could handle not smiling, or charming people. Right?

Laughter didn't equal charmer, did it? Was it cheating on the bet if he asked her? Aw, hell. He had to forget about it and concentrate.

If he were here as a ranger, he would have had backup to send into the bar and check out who seemed to be watching them. Or not watching them. He couldn't make a determination.

"I might…" he began, but the bar door opened, and the guy he'd noticed meandered slowly out, heading in the opposite direction. He staggered a bit from side to side. So maybe they'd both been watching for cops.

About to nudge Kenderly and share a staggering story of his own, he stopped himself. Would that be charming? Wait a second. Was everything he said really that predictable? Damn, it was going to be a long two hours until this bet was over.

Coffee gone, more tense than they'd been at the apartment before she kissed him—it was time to make a move. "You ready? Remember what we're going to do?"

"Sweet Thelma, it's about time. This has been the longest hour of my life. And, yes, I remember." She sprang from the bench, running straight to the sedan.

He ran after her. "Wait. Honey. I didn't mean it," he shouted and waved his arms.

She spun around, and the few contents she had in her borrowed purse fell to the street, rolling under the car, bouncing off the curb. He ran to her side. Better than they'd planned.

"Let me help." He crawled under the car, snagging the lipstick, but looking for anything unusual.

No one was around. No one rushed from a hiding place. No one paid them any attention.

Kenderly was on her knees, gathering some pennies, but looking at him. He nodded. By the time he was out from under the sedan, she had the car unlocked and was sitting in the passenger seat. He sat behind the wheel, and seconds later they were around the corner.

Another corner. He knew exactly where he wanted to go. They'd planned it. He drove straight to a parking garage, third floor, throwing the car into P in the back corner. He popped the trunk, and they were out the doors. At the trunk he keyed the entry code to the gun lock-box, and there was the case. Kenderly put it in her purse and slung the strap around her neck. She was turning to leave when he picked up the captain's Glock and extra magazine. He shoved the weapon into his belt and covered it with his shirt.

The whole episode took four or five minutes. Tops. It didn't look like they'd been followed, but he couldn't be certain. As Kenderly was about to fly through the outside door, he yanked her behind him.

"We walk to the bus stop. Very quickly, but we walk." He checked his watch. "It still has a couple of minutes. When I see it, we cross the street."

Kenderly bent and rested her hands on her knees, catching her breath. "I can see why you like this work."

"Huh?"

"Being undercover, all these getaways. They're addictive."

He took her hand when the bus stopped at the light on the corner. "Here we go."

"All right." She casually licked her bottom lip, still bright red from the garish lipstick.

He didn't care. He kissed her quick on the mouth, checked the street again—for whom, he didn't know—and pressed the bar to open the door. Her "ha" echoed behind them as they got on the bus.

A block later he was still looking around to see if they'd been followed.

"Oh, wow. That was awesome." Kenderly adjusted the scarf and pushed her sunglasses higher on her nose. "If someone wasn't trying to kill me," she whispered, "this would just be amazing. Don't you love it?"

"No. It's dangerous."

"Come on. Even just the tiniest bit?" She slapped his knee.

"I haven't had time to think about it. We've been thrown a lot of surprises."

"Is it always like this?"

"I wouldn't know."

"What do you mean?" she asked with a curious face that was cute even with the heavy makeup.

"I mean that this might, sort of be...like my first..." He nodded his head, hoping she'd catch on without him having to admit it out loud.

"What? Ooohhh. Really? You mean I'm your first?" she asked a little louder.

Heads turned. An older gentleman with a cane winked. A mom moved to the front with her child.

"No. Wait. That's not what I—you don't understand." He wanted to set the conversation straight with the passengers, but he couldn't.

"You don't have to explain yourself, young man," a white-haired lady said two rows back. "It takes courage to wait for anything in this day and age."

"Yes, ma'am. I mean, you misunderstood. She's not talking about sex."

"Oh my, is that what she meant?" The older woman feigned shock.

"You're just giving me a hard time." He smiled and did what came naturally...he took a few minutes of harmless flirtation to catch his breath and keep an eye on traffic behind the bus.

The woman—named Frankie—got off, and he turned back in his seat. Kenderly had an all-knowing grin.

"What?"

"I win."

Damn. He'd lost the bet. No question. For the rest of the day, he was hers to command. At least he was armed.

KENDERLY FELT LIKE a spy in a movie. Their plan had worked. Completely. Wonderfully. They had the jewelry box. And she'd won the bet. She could ask Garrison to do everything for the rest of the day.

After running in shoes that were a little too big, maybe she would ask for the foot massage he'd suggested. It would serve him right if she did. Actually, the idea of a full body massage wasn't so lame at all. As soon as they found out what was inside the case. She patted the rectangle safely in Rose's purse as they climbed the stairs to the apartment.

"Stay here." Garrison pointed to a step halfway up the last flight.

She did as she was told while he entered the apartment, checked things out and waved at her to come inside. He was looking through a crack in the shade when she turned the dead bolt into place.

"Still no sign of the bad guys?"

"Something is very wrong or we're very lucky."

"I'm going with lucky. Come on." She patted the seat next to her on the couch. "Do we need to document this or anything? Forget that I asked that. I'm not waiting."

The jewelry box sat in her lap. She couldn't be patient. Garrison stood in front of her, almost at attention. She hesitated and he gave a nod. She closed her eyes—either wishing or praying—and flipped open the lid.

"We need a computer."

She opened her eyes and found a flash drive. "Nothing else?"

"This is good news. That might be a money trail. Mind

if I keep this?" Without waiting on a response, he snatched it from the box. "Does your friend have a laptop?"

"If she does, which isn't likely, she probably took it with her. I haven't seen one here."

He wandered around the room. She had no clue what he expected to find now. He'd already been through the apartment and knew what was in every corner. He tossed the flash drive in the air, catching it like a baseball. "Looks like we have to wait to find out what's on this thing."

"We could go somewhere…"

"We risked a lot to get this today. I'm not putting you in danger like that again. Nope, we wait. We're safe here and should stick it out until we hear from Jesse."

"So we're stuck here for two more days, then we call Waco? Meanwhile, every person we know believes we're wanted for murder."

"Better that than in the hands of Tenoreno because we're too curious about what's on this thing." He tossed the flash drive, caught it and shoved it in his pocket. "The tech crew would remind me that it's better for them to take the first look at it anyway. But, yeah, I'm curious, and my body's pumped from outrunning them earlier. It's going to be hard to sit still for two days."

"It's sort of a letdown after finding it." She toed off her shoes and remembered the heavy makeup. "I'm going to get this stuff off my face. Be right back."

When she had finished washing her face, Garrison was in the kitchen. Wig on the table, button shirt on the back of the chair, face being scrubbed in the sink. She just stood there. Staring. So glad to be simply watching and not running from yet another man wielding a gun.

"Hey, you lost the bet." She handed him the dish towel to dry his face.

"I sure did," he mumbled behind the towel. "Ready to eat? As my first command, I'll make dinner."

"I've given it great consideration, you know."

"You have?"

"Yes. I really think I need that back massage you offered."

"That wasn't an offer, sweetheart. It was a request." He opened the freezer, taking a box down before it really registered that dinner would be from a frozen package.

"It was a good idea. I'm still stiff from bouncing on the back of your motorcycle."

"I'll put a pizza in the oven, and you get out of your shirt and pants."

"What?" She wasn't certain he heard her since he kept talking, issuing instructions.

"Grab that sheet you used last night. I think I saw some lotion on the dresser." He quirked an eyebrow in her direction while folding the pizza box to fit the trash can. "Do you expect me to massage you through your clothes?"

"Well, yeah. I thought you'd rub my shoulders a while."

"Trust me." He winked. "This'll be great."

She didn't feel in charge while grabbing the lotion, sheet and a towel. But before marching back into the living room and telling Ranger Travis a thing or two about flipping the tables…she changed clothes, borrowing a workout top and yoga pants from Rose.

Much more confident, she gathered the items and was ready to put Garrison in his place. He wouldn't be getting her out of her clothes unless she decided. And at the moment she hadn't decided.

Chapter Fourteen

The window blinds swung into the wall as Garrison turned to face her and dropped them, once again caught keeping watch over the parking lot. He tilted his head sideways and quirked a brow as if he knew something she didn't. Did he?

"Is this a problem?" She pointed to her borrowed out-fit.

"Not for me. Lotion or oil?" His hands each held a bottle. "I found some on the counter."

The coffee table was pushed out of the way, now in front of the door. The couch cushions were on the carpet. He stood next to them ready to start. Her body tingled a little—okay, a lot—imagining his hands rubbing the kinks from her neck. "I brought sheets, so…um…oil."

"I'm at your service." He bowed and dropped to his knees, hiding his face. So if he was laughing at her, she couldn't tell. Or maybe not laughing, but absolutely commanding with his presence.

Why did she no longer think any of this had been her idea? She was so determined back in the bedroom that she could bring him down a peg or two. She wanted a massage. Her body ached and needed to relax after the rush from earlier.

Or did she need something more?

Could she allow his hands to touch her body and still keep him at a distance? Just how did that work with a heart?

It hit her like a sledgehammer to the side of her head. She could fall in love with Garrison Travis. Easily fall in love with everything about him. Of course he'd rescued her numerous times, and the adrenaline high probably had something to do with it, but she actually *liked* him.

If the average date was three hours, and they'd already spent forty-eight together... That would be...sixteen dates. Maybe it wasn't unrealistic to think she could be halfway in love with him already.

Of all the things she knew she'd have to give up in order to stay alive...her job, her friends, a career she was hopeful about. He would be the hardest.

When she'd walked into the room, she'd been uncertain of Garrison, uncertain that she could keep him in line. Why did she really want to?

"We going to do this?" he asked.

"You know what? This isn't going to make any sense to you at all." She spread the sheet open, concentrating on how it drifted across the cushions. It hid her from his view for a second. Long enough for the outline of a plan to set itself in her mind. His curious eyes locked with hers above the floating white cotton.

Garrison didn't need to say a word. He drew his breath in deep, straightened his shoulders so his chest stuck out a bit more. She could see that he knew what she was about to propose. His eyes asked exactly what had flashed through her mind. The ultimate question...was she certain?

She was. Sixteen dates or forty-eight hours hiding from an assassin. It didn't make any difference. She wanted this funny, slightly arrogant, very charming man.

But more than that, she needed to be wrapped in his arms and feel safe.

Not abandoned.

She swallowed hard and stretched her fingers. "I've never managed to pop my knuckles like other people."

He cracked his own and they laughed, but he remained silent. It left the decision with her. He stayed on his knees. She joined him but on the opposite side of the cushions.

"Lay down on your stomach, please."

He did without any hesitation.

"I should have said to pull off—"

His shirt quickly went over his head and landed near the wall.

Kenderly popped the cap and squeezed a generous amount of oil in her hands. She'd never given a man a massage—or anyone else, for that matter. Nothing more than using her nails on a customer's scalp during a hair wash.

The oil felt cool, so she rubbed her palms together before touching them to Garrison's shoulders. The muscles tensed and relaxed under her fingertips. She kneaded across the corded sinew, experiencing the restrained power within her touch. She formed a fist and twisted it gently down his spine, adding oil and keeping his skin shiny.

Garrison's arms were stretched out in front of him, crossed at his wrists. She tugged a little, massaging his upper muscles all the way to his fingers. She repeated the same with his other arm, then began his back again. If the short moans and sighs were an indication, she was catching on to the art quickly.

All the while, he kept silent, allowing her to guide their encounter any direction she wanted. She worked her way to his waist. He was still wearing his jeans and boots.

"Why were you so scared to be alone last night, Kenderly?"

"I… I just panicked for a minute."

"A minute?" he asked in a muffled sort of voice.

She continued to knead his tight shoulders. The muscles relaxed but not the feel of his strength. She was safe, and it was a wonderful, heady sensation. "I was abandoned when I was a child."

"How old were you?"

"Close to seven. At least I think I was. I had it in my head that it was my birthday."

"You didn't know for sure?"

"Not really. I couldn't read. All I had was a balloon and my sweater."

He lifted a shoulder attempting to sit up, but she pushed him back to the sheet. "Did they find your parents?"

"I knew that I'd been staying with my aunt Soppie for a couple of days. At least someone who let me call them aunt Soppie. The police searched the mall, but all they could really do was wait for someone to report me missing."

"And no one ever did?"

She didn't hear pity in Garrison's reaction so she plunged forward, with more oil on her hands. "No one. I went into foster care. There are horror stories out there, but mine's not bad. I was placed with a genuinely loving couple. Georgia died about three years ago. Wiley died shortly after I went to live with them."

Tired of leaning awkwardly over him to reach his far side, she straddled his jeans-covered thighs.

"You…um…consider yourself lucky, then?" he asked with a hitch in his voice.

"How lucky is a person who knows nothing about their parentage or where they came from? Or even what day their real birthday is?" She sat straight, arching her back in a stretch, then she pressed her palms into his flesh again. "But, yes, Georgia was nice to me. She didn't have any children of her own and didn't foster anyone else. There wasn't any jealousy or fighting. I mainly stayed to myself."

The cords in his muscles rolled under her fingers like cords in a thick rope.

"Where was this?"

"A little town near the Gulf called Victoria. Enough about me." She hadn't predicted this turn in the conversation. It wasn't exactly the sexy foreplay she'd envisioned.

"I like hearing about you."

She needed to forget her lonely past and now lonely future. Instead, she needed to celebrate the moment with Garrison.

KENDERLY'S RHYTHM AND deep massage changed as her nails barely scraped the skin on Garrison's back and shifted to his sides. Circle after circle got lower and lower—closer to his abs and sometimes dashing under his belt.

Being turned on seemed like a trickling creek compared to the rushing white water racing through his veins.

He'd watched the clock on the stereo slowly tick by. He gulped, trying to swallow with his dry throat. He wanted to flip over and give Kenderly the same torturous treatment she'd given him for the past half hour.

As good as her massage felt, he was sweating bullets from the sensuous overtures. There wasn't any mistake about where she wanted this to go.

His only question was when? She'd won the bet. She was commanding him for the rest of the day. He was close to taking the decision out of her hands.

"Think you could face me?"

She made no effort to move from where she sat on his thighs, so he didn't hesitate. He twisted, and she had enough weight on her knees that he flipped around, staying under her.

A little more oil on her palms, and his chest was covered…and on fire.

The thought of ripping her skimpy clothes from her body and rubbing their bare skin across each other entered his mind more than once. More like every other heartbeat. His hands gripped her hips, trying to maintain his sanity as she rocked across his manhood.

"Look at me," she whispered.

He forced his eyes open when she stopped massaging his chest. She took a lone fingernail and parted his chest hair from his neck to his navel. He thought he might bruise her. His grip was tight on her slender hips as she unbuckled his belt and reversed his jeans zipper. He bit his lip to stop from shouting.

But complete relief wasn't to be his. She took his hands in hers and guided them to her waist, then up to her firm rib cage.

He gave her the same feathery treatment. His thumbs brushed across her nipples, which fought to peak through the workout bra. She closed her eyes and threw back her head as she'd done several times over the past two days. This time he didn't hesitate. He dove forward, bending her backward just far enough to catch the delicate white of her throat with his lips. He limited his kisses to her collarbone.

Restraint. Patience. Two of his evils, not virtues.

Instead of helping himself to the delights of her swelling breasts like a man needing a drink in the desert, he held her closer by wrapping his arms around her completely. There was no hiding his desire. She still sat in his lap and could feel his erection.

The yoga pants did nothing to hide the shape of her body as it molded around him. If it weren't for the jeans, he would have been inside of her—that's how badly he wanted her.

Jeans were a good thing, or he wouldn't be able to wait for her to make the decision about what came next.

Aw, hell. He couldn't wait.

He let his lips give up their hard-won territory of her magnificent skin to make his move. He was one move away from setting her to the side and shucking the barriers between them when she smoothed one cheek with her palm.

Then Kenderly took his face between her hands and kissed him. She opened her mouth, inviting his tongue deep inside as their lips devoured each other, exploring the intimate warmth.

No explanations or reasoning. If they talked he might try to convince her it wasn't right, convincing himself again that it shouldn't happen. And making love to Kenderly—right or wrong—was going to happen without regrets.

His hands skimmed her sides and tugged at the bottom of her workout bra while her fingers clung to the back of his neck. He could have left it hanging around her neck when the perfect globes were released. Kenderly helped him out by pulling it off over her head while he leaned back against the pillows and stared.

Had he ever seen breasts before? He had, but not like these. Kenderly's were perfectly round with a dusky pink nipple. He barely outlined each one, cupping the undersides gently, extracting a deep moan as his thumb brushed across the center.

She shivered and he noticed. He watched each of her

reactions, her quick drawn breath when he tweaked her nipple to attention. The surprise as her eyes opened wide when his knuckle grazed her most intimate place, still resting near his.

"Let's move to the bed."

"Shhh." She leaned forward, laying her finger across his lips, dusting his abs with her breasts. "I won the bet, remember? I get to decide what happens when."

Stretching out against his body, she caught his hand intimately between them. He took care of the rest until she gasped with relief and her body calmed on top of him.

He stayed put. Unable to jeopardize what should come next. She was in command, after all, and might try to teach him a lesson.

"Now."

Barely a whisper or just the outline of the word with her lips. He didn't care if it was his imagination. He couldn't wait any longer and grabbed her waist, flipping their positions.

He supported them with one arm so he wouldn't crash down on her with all his weight, until he realized they still had clothes on. Her hands shoved at his jeans at the same time he tried to kick free of his boots. He thought he'd been smart keeping them on earlier. A layer of protection to keep from making love to her.

Kenderly was like no other woman. She tugged at the yoga pants. He helped.

Lying next to each other as intimate as two people could be, he'd learned at least one lesson. He couldn't keep his hands off her.

And drove into her body, which was completely ready for him. He doubted he'd ever be able to be hands-off with her. And he didn't want to be. That was the biggest surprise of all.

THE WONDERFUL SENSATION surrounded her completely. She closed her eyes and was consumed, completely safe. Each intimate stroke, each soft touch, each gentle teasing kiss kept the illusion that no one could hurt her again.

Garrison explored her everywhere. The light hint of the back of his hand flickered across her ribs. The slight graze of his scruff of a beard across her breast. Fluttering awareness overcame any hesitation she might have had that this was the right thing to do.

Her body and mind needed this release.

Their bodies fit tightly together. Garrison didn't leave any part of her untouched. The rhythm might be as old as the world, but newer than fresh raindrops for them. They rocked and strained, pushing themselves to their limits and enjoying every second of it.

Just when she didn't think she could take another wondrous second, she exploded like a string of firecrackers. The climax shattered her into fragments, and Garrison was there, holding her, pulling her back together. He kept her safe so she could do the same for him moments later when he reached his own pinnacle.

Chest pounding, gulping air through his mouth, eyes rolling slightly back in his head…he collapsed on top of her. She loved it. Every second of it. She ran her fingers through his sandy hair, super glad they hadn't dyed it black. She brushed a few beads of sweat from his brow with her finger.

She pulled another sheet over them and rested her head in the crook of his shoulder. She was completely content and refusing to think about men trying to kill them. "I hardly know anything about you."

"Sure you do. No one except Jesse knows my aunt's address. Hey, you've even met my dogs." He stroked her arm, then drew circles over her skin.

The simple gesture sent shivers down her spine. "Come on, Garrison. Spill something. Any little secrets hidden in there?" She tapped his forehead, then smoothed his wrinkled brow.

"I'm an open book."

"That's hard to believe." *Then again.* "Maybe you do believe that. So I'll just ask what I want to know. How did you get your name? Garrison is like a fort, right?"

"It's also a couple of famous Texas Rangers. Including one of the original commanders. My dad was a big history buff. I can't tell you how many times he stopped by the museum near our house." He continued to drag his fingertips across her hot body.

Kenderly wasn't certain if the gesture was calculated to turn her on again or if he was just comfortable with her. "And you grew up to be one? That's awesome. What's his name, your dad, I mean."

"William," he whispered. "He was shot and killed in the line of duty when I was fourteen."

"I'm sorry, I didn't mean to pry or bring up bad memories."

"No bad memories there. Besides, it was a long time ago. He worked with the Texas DPS. One day, making a routine speeding stop, he was shot. That's about all I know. About all that anyone knows. The shooter was never caught. Dad radioed dispatch, left his vehicle, and the next thing is a 911 call from a driver who saw him fall to the ground."

"That must drive you crazy. Not knowing why..." She'd thought about why she'd been abandoned at the mall. "Georgia always told me to imagine the good reasons. That my biological mother must have wanted a better life for me. I got it, but others don't."

"It was my dad's dream to become a Texas Ranger,

you know?" His hand wrapped around her upper arm. "After he died, I swore I'd do this for him. I sort of hauled Jesse right along with me. Everything clicked. It all made sense."

"That's a nice way to honor your father."

"Hey, it's something I wanted, too. My mom...not so much. She hates that I went into law enforcement."

"Have you been in trouble to make her worry? Good grief, I bet she's scared for you now. There's no way she hasn't seen the reports about us on TV, and I know you haven't called her."

"She knows I'm safe. Jesse would have taken care of things." He shifted to his side, head resting on his elbow now.

"I hope she does know. It must be crazy being worried about you all the time. I've only been a part of your life for a couple of days, and I can already see that."

The sheet drifted lower when Garrison moved to his side. When it continued to glide down to her hip, his hand floated across her bare skin.

Kenderly's body was hungry for his touch. There were so many emotions running through her. It was a constant mixture of excitement from their attraction and the fright of hiding. But what girl wouldn't want to be in the arms of a man protecting her? This adventure was surreal.

Something she'd never imagined would happen to her. And was still a mystery about how it would end.

"What's your next command, sweetheart?"

More commands? He was hers for the day. His skilled hand brushed her breast. The answer might have been hers to decide, but the hints of what he wanted were very plain.

"Well, at the Best Little Hair House in Texas where I work, we have a saying."

"Wait a minute." He paused, laughing under his breath and rolling on to his back. He pulled her on top of him, fitting his hands onto her waist. "You actually work at a place called the Best Little *Hair* House?"

"As I was saying." She swatted at his wandering hands. "Our policy is lather, rinse…repeat."

"Lather, rinse, repeat? I don't get—oh, repeat? That's your command?"

"That's…right." She smiled wide enough that Garrison Travis would be proud of her.

His hands cupped both her breasts, and she began the ascent to heaven again.

"If it's company policy…"

Chapter Fifteen

Garrison propped the blinds open just enough that he could see through them sitting on the corner of the couch. The parking lot was silent. No sign of the dog walker. The lamp pole was collecting some crickets at its base. He dug into his front pocket and snagged the flash drive, turning it over and sideways.

A regular flash drive. Nothing special. It could be bought at any checkout and probably had been. But Isabella Tenoreno wouldn't have made the purchase. Other people did her shopping.

"If you keep rubbing that thing like Aladdin's lamp, will it give up its secrets? Or maybe yours?" Kenderly leaned against the wall separating the room from the kitchen. She wore his T-shirt and the underwear he'd bought her. "Don't you still need a computer?"

Long blond hair—scratch that. Her hair was still every shade of blond he'd ever seen. Every time she turned her head, he saw a new color. It fascinated him. He'd never been fascinated by hair before.

He needed to concentrate on something—anything— or he'd take her back to bed. "It's hard to believe we have one crucial clue, and it has to be tucked away instead of turned over to clear our names." Garrison stuffed the drive back in his pocket.

Going back to bed might not be a bad idea. They were supposed to lie low another day before calling Jesse back. Then what?

"Whatever's on that drive started this entire mess. Didn't it?" She moved to sit in the middle of the couch.

Until he knew for certain, all he had was a theory— a strong theory—but nothing more than that. "I don't know, Kenderly." He slid off the arm to a spot next to her.

"Two women have been executed for no apparent reason. It had to be planned. Not random. So one of their husbands has to be responsible."

He pulled her into his arms, tucking her head under his chin, wanting to comfort her. It surprised him as much as the conversation. He couldn't have pictured this two days ago. "Who else would risk the wrath of the two biggest crime families in Texas?"

"No one? What good came out of killing them? What purpose did it serve?"

"Damn, I want a computer to find out what's on this thing."

She pulled back. "I know we're supposed to stay hidden, but I can't stand not knowing what's there. It's driving me crazy. What about the library?"

"What about it?"

"Garrison, we could read what's on the flash drive at the library's computer. Who would know?" She spread her fingers across his chest. "Even if plugging it into a computer activated a tracer or something, we could be gone before they find us."

He wanted to kiss her and twirl her around the room. It would let them know what they were dealing with. "That's right. Who would know?"

"Let's get dressed."

"Right after—"

He swooped in and let his lips have their way, putting his brain on hold.

GARRISON FOLLOWED KENDERLY into the library, keeping three or four people between them. He was wearing the curly black wig again, but this time without the heavy makeup. He didn't have the stamina to wash it off again. He'd already asked how women do that to themselves on a daily basis.

Kenderly had just laughed at him and kept getting dressed.

The plan was to sit next to each other at the library's computer center. She took a seat, and he had to wander for another ten minutes before the one next to her opened up. He glanced at her screen as he passed behind her. She was reading articles about the murders and about them as suspects.

"Don't push your luck," he whispered.

"The library will close in ten minutes. Please, bring your articles to the checkout." The voice through the speaker did one thing for them. It cleared out the area as the other patrons closed their notebooks and signed off.

Garrison plugged the flash drive into the slot. He was taking a huge risk by coming to the library and exposing them. Opening the files was just as risky. He clicked on the buttons, Kenderly moved to his side.

Several numbered files. Only one had a name. He double clicked "Kenderly."

My dear Kenderly,
Thank you for being such a wonderful friend to me and Trinity. I am sorry we won't meet again, but leaving in secret is the only way we can escape.

We decided that we want our freedom. We can no longer live this life knowing the horrible things about our husbands that we do. This is why we are leaving, never to return, and no one must know where we are.

Please, deliver the information from the files to the authorities. There is a list of information I copied from my husband's computer. We do not know who you can trust, but every name in that file has accepted bribe money. Many others have received money from our families to do illegal things. Some files involve the Roscos, but most are about Paul. The files should be enough to prosecute my husband for his sins.

We trust you to know what's right and to find someone to help you. Because, sweet girl, our husbands will come after you. Being the last person outside our home that we spoke with, they will suspect that you helped.

It is very important that you take the files to the police and get protection for yourself. I am begging your forgiveness for putting you in this situation. Isabella

HE PROBABLY SHOULDN'T HAVE, but he opened one of the numbered files. Three names down, there was an easy one to recognize, then another…and another. He closed the file, stuck the drive deep in his pocket, grabbed Kenderly's hand and practically yanked her from the small study room. They wove their way through the library until Kenderly pulled her arm from his grasp.

Kenderly wiped her eyes. "Isabella's note had been so hopeful of a new life. Oh, God." She covered her mouth. Of course she was upset. She hid her crying from being heard by library patrons leaving with their books and videos. He pulled her closer, tucked under his arm.

"Come on, let's get out of here." Garrison's heart raced. This was exactly what they needed. "No reason to wait. We need to get to Waco. Pronto."

He didn't think that she knew what they'd just stumbled on. Hell, he didn't know much. Isabella Tenoreno hadn't just put together a list of names. She'd copied ledgers.

"What did you see?"

"This flash drive is the jackpot of jackpots for a prosecutor. A lot of important names are on the list."

They were in way over their heads. This information couldn't sit in his pocket. They couldn't take a chance that these files never made it to someone legit who could use it in court.

"How are we going to get to Waco?"

"Good question. We have about six bucks left."

"Should we just call your friend Jesse? Couldn't someone from Austin pick us up? We could go back and email it."

Lights at the back of the room flipped on and off. They had timed their visit perfectly in case the flash drive triggered some type of trace.

"I can't call just anybody."

"Why not? You've called Jesse before. Even if your friend can't help, he could find someone who can."

"If we wait around," he whispered, "Tenoreno's people will find us. I'll be honest with you, Kenderly. We've underestimated this crime family's reach. I wouldn't put it past them to be listening to conversations in and out of Company F. It's probably one of the reasons Oaks set up this operation limiting the people who knew. We need to get to my company commander. Major Parker will know how to handle things."

"And your certain his name isn't on the list?"

He nodded and grinned. For a hairdresser, Kenderly Tyler was fast catching on to the concept of trust no one. "I don't have any doubts about Parker. You ready?"

"I'm okay now. You don't have to squeeze so tight." She wiped another tear and turned her face toward him.

He gave her a quick kiss and knew exactly what they needed. "The quickest way to get this in Parker's hands is for us to get to Waco. We need transportation and my motorcycle will still be at my aunt's house. The police had no reason to confiscate it. We can take the bus nearby."

"What if they're watching?"

"I can sneak in the back. My bike will fit through the door on the side of the garage. You can stay about twelve blocks away. There's a supermarket by the bus stop."

"Garrison?" She was squeezing his hand this time. "I'm really afraid. Are you sure this is the right thing?"

"We don't have a choice," he whispered.

The bus was about two blocks away. He took a couple of steps, but she stopped dead in her tracks.

"What did you see when you opened that file? There were names, but what frightened you?"

He smiled. Yeah, this time it was calculated. She'd called him on it countless times in the past three days. This time she needed him to charm her. He needed her to believe that everything would be okay.

"Motive. Proof. Enough to clear our names, get you some real protection at a safe house and prosecute Paul Tenoreno and a lot of other people."

"How on earth did you ever think you were a good liar?" She laughed and pulled him forward. "Whatever is on that list and has you this motivated scares the living daylights out of me. I trust you, Garrison. You stay confident and cocky. It makes me feel safer."

She wouldn't feel safe at all if she knew he'd read a whole lot of dollar signs next to the name of the deputy first assistant attorney general of Texas. Walking into a police station was a death sentence for them.

Trust no one else. No police. No state trooper. No elected official. He hated to add Rangers headquarters to the list, but he did. He could trust two people with this information. Two rangers.

The entire bus ride had him looking over his shoulder, watching to see if any cars were trailing them. But no one was there. If the Texas mafia knew where they were, they wouldn't be riding on a city bus.

"I'll meet you in the fruit section in one hour. Got it?" He reluctantly left Kenderly at the store next to the market. He looked backward one time, saw the fear in her eyes and ran the blocks to the house, cutting through a few yards without back fences.

He was breathing hard and watched the light blue house belonging to his aunt. He'd told everybody he was staying here to get the yard ready for the next college student. The bushes were grown up, and he hadn't realized just how difficult it was to see into the yard or along the side of the house.

No cars parked on the street with an unknown person sitting there. No one walking the sidewalk. It was a quiet Sunday evening. Quiet, and the coast seemed clear for stealing his motorcycle from a crime scene.

The yellow tape was across the doors to the bullet-ridden house and garage. He hopped over the back fence and took his keys out. No alarms sounded. No police lights flashed. Maybe he was in the clear. Maybe something would go right, and he could get Kenderly to safety.

Darkness surrounded him. He let his eyes adjust, and the open door to the yard let in enough light to see. That feeling of something wrong crept up the back of his neck. He knew it before he saw it.

The beam was a motion detector. He'd seen a couple before. The police wouldn't have these resources. One guess who did. The murdering son of a bitch was as smart as he was big. He was probably nearby. Probably had a tracer on the bike. Would be on him as soon as he turned the corner.

He had to think. If it was just him, he'd face this guy without worrying about the consequences. But it wasn't him. The only thing on his mind was Kenderly. Her beautiful face lying lifeless like Isabella and Trinity made bile rise in his throat.

She'd be waiting on him. Pretending to look at veggies and fruit. Where would she go if he didn't get back to her?

"Dammit!" He fished the flash drive from deep in his pocket. He had to hide it. Had to keep it safe as much or more than either of them.

Aunt Brenda had cases of water stacked in the back. He slit the top plastic and emptied a bottle from the middle. It was a good hiding place, but he needed a plastic bag to keep the drive dry.

Drawers. Garden supplies. Plastic wrap.

The drive was secure as he switched the top case of water to the middle. If they were caught he'd know where it was. Staying alive to tell someone was his next goal.

Next split decision. Pick up Kenderly before she freaked and called the police. If the deputy first assistant AG was on the take, then the responding officers would be, too.

The sound of squealing tires got his attention. He straddled his bike, started the engine and pushed the door opener. The drive was clear. He had twenty feet of driveway to clear before he could cut across the front lawn.

He ducked his head even with the bike handles, not waiting for the door to open completely. Headlights on the street. Five feet till the lawn. He barely heard the gunfire before he fishtailed into the grass. He felt the second shot rip through his arm as he zigzagged into the street. The handgun at his back was useless. He couldn't fire. He needed both hands and was losing a bit of strength in his left. He had to shake this guy.

The yards without fences!

It would be tough but worth it.

After the first yard taken, he could at least drive in a straight line in the alley. If he'd been staking the scene, he would have placed a tracking device on his bike. If they had, he'd cross that giant obstacle when he got to the store. Find the device or ditch the motorcycle after all.

Second yard and back on the street. He blasted through the stop sign. Gunned the bike hoping this street would be as deserted as the rest. He passed the street for the store, seeing if he was followed. High beam headlights turned behind him. He watched for another house without a fence.

Took the turn. Back in the alley he darted forward, then spun to a stop and U-turned back to the same house. That maneuver might gain him an extra minute. He went back through the yard, passed somebody coming out the back door shaking his fist, turned right and hit the yard of another fenceless house in the direction of the store.

No sign of the murderer's car. He circled the block.

Two more streets, and he was in the shopping center. He parked across the street, giving his bike the once-over and locating the tracker. He'd seen enough movies to know he needed to keep it moving, so the piece of slime following him would be following someone else.

Spinning through the parking lot, he tossed the device into the back end of a pickup heading the opposite direction. He glanced at his watch. Late and light-headed, he sped to the back entrance of the market. There wasn't a way to hide the red stain on his arm, or the trail of blood running down it.

Might be a graze, but it still burned and bled like the devil. He needed his shirt, but not the bottom of it. He pulled it over his head, his left arm demanding a little more care now that he was off the bike and thinking about it.

Damn, the wound stung. Throbbed. Ached.

He ripped at the seam with his teeth. He was either weak from the shock of being shot, or T-shirts weren't as easy to rip apart as on TV. He found a nail close to the trash and finally got a strip of cotton. He tied it around his arm after wiping at the blood. Stained looked a lot better than dripping.

Then he ran—not as fast as he had after dropping his witness off—but he ran.

Veggies. Nothing visible from the front of the store, so he pushed his feet to the left. He darted in between carts and old gray-haired ladies begging forgiveness as she set them from his path. A stack of potatoes came into view. Lettuce, tomatoes, onions, but no Kenderly.

Quickly searching each row, he ran the back aisle of the store again. Swallowing the fear that threatened to stop him.

Then he saw her.

Grocery cart overflowing. Head down reading the label on a can of something. She put it back on the shelf and saw him. He looked past her to the opposite end.

The murderer was steps behind her.

"Run!" he shouted and pulled Oaks's weapon from his waist. He couldn't pull the trigger here, but the bastard now knew he was armed.

Kenderly's feet slipped a little, she started to fall, caught herself on the shelf and knocked cans to the floor. She made it to his side, steering clear of the gun. He pushed her behind the end of the aisle. Tenoreno's man disappeared.

"They found us?"

It was a rhetorical question, not needing an answer.

"Back door, sweetheart."

A decade of law enforcement and a lifetime of pretending to be the toughest kid around kept him calm. The wound to his arm slowed him. Kenderly's presence made him more cautious. He directed her to behind the refrigerated food displays and pointed toward an employees-only door.

Having his weapon drawn caused civilians to run in the opposite direction. After a few screams from those gray-haired ladies, Kenderly pushed through the swinging doors just as the intercom buzzed to life.

"Hey, Texas Ranger," a raspy bass voice said.

He jerked Kenderly to him and put his back to the wall, searching for a path outside. An exit sign caught his eye, and he pointed to it, giving her shoulder a nudge.

"I'm not leaving without you."

"You have to, babe. It's the only way. Get going and call Jesse for help."

"Garrison, you don't understand."

"You have to run. Go. I'll keep him here long enough for you to get—"

"I can't drive a motorcycle!"

"Texas Ranger dude, I know you're still in the store. I also know you don't want anyone to get hurt. If you give yourself up, I'll let these nice people at the front door leave."

"Dammit."

"I'll count to ten."

The countdown wasn't slow. He had a few seconds to make a decision. "All right!" he shouted through the door. "I'm coming out."

"I want the pretty lady, too."

"Hide, Kenderly. There's gotta be an office back here. Find it. Lock the door and hide. Call Jesse," he whispered. "Trust no one but him."

"I don't know if I can."

"Two…"

"Don't hurt anyone," Garrison shouted again. "We're coming." He turned back to Kenderly. "The drive is in the water at the house."

"You can't go out there. He'll kill you." She grabbed his arm and looked at the makeshift bandage. "God, are you shot? When did he shoot you? Oh my God."

He kissed her. As passionately as he could get during a situation like that, pressing the gun into her hands. Then he pushed through the swinging doors.

"Don't shoot."

"Now, buddy, what makes you think I won't?" the voice asked, still on the intercom. "You've seen me work."

Garrison ran down the aisle to the front. The intercom was still on. Screams echoed through the store.

A lone shot.

Chapter Sixteen

Kenderly stared at the gun in her hands. She jumped with the firing of a single shot and dropped the weapon. She knelt to the floor and couldn't get back up.

Garrison? Was he dead?

"Don't shoot."

At the sound of his voice, relief shot through her as fast as any bullet. Air rushed back into her lungs. She was weak at the thought of him lying on the cold linoleum floor. It seemed like an eternity and had only been a split second.

"Ranger Travis, words aren't necessary," the intercom voice said. His lips must have been too close to the microphone. He sounded as distorted as his mind must have been.

"Why don't you show your face, you ugly son—"

Garrison's voice sounded strained as he shouted. No more shots. No more screams. She once again was cradling the gun he'd handed her...this time tight between her breasts. She couldn't stay here. Where could she hide?

"Miss Tyler," the voice taunted, close to the microphone like a child playing, "it's no use hiding. You can't get away. Come on out, unless you want me to hurt some of these people, or I could just hurt your friend over and over. You know what will eventually happen."

If she went out there, no one would ever find the flash drive. But if she were honest with herself, she didn't hold out much hope that she could resist this killer's threats. How could she live with herself, knowing she'd caused anyone's death?

She ran for the phone inside the office, locking the door behind her. The number she'd memorized went to voice mail. "Jesse, this is Mr. Travis's dog walker. If you're in Austin, there are special instructions with the water."

"Where are you, my little pretty lady?" the voice sing-songed over the intercom.

She couldn't leave Garrison. He had gone out there to save innocent customers, but he would kill her himself if she walked out front and just gave up.

"This is 911. Please, state your emergency."

"I'm at the market on Forty-First Street. Someone has a gun and is threatening to kill everybody."

"I need you to stay on the line, ma'am. Can you do that?"

The doorknob rattled. The door shook.

"Please, let me in. Oh God, please, don't leave me out here to die. He's shooting people." A customer in a checkered shirt pounded with his palm on the door's glass. "Open up."

It wasn't the man chasing them. This man was slender, a slighter build, and his eyes were totally different. He looked as frightened as her.

"Hold on, I need to let this customer inside." With shaking hands, she left the receiver off the hook and unlocked the door. The man burst through, locking the door behind him. He threw his hands in the air when he turned and saw her gun.

"Oh no, wait." She set the gun on the desk, anxious to get back to the phone call. "I'm not going to hurt you."

"What a shame." He swiped the gun, tossed it to his other hand, like someone used to handling a weapon, and pointed it at her chest.

Isabella's murderer had a partner. Big surprise. But the cops should be on their way. The 911 operator was listening.

"So there are two of Tenoreno's men here with guns," she said for the operator's benefit. "Please, don't hurt the innocent people out there shopping."

"They want you alive. So no trouble, or the boyfriend gets it first. Let's go." He jerked the barrel toward the door and clicked a button on his cell. "Got her. Back. Got it."

He shoved her between her shoulders toward the door that should have taken her to safety. She wanted to slow down, but he didn't allow it. "Where's Garrison? What are you going to do with us?"

The question she wanted answered at any minute was *what are you going to do when the police arrive?* She searched reflections in windows…no flashing lights. She'd put in the call. They should be there any minute.

The black car that had followed them the day before was parked in a fire lane on the vacant side of the building. Her feet crunched broken glass. She took a real look at her surroundings.

The neighborhood wasn't as nice as she'd first assumed. Half of the parking lot lights around her were broken or out. It was doubtful the security cameras still worked. Less doubtful that anyone would help her.

She was alone.

Uncertainty consumed her. She didn't want to die. Especially not today. She'd just begun to live. Her knees grew weak. The man shoved her again. Apparently she'd stopped next to the Dumpster for a convenient shot to the back of her head.

"Remember what I said about cooperating. Not a peep. You got it?"

She nodded as she walked next to the dimly lit car. So they must really want her alive. At least for now. "Where's Garrison?"

He didn't have to answer.

She recognized the ski mask immediately. He had the same build, the same walk and the same confidence as the man who'd shot Isabella. Garrison walked in front of him with his hands behind his head. Once they were side by side, she saw the gun in the murderer's grip.

"You okay?"

She nodded without moving too much, completely unable to push a yes through her lips. She hadn't ever been this frightened. It was debilitating and far worse than escaping over the balcony on Friday.

This time she had a chance to contemplate what might happen. They handcuffed Garrison and shoved him face-first on to the back of the car.

Then the smaller man who had tricked his way into the office began patting her down. His hands took in every contour of her body. Every pocket, the inside of her bra. Garrison struggled to stand up, and the big man shoved his cheek against the trunk, lifting his wrists higher into the air, pinning him there.

"What the hell are you looking for?" Garrison said.

The man was about to descend into the front of her jeans when the murderer who killed Isabella waved him to a stop. They stood there, him behind her, arm wrapped around her waist, his fingers at the top of her jeans about to violate her.

Dim light or not, there was enough to see the sizzling hatred in Garrison's eyes as he pushed back again and again. The makeshift bandage slipped from his strong arm. His wound, raw and visible, bled and dripped to the dusty metallic paint.

"That isn't necessary," he gritted and stood.

"Please, stop. He's hurt."

"Shut up," the checkered-shirt jerk who'd fooled her said. He continued his search on the outside of her jeans.

It was humiliating, but it had almost been so much worse. As it was, tears sprang from her eyes and blurred her vision. She had no weapon for him to confiscate, or she would have used it on him inside the market. He nodded to the big man.

"It's going to be okay. No matter what—" Garrison tried to reassure her and received a blow to his temple with the man's gun.

Why weren't these men in a bigger hurry? Did they know the police would be delayed? She'd left the 911 operator on the line. Had Garrison been right not to trust the cops?

One more time she was shoved, tripping and falling to the pavement, only to be lifted by her arm. The murderer faced Garrison, but not before she saw the blackness in his eyes. He wanted to hurt people, and this time it was their turn.

The car door opened, and she was shoved into the backseat. Her arms were yanked behind her back and handcuffed. She'd barely scrambled to a sitting position when she heard the scuffling behind her. As she watched in the rearview mirror, the two men took turns throwing punches, hitting Garrison.

The car rocked as Garrison fell over and over. He was defenseless. Another punch took him to his knees and out of her sight. She could only see the top of his head.

Isabella's killer kicked him, grabbed a fistful of hair, keeping him upright, hitting him again. They bent over him, disappearing, then Garrison was thrown inside, his face landing in her lap.

Standing close to the door, the man who'd been chasing them took off his mask and handed it to the checkered-shirt liar. He placed the heavy wool ski mask backward over her head.

The men didn't talk. After the car turned a couple of times, the accomplice got out. She could tell it was him because he'd said "I'll find it" before slamming the door.

The mask over Kenderly's head smelled like a cheap aftershave. Why it was on his hair baffled her, but it was only a fleeting thought. She was getting sick from the odor, the rough car ride and wondering how badly Garrison might be injured.

Kenderly could barely see Garrison's face through the weave of the mask. He was still out cold in her lap and hadn't moved. She didn't think he could be faking such unconscious perfection. They hadn't bothered to blindfold him like they had her. The thought that he'd been drugged fleeted through her mind along with all the other details she was trying to rake in.

The longer he didn't move, the more it made sense. He would be much less trouble drugged. She fought back the tears and the feeling of total helplessness.

What could she do? Her wrists were bound by handcuffs. She was blind to her surroundings. Even if she could get out of the moving car, she wouldn't leave Garrison behind.

Think. Think. Think.

Yes, the Texas Ranger who had been protecting her with his life would want her to leave him behind and escape. She hated that option. But if she could, she would. It was their only chance at survival. If she could get out of there, she could bring someone back to help Garrison.

Back to where? For every answer, she had more questions spring up.

The man who had been chasing them wouldn't care about her personally, so attempting to reason with him wasn't an option. She'd already heard Isabella beg for her life, so that wouldn't work. The man had no heart and no soul. She couldn't bribe him. She had no money.

The sound of traffic disappeared. Their captor didn't play the radio or music. He didn't talk or even breathe hard. If she spoke to Garrison and tried to wake him up, the murderer would hear.

What was she supposed to do? She was only a hairdresser. Her training hadn't included escape artist techniques or hand-to-hand combat. Even after two days, her on-the-run skills weren't very good, either.

There were too many thoughts in her head, and she didn't know how to sort through them. Or maybe there weren't any ideas at all, and she was as helpless as she appeared.

Why not just kill them? Were they being taken to a location where their bodies would never be found? But they'd drugged Garrison instead of killing him.

Or had they? She could feel his warmth penetrating through her jeans to her thighs. She leaned forward and felt his chest rise. He was alive.

Why?

What did they want?

The flash drive. That's why they'd been searched so thoroughly. They wanted the flash drive.

Chapter Seventeen

Jesse Ryder played the phone message again. When he'd first arrived back at headquarters his hair had been dripping from his shower. He was surprised he'd gotten all the soap off after he heard the general ringtone.

"Something has happened. He must have found the evidence he was searching for."

"We're waiting on facts, Ryder," the major answered sternly.

Jesse noticed the differences, though. His superior was stiff in the chair, not flipping a pencil with one hand while he tapped his chin with the other. His feet were squarely under him, not propped up on the corner of his desk. This time he hadn't drawn a conclusion about the correct course of action.

"I do know it, sir. There's no logical reason to leave me a message like this if they weren't in danger. I told them three days. It's been two. Travis should check in tomorrow." He hesitated to say the next words, but what the hell. "If we wait until we know there's trouble, it'll be too late to get there. Sir."

"And you believe that the 911 call at the grocery store involved Travis and Tyler? Did you get a copy of the tape? You might recognize the gal's voice. Run it down

for me." The major's finger began tapping his chin. He
was ready to listen.

"Multiple witnesses on the news report said the
masked man demanded that the Texas Ranger give himself up. Reports say the ranger looked like he was ab-
ducting a woman, and was safely in the storage area. The
threat of shooting hostages got him to surrender to the
man threatening customers out front. Witnesses didn't
see the woman again. We're waiting on the security footage, but the police department didn't seem very forthcoming. The sergeant I spoke with might as well have
accused me of trying to cover up for Travis."

"You think it would be any better if you were in Austin? What do you hope to find that the police can't?"

My best friend. Alive.

"I think Travis uncovered something important
enough to get Kenderly Tyler to call me while he stalled
at the front of the store. It's a cryptic clue, and we'll be
lucky if we find it before Tenoreno's men do."

"Why not just tell you what's going on?" He looked
at Jesse, expecting an answer.

"Perhaps they believe that two crime families might be
listening. Even Johnson was surprised at how quickly the
police and media began calling Garrison Travis a murderer. We already knew Tenoreno was paying officials.
We just can't prove it."

"You don't believe the media jumped on the chance
to sensationalize because of our Ranger history?" the
major asked.

"Partly. Don't you think they were hasty?"

Jesse forced himself to stay at attention. Any other
stance would have him anxiously drumming his fingers
or performing some other tapping while waiting on per-

mission. Didn't really matter. He was heading to Austin to help his best friend, no matter what his directive was.

He was done sitting here at his desk or trying to get shut-eye at home. Garrison's dogs were whining to get outside or whining to get into bed with him. Pets he could take, but waking up face-to-face with dog breath was pushing their friendship to the limit.

"We're losing time, sir."

"Take Johnson with you. Lights all the way. I know you aren't traveling at the speed limit anyway. Let me know when you arrive." He stood. "In fact, keep me apprised of every move you make."

Jesse was dismissed. "Thank you, sir."

"Don't thank me yet. You have to deal with headquarters. I'll be making that call after you've gone." Parker picked up the phone from his desk. "Easier to ask forgiveness than permission. Hit the road."

"Understood."

He did understand. He hadn't been in Company F all that long, but he knew that his commander was getting his head chewed off at regular intervals from the top brass.

He tapped Bryce's desk as he passed. "Grab your weapon, Johnson. We're heading to Austin."

"I thought the company had been ordered to stand down. That there would be consequences from Austin if we investigated." Johnson was correct.

There might be reprimands for their permanent records, but he had to find his friend. He wasn't getting any psychic message or anything. Far from it. Garrison Travis was the last person on earth Jesse would ever correctly predict. In all their escapades and adventures together, this was the first time he'd ever known his friend was in serious danger.

It was the first time Jesse knew he had to help.

"Orders change. I'll fill you in on the details when we hit the road."

Both men unlocked drawers, removed weapons and ammo, then left the building.

"Any idea what we're going to find? Or how to find Travis and the woman?" Johnson asked when they got to the parking lot.

"Not a clue. But we will. Even if we have to beat down Tenoreno's front door."

Chapter Eighteen

Garrison's skull pounded harder than on the day after he'd graduated from the police academy. This hangover was the absolute worst. He tried to grab his aching head, but his arms were pinned behind him.

He cracked one eye open. At least there was darkness. Light would have been too much to handle. He was already sitting upright. That was a start. Or a really bad sign.

"Damn, that must have been some good tequila."

"Garrison? Are you really awake this time?"

This time?

He knew that voice. Remembered his hands on her perfect body. Then his hands were replaced by a guy in a checkered shirt. Was this a dream? His hands were pinned again, he couldn't do anything. There was pain. Everything hurt. Things went black.

Memory or imagination?

"Kenderly?" he croaked through a dry, odd taste in his mouth. *Handcuffs.* He recognized the feel of the metal bracelets. It wasn't his imagination.

"Thank goodness. I don't know how much longer I could take being alone in here."

He had a vague memory of being caught in the soup

aisle of a grocery store. That made for a weird dream. "Where's here?"

"I'm not sure, but I think we're back at Isabella's house. At least somewhere on the estate. They covered my eyes with a ski mask, but we didn't drive far, so it seemed logical to assume they'd take us here. Right?" She must have been shifting.

He heard metallic noises, but couldn't focus on anything. Or feel much either. "Why aren't we dead?"

"I'm fine. Thank you very much for asking. No one's done anything except lock my hands to a chain on the floor and slap me once or twice."

"My head's a bit foggy regarding some details. More like all the details. Are you really okay? Or are you just staying strong?"

"I think he split my lip. Other than that, I'm fine. Sorry for taking your head off."

"Sweetheart, if you could take it off, I'd let you. It hurts like a son of a bitch." His mind's picture of her lip bleeding, her unable to touch it, worried about him…it won out over the fact he still saw four of his shoes. She would have been worried. Probably still was. He tried to be hopeful. "What did they hit me with—a sledgehammer?"

"They did hit you pretty hard, but I bet it was whatever they gave you to knock you out all this time. It's been hours. Long, scary hours here by myself."

Whatever they were both handcuffed to rattled as she jerked against it. Maybe something bolted to the floor. Kenderly had to be cuffed and connected to him with a chain or something. She'd moved, and his wrists were pulled. He couldn't be certain and didn't have enough strength in his arms to pull to see if it was a possible escape.

"Remind me to say no to drugs."

"Sure." She sort of laughed and cried at the same time. Then it was just an all-out cry. If he could have seen her, he might have lost his composure. Odds were they were going to die soon, and it wouldn't be easy or as quick as what she'd witnessed when they'd first met.

"It's okay, Kenderly." He was lying through his teeth. These men were going to get ugly and use them against each other. "Look, if you have a chance to save yourself, take it."

Nothing was okay about their situation. No one knew they were missing. No one knew they were anywhere close to here. Tenoreno could have them disappear. Easy.

In pieces.

With his memory returning a little more each minute, he was surprised he'd awakened at all. Tenoreno knew about the flash drive. It was the only bargaining chip Garrison had to try and save Kenderly.

"Sorry." She sniffed. "I'm just so glad you woke up. Now we might have a chance to get out of here."

He wanted to tell her the truth, but what good would that do? Make her spend her last hour crying or hysterical? Okay, she hadn't been hysterical up to this point in their adventure.

In fact, she'd been damn smart about things. She'd been a good sounding board and had come up with a lot of the ideas they'd used. But he still wasn't telling her the truth. Take away someone's hope and that was worse than…

"Garrison?"

"Yeah."

"You wouldn't happen to be able to break your thumb to slide the handcuffs off. Or maybe dislocate your shoulder? No, that wouldn't do anything. What about stepping through the loop of your arms to bring your hands in front of you? We might be able to find something to pick the handcuff lock."

"I thought I was the one who had been drugged." He wished he could do one of those tricks.

"I just thought it was worth a shot. I've been trying to think of something, anything, that would help if you woke up. I mean when you woke up." She shifted again, and his hands were pulled a little farther from his back. "Speaking of shots, how's your arm?"

"Sore. Stiff. Better than my head. Seeing myself hurl twice with this double vision isn't going to be fun. But I'm optimistic." He yanked at the handcuffs.

"Ow, that sort of hurt."

"That confirms that our cuffs are connected by a chain. These things are not coming apart. If I pull, I'm going to hurt you." He was still feeling the effects of whatever drug they'd used on him, so he didn't have much strength anyway.

"I'm not finding a lot of positive in this experience, Garrison."

"Did they question you? What did they want? Do they know about the info?"

"Isabella's murderer—who is more frightening to look at without his mask—asked me a couple of questions. But then he got a call, nudged you with his toe and left."

He couldn't detect any additional shaking in her voice. She just sounded scared. "Do they know about the flash drive?"

"Yes. Do they want to know if we have it? Yes. Do they know what's on it? No."

"Kenderly, you can talk to me. Unless you're upset that I screwed up. I don't have enough words to say I'm sorry. I didn't realize the guy had a partner."

"That's right. I think Isabella's murderer dropped his

pervert of a partner off at your aunt's house to look for something," she whispered. "I heard they don't know what's on the flash drive. They were talking about it when they threw you in here. Apparently you are heavier than you look."

"It's my boots. Why are we whispering?"

"They may be watching us or recording our conversation," she continued with her extra breathy voice.

"You really have watched a lot of crime shows on television."

He didn't think there were any recording devices in the room. No blinking red light or visible camera. No two-way mirror. But he couldn't see all of the room. He knew the door had opened on the wall behind him.

"We live in a very electronic world. Why wouldn't they be listening—" Were her heels scooting against the floor? There was a lot of slack for his arms after the noise. "See. They knew you were awake."

He didn't see anyone or hear footsteps, but needed to get the game going. "Before we get started, fellas, I want you to know that you can let Kenderly go. She doesn't know anything and has been trying to get away from me for three days."

A solitary clap, followed by another, echoed throughout the room. "Nicely played, Lieutenant Travis. But also quite false." Paul Tenoreno walked in front of him.

"Nice suit, fancy ostrich boots, manicured nails—all the signs of a person with money. Should you be visiting the dungeon? Or getting your own hands dirty? That's taking a big chance with your freedom."

He was a short man, no more than five-eight, unless you were sitting on the floor and could only see his kneecaps.

"Don't be absurd. I know all about you, Garrison Travis. You have a twin sister, aunt, mother and what a trag-edy, your father was killed when you were a teenager. So don't think you can lie your way out of this. There is no way out."

"Me, lie? Naw, you got that all wrong, pal. I'm a Texas Ranger. We're the freaking oldest law around and han-dle things the old-fashioned way. We don't need to lie."

His head whipped back on the receiving end of a left cross. He forced his jaw to move from side to side, crack-ing it back into place. Tenoreno had jabbed him hard. "Dammit. I honestly didn't think you'd do that."

"Come on, Garrison. How do you think I got to where I am today?" He smiled and splayed his hands in an in-nocent gesture.

Garrison's wrists were jerked away from him. He felt the tug stop and turned his head, attempting to see the scuffle he heard. He saw the murdering bastard who had pulled the trigger held a gun to Kenderly's head. He pulled her by the long strands of multicolored gold and forced her to kneel.

Garrison didn't want to panic. He had to stay calm, keep a cool head, think through what needed to be done. He couldn't. That was Kenderly.

As much as he tried, he couldn't fake it. He'd seen what that scar-faced monster had done to two women. Kenderly's hands were still behind her. Garrison tried to reassure her. The terror in her dark brown eyes spread quickly across her face.

The soulless bastard twisted his fist in her hair, butted the barrel against her temple.

"You see my dilemma. I only need one person to get what I want. We threatened your…health shortly after your arrival. Miss Tyler cares for you and begged for your life. But I believed her when she told us she doesn't possess the information I require."

"We didn't find anything. The jewelry case was empty. Maybe whatever you're looking for fell on to the lawn when we climbed over the balcony. Why not just let her go?"

Tenoreno nodded. His hired thug tugged harder. Kenderly cried out. She was trying to be brave, but the tears streamed down her cheeks.

"We don't have it." He needed time. *Think*.

"That I already know. Where did you hide it?" Tenoreno nodded again.

Garrison's heart stopped as he watched the trigger being squeezed. Kenderly screamed on a long sigh. He shouted no or screamed it himself.

The revolver clicked on an empty chamber.

"Stop. All right." He shook his head, unable to get the image of Kenderly lying dead in front of him out of his mind. "We hid it. But we go together. That's the deal. You want it back? We go together."

When Tenoreno found the flash drive, they'd be dead anyway.

"Tell me what you saw. Prove that I should invest additional time in this venture."

Garrison didn't answer. It went against everything in him. Everything true and right that his father had instilled bounced around in his head, contradicting what his gut told him needed to be done. He heard his mother's voice, too. Begging him to stay alive. Anything he could do to prolong their lives gave them a fighting chance to get away. To jump on a possible mistake.

Staying alive longer...a fighting chance.

Tenoreno looked bored. He flicked a finger, and Kenderly cried out in pain as her head was yanked backward. "Do I really need to have Thomas pull the trigger again? This time it might have a bullet in the chamber. Do you wish to see your friend's brain all over my walls?"

"Garrison?" His name whispered from Kenderly's lips said more than he could express. She didn't have the information that could be given to Tenoreno.

Kenderly's eyes locked with his, pleading for him to say something, to save her life. Her eyes were blacked from the tears ruining her makeup again. Her cheekbone was swollen from being hit. Her bottom lip had been split, and a dark stain of blood trailed across her chin. The revolver's barrel pressed against her had scratched her temple.

The bastard Thomas played with the trigger. His finger tapped it like Morse code. But it wasn't Morse. It was itching to pull it for real.

Garrison strained at his chains. They weren't giving an inch more. He couldn't break away and save her. "Files. Names. Dates. Payments."

"A good guess, but I'm waiting for my proof." Tenoreno crossed his arms and didn't appear patient.

"The deputy first assistant AG of Texas," Garrison blurted.

"That wasn't difficult." He flicked his finger, and the gun disappeared into his man's pocket.

"Dammit, let go of her."

His words had no effect. She was jerked to her feet and then out of his sight.

"Take her to the van," Tenoreno directed, pulling his own weapon from inside his coat. "And send Leonard in here for Mr. Travis."

"Where are you taking her?" Garrison yanked on his cuffs, wishing he could break his thumb and get free.

"Don't worry. You'll be with her. One wrong move while we're retrieving the flash drive, you even blink wrong and she's dead."

"You're going to kill us anyway."

"You know, Travis, I'm not such a bad person. Not as gruesome as you might think. I've got a proposition and a way for your friend to disappear."

"And you think I'll believe you? Why?"

"All you have to do is cooperate. Just follow through on the headlines that are already out there." He leaned against the wall, cocking his head to the side like a big shot, gun relaxed in his hand.

If Garrison were free, he'd take care of this mafia wannabe with one punch.

"Plain speak, if you can. Enough with the riddles. What do I have to do to get you to let Kenderly go?"

"Take the fall, Mr. Travis." He pulled a flash drive from his pocket identical to the one hidden. "I got a ton of these being dropped off at papers and the news programs. You admit that you murdered Isabella and Trinity, and we're done. You go to jail, and she gets a fresh start in the state of her choice."

"It won't work."

"Sure it will. If she opens her mouth, you die in prison. If you don't get convicted, she dies in her new town. I've seen the way she looks at you. She'll do anything you tell her. Course, she stays as my…guest until we're square. She can earn her keep with free haircuts for all the boys."

"It won't work. Nobody will believe I've been working for you."

"People will believe anything." He held his palm toward the door, stopping someone from coming inside. "Especially since you're a lofty Texas Ranger. You're going to take the Rosco family down with you. It's brilliant."

The gun barrel bounced up and down like a presentation pointer.

Was he for real?

Tenoreno might just be crazy enough to believe himself. But Garrison wasn't. If he agreed to this insanity, the Rosco family would have him killed as soon as his butt hit a jail bench.

"What's your answer, lawman?"

There had to be an ulterior motive. Why did he want to involve the Texas Rangers?

Garrison didn't know, but there was only one way to find out.

"I'll do it."

Chapter Nineteen

It had taken the entire two hour drive from Waco to Austin to clear the bureaucratic tape for permission to search the crime scene. When Jesse arrived there were police cars blocking the house and another argument about jurisdiction.

Johnson was on the computer in the car while Jesse leaned on the hood. Three Austin cops stared at him. He wasn't new to how agencies worked together. He'd been with the Texas Department of Public Safety long enough to have experienced his fair share of joint law enforcement.

This was different.

He hadn't been allowed to search on his own. Hell, he hadn't been allowed to stand in the background and look over someone's shoulder while they searched. These officers were treating Johnson and him like suspects. There was nothing relaxed in the posture of the policemen watching him. They looked ready for a fight.

Same as him.

"Any luck, Johnson?"

"No. It's the middle of the night, and no one's picking up, not for me, not for the major." He stood, leaning his elbow on the top of the car. "Oaks pulled through. He's still in ICU with his wife. Guards—from headquarters and the Austin PD—are outside his door. My buddy there didn't know if they were protecting the captain or if they were there to arrest him."

"Something smells like rotting fish." He lowered his voice, nodding to their own guards. "I've got a bad feeling about this."

"Your turn to try the major."

Jesse didn't get it. He'd just said the major hadn't had any luck. So why would he... Once Johnson raised his eyebrow and darted his eyes toward the car, Jesse smartened up. Tensions were high, and Johnson wanted privacy. Got it.

Once inside Johnson snapped his seat belt. "I think we'd be better off leaving for the moment." A police officer ran down the front steps of the battered house. "Now."

Jesse didn't argue. The surrounding officers slowly approached the vehicle, hands on their weapons. He put the car in Reverse and gunned it, weaving backward through police cars and civilian cars parked on the street.

He spun the wheel, threw the car in Drive, praying that his transmission wasn't stripped, and gunned it again.

"Mind telling me what that's all about? And how the hell did you know it was about to happen?"

"Don't stop. We need to find a place to chill for a while." Johnson grabbed his cell from his shirt pocket and began playing a video.

"Is that the news?"

"Yeah. Keep driving."

Jesse listened to the male newscaster. "While this isn't the first time that a Texas Ranger will be indicted or brought to trial, it will be the first time in modern history. WGPN has an anonymous source that evidence has been found linking Lieutenant Garrison Travis to the Rosco family business interests. It's long been suspected that the Rosco family has ties to the drug cartels in Mexico. Authorities are reporting that the rangers in Company F will be temporarily detained until more information is available. Company F is based in Waco where the…"

"What evidence?" Jesse asked.

"Another online source reported a second bank account with payments directly from the Roscos."

"You don't believe that, do you?"

"No. You two haven't been in the company long, but that man bleeds Lone Star red, white and blue."

"You got that right." Jesse hit the main thoroughfare and slowed to blend in with traffic.

"I was at his house yesterday. Remember? If Travis had extra cash, he's not the type who could hide it for long. He'd be living large."

"You think Major Parker is up now?"

Johnson nodded. "You got a place in mind to lay low?"

"We're driving back to his aunt's, taking charge and getting inside. Period. Kenderly Tyler told me to look in the water. I don't think she'd have risked a call before dialing 911 in order to give me false information. We need to find the real evidence."

"Agreed. It probably looks like a normal flash drive. They don't hold up in water so what do you think she meant?" Johnson asked.

"No clue. If being accused of murder wasn't enough, the press accusing him of being dirty will kill Garrison. Is anyone out there on his side?"

"We are," Johnson reminded him matter of factly.

"If Garrison and the woman are still alive, we need to find them. How's that going to happen if we're all in jail?"

"Maybe that's the plan. The evidence that WGPN claimed is exclusive is showing up on multiple sources."

Johnson looked up from scanning his phone. "That's not a coincidence. Someone sent out multiple copies."

"You know these families better than anyone in the state. What's Tenoreno's game plan? What's he trying to do?"

"It looks like he's setting the Rosco family up to take the fall for killing his wife. We have to make that assumption, since they're the ones implicated."

"And why involve Travis?" Jesse asked.

"It sidelines the Rangers. Maybe Oaks was closer to something than we know. We need to find the real evidence." Johnson continued staring at him. "Are you going to force me to ask where you think we should start?"

"The garage. Just makes sense. The two of them found some kind of evidence. He's out of money. Can't risk a call to me. Travis came here for his bike. Transportation to Waco, to the men he trusted to turn himself over to. He knows he's compromised, stashes the evidence nearby. Then heads out hoping to lose Tenoreno's men, can't and then we have an incident at the market that's less than a mile away."

"So you're thinking there's some type of water in or close to the garage."

"Damn straight."

"Now we just have to get it *out* of the garage without being arrested." Johnson shoved his glasses up his nose.

And determine where to find his best friend and the eyewitness. Then clear their names of murder charges. Then save the day. No problem. Typical Texas Ranger stuff.

"Aw hell no," Johnson exclaimed, reading his phone. "They caught him. They just announced he'll be turned over at the county courthouse within the hour."

Chapter Twenty

"This is the wrong way. We're heading south. My aunt's house is north," Garrison whispered. Kenderly had made the same assumption when the tall office buildings of downtown Austin came into view.

They were in the back of a van again. This one had a little more room than the delivery truck of a couple of days ago. It had two small windows high in each back door. They could see each other from the headlights shining inside.

Two armed men sat in the front. The checkered-shirt pervert was driving. The other one pointed his weapon straight at her.

"I wish I could hold your hand or something. Or maybe have you tell me what's going on."

The man in the passenger seat faced forward, and Kenderly twisted closer to Garrison. She didn't know how she managed, but she did.

"Maybe we shouldn't push our luck trying to snuggle."

"Shush. I've been dying to tell you this," she whispered. How did he keep his sense of humor in a situation like this? "I called your friend Jesse when I was in the market office and told him about the flash drive. You don't think that checkered-shirt pervert found it, do you? Jesse will help us, right?"

"If he can."

"What's going on, Garrison? What did Isabella's husband do to you?"

"Damn, you're wonderful."

Had she heard him right? She scooted as close as she could, resting her head awkwardly on his shoulder.

"I mean it," he said, kissing her forehead. "You're just…terrific."

"Oh, golly gee, I like you, too." She answered with old-fashioned sarcasm, then tilted her face to where she could see him. "What is this, seventh grade?"

"Can't a guy give his girl a compliment and tell her he likes her?"

"Here? We're going to share our feelings while handcuffed, in the back of a van taking us to who knows where, with guns pointed at us? And seriously, Garrison… I look a mess."

"Yeah. It'll be a story to remember. Grandkid worthy, maybe."

What?

Lieutenant Garrison Travis, named after two famous Texans, raised his eyebrows as if asking her a question, then winked at her. He kissed the tip of her nose and made her want to cry at the beauty of it. Even handcuffed and probably headed to a grave in the middle of nowhere. His confession was absolutely beautiful.

Even if it did seem like their timing was always off. "I'm really glad it was you who came to rescue me."

"Sweetheart, this is definitely not my best work. Good thing I can't reach more than your nose," he whispered. "Your bottom lip looks like it hurts, and I wouldn't be all that gentle."

She stretched and he stretched, and they met in the middle. He wasn't gentle. The van bumping along made it worse. But since it might be her last kiss ever, she pushed through the little pain and shared it with him.

"You sure do like showing me I'm wrong." He kissed her again. Softly. Grazing her lip with a gentle touch. "Um…you were telling me about your call to Jesse. I assume you left him a message."

She nodded.

"Hey, get away from each other," the checkered-shirt criminal shouted from the front.

"Stay where you are, Kenderly. Go ahead. Shoot us. Then the deal's off. Tenoreno will forgive you. Won't he?"

They hit a bump and readjusted. Garrison ignored the grumblings, focusing his stare back on her.

"What are you talking about? What deal?" She was afraid to ask but had to know.

"The one I made to be the fall guy for a crime boss."

"You did nothing of the sort." She couldn't believe that he'd agree to that. He'd spoken with so much pride about fulfilling his father's hopes and dreams. "What about the spotless Texas Ranger reputation?" Her voice had grown louder, but she was suddenly furious. He had to be doing this for her. Then, in a softer whisper, "You've got a plan, right?"

"To stay alive?" His smile split his face.

It was the smile from when they'd first met. The one she'd been warned about. The one that convinced her he wasn't telling the entire truth. He had a plan, all right. But what if that was what he was stretching the truth about?

"Remember one thing for me, Kenderly. Tenoreno has no intention of letting either one of us live. There's a lot at stake here. He murdered his wife to keep a lid on it. He murdered Rosco's just because she was there."

"But if he's turning you over to the police, can't they

help us? What if we tell the truth? Won't your friend find the flash drive? That proves he's guilty."

"He's already sent a different one framing me to just about everyone in the media. I don't think we can count on the police. Tenoreno's got high-ranking officials on his payroll."

She was scared again. They'd gone from witnesses to murder suspects to confessed killers in less than four days. How could this happen? Bad luck? Would it end with Tenoreno winning? Would they really be dead?

She couldn't question him further. She had nothing to say. No ideas. She wanted to wrap her arms around him and couldn't. She wanted to hold on to him and never let go.

The van turned and slowed to a stop.

"Remember. No one in uniform is going to tell you the truth. They either want you to believe a lie, or they've been fed the lie to repeat. But you can trust Jesse. Get out of here. Find him. Promise me."

"I promise."

She hoped and prayed that he did have a plan and that they'd be running in a few minutes to find someone with a handcuff key.

"Step out of the vehicle. Nice and slow. Get those feet on the ground fast."

Blinded by more flashlight beams than she could distinguish, she couldn't see who was holding them. Then she realized there were flashes a few feet behind them. She heard the whirring of a professional camera.

Both she and Garrison followed the step-by-step instructions exactly. With their hands behind their backs, they were unable to hide their faces. As bad as she looked, the bruises developing on her face would not hide her identity. Even a kick to his head wouldn't hide Garrison's distinctive features.

"Where are we?" she asked once she had both feet on the sidewalk, still blinded by cameras. "What's going on?"

"The county's booking your boyfriend for murder. That's what." The voice belonged to a woman in a police uniform.

"We didn't—"

"Kenderly, don't say a word. You'll be out of here in two shakes. Ignore the taunts and don't answer them— any of them." Garrison was escorted in front of her.

This time the men surrounding him were in different uniforms. There were a couple of men in suits, but none of them wore a white hat representing the Rangers.

"It'll work out," he said, twisting in his escorts' hands. "And remember what we talked about." He was pulled from her and disappeared into the crowd.

The media frenzy gathering for Garrison's arrest was in front of the courthouse. She was still in handcuffs, walking uphill about fifteen feet behind those surrounding him. They continued leading her hero to a podium, but she was held on the outskirts of the crowd. Her body recoiled at the checkered-shirt's hands grasping her arm. The memory of his search for the flash drive made her gag.

Someone spoke at the podium in the distance, but she couldn't focus on his words. Cameras and lights were pointed toward him, leaving her in the dark. The vile checkered-shirt creep turned on a flashlight and pointed it at her face.

"Lieutenant Garrison Travis has a statement to make," the voice she couldn't see announced.

She wished she could swat the bright beam from her eyes. She could only assume that she was spotlighted to remind Garrison she was still in danger. She didn't want to be. She yanked on her arms. Twisted. Tried to fall to the cement. The flashlight wavered. But never dropped.

"I guess by now you all know who I am. I'll be saving the taxpayers some money by waiving my right to council and pleading guilty to the charges."

"No—" she wailed, only to be cut off by a hand over her mouth.

"This is really unusual," one of the voices from the crowd shouted. "Why the makeshift press conference in the middle of the night?"

The blinding light turned off, and she could see Garrison being led away. She was crying at the thought of never seeing him again. Maybe a little because the next few moments seemed so bleak.

"We're taking Miss Tyler to get debriefed," checkered-shirt said.

She didn't know who was listening to him. Her eyes were a bit blurry from the tears, and she couldn't see until she blinked them away. There had to be a place where she could make a run for it.

They walked on a sloped hill, but even then she was so weak she didn't think she could outrun two very fit men—or even unfit men. Emotions and fatigue were wearing her down. They drew even with the van again, and the man from the passenger seat opened the door.

A booted foot kicked out, connecting with his head. The man crumpled to the ground. The checkered-shirt pervert reached for something but let her go.

Kenderly ran. She didn't look back. Her hair blew in front of her face, she flipped it away and darted in front of an oncoming car. She was across the street and ran through an opening in the wall.

Furiously pushing the elevator button, she read that it

was the county jail and courthouse parking. She got on the elevator and rode it to the top floor. She ran in between the only two cars parked next to each other.

"Of all the rotten luck," she huffed. "No one's going to help someone in handcuffs."

Collapsing, she leaned on the tire and sat, forbidding any more tears to come, refusing to let herself panic. She'd gotten this far.

"Maybe I can break my thumb," she mumbled.

"Why don't you come with us instead?" a man in a suit and glasses asked her.

Kenderly bolted in the opposite direction, but within seconds two men grabbed her by the arms. Practically lifting her off the ground they ran down the ramp to a truck parked on the level below.

"Wait a minute. Where are you taking me? If you're going to kill me, just get it over with."

"You don't mean that. You didn't sound like the quitting type. Never give up. Kenderly, do you recognize my voice? I'm Jesse Ryder, Garrison's best friend and partner."

Talking didn't slow him down, but his words certainly did relax her. They got her on the floor of the truck and were leaving the garage in record time. Jesse drove, and the second man took out his keys.

"Let's get these things off you. Can you lift your arms any?" She did and he unlocked the cuffs.

"Is it okay to sit in the seat now?" She rubbed her wrists and rolled her shoulders, constantly looking behind them. No one followed. "They're going to realize I'm gone. Those men—"

"We took care of them. We need to get you out of here."

"Not without Garrison. They're going to kill him as soon as he makes a statement."

"I agree. It's logical. Why else would they have a press conference at this late hour unless that's exactly what they intend to do," Jesse said.

"That's true," the other man stated. "We need backup."

"There's no time. Believe me. They won't risk you or anyone else talking to him. Tenoreno doesn't want any delays." She argued, feeling as if she was an expert on Paul Tenoreno. "Garrison is in serious danger. There's no time. You're the only chance he has to get out of there."

She was about to plead, but one look at their faces and she knew they believed her. Their hesitation made her ask, "What now?"

"Just one problem," Jesse mumbled.

"We show our faces up there, and we'll be arrested," Glasses said.

"What's your name?" she asked. "Don't you have guns?"

Jesse didn't wait at the red light. He turned right from the middle lane, taking her farther from Garrison.

"Bryce Johnson, and yes ma'am, we have guns." He turned in his seat, pulling the seat belt closed, quieting the warning ding sounding throughout the cab.

"Then, why can't you use them?" She sat forward until her head was between the seats, and she could look at both men. "I'll drive the getaway truck."

Chapter Twenty-One

Garrison couldn't see Kenderly anywhere. There was a gun in his side. He was headed into a courtroom that had his name all over it. These guys weren't wasting any time. They were going to tape his confession and get him arraigned.

He doubted he'd make it to a holding cell alive.

No regrets on choosing this path. Neither of them would have made it this far if he hadn't agreed. If he could get these cuffs off, he would have a fighting chance. A slim fighting chance was better than none at all.

Had to be soon or there'd be no chance to save Kenderly.

It surprised him just how much he'd meant it when he'd talked of sharing the stories with their grandkids one day. At this point it seemed like an unrealistic dream. Kenderly was the first woman he'd ever had a thought like that about.

If they got out of this alive, it was worth seeing if the dream could happen.

Pushed, shoved, tripped along the way... He took all of the abuse from law enforcement officers, knowing how he'd feel by a betrayal like this.

Three county deputies propelled him into the court-room chambers. They stood guard after pulling out a chair and gesturing for him to sit. They didn't speak. He couldn't tell if their looks were honest disgust or dishonest smirks.

Commotion at the back of the room. He didn't care. He calmed his heart rate, preparing to focus the last bit of his energy on escape.

Kenderly needed him.

He memorized the room. Estimated the distance between each guard. Looked to see if their weapons were secured. The deputy farthest from him had his thumb break unsnapped on his holster. He could be compromised, his weapon stolen faster than the others.

Once he made a break, it was useless to try and quiet the other deputies. There was nothing in the room to keep them from yelling. He'd have to run. Take the hallway the judges used, either direction would have a staircase to the bottom floor. He was only one flight up, he could do that in seconds.

The trick would be to get out of the building. Finding a door that wasn't already surrounded, expecting him, with a dirty cop there ready to pull the trigger.

"I don't care if he's refused council or not. The state's attorney's office doesn't want anything called into question. We need a certified signed confession to what he stated earlier. Now, step aside."

He knew that voice and suppressed the urge to turn around to acknowledge Bryce Johnson. Garrison forced himself to remain seated at the table instead of making a move. He waited and made eye contact with his colleague. Then he darted his eyes toward the vulnerable guard.

"Get these handcuffs off him immediately." Johnson directed the guard he'd spotted. He slammed his briefcase on the table, took his glasses off and wiped them with a glass-cleaner cloth.

Garrison had seen him do the same thing in their offices daily, but never with this much determination. A guard slowly approached but unlocked his cuffs without a debate. Grabbing the deputy's sidearm, he knocked him to the ground, dragging Johnson across the deputy's chest.

Garrison pulled the other ranger in front of him. There was video in the halls so he staged it to look like Johnson had been taken hostage. That cover would only last a short time. It wouldn't take long for them to discover his fellow ranger had posed as a lawyer to get near him.

"Don't shoot. Put your guns down, you fools," Johnson screamed like a frightened girl, causing the other two deputies to hesitate. They worked together, backing from the room into the hallway reserved for court staff.

As soon as they were through the door, Johnson spun and led the way to an elevator. "Our ride's on the north side of the building. This way. Ryder's waiting with Kenderly. She insisted on driving the truck."

"She would. The doors will be covered by now."

"Use me as a hostage again."

"No. You're staying here."

"I've got news for you, Travis. All of Company F is being detained. I'd rather my stay be in Waco instead of County. I've put a few of the crazies behind bars here."

"That's it." The elevator doors opened, and Garrison jerked Johnson back and led him farther down the hall.

"I have a better if not riskier idea." He spun the deputy's gun and let Johnson take it. "We're going out the prisoner corridor. There's a second-floor bridge to county lockup."

Johnson fished out his badge and put it on his pocket. "I got you. Prisoner. Ranger. This should work."

JESSE RYDER WAS perhaps even more stubborn than Garrison. He wasn't letting Kenderly drive, and he insisted that she lie on the floor of the backseat, so no one would see her. She wasn't stupid. His plan was safer. She understood completely.

And he was right that Garrison would probably sock him for leaving her alone. Look what had happened the last time they'd been separated.

She'd spoken her thought that it might take more than one ranger to bust another out of jail. They'd both laughed.

There really was something about a Texas Ranger creed or code that Garrison was going to have to explain one day.

"Any sign of them?" she asked.

"Nope. But no one's running out of the courthouse like a maniac is loose with a gun yet, either."

"And you expect that?"

"People running out, cops rushing in. Something like that, yeah."

"So how are they supposed to get out of the building? Think you need to take a look around?"

"Johnson has a phone. When they know, I'll go."

"And I thought Garrison didn't communicate well," she mumbled. Her arms and back were killing her. She was starving and probably dehydrated, to boot. She stretched and relocated to the corner of the seat, keeping herself out of the window as much as possible."

"You really should stay on the floor."

"I can look at what's going on for myself this way, and you won't have to talk at all. You should be happy."

"It's safer."

"Listen, I've been through an awful lot in the past twelve hours. I've been threatened, had a gun fired at my brains—empty, but it was frightening. And I'm worried. I promise to sit here in the corner and not show my face." Not to mention thinking Garrison was dead—more than once. "It's been a hell of a day."

Dawn was breaking behind them. The orange and yellows were reflecting off the windows in the jail.

"What happens now, Jesse? Let's say they do get out, and no one shoots them again."

"Again?"

"Are we all fugitives? Where do we go? How can we possibly get out of this city with the police and the sheriff's department and, shoot, let's not forget the other rangers on the prowl?"

Maybe it was the lack of sleep or everything finally staring her in the face, but she felt kind of loopy. Maybe the bubbling anxiousness starting to shake all her insides was what hysteria felt like. She didn't know and had little control. The feeling wouldn't stop or go away.

"When does Paul Tenoreno and the men he has do his dirty work get his comeuppance?"

"I don't have all those answers, Kenderly. We take things one step at a time. And I promise you. Garrison will be cleared and Tenoreno will go to jail."

She kept her face pushed back in the corner of the seat. Right up to the time the police cars began circling the building. Jesse started the engine, but they cut him off. He immediately began calling his partner's cell. No luck.

With no way out, she watched the ranger switch off the engine and drop his badge and weapon in a compartment under the console. "Kenderly, the officer is coming my direction. If you can get out on the passenger side, you might be able to make it between those parked cars without him seeing you. The other officers are heading to the courthouse. Can you do it?"

"But—"

"No buts. Take my phone and credit card, password's seven nine eight three, and zip code is seven six seven nine nine." The phone and small card holder slid over the console, and she grabbed both. "Got it? Garrison will find you. Remember that. Ready? Go now."

Jesse got out of the truck at the same time she opened her door. As she snuck to the other side of the street, she heard him confronting the police officer, asking questions, raising his voice and being slammed into the front of his truck.

She stuffed the phone in her bra. If it was on silent, she wanted to feel it ring.

Jesse was still drawing attention to himself when she snuck to the next car, and the next. There was construction equipment along the street. She stood up behind it and turned into the parking lot, leaning against the stone wall that separated it from the street.

Her heart raced and her hands shook. She shoved them through her hair and wondered how she could do this on her own. She sank to the ground, unable to keep her knees from buckling.

What if none of them got free? She took a deep breath, then another. Sirens sounded around her. She jumped with the vibration of the phone but pulled it free and started swiping to answer it.

"Jesse?"

"Garrison? It's me."

"Thank God, Kenderly. I'm coming to you. Just tell me where you are."

"Across from the courthouse. Jesse was arrested. Is Bryce okay?"

"Sweetheart, be a little more specific." He was running. She could hear him breathing hard.

"There's construction across the street. I'm against the wall."

"Listen carefully. Do you know how to get to the capitol from there? Johnson said that you and Jesse were on Eleventh Street, same as the capitol. Can you get there?"

"I think so."

"No, sweetheart, you can. We got this. I'll stay on the phone with you. Come on. You walking yet?"

Hysteria or shock was wearing off. She inched her way up the rock wall and saw an exit the direction she needed to go. The police were focused on the opposite side of the street, but she didn't want to risk it.

"What about Bryce?" she asked again.

"He's headed to headquarters to get Jesse out. You know this city. Where can we meet?"

"I'm heading to the west entrance to the capitol grounds. We should be closer to that side. The actual park won't be open at this time of day." She was thinking straight once more. The anxiety that had overwhelmed her for a moment was gone. "Are you okay, Garrison?"

He was still running but answered yes.

"I've met friends across the street from the park on Twelfth, there's a small monument in the greenbelt." She picked up her pace, ready to be back at his side. "I'll wait for you there."

"Sure thing. They didn't get the evidence."

"They mentioned that." So that would be their next move, back to his aunt's house again. "Going there hasn't been very lucky for us."

"I… Maybe you should sit this one out, babe."

"No way. I'm safer with you than anywhere else." And saner. If they lived through this, they could laugh at her going crazy together. "Remember what you said about great stories for the grandchildren?"

"Yeah," he spoke on a marathon breath.

"I'm going to hold you to it, Lieutenant Travis."

Kenderly stood at the statue. Content to just hear Garrison's heavy breathing.

"Don't jump," he said.

She turned around and there he was. She'd never been so glad to see someone in her life. They hung up, and she ran across the street to him, flying into his arms. Not thinking until afterward about his injuries. They didn't seem to matter as he held her to his chest and kissed her as if they'd been apart forever.

"Let's get out of here," he whispered before kissing her again.

Chapter Twenty-Two

Kenderly was quiet and drifted off with the swaying of the cab. Garrison was a lifetime away from relaxing. He couldn't think that she'd relaxed as much as she was just plain exhausted. He'd had a restful drug-induced nap, but she'd been awake for twenty-three hours. The past day had been nonstop action.

If he could think of any place safe, he would have taken the taxi there. He wanted to leave the city with her in his arms and just disappear. As soon as they stepped back on the street, she'd be back in danger again. There just didn't seem to be a path that would keep them out of the line of fire. He skimmed her bruised cheek with the back of his fingers.

It made him choke up just thinking about her begging for his life. Choke up worse when she didn't beg for her own. He hadn't known many women—other than his sister—who could be this brave.

The cab dipped into a pothole, waking Kenderly just as they reached the parking lot near the market. Garrison used Jesse's card to pay, then they took the long way around back. As soon as they turned the corner he saw his bike was still hidden in the alley.

"I didn't think it would still be here."

"Why not?" Kenderly yawned. "It hasn't been twelve

hours since we left. It only feels like it's been a week. Just like it seemed an eternity when you were unconscious."

Kenderly weaved as she walked, but she was still hanging in there. He held on tight to an amazing woman. He hated the thought of losing her again, realizing his fear would stay with him a good long while. For the first time, he came close to understanding what his mother went through after losing his dad and watching both of her children go into law enforcement.

He cared deeply for Kenderly. If their relationship could survive starting this way, it might just survive an average day-to-day life without hiccups.

"How are you going to start that? Didn't Tenoreno's men take your keys?"

"I can pick the storage compartment lock. I have a spare inside. I just need to find a piece of wire. There should be some here in an alley."

"Well, while you do, I'm going to sit down over on these steps and rest my eyes for a few seconds."

The adrenaline had worn off as evidenced by her falling straight to sleep while resting her head against the brick. Garrison found his wire, picked the lock and obtained the key. Everything was ready to kick-start and go, but he sat on the seat and watched her.

His mind hadn't worked past retrieving the flash drive and getting the hell out of Austin. Well, except about staying with Kenderly. That was a given. It had to happen.

So they'd pick up the flash drive and then... What would happen to Tenoreno?

Where could they go that they wouldn't be found? He left the bike and sat next to Kenderly. "I need your help."

"Hmm."

"We need to access the files and see what state prosecutor hasn't been purchased. Or find a judge who's safe to ask for a warrant. Then we can turn over the flash drive and go into hiding until the trial."

Libraries and computer stores wouldn't open for another three hours. There were too many cameras at all-night super stores. So what choice did they have? What were the remaining options?

"Kenderly, wake up. Where's a place we could open the files on the flash drive? I don't want to push our luck hanging around Austin waiting on a library to open up."

"Borrow a laptop," she mumbled before dropping her head on his shoulder.

"Borrow? From who?"

"Don't you have any friends?" she mumbled into his shirt.

"Not here, but you do. Don't you, sweetheart?"

"My friends aren't awake at this time of day." She pushed her hair away from her face and stretched an arm to wake up. "Actually, doesn't your dog walker live across the street from your aunt? Why not email the files from there?"

"It'll all be a moot point if the flash drive isn't in the dang water bottle."

"That is so clever of you." She swatted lightly at his shirt. "I had no idea what you meant when you said it was hidden in the water. I still might be a little loopy, though."

Kenderly stood and shook her head. She walked forward a few steps, stretching her neck and then waving her arms. She bent over and touched her toes. Garrison raced forward and swatted her behind. Things were tense. The city of Austin seemed to be trailing them, but he still wanted his hands on her.

She was working on her last ounce of energy but still had a smile for him.

He straddled the seat, and she hopped on behind him. He pulled her close, very familiar with the shape of her thighs.

"Now that I'm awake, remind me why we need to get the flash drive right this minute. You think someone's watching the house, right? And most of the city is looking for an escaped prisoner—meaning you."

He twisted enough to reach one of her hands. He lifted it to his face and brushed his lips across. He swallowed hard, not wanting to tell her the truth, wanting to protect her from it. But if something happened to him, she needed to know what to do.

"With my confession, Tenoreno brought Company F under serious question. The accusations have brought a halt to all the investigations there. Johnson told me a couple of things that are going to go south real quick if it's not resolved fast."

"I couldn't believe you made that false confession. I know how much it means for you to be a ranger. You trust those men, and they may never trust you again. Why would you?"

To save you.

He couldn't tell her she was the reason he'd do it again in a heartbeat.

"Here's where it becomes our problem. We've got nowhere to go. What if we wait, and Tenoreno's men find the evidence? What if he doesn't take any chances and just burns the place down?"

"If he catches us again…" She brushed his hair, skimming his scalp with her nails. "He's going to kill us this time, isn't he?"

He confirmed with a nod. "Finding the flash drive and delivering it to someone who has not been paid off by Tenoreno is the only way we're going to survive. I think he knows that, too. So his men are going to shoot to kill this go-round."

"All right. I'm ready." She wrapped her arms around his waist. "I'll have you know this is going to be hell on my hair again. I take no responsibility for what I'll look like later today."

He laughed. "Sweetheart, no one's going to notice your hair with that awesome shiner you have."

He gunned the bike to a start while she said a loud "what" in his ear. They could only take the motorcycle so far before the engine would alert anyone watching the house. Having it after as a means to leave town—that's why he wanted it close by.

He pulled up on the sidewalk around the corner from his aunt's street. He rolled forward until they could see the house. Parked in front of the driveway was a cop car, cigarette smoke curling from the open window. He pushed them down the sidewalk, back into the access alley behind a privacy fence and under a low overhanging tree.

"I'll get the flash drive. You stay with the bike."

"Can't I come with? I haven't had much luck on my own."

He kissed her, loving every second he spent with her in his arms. "I'll slip around to the back, jump the fence, get the drive and a bottle of water for you. I'll be back in a shorter time than it takes to make Bear fetch a ball. Easy."

"I'm holding you to that."

He removed the gun from his waist and checked his ammo. Not much. He had to trust this was going to work without problems.

KENDERLY WATCHED GARRISON jog through the alley. He would be crossing the street midway at the next block to

avoid detection. So she knew it would take a few minutes. It was a lot more dangerous than his smile let on.

All she had to do was wait. Simple. Sure. Just waiting
had nearly gotten her killed yesterday.

The old alley between the houses had tall grass which
was wet with the early morning dew. She was afraid to
sit, fearing she'd fall asleep as she'd done earlier on the
back steps of the market.

So she waited. Impatiently. She checked the time on
Jesse's phone about every thirty seconds. The bungle of
numbers he'd told her for his password were long forgotten or she would have found what media was saying
about their escape. She was just putting the phone in her
back pocket again when she noticed a car moving at a
snail's pace.

The motorcycle was back far enough it couldn't be
seen from the street. The car passed, and she ran to the
edge of the fence. It pulled through the stop sign and
turned the corner. The familiarity of the man behind
the wheel was probably her imagination. She hoped she
wouldn't be reacting to all dark sedans with almost black
windows that way for the rest of her life.

She kept leaning on the fence when a large man jogged
across the street. She pulled back, hiding. It was Thomas.
She was certain of it. The same murderer who'd held a
gun to her head and pulled the trigger. She'd made peace
with God because she'd thought she was about to die.

The nightmares about him would come for many,
many years.

Garrison! Shoot to kill.

The words battled in her heart and mind. She was safe
where she was. Garrison could be in and out of the garage before Tenoreno's man even reached the house. But
what about the cop sitting out front?

She rushed across the yard, pausing at the corner of the house, feeling like a thief. Thomas was slowly sneaking up the sidewalk, acting like a regular person. But he'd never look that way to her. He was a murderer. She couldn't forget the hatred in his eyes or the delight he took pulling the trigger.

He would kill again. She was certain of that. She saw him raise the back of his loose black shirt, pulling a silver gun and pointing the long, black barrel toward the sky. He was going to kill the police officer and then Garrison.

If she watched him kill another person, she wouldn't be able to live with herself. He was almost at the back of the cop car. The sun glinted off the gun as he dropped it behind his thigh.

"Hey! He's got a gun!" came out of her mouth before she'd thought through what to do next. Thomas turned toward her.

The cop's door flew open, weapon drawn, body ready for a fight. He saw Isabella's murderer and relaxed, nodding his acknowledgment.

The fact that they knew each other glued her feet to the driveway she stood on. Thomas was off to his right, running toward the garage. He was soon hidden by a hedge that separated the houses.

The cop was halfway down the street, heading toward her.

She turned, running across the wet grass. She slid to her knees when she turned away from the motorcycle. She couldn't go back there. She couldn't hide in one of these homes or ask for help. Since the police officer was after her, no one would take her word over his.

He was on top of her in no time at all. He covered her mouth with his hand and dragged her back to his car. She fought every inch of the way, but had no real strength left. He threw her in the backseat and locked her in a nightmare.

"Stay inside, ma'am. There's an armed felon nearby."

That would be Garrison. The dirty cop held his gun and pointed toward the house. She didn't hear anything about backup coming to this address on the police radio. If the cop was dirty, as she suspected, he'd let Thomas murder her.

From where the officer's car was parked she could still see him watching the garage from the corner of the house. It seemed such a long time ago that she'd jumped off that porch and into Captain Oaks's car.

She couldn't see Tenoreno's man. Could barely hear anything outside the car at all.

She kicked and pounded and cried.

There was no way she was getting free or out of here alive. No way.

The officer moved to the yard and into the garage. He came out again, shaking his head. That's when she noticed that Thomas was near the car. His hand was on the passenger door. She pushed as far to the other side as possible. He would use her to draw out Garrison.

Her sacrifice would have been worth it if she'd saved someone's life. But she hadn't. And now if she was used against Garrison...

She was a fool.

Chapter Twenty-Three

"Dammit!" Garrison shouldn't have left her alone. Nothing had gone right—almost nothing—so he should have learned his lesson. But he'd left Kenderly on her own again, and there she sat in the back of a dirty cop's car.

Why couldn't they catch a break?

Tenoreno's man, Thomas, had gotten to the garage a minute too late. Garrison was clearing the back fence when he'd heard Kenderly's shout, warning the officer. He didn't blame her. She had to warn him. Just their luck that he was on Tenoreno's payroll.

Pausing in the overgrown hedge between the houses, he watched. Gun in one hand, and in the other was the flash drive still stuck in the water bottle. He couldn't let Kenderly be threatened or touched again. He'd meant every word he'd said in the van. She was wonderful. And strong. How had she not fallen apart after having a gun to her head?

Thomas didn't need permission to shoot today. When he squeezed the trigger this time, a bullet would be firing into Kenderly.

Where could he stash the water bottle? The neighbor didn't have a storage building. No woodpile or trash can nearby. The garage was attached to the house and not accessible. Nothing besides a swing set and a couple of kids' bikes.

The passenger door was pulled open, Thomas would have Kenderly, yanking her out of the car in seconds. Garrison did the only thing possible, he shoved the water bottle into the thick branches of the hedge and pushed through. He could come back for the evidence. Right now, he needed the gun away from Kenderly.

But first things first. He aimed his weapon. He was a good shot, but the line of sight wasn't clear. He could hit Kenderly or… Damn, they actually needed him alive to face the murder charges. He stepped over a bicycle. The image of his aunt's paper thin walls popped into his head. Thomas or the cop could fire and hit one of the neighbors inside their home.

He had to keep the fight in his aunt's yard and somehow not fire his weapon. How was he supposed to keep criminals from shooting? He holstered his gun.

"This should be a hell of a fight," he mumbled to himself. Garrison walked quickly and silently along the hedge. But when Thomas latched on to Kenderly's arm he shouted to get his attention.

"I sure hope you're carrying some ID, you son of a bitch. When we're done, they're going to need to identify the body. Can you handle someone closer to your size?"

Thomas stood, his body still blocking the way out of the vehicle for Kenderly. While swinging his weapon around, Garrison charged the last twenty feet.

Garrison slid feet first, using Thomas's ankles like second base. He popped back up, elbowing the gun from his opponent's thick hands, following it with a left punch to the gut. They danced apart like in a boxing ring, hands up, bodies angled for the first jab.

Thomas roared, dipped his head and charged like a

rhinoceros. He crashed into Garrison, slamming him to the ground. The force took both of them into the neighbor's front yard.

If he could just get up… But Thomas trapped him in the wet grass and punched the side of Garrison's aching head. Garrison punched back, sending two jabs to Thomas's right kidney.

There was another punch to his jaw, and Garrison couldn't get free. He needed Thomas off him, but he couldn't budge him. He drew back his arm, aiming to hit below the belt—

Where was she? He saw the cop creeping closer to his squad car, Kenderly leaning from it to get the gun. "Look out."

The cop jumped forward, pinning her arm under his shoe just before she reached his weapon. The cop leaned down, and she screamed.

"Kenderly?" She didn't answer.

Garrison shoved with all his might. He had to get to her. Finding strength he didn't know he still had, he forced Thomas backward. They both scrambled to their feet. Circling. Ready to attack like wrestlers.

Kenderly was still on the ground. "Get up." The cop nudged her with his boot. She got slowly to her knees, then grabbed the door to help.

Garrison tried to fake Thomas out in order to get to Kenderly, but his opponent planted his feet firmly between them.

The cop tried to lift her with one arm. When that didn't work, he shoved his weapon under her arm and attempted to help her to stand. Garrison caught his breath trying to determine how to get her out of there. She used the outside of the door to pull herself up.

Dammit. He couldn't pull his gun since the cop still had his weapon practically in Kenderly's face.

"Give me the gun and the girl," Thomas growled at the cop.

Behind them he saw Kenderly perk up. Her eyes connected with his. Thank God she was faking it.

The cop reached around her. She shoved the door, slamming it into the cop's arm. He lost his weapon. The gun bounced away from the patrol car, Kenderly went after it but hesitated before following it under the car.

"Dammit, run!" Garrison shouted at her, reaching for the gun at his back. "Get out of here."

Before he could get a firm grip, he turned into a right cross from his opponent. His vision spun with the rest of his head as he fell to the ground. In the blink of Garrison's eye, Thomas had his hands around Kenderly's throat.

The look of desperation he'd seen on her face at Tenoreno's was back as she clawed at the thick hands choking the life from her.

"Where is the flash drive?" he gritted out between his teeth.

Garrison drew on all his strength and rammed Thomas in his side, breaking his hold on Kenderly. They fell on to the rear of the car, then rolled to the pavement on the street. He heard Kenderly coughing, still on her knees. Thomas's hands quickly circled his own windpipe, cutting off the oxygen.

Garrison pulled both thumbs backward, forcing the release. "You. Can't. Win." He fought to say the words between punching and getting punched.

The pavement hadn't grown warm yet, but the sun reflected off metal and into his eyes. The gun. He and Tenoreno's man rolled over and then back again. He'd lost sight of Kenderly. He finally twisted away and kicked his opponent's chest.

Barely an umph escaped. He kicked again, and the guy knocked him on his back. Garrison rolled to his feet and connected with a rib. He remembered how much his head had hurt after yesterday's encounter. He kicked out again.

Garrison was brought back to the ground by another twist and tug on his foot, but this time he lashed out, following with a roll forward. Thomas couldn't pursue Garrison to his feet and wasn't prepared for the boot at his throat or weapon in Kenderly's hands.

"Drop it!" Kenderly shouted at the cop who was reaching for his gun. "I've had a horrible day, so don't tempt me to shoot this thing. I'm probably a terrible shot, but I'm bound to hit something."

Garrison scooped up the deputy's gun, pointing it at Thomas. "That goes for you, too. Don't tempt me." He stood shoulder to shoulder—or as best as he could—next to Kenderly. "You okay?"

"For the moment."

"Let me have that, sweetheart." He took the second gun from her shaking hands, then turned to the cop. "Cuff yourself to the live oak."

Someone in the neighborhood was bound to have called the police about the fighting. Good or bad, they'd be arrested, and Thomas would probably walk.

"Cuff your right wrist. Now around the tree. That's right." Out of the corner of his eye he watched Kenderly direct the cop.

"Get in the car, Kenderly. We need to move it."

"But what about—"

"He's coming with us. Yeah, big guy, let's go. No tricks. Just get into the car." Thomas followed the instructions once both guns were trained on him, and Garrison locked him inside.

Kenderly got close, wrapping her arms around his waist. "I'm so sorry, Garrison. I thought he was going to kill the officer. It looked like he was. I couldn't stand there and do nothing. Not again." Her voice trailed off. He knew what she was remembering.

"It's okay. We've got him. And now we have a laptop."

"The one in the car?"

"Yep. If that won't work, we'll go buy one with Jesse's credit card. All we need is a little time and to verify that none of the rangers are involved. Come on, get in."

He ran back to the hedge, found the bottle and got in the driver's seat, pulling away before the sirens made an appearance from the other direction.

Garrison grabbed Kenderly's hand in victory. "Looks like something finally went right for the good guys."

Chapter Twenty-Four

The files were sent to the state attorney general's office. Kenderly's joyous whoop could probably be heard all the way in Dallas. The relief she felt would have been even greater if Thomas, the murderer, wasn't still in the backseat.

Garrison had spoken to the commander of all the rangers after opening the files. Just as he said, there were no Texas Ranger names on it. The list was very thorough and not very long. Only a few local cops, but numerous attorneys who had been appointed to high positions within the state.

Sometimes just a campaign contribution was listed, but the file contained personal notes from Paul Tenoreno. He was meticulous about meetings and conversations. Right down to the politician's dog's name.

An impartial prosecutor should have no problem going to trial with the evidence against Tenoreno and Rosco. Isabella's notes even said where she'd hidden the handwritten ledger kept by her husband. No wonder he was so desperate to retrieve the flash drive.

"I think we've accomplished the impossible." She was definitely on a victory high, but the feeling was wearing off fast.

"Tenoreno still has to go to trial." Garrison's voice was

somber, bringing reality back. "We still have to testify. It might take a while, Kenderly."

They'd both have to give official statements about what happened. But for now, in this moment, they were safe and could rest. She glanced over her shoulder at Thomas, who looked totally undisturbed by it all. His lack of concern frightened her almost as much as when he was about to kill her.

"Want something to eat? I still have Jesse's credit card." She realized Garrison wasn't serious, but she played along. They could relax just a little. Couldn't they?

"What about him?" She pointed to the murderer in the backseat. "And don't you think that the police will be wanting their car back?"

He playfully hit the steering wheel. "Probably. I prefer my truck anyway."

"Not the motorcycle?"

"Well, the bike does get you close to me. But the truck usually works out as the better date vehicle." Garrison smiled and arched an eyebrow.

"If you're attempting to ask me out on a date…" She pointed toward their prisoner again. "Can we get rid of him first?"

"I think Rangers headquarters here in Austin is an excellent place to do both."

"You are totally right."

The man in the backseat didn't do anything except glare. Maybe he knew the futility of trying to escape, or maybe he had nothing to say. She didn't mind. He stared at her, and the only thing she could do was shut her sore eyes and face forward.

"I'm going to have one whopper of a shiny black eye," she continued. But from the little she'd seen of their passenger, Garrison had paid him back ten times over.

They'd come close to dying so many times. Remembering the ordeal of the past four days left her shaking. She laced her fingers together to keep them still. She avoided looking at anything except the cracked nail painted with her favorite polish.

"You okay, Kenderly?"

"Sure. Why wouldn't I be?"

Thomas Whatever-His-Name-Was laughed. In fact he laughed so hard he sounded as if he was wheezing.

"Why is he laughing?" She turned to the man who had spent four days trying to kill her. "You're going to jail for what you did to Isabella and Trinity. I'm going to make sure of that."

"I'll be out of jail before you can wash the makeup off your face." He lurched toward the plastic window. She flinched, causing him to snicker more. "I'm laughing at you, sweet pea. You think this is all over? You'll never be safe. I'll be out walking around, back working for Tenoreno or somebody else, and you'll be stuck in a dingy hotel room."

"Shut up. Just block him out, Kenderly. Don't listen."

She was glad Garrison knew where he was going. She couldn't concentrate on roads or street signs. He reached across the space separating them and held her hand.

"That's right, honey." Thomas tapped on the window. "Don't listen. But it doesn't matter. I know everything about you. Little that there is. I *will* find you, and then I'll rip your heart out."

Garrison flipped a switch, and the sirens started. He ran red lights and pulled into a parking lot a couple of blocks later. He flew out of the car with his gun drawn and yanked open the back door.

"Out. Get out, so I can—just get out."

Did he think he was going to fight the man again?

Kenderly jumped from the car. Thomas was still taking his time. She was sure the criminal saw the rangers rushing from the building and took his time trying to get Garrison riled.

She didn't want any more fighting and ran to the front of the squad car. By then Garrison wasn't alone. Several rangers took Thomas, cuffed his hands and led him to a different door. Two men she recognized as her rescuers from the night before greeted her and escorted her inside.

"You need a doctor, Kenderly. I didn't realize how badly you'd been hit in all the rush to rescue this one's backside." Bryce stood a little straighter and shook Garrison's hand, who now stood next to her.

"He's not going to make bail. No matter what he thinks, says or begs. I promise you that, Kenderly." She looked up at him. His touch gliding across her skin was as soft as a butterfly's wings.

"Hey, bud." Jesse stuck his hand out, but Garrison pulled him into a bear hug.

"How are my dogs?"

"Fine?" Jesse reached for his phone.

"Are you asking me?" Garrison put his hand over his heart, exaggerating every word and smiling.

"Give me a second." Jesse waved him off and walked away.

Garrison faced Bryce. "He forgot to get someone to feed them today, right?"

"Hey, I'm innocent in all this." He threw up his hands in surrender but grinned before pushing the glasses back high on his nose. "He's right, Kenderly. We're going to protect you. You brought down two of the toughest crime families in the state."

She shook her head. "I didn't do it. Isabella is the one

who had the courage to make her life better. She's the one who deserves to be called a hero."

The men nodded their heads and didn't argue.

"You guys are a mess. We need to get you two to a hospital."

Kenderly sat on the bench, exhausted. Moving another inch seemed way too hard. Whatever adrenaline high she'd received from actually winning their fight with Thomas and the police officer had worn off. It had been replaced with a fear she didn't completely understand.

Bryce attempted to convince them to get checked out by doctors until Garrison held up his hand.

"We're not going anywhere, pal. We've been on the go for days and deserve to sit down for a while. But you could spring for a couple of deluxe breakfasts. And pick up some coffee. Mine's black all the way. Kenderly wants a grande café au lait skinny extra foam." Garrison turned Bryce around and scooted him away from the hall bench. "Are you writing this down? It's extra foam. Bacon, not those flat sausage patties." With both men gone, Garrison took her hand and led her down the hall.

Impressive. He remembered her coffee order. She liked that he could momentarily take her mind off the greater problem of staying alive. But the rush of uncertainty hit her again. What was going to happen with the rest of her life? Would she constantly be looking to see who was behind her instead of planning for a future?

It couldn't be a pleasant way to live. And more than likely was the reason Thomas, the murderer, had finally used his voice…trying to scare her.

Once the door was closed in a small conference room, he pulled her into his arms, snug against his chest. She leaned back, and he caught her lips in a kiss. His fingers caressed her skin. She jumped at the contact but remembered who had her in his grasp. Relaxing in the wonderful feeling of his soft control of their touch, her body went all tingly, wanting more.

Garrison swayed backward, gulping for air, tilting his forehead to hers and dropping his hold to her waist.

Something happened between them. She didn't know if a gradual relationship would have developed this way. Between her mundane life and his exciting one, they may never have survived. But after this long weekend together, she knew she wanted to try.

She wouldn't be scared.

Life was an adventure, and she planned to live it.

"We only have a couple of minutes before they separate us and start asking questions." Garrison's deep voice took on an excited anticipation. "I just wanted to say that…that I…um… I think I'm on the verge of falling for you hard, Kenderly Tyler."

"Don't worry, Lieutenant Travis. I'll catch you." She kissed him quickly, gently. Then whispered, "I'm stronger than I look."

"No arguments there."

A knock on the door made him break away from her. They were joined by several men, all with badges on their belts.

The men gestured for Garrison to leave.

"I'll see you for breakfast."

"Breakfast," she mumbled to herself.

Garrison was the last connection to her past. A part of her life she could never return to. He wouldn't leave her. Not after saying that he…that he what? *Might* fall for her? That wasn't the same as saying he had. It wasn't the same as saying he would.

Panic hit.

Alone. Defenseless. She was just a beautician, all on

her own. If she disappeared, no one would know. She wasn't prepared to take down the Texas mafia. How could any of these men think she could do this?

No! She wouldn't be scared. She would have a life. And when the door shut, everything was different. She would force herself to be different.

The person she'd found hiding deep inside over the past four days would stay strong. The new her had no doubt in her mind what she wanted. She wanted to share her new life with Garrison.

"LOOKS LIKE YOU'LL have your choice of assignments now, Lieutenant. Eventually. We'll need all the hubbub to die down, of course. Your confession is going to confuse our public image for a while."

Garrison felt a hard slap on his back and was not so subtly turned toward an interrogation room by a major he recognized from a seminar months ago. He hadn't caught his name while getting one last look at Kenderly. She'd looked alone and—

It hit him like a truck. No. She looked abandoned, and he was the one deserting her.

"Is there no way we can stay close by? I mean, where she can see me. She looks sort of lost."

His escort just clapped a hand on his shoulder and gestured they sit down.

"We know you're tired, Lieutenant. We'll try to get your testimony recorded as quickly as possible. But you know how important it is to get this down while it's still fresh in your minds."

There was no way around the separate rooms and individual interviews. Garrison had no illusions; it was an interrogation. They'd deliberately brought in a friendly face, but he was almost certain the major had given a talk about debriefing tactics.

Garrison would emphasize the importance of Kenderly's help and the need for her testimony. That they would keep her safe in protective custody. He might not get to see her for a while. Okay, he knew that would be the case. They'd probably keep them separated at least until they could check out their stories.

"Are you going to want a lawyer? Are you certain you don't need emergency care?"

"I'm fine for the moment, sir." Might as well relax and get on with it. "Just hungry like usual, and I'll need a heck of a lot of coffee. It's already been a long day."

"I bet it has. Why don't we just start at the beginning? I've got someone working on that coffee."

The next few days were going to be rough. But the Rangers wanted him in the clear as much as he did. Having one of their own involved with a crime family would call into question a lot of their cases. Clearing him would be the best thing for all involved.

"I'm familiar with procedures, sir. Before we get started, I'd like to go on record regarding the threats the man I had in custody made against Miss Tyler. I believe he's a flight risk, but his threats put her at a high risk. Do we need to wait on a prosecutor?"

"We're reviewing the documents you emailed. We were also able to obtain a warrant which is being served as we speak. Thomas Dimon will not be released on bail. Do you have the original flash drive?"

Garrison's body relaxed. His spine was no longer stiff, and his shoulders dropped. Both physical testaments to the tension he felt regarding Kenderly's safety. He plucked the drive from his pocket and set it on the table.

"My phone has pictures of the murderer leaving the scene Friday."

"Let's start with why you were there."

"On Tuesday of last week, I received a call from Captain Aidan Oaks…"

He told his story, and a doctor checked him out, leaving a bandage around his arm and certifying he was physically fit.

With every mention of Kenderly's name, he thought about the last look she'd given him. He should have told her what to expect, but he didn't want to risk influencing her statement.

He'd arrested his fair share of people. He'd escorted witnesses—from both sides of the law. He'd been on stings, car chases, government details… Sitting on this side of an in-depth interrogation wasn't pleasant but would give him insight to the future ones he conducted.

During each interview, he was asked whether he thought Kenderly Tyler, beautician at the Best Little Hair House in Austin, was legit. Each time he cracked a smile, thinking about their wigs and makeup.

Each time he was asked if he thought Kenderly was capable of the murders of Isabella Tenoreno and Trinity Rosco, he said it was impossible.

The questions didn't stop—breaks were few and far between. He didn't mind. It meant they'd be finished quicker. The men treated him like a hero and were friendly enough, but none of them would tell him about Kenderly. No one answered his one question…was she all right?

Chapter Twenty-Five

"Thomas was right. The motel is dingy," she spoke softly to herself. After a week alone, sometimes she needed to make certain her voice still worked. Dingy and dark, especially with the curtains drawn.

Kenderly paced. She wasn't a pacer, yet…she paced. She'd actually paced more in the past week than she'd thought humanly possible. Then again, she hadn't been outside Rangers headquarters or motel rooms for over a week.

The unknown bugged her. The not knowing where or how long. Everything about starting over. Would she ever be safe? It all bugged her. They had Thomas Dimon in custody, and she'd been assured he wouldn't make bail. They'd indicted Paul Tenoreno, and he also hadn't made bail, which was a huge relief.

But she'd lost control of her life because she had been in the wrong place at the wrong time. At least she wasn't crying about the situation.

But maybe she wanted to, just a little.

She'd thought she'd grown very close to Garrison, and then he'd just left. His last words had been about breakfast. Two days of being deposed or debriefed and feeling alone. She wasn't allowed to call anyone except an attorney. After they assured her no charges were being brought, she didn't need one. She was told time and time again what she couldn't do. Then another week of just sitting, hidden in several run-down motels.

Not one person had mentioned anything about her future. The more they veered away from the subject, the more her brain dwelled on it. And on Garrison.

So she paced.

The men in and out of Company F's headquarters looked like genuine Texas Rangers—boots, jeans, dress shirts, guns and white Stetsons. It was sort of hard to think of Garrison Travis as one of them. He was her personal hero in a curly wig.

But wasn't he the one who put you in a room with strangers and just left?

It was easy to remind herself just how heroic he'd been with each retelling of their adventure to another prosecutor with a video camera. But it was harder to believe when she was alone in a new motel room every night. The prosecutors reminded her how well they'd do with the evidence and testimony. But it was no consolation to walking away from everything she'd built for herself or business.

It just didn't help that she was so completely alone. It gave her too much time to play the what-if game. What if things had been different?

"Blah, blah, blah." Tired of talking to herself again. "It doesn't matter now."

She'd made her decision to honor Isabella and Trinity by testifying, no matter what. She crossed her arms and looked out the window, longing to be outside in the fresh sunshine.

Kenderly stretched her neck from side to side to re-

lieve the stiffness. "How can I be so stiff from just pacing? This is never going away while I'm sleeping in a
motel bed."

"I still owe you a back massage." Garrison was in
the doorway.

Shiny boots, black jeans, crisp white shirt, white hat
and a genuine glad-to-see-you smile that she'd sorely
missed. It was so corny to think that she'd missed him
more than anything in her life. They'd known each other
for so little time, but she did. She couldn't hide how seeing him made her happy.

"I DON'T THINK you'll want it here, though." Garrison
loved the unreserved joy on Kenderly's face when she
saw him. She no longer looked abandoned, just impatient. "How you holding up?"

It was good to see that she'd come out of this whole
thing relatively unharmed. The one conversation he'd
had about Kenderly was with Major Parker and Captain
Oaks when they'd asked what Garrison wanted as his
next assignment.

"I don't suppose reminding you that fraternizing with
a witness is against the rules," Oaks had warned.

"What about protecting a fiancé?" he'd asked.

"That, son, is something I can work with." The captain had laughed.

Garrison's short conversation with Oaks had surprised
him, but he was comfortable with the decision. As long
as Kenderly liked the idea and things worked out. They'd
have lots of time to get to know each other while he
served on her protection detail.

"Garrison!" She flew into his arms.

"No one would tell me a damn thing until this morning," he whispered. "You should be happy to know they're taking your safety very seriously."

"Well, being safe is extremely lonely." She stepped back when Jesse and Bryce walked in the room.

"Go ahead and kiss her," Bryce said. "No one's coming."

Both men faced the hallway, giving them privacy— of sorts.

Garrison didn't hesitate. He scooped Kenderly to his chest, feet dangling in the air. She tasted as good as he remembered. Her response showed that she'd missed him as much as he'd missed her.

He let her slide down the length of him and kept her close. "Damn, I missed you."

"Me, too. They said it might be months before we go to trial. Will you be able to visit or write or call? Or forget about me altogether?"

"That's never going to happen, and you don't have to worry about visits. I'm going with you." He was more determined than ever. Nothing would keep him from loving her.

"What? No one mentioned anything about you. But wait. Are you sure? I mean, they're talking about months. Are you going to be away from crime fighting the entire time?"

"You don't want me on the detail?"

"Oh no, that's not it at all. I want you to be on my detail for life. I mean…you don't have to, if you don't want to." Kenderly looked so forlorn, yet hopeful.

"Sweetheart, you know what happens if I leave you alone. There's no tellin' what trouble you'd find."

"That is so true." She laughed, making him want to kiss her again.

"I'm not letting you out of my sight." He kissed her

again before any of his superiors marched into the room. "Besides, it'll give us plenty of time to create more of those porch swing stories for the grandkids."

* * * * *

Don't miss the next book in Angi Morgan's miniseries,
TEXAS RANGERS: ELITE TROOP,
when SHOTGUN JUSTICE goes on sale next month.
You'll find it wherever Harlequin Intrigue books
and ebooks are sold!

#1623 NAVY SEAL SURVIVAL
SEAL of My Own • by Elle James

Navy SEAL Duff Calloway's vacation turns into a dangerous mission when he meets Natalie Layne. She is in Honduras to rescue her sister from human traffickers—not to fall in love with a sexy SEAL.

#1624 STRANGER IN COLD CREEK
The Gates: Most Wanted • by Paula Graves

Agent John Blake is hiding in Cold Creek to recuperate from gunshot wounds. He never expected to thwart an attempt on Miranda Duncan's life—or to find himself falling hard for the no-nonsense deputy.

#1625 GUNNING FOR THE GROOM
Colby Agency: Family Secrets • by Debra Webb & Regan Black

PI Aidan Abbot is undercover as Frankie Leone's fiancé to clear her father's name. But the closer he gets to the truth, the more Aidan wants to protect the woman he was never supposed to fall for.

#1626 SHOTGUN JUSTICE
Texas Rangers: Elite Troop • by Angi Morgan

When a serial killer targets Deputy Avery Travis, it is up to Texas Ranger Jesse Ryder to protect her. But he'll discover that falling for his best friend's little sister is almost as dangerous as the killer stalking them.

#1627 TEXAS HUNT
Mason Ridge • by Barb Han

The man who once traumatized Lisa Moore is back—and he's deadly. Lisa turns to her childhood friend, Ryan Hunt, who risks his life and heart to help. But can Lisa ever truly escape her past?

#1628 PRIVATE BODYGUARD
Orion Security • by Tyler Anne Snell

Bodyguard Oliver Quinn can't deny his history with his new client, PI Darling Smith. But keeping her safe from a killer comes before exploring their lingering feelings.

YOU CAN FIND MORE INFORMATION ON UPCOMING HARLEQUIN® TITLES, FREE EXCERPTS AND MORE AT WWW.HARLEQUIN.COM.

HICNM0216